KAT MARTIN

AGAINST THE
MARK

WITHDRAWN

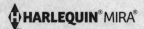

Recycling programs
for this product may
not exist in your area.

ISBN-13: 978-0-7783-1467-7

AGAINST THE MARK

For questions and comments about the quality of this book, please contact us at CustomerService@Harlequin.com.

Printed in U.S.A.

™ www.Harlequin.com

To the men and women in our armed forces for their dedicated service to our country and our freedom. God bless you all.

One

"**Y**ou dirty, no-good, low-down son of a bitch."

Ty Brodie's eyes widened at the sight of the little man standing, fists clenched and red-faced, in the doorway of Riggs and Brodie Private Investigations. "What the hell?"

Pug Calloway was no more than five foot five, barrel-chested and brawny, and he was fire-spittin' mad.

"Mess with my wife, will you?" Pug swung hard, but Ty, being six-two, dodged the first punch simply by stepping out of the way. "Hold on, Mr. Calloway—you've got this all wrong."

"Bullshit! I saw you with my Nettie down at the Cockadoodle Inn." Another punch sailed out, straight from the shoulder. Determined not to hurt the older man, somewhere in his sixties, Ty danced backward out of arm's reach.

"We were talking business, Mr. Calloway. I'm a private investigator. Your wife hired me to look into some personal matters for her."

"Liar!" Pug's left arm shot out, two sharp jabs that

sailed harmlessly into the air, followed by a right cross that would have been painful if it had connected.

After five years in the Marines, Ty was more afraid of hurting the old guy than Pug doing any real damage.

"Listen to me, Mr. Calloway—"

Pug swung a punch that whizzed past his jaw. "She's mine, you understand? You stay away from her!"

"Dammit! I wasn't trying to steal your wife!" He clamped a hand over Calloway's head, holding him back as the little man swung several more harmless blows. "All right, Pug—that's enough."

Ty shoved the shorter man backward hard enough to make him stumble. He heard a noise behind him and glanced over his shoulder to see his next-door neighbor, Ellie Stiles, standing beside a long-legged, good-looking blonde in tight jeans and a crop-top that showed tanned skin and a sexy silver belly-button ring.

He flashed a grin the instant before Pug Calloway's fist connected with his nose. Ty flew backward, tripped, went ass-over-teakettle and landed hard, the impact sending him sliding across the tile floor to wind up at the women's feet.

"Don't call me Pug," the little man growled. "Only my Nettie calls me that."

Ty glared up at Pug, whose fists were still clenched, ready to hit him again. Catching a glimpse of the pretty blonde's smile, Ty felt a rush of heat to the back of his neck that slowly crept into his face.

"For chrissake, man. I wasn't trying to steal your wife." Nettie was old enough to be his grandmother. He used the hem of his white T-shirt to wipe away the blood leaking out of his nose. "Nettie hired me to follow you. She thought you were cheating on her."

Pug's bushy gray eyebrows shot up. "That's crazy.

Why would she think that? I love Nettie. I'd never cheat on her."

"Yeah, well, that's what I told her." He rolled to his feet, checking his nose, relieved to find it wasn't broken—it just felt that way. "Now if you don't mind, I have better things to do than solve your marital problems."

Pug just grinned. "She really thought I was cheating? She was jealous?"

"Yeah, so why don't you go home and show her how much you love her? You might use some of that energy you're wasting on me for a better purpose."

Pug's irritating grin widened. "Good idea." The little man started walking, stopped and turned back. "Sorry about your nose."

Ty scowled as he shoved to his feet. "You'll be even sorrier when you get my bill."

Pug just smiled. Chest puffed out, he headed for the door. The P.I. office occupied the lower floor of the house Ty's partner, John Riggs, lived in with his wife, Amy. It had once been the guesthouse on Ellie's Hollywood Hills estate. The smaller house had been a wedding gift from Ellie, the silver-haired woman now standing at the bottom of the porch stairs.

Remembering she was still there, Ty turned, and Ellie handed him a wet washcloth she had retrieved from the bathroom.

"Thanks." Tipping his head back, he pressed the cold cloth beneath his nose, stanching the flow of blood. He tried not to look at the blonde, who was still grinning, digging a pair of dimples into her cheeks.

"I see you had a little misunderstanding with Mr. Calloway," Ellie said dryly. At seventy-one, she was still pretty, still kept a trim, athletic figure. She lived in the big house up the hill, and her mind was as sharp as the day she was born.

"I guess when you referred his wife to me as a client, you neglected to mention her husband was the jealous type."

Ellie sighed. "Well, knowing Pug and Nannette for so many years, I suppose I should have said something."

Ty grunted. "I suggest you make sure things get straightened out between them."

"Oh, I will." She hid a smile as she turned. "In the meantime, I've got another client for you. Tyler Brodie, I'd like you to meet my grandniece, Haley Warren. Haley's out here from Chicago. Her grandmother was my sister."

Just to regain a little of his dignity, Ty let his gaze roam over her, starting at the frosted-pink toenails peeking out of strappy high-heeled, open-toed sandals, sliding up a pair of long legs in snug-fitting jeans, across that bare midriff with its glittering belly-button ring over a set of nicely rounded breasts to a pretty face framed by long, softly curling honey blond hair.

She had big blue eyes, and an Angelina Jolie mouth that made him think of dirty sex. Maybe she read his thoughts for a faint blush rose in her cheeks.

Good. A little payback only seemed fair.

Besides, she was a real pleasure to look at. Not beautiful in the classic sense like some of the women he knew, but with those dimples and big blue eyes, she was way beyond cute.

"Nice to meet you, Ms. Warren."

The smile was gone and she assessed him coolly. "Aunt Ellie tells me you're a friend, as well as an investigator."

"I like to think that's true."

"Of course it's true," Ellie said. "That's why I know we can count on Ty to help us."

Wariness slid through him. Ellie had a way of bringing him clients who were nothing but trouble. "How's that?"

"Well, you see, three months ago Haley's father died when his powerboat exploded."

"I'm sorry for your loss," he said to her.

Grief flashed in her eyes an instant before she glanced away. "Thank you."

"At the time everyone thought it was an accident," Ellie continued, "a gas leak of some kind that turned deadly. Haley's stepmother doesn't believe it. About a month ago, Betty Jean started emailing Haley, trying to convince her to come to Los Angeles and help her find out the truth."

Ty focused on the leggy blonde. "And you think she's right because…"

"I don't know if she's right or not. I've never met her. Before he died, my father and I had been estranged for nearly five years, ever since he left my mother and ran off with another woman."

"Betty Jean," he said, just to make sure he was getting this straight.

"That's right. After he moved to L.A., Dad tried to mend our relationship, but I just… I couldn't get past his desertion." She glanced down and her eyes misted. "Now my father's gone."

Ty nodded, beginning to get the picture. "So your dad's dead and you regret not mending your fences."

"Yes, I do. Very much. But the thing is, some of the things Betty Jean says make sense. I owe it to my father to find out what really happened."

He flicked a glance at Ellie, whose features looked

a little too bland to suit him. "I take it you're here to convince me to help her."

"That's right. You know how good you are at these things, Tyler. I know Johnnie's out of town but Haley will be helping you. That'll save you from having to do everything by yourself."

Haley would be helping him. He could think of any number of things he'd like her to do for him, but none of them had anything to do with business. The fact was Haley Warren was Ellie's niece. Seducing her probably wasn't a good idea.

"Have you talked to the police?"

"Betty Jean has," Haley answered. "The police said there was nothing to indicate any sort of foul play. But my stepmother isn't convinced and if she's right—"

"I'll tell you what. I'll look into the circumstances of the accident, see if anything looks suspicious. I've got friends in the department. If something's not right, I'll talk to them myself."

Haley reached over and caught his arm. He felt a little zing of awareness and figured she must have felt it, too, since she stepped back as if she'd been burned.

She glanced away, took a deep breath and forced her eyes back to his face. "I want to be involved in this, Mr. Brodie. I need to find out for myself. I owe it to my father to find out the truth."

"It's just Ty, and I can get things done faster if I work alone."

"I want to be there when you talk to Betty Jean. I want to hear what she has to say."

He figured Haley also wanted to find out why her father had dumped her mother and run off with another woman. Probably someone younger and prettier, the usual motivation. Truth was, it didn't really matter if Haley went along. And it might help the stepmother open up.

"All right, when I go you can come with me. Make an appointment with Betty Jean, and you can fill me in on what you know on the way. I gather you're staying with your aunt."

"That's right."

"When would you like to go?"

"How about tomorrow morning?" Ellie suggested, the twinkle in her eyes warning him he had just stepped into another of her traps.

Or maybe he was just being paranoid. Maybe this time Ellie was just trying to help her niece. He reminded himself that as pretty as Haley was, getting involved with her wasn't an option—not for either one of them. Not when Ellie Stiles was such a good friend.

Night had settled over the valley below the house by the time Haley got home after supper. Her aunt Ellie had taken her to a little bistro called Le Petit Four on Sunset Strip, and though the food was excellent, Haley hadn't really been hungry.

She hadn't had her usual appetite since she had received the news of her father's death. But she had already lost four pounds so she'd forced herself to eat, and the broiled halibut with a Parmesan crust and lime butter had been delicious.

With a tired sigh, she drew back the blue satin coverlet on her bed in the guest wing of her aunt's opulent Hollywood Hills home and slid between the Egyptian cotton sheets.

The house was at least eight thousand square feet, perched on a hillside, modern in design, white stucco with dark brown trim, a flat roof and a four-car garage. There was an infinity pool on the lower level of the yard, a deck off the living room and bedrooms that stretched across the entire back of the house, with spectacular views of the L.A. basin.

With its twelve-foot ceilings, the inside was equally impressive, the decor also modern, a showcase for the valuable contemporary art collection Ellie and her late husband, movie mogul Harry Stiles, had amassed before his death.

Haley hadn't been to visit her aunt since her parents divorced five years ago. At the time, she had just turned twenty-one and was finishing her degree in fine art at the University of Chicago. Art was an interest she and her parents had shared, kind of a family tradition that even her great-aunt and her husband, Harry, had enjoyed. Allison Warren, Haley's mother, had started taking her to galleries when she was just a child.

Armed with both an art history degree and one in art design, for the past four years she'd been working at the Seymour Gallery in downtown Chicago. She'd hoped her dad would come to one of the openings she arranged for both up-and-coming and well-known artists.

Her heart squeezed. She'd always believed that in time she and her dad would talk things out, breach the rift between them. But the years had slipped past and now her father was dead.

Not just dead, Haley amended.

According to her stepmother, her father had been murdered.

Haley thought of the woman she had never met. *Betty Jean.* She sounded like a waitress in an Alabama biker bar. Or some kind of country bumpkin. *Have you heard the joke about the traveling salesman and the farmer's daughter, Betty Jean?* Just the whisper of her name at the back of Haley's mind made her stomach burn.

The woman had to be some big-busted bimbo with bleached blond hair and no morals, just the sort a good man like James Warren would fall prey to. Nothing like her mother, who enjoyed the opera and symphony and was a patron of the arts.

Her father had been extremely intelligent. Before the divorce, he had been working for her grandfather as president of the Wentworth Insurance Group. Then he'd met Betty Jean Simmons when he was in L.A. on business. Six months later, he quit his high-powered job, left his wife, abandoned his daughter and moved to California.

Tomorrow Haley would meet the woman who had destroyed her family.

A light knock sounded at the door. Haley turned as the door cracked open and her aunt poked her head into the bedroom. "Oh, good, you're still awake. So, what did you think?"

Haley scooted backward until her shoulders came up against the headboard. "What did I think about what?"

"Why, Tyler, of course."

She thought of the man her aunt had insisted accompany her in the morning. Tyler Brodie. "He looks like a college boy. And he fights like a wimp."

Ellie laughed. "He's thirty years old, and he's no wimp. Ty spent six years in the Marines before he moved here from Dallas. He just didn't want to hurt poor Pug, is all."

She remembered the punch Ty had taken and bit back a smile. Clearly, he had been trying not to hurt the older man.

"He's good at his job," Ellie added. "If the accident

that killed your father was more than that, Ty will help you find out."

Ellie had told her a little about Tyler Brodie. That he was raised in Texas and had been working as an investigator for the past three years. She'd neglected to mention he was handsome as sin with a body to match. Tall and rangy, with dark brown hair a little too long and interesting hazel eyes that seemed to change color with the light.

He had shoulders that would fill a door frame and an impressive set of biceps that stretched the sleeves of his plain white T-shirt and hinted at the solid muscles underneath. He had a V-shaped body with a lean waist and long legs that ended in a pair of scuffed leather cowboy boots.

"I hope he's as good as you say. I guess we'll know more after I talk to Betty Jean."

"So you called her?"

Haley nodded. "We're supposed to be at her house at ten tomorrow morning."

Ellie smiled. "Then I guess I'd better let you get some sleep. Good night, dear. I'll see you in the morning."

"Good night, Aunt Ellie."

Her aunt closed the door, and Haley's thoughts returned to the man who would be taking her to meet her stepmother. Her girlfriends in Chicago would call Ty a hottie. Fortunately for Haley, she had never been one of those women who fell dumbstruck in the presence of a particularly virile male.

The only reason she was letting him come along was that her aunt had insisted. Brodie was a trained investigator. Since Aunt Ellie had even more money than Haley's mother's family and was paying his fees—

however extravagant they might be—Haley had agreed to accept his help.

Besides, the thought of facing Betty Jean Simmons—now Warren—by herself was daunting.

Haley closed her eyes, shutting out the distant spots of colored light blinking through the huge plate-glass windows on the far side of the bedroom. She should have closed the drapes, but the lights kept her mind off the meeting she dreaded in the morning.

And any unwanted images that might pop into her head of Tyler Brodie.

Two

The following morning, Ty drove from his condo to his office a few miles away to meet Haley Warren, Ellie's niece, the sexy little blonde he couldn't lay a hand on.

He owed Ellie Stiles. The wealthy older woman was the main reason he was now a partner in Riggs and Brodie Investigations. He had met her through Wounded Warriors, a charity where she worked helping disabled vets.

Ty had been visiting friends who'd been wounded in Afghanistan. He'd met Ellie and they'd struck up a friendship. Next thing he knew he was working part-time, then full-time for Johnnie Riggs. Now they were partners. He had a job he loved and was good at, and he owed it all to Eleanor Stiles.

When a knock sounded at the office door, he got up from his desk and walked over to open it. In a pair of cream slacks and a long-sleeved, blue silk blouse the color of her eyes, her hair done up in one of those complicated French braids, Haley looked classy and slightly remote.

He tried not to think of the silver belly-button ring beneath her clothes, at odds with the don't-touch-me outfit she was wearing.

Clearly, her conservative dress had been chosen for her first meeting with her stepmother. Probably the exact opposite of the style she figured her mother's competition would be wearing.

"You want a cup of coffee or are you ready to go?" he asked, glancing at the pot on the counter he'd brewed earlier.

"I had more than enough at Aunt Ellie's."

"Good, then let's get out of here." He guided her back out to the newly completed office parking area.

Before he and Johnnie had become full-fledged partners, they hadn't needed that much space. But with their clientele growing, they had added an outside door and flattened some of the hillside to form a place for their clients to park.

"We can use my aunt's car if you don't want to drive," Haley said.

"We can take my truck." A black Chevy Silverado with custom chrome wheels. He really loved that truck.

Haley looked down at the scuffed cowboy boots he was wearing. "Ellie says you're from Texas. I should have figured you for a pickup man."

One of his eyebrows went up. "What, you don't like trucks?"

She grinned, cutting those cute little dimples into her cheeks. "I'm from Chicago. We mostly ride in taxis."

Ty's mouth edged up as he pulled open the passenger door. Admiring the curve of her ass in the tailored slacks, he set his hands at her waist to help her into the cab and felt that same zing he'd felt earlier. It must have hit her, too, because he heard her slight gasp.

She wasn't as tall as he'd first thought, maybe five-seven, but all the curves were in the right places and those pouty lips were enough to get his blood flowing south.

"What's Betty Jean's address?" he asked, forcing his mind back to business. Haley had told him the woman lived in Torrance. She rattled off an address on Merritt Street, and he punched the numbers into the GPS on his dash.

Ty fired up the powerful V-8 engine, released the parking brake and they rolled off down the hill toward Sunset Boulevard.

"It'll take us a while to get there," he said as they merged into traffic. "You can fill me in on the way."

He knew some of it already. Yesterday, after Haley and Ellie had left, he'd booted up his computer and done some research on James Robert Warren. Fifty-three years old, married to Betty Jean Simmons four years and two months—as soon as his divorce was final. He'd attended Michigan State University, but dropped out in his senior year and married Allison Wentworth, one of the wealthy Chicago Wentworths.

From the photos Ty had found, he was a good-looking kid who'd grown into a handsome man. In school, he'd been athletic and popular. But none of that really mattered. What mattered was why the man was dead.

Haley leaned back in her seat. "I don't know that much about what happened, just what the police told my mother and what I read in Betty Jean's emails. The cops believe gas fumes built up in the galley of the boat. They think maybe a burner on the stove was on but not lit, and when Dad started the engine, the boat blew up."

"But you and Betty Jean aren't buying it."

"The thing is, my dad knew everything there was

to know about boats. He owned one as far back as I can remember. Boating was his passion. And he was ridiculously careful. He would never leave the propane turned on. And even if he did, there were alarms and safety measures that should have warned him. Betty Jean thinks someone must have done something to cause the boat to explode."

But accidents happened all the time, even to people who were careful.

"What else?"

"The boat was a twenty-six-foot Pacific Flyer my dad kept in a slip at Marina Del Rey. His office was located in one of the high-rise buildings nearby, so the boat was close. Betty Jean said he went to the marina almost every day."

"What kind of work did he do?"

"He was an investigator for Allied Global Insurance."

On the internet, Ty had run across his name on a roster on the Allied company webpage.

"Dad was a police science major in college. Then he met my mother and they fell in love. Instead of going into police work, he wound up working in the insurance business for my grandfather."

"That would be your mother's father, right?"

"That's right. Dad was really smart, and it didn't take him long to become a vice president."

Of course it didn't hurt that he was married to the boss's daughter.

"When Grandpa got sick, Dad took over as president of the company."

"Then a few years later he meets Betty Jean and quits," Ty said. "Uses his background in insurance to get another job, but this time as an investigator, the kind of work he had wanted to do for years. It makes a certain amount of sense."

Haley arched a blond eyebrow. "Do you know how much an insurance investigator earns?"

"I'd guess sixty, maybe a hundred thou a year if he's good."

"In Chicago, Dad made over a million dollars a year."

Ty flicked her a sideways glance. "Earning a lot of money doesn't always make you happy."

"I wouldn't know. What I make barely covers my monthly expenses."

"I guess you don't work for your grandfather's company," he said dryly.

Haley ignored the gibe, though the tick in her cheek said she hadn't missed it. His guess was she didn't miss much.

"I was an art major in college. I work for the Seymour Gallery in downtown Chicago. I plan openings, work with up-and-coming young artists, cater to famous ones."

"They let you off work to come out here?"

"I took a leave of absence. I had some savings, and Aunt Ellie is helping by letting me stay with her."

He mulled that over, beginning to understand how important this was to her, and brought the conversation back to where they were. "So your mom was into art and your dad was more an outdoor kind of guy."

Haley nodded. "Dad loved sports. Boating, mainly. He loved to fish, but he also played racquetball and tennis. He played golf a lot when he worked for my grandfather, and he was really good."

"He like art?"

"He liked the old masters. My mother prefers modern art." Her features softened. "He was a great dad.

I shouldn't have condemned him for leaving. He was a man. Sometimes men fall prey to a certain type of woman."

Ty was smart enough to let that comment slide. "Your dad became an investigator. Is that why you think he might have been murdered? He was working on a case, maybe getting close to finding out something someone didn't want him to know?"

"That's what Betty Jean thinks. She said she needed me to come to L.A. so we could figure things out."

He didn't press for more. Odds were the explosion was exactly what it seemed, but he didn't have enough information yet to make a judgment call.

Ty fought his way through traffic, finally got off the 405 Freeway in Torrance and followed the GPS directions into a neighborhood of middle-class, single-family homes. Haley's blue eyes went wide as he pulled up in front of the address on Merritt she had given him.

"I can't believe this."

It was a modest gray stucco house with white trim, a small, well-maintained front yard, and a two-car garage. "What?"

"My parents…" She shook her head. "My parents lived in Lake Forest. Their home made Aunt Ellie's place look small."

Ah, poor little rich girl. Until his uncle recently died and his family ranch in Dallas had been sold, Haley would have been out of his league. He had plenty of money now, but he wasn't raised to the high life, and he had nothing in common with a girl who was.

In a way he was glad. Made things a whole lot easier.

"Like I said, money doesn't always make you happy." He turned off the engine, cracked open the door and went around to help her down from the cab.

Haley didn't wait. He wondered if she was worried about that little jolt that leaped between them whenever he touched her. He sure as hell was.

"You ready for this?"

She nodded. Her face was a little pale, but he could read her determination. She took a deep breath as they walked up the cement path to the front porch. Bright red geraniums bloomed in a pot beside the door, and a hummingbird feeder swung from the rafters overhead.

Haley rang the doorbell and it opened a few seconds later. If she'd been expecting a trashy little number with too much perfume and big, perky breasts she was sorely mistaken.

"Haley! I'm Betty Jean. I'm so glad to meet you!" The woman threw her pudgy arms around Haley's neck, went up on her toes and hugged her. She was short, no more than five foot two, wide-hipped, and though she did have oversize boobs, they were definitely her own, with a little too much wear and tear to be perky.

"Oh, dear. Where are my manners? Both of you... please do come in."

"I'm Haley's friend, Ty Brodie," he said, giving Haley time to recover and figuring he might as well get the introductions out of the way. "Pleasure to meet you, ma'am."

"It's a pleasure meeting you, Ty." She returned her attention to Haley, who hadn't yet said a word. Betty Jean's eyes filled. "Why, you're even prettier than your daddy said. Of course I've seen pictures, but they didn't do you justice. Jimmy loved you so much. He talked about you all the time."

Haley swallowed. Her bottom lip quivered an instant before her composure returned and her features hardened. "Jimmy? You called my father Jimmy?"

Her stepmother's eyes rounded as if she'd said something wrong. "Why, yes. He just…he never looked like a James, you know? We used to laugh about it." More tears welled and spilled onto Betty Jean's plump cheeks. "You'll have to excuse me. I just…I miss him so much."

Pulling a tissue from the pocket of the turquoise Capri pants she wore with a flowered turquoise top, she dabbed her eyes. She was in her early fifties, with short, curly blond hair with dark roots that had begun to show. She was round-faced, but appealing in a sweet, homey sort of way.

"Would you like a cup of coffee, or maybe a glass of iced tea?"

Haley seemed to be getting over her shock. "Tea would be nice."

"That'd be great," Ty said.

They made their way through a living room that was clean but cluttered with knickknacks, everything from ceramic squirrels to Hummel figurines, into a modest kitchen with yellow ruffled curtains at the windows.

"Just sit right down and make yourself at home."

Haley made no move, just stood there staring in stunned disbelief as Betty Jean rumbled around the kitchen. Ty guided her into one of the captain's chairs at the maple table, and she sank down heavily.

Ty figured if he wanted to get this over with, he had better take charge of the conversation. "Haley asked me to come along because she thought I could help you look into your husband's death. I'm a private investigator, Mrs. Warren. I'd like to hear why you think the explosion that killed James Warren was more than an accident."

She set a glass of iced tea in front of each of them,

carefully placed a sugar bowl and spoons on the table, then sat down across from them.

"To tell you the truth, at first I didn't. I was too grief-stricken to do anything but mourn Jimmy's loss. But little by little, I started thinking about the accident. I began to go over the details, try to work out what went wrong."

Ty heard the sincerity in her voice. It was clear the woman believed what she was saying. In a robust sort of way, she was attractive, her figure plump but curvy, and though there were tiny wrinkles at the corners of her eyes, her cheeks were smooth and her smiles were guileless and warm.

Ty wondered what Haley's mother was like.

"And?"

"And the more I thought about it, the more certain I became it wasn't an accident at all."

Three

Haley sat mostly in silence as Ty questioned Betty Jean. She was still trying to wrap her head around the fact that her intelligent, incredibly attractive father had left her sophisticated and beautiful mother for pudgy Betty Jean Simmons. But he had, and now wasn't the time to examine why.

She forced herself to concentrate on the conversation.

"I did a little preliminary research," Ty was saying. "From the articles I read in the newspaper, either the galley stove was left on or there was some kind of a leak in a fuel line. Fumes built up in the cabin. When your husband started the engine, the boat exploded."

Betty Jean shook her head. "Jimmy would have checked for something like that. Whenever we went boating, he was always very careful."

"Accidents happen, Mrs. Warren."

"Please…I'm just Betty Jean. And Jimmy told me there was some kind of alarm that warns about a gas buildup."

"That's right, but those things can fail."

"What about the fan? I know there's something that blows out the fumes if they build up, right?"

"A bilge blower. In case there's a spark when the bilge pump turns on. But again—"

"There are other things, Ty, information the police won't believe because I don't have any proof."

Haley's interest picked up. "What kind of things are you talking about?"

"It all started three years ago when Jimmy was called in to investigate a smoke-damage claim at the Scarsdale Center—that's one of the more prestigious art galleries in town. There was a fire in the Old Masters section. The flames didn't do much damage—it was the smoke. The investigation was purely routine. The claim wasn't even that large, just the cost of cleaning the paintings. But as the work was being done, one of the experts working on the pieces began to suspect that two of them were forgeries. It didn't take long to prove she was right."

"So the claim went from a relatively small amount to a helluva lot of money," Ty said.

"That's right. The pieces, a Titian and a Caravaggio, were insured, and they were valued in the millions. Jimmy worked night and day, trying to find out what happened, but he never did. The gallery people went back through the provenance—that's the chain that starts with the painting's origin and goes all the way to its current owner or location. Everything appeared to be completely in order."

"Which meant the real pieces arrived at the gallery, but were switched after they got there."

"That's right. But as hard as Jimmy worked, he never figured out how the original pieces were stolen and replaced with forgeries."

"There was nothing on the surveillance videos?" Haley asked. "Nothing in the background checks of the people who worked at the gallery?"

"Not a thing."

Just to give herself something to do, Haley took a sip of her iced tea. She was a little more impressed with Ty Brodie than she wanted to admit. He actually seemed to know what he was doing. "So what does any of this have to do with my father getting killed?"

Betty Jean sagged like a balloon leaking air. "I don't know. All I know is that Jimmy took his failure very personally. He never completely gave up his investigation of the theft. I think lately something may have happened. He mentioned the old case several times. Maybe he found something, discovered some new information that would lead him to the people who stole those valuable paintings three years ago."

"You think they killed him to stop him?" Haley asked.

"It's possible. And if Jimmy was murdered, I want his killers brought to justice."

The thought made Haley's stomach tighten. She would definitely want that, too.

"So you've gone to the police with your suspicions?" Brodie asked.

"I spoke to a detective named Cogan. He gave me about five minutes, then told me I was just grieving. That in time I'd be able to accept what had happened."

"Charlie Cogan is an okay guy, but he's up for retirement. He isn't interested in doing much of anything right now besides running out his time and taking up residence in a rocking chair."

Betty Jean's shoulders straightened. "Detective Cogan didn't believe me. What about you?"

Brodie seemed to be thinking over his reply. Haley watched him idly run a finger through the condensation on the outside of his glass. His lean hands were tanned and calloused, as if he was used to hard work. His scuffed boots and slight Southern drawl made Haley wonder at his Texas background.

"At this point, what I believe, Mrs. Warren, is it's all just conjecture. As you said, there isn't any proof."

"Betty Jean." She flicked Haley a glance, but her attention returned to Ty. "How much do you charge, Mr. Brodie? I have a little money, some Jimmy saved from his retirement fund when he quit his job in Chicago, but not a lot. Jimmy believed in enjoying life, and so we did. We bought a motor home and traveled around the country. We went on cruises. We even went to Europe once."

Haley's mouth thinned. *Gold digger.* Her dad had left Wentworth Insurance with millions from his pension fund. Her mother would certainly have gotten her share in the divorce, but there must have been a lot left over. Now it was gone.

"Ty's fees are already being paid," Haley said a little tartly. "I'm just as determined as you are to find out what really happened to my father."

The older woman's features looked uncertain. "Oh. Well, then. I won't worry about it." She turned, smiled warmly at Ty. "I'm very happy that you'll be helping Haley and me. With all of us working together, I'm sure we'll be able to bring peace to Jimmy's memory."

"James," Haley corrected.

Betty Jean flushed and made no reply. When Haley looked at Ty, his hazel eyes held a trace of pity. It made her feel oddly guilty.

"I need a recent photo of your husband and access to

his belongings," Ty said gently. "There might be some-thing there that will give us a clue."

"Of course. His clothes are still in the closet. I couldn't... I wasn't ready to give them away. The stuff from his office and everything else is in boxes in the spare bedroom. There are some pictures in there, as well." She sniffed and glanced away.

Ty reached over and squeezed her hand. "I'll take a look, see if anything interesting turns up. You don't have to be involved."

Betty Jean released a shaky breath. "Thank you."

Ty cast Haley a glance. "You can come or you can stay here. Whichever you want."

Her chest tightened. She thought of sifting through her father's personal possessions, things he had amassed in a life she knew nothing about, and a lump formed in her throat. It didn't matter if she disliked the woman he had married, she should have called him, come to L.A. to see him, straightened things out.

He was her father and she loved him. And she had utterly failed him.

"I'll come with you," she said. Taking a deep breath, she followed Ty down the hall.

"You okay?" Haley hadn't said a word since they'd left her stepmother's house. Ty maneuvered the pickup through the freeway traffic. A car horn honked and the SUV ahead of him slammed on the brakes as the traffic slowed to a crawl again. He'd never really gotten used to it. He liked the open spaces of Texas, but he liked the action in L.A.

She stared down at her hands, looked up at him and shook her head. "Nothing's what I expected. My father's life...the way he lived here...was completely different than it was in Chicago. It was like he was a totally different person."

"People change."

"Maybe. Or maybe there was a part of him I never really knew."

A big part, it looked like to Ty. The camping equipment they had found in the garage, the albums filled with photos of James with Betty Jean in front of their motor home, the couple on deck during various cruises, sailings on the Carnival line, nothing fancy.

Betty Jean had sold the motor home, but Ty had seen pictures taken of them inside the vehicle, laughing as one or the other cooked dinner, a candid shot of James in his underwear, grinning like a kid. He looked relaxed, completely comfortable in his own skin. From what Ty had seen in that album and among his possessions, James Warren was a happy man.

He glanced over at Warren's daughter, sitting stiffly in the seat beside him. "We didn't find anything, Haley. Not in all those boxes. I think you need to accept the fact your father's death was an accident."

She straightened. "We haven't looked through everything. We haven't gone through his computer."

They had loaded her father's desktop into the back of the pickup along with his laptop. His iPad was missing, probably destroyed in the explosion. Betty Jean said that his cell phone had been recovered, but it was melted and mostly destroyed.

"We'll take a look, but don't expect to find anything."

Her mouth tightened. "You just don't want to do this. You've made up your mind and you don't want to be bothered. Unfortunately, I can see we're going to need some help. Whatever my aunt is paying you, I'll double."

Irritation trickled through him. "I thought you didn't have any money."

"I don't have much. I can borrow what I need."

"From your mother?"

Haley ignored his barb. "It doesn't matter where I get it. The point is, if you'll help me, I'll make it worth your while."

Ty's jaw tightened. "I'm doing everything I can to help you, and for your information, sweetheart, I'm doing it gratis. Ellie's a friend. I'm doing this for her, and I'm not quitting till we know the truth."

Haley fell silent, her features contrite. When she wasn't frowning, she was a pretty little thing. He hadn't missed the turmoil in her eyes when she had met her stepmother. She was determined to dislike the woman who had ended her parents' marriage, but a lady as warm and sincere as Betty Jean was hard not to like. And she had clearly been in love with her husband.

Ty didn't think Haley was anywhere near ready to accept that.

"Thank you," Haley said. "I appreciate your help."

"No problem."

"I've been thinking about the case…is there any way we can get a look at the police file on the art theft three years ago?"

He flicked her a glance. The lady was no dummy. He felt that same pull of attraction that had hit him the moment he had seen her in his office. And he admired her tenacity, even if it did mean doing a lot more free work.

"I've got friends in the department. I can get a copy of the police report."

She smiled, a wide bright smile that showed her dimples. "That'd be great, Ty." She hadn't smiled all day, and it knocked the wind right out of him. He had the nearly uncontrollable urge to kiss that pretty mouth, nibble a path all the way down to her silver belly-button ring. *Damn.*

"Let's see what's on those computers first, okay?"

"Okay."

Ty didn't say more. All of a sudden, his jeans were fitting too tight, and he was trying to convince himself it didn't matter if she was Little Miss Chicago socialite and he was a down-home Texas country boy.

Women had always liked him. On any given day, there were usually one or two ready to please him. He threw a sideways glance at Haley and knew she wouldn't be one of them. She treated him more like a hired hand than a man she considered her equal.

Taking her to bed wasn't going to happen.

Ty told himself it was a damned good thing.

Four

H aley sat out on the deck of her aunt's sprawling Hollywood home. The L.A. Basin stretched for miles below her, the view a little hazy this warm May afternoon. A Jacuzzi bubbled next to the infinity pool below, beckoning her in that direction. She could use a little stress reliever. Maybe she'd try it later.

She checked her watch. Three o'clock. She'd been trying to do a little sketching, but her mind kept wandering. Charcoal drawings were her hobby. She loved art, but she had never been good enough to be a successful artist herself. Still, it was fun to dabble. And the process usually helped clear her head.

Not today. Since Ty Brodie had dropped her off at home and headed down to the police station, her mind had been on the report he was in the process of obtaining.

She glanced up as the big glass patio door slid open and her aunt stepped out on the deck. A petite young woman with a very pretty face and long, straight blond hair walked out beside her.

"You have a visitor," Aunt Ellie said.

Haley set her sketch pad aside and rose from her lounge chair, certain who the woman was. "You must be Amy, John Riggs's wife. Aunt Ellie's told me a lot about you."

Amy smiled. "I'm Johnnie's wife. I've been looking forward to meeting you."

Haley smiled back. "Me, too."

"I'm afraid I must run," Ellie said. "I've got a botanical society meeting. I'll be back in a couple of hours."

"I hope I'm not intruding," Amy said.

"Not at all. Why don't we sit at the table? Would you like a Coke or a glass of tea or something?"

"I'm floating now." They sat down in one of the orange-striped chairs at the round, glass-topped table. "I hear you're working with Ty."

Haley's stomach lifted. She had no idea why. "That's right. I imagine Ellie told you I came out to investigate my father's death."

"Yes. I'm sorry to hear about your dad."

Haley swallowed past the lump that suddenly rose in her throat. "I hadn't seen him in years, not since he divorced my mother. He wanted to mend fences, but I was too stubborn. Now he's gone."

"Time goes by so fast sometimes. Ty'll help you figure out what happened. It won't bring your father back, but it might give you some closure."

"He seems good at his job."

"Oh, he is. That's why he and Johnnie are working together. My husband has a steady clientele and he's always busy. After we got married, he wanted more time for *us*. Ty had been working for him a couple of years. A while back, they decided to become partners."

"I see."

"Ty's a really good investigator. Johnnie says he's a natural." She grinned. "He's also a total hunk. But I guess you must have noticed that."

She'd noticed. She was a woman, after all. "He's a great-looking guy—no question about it. I'm just not interested."

"Not that it's any of my business, but why not?"

Haley shook her head. "Let's just say, my relationships with men have been less than satisfactory. I enjoy a man's company, but the rest of it..." She shrugged. "I'd rather just stay friends." She had no idea why she was talking about any of this with a woman she had only just met, but she liked Amy Riggs. Ellie loved her and she could use a friend while she was in L.A.

Amy was nodding. "Probably just as well. Ty has a bevy of women chasing after him. He's not a man-whore or anything like that. Women just like him and he likes them back. Ty's like Johnnie. They're extremely potent men."

Ty certainly gave that impression. With his wide shoulders, long legs and movie-star-handsome face, Ty Brodie was an amazing-looking man.

"Since you're married, it's probably different for you, but for me, when it comes to...umm...sex, I don't see what all the hoopla is about."

Amy grinned. "Before I met Johnnie, I would have agreed." She smiled dreamily. "The first time I saw him, I couldn't take my eyes off him. All I could think of was what it would be like to have a sexy man like that take me to bed."

Haley thought of the little zing she felt every time Ty Brodie touched her. It didn't mean anything. Just that she was a woman and he was a man.

And she had been down that path before. She'd tried

sex a couple of times with guys she'd thought were attractive. When it was over, all she'd felt was empty and disappointed.

She went for a change of subject. "Ellie said your husband would have taken the case but he's out of town."

"Johnnie's in San Diego digging up information on somebody or other. He didn't tell me his name. I don't think he wants me to worry, but of course I do anyway. God, I really miss him."

Haley couldn't imagine feeling that strongly about a man. "You're a teacher, right?"

Amy nodded. "Kindergarten. I love kids. I think Johnnie and I might try to start a family next year."

Haley made no reply. The subject of children bothered her. She didn't believe in marriage, and she was one of those women who felt kids deserved a traditional family. Since marriage wasn't in her future, kids weren't, either.

She looked up as the patio door slid open again and Tyler Brodie stepped out on the deck. Still wearing the jeans and yellow, short-sleeved Izod pullover he'd had on that morning, he had clamped a blue-and-white Dodgers baseball cap over his head, making the ends of his slightly too-long hair curl over the edges. He ambled toward them in that loose-limbed way he had of walking, like he had all the time in the world.

Haley felt a little kick she hadn't expected and totally did not want to feel.

"I rang the bell," Ty said. "When no one came to the door I used the key Ellie keeps under the flowerpot. Dumb idea, but she doesn't care if I use it, and I figured you'd be out here." He grinned at the petite blonde. "Hey, Amy."

"Hey, Ty." Amy glanced from one of them to the other. "Listen, I've got to run. It was nice meeting you, Haley."

"You, too, Amy."

"Next time my sister, Rachael, comes by, I'll bring her over. You might recognize her—she plays Detective Reynolds on L.A.P.D. Blue. It was a new show last fall."

"So she's famous?"

"Not so much. It isn't that big a part, but she's really good in it. I think you'll like her."

"I'm sure I will." Particularly if Rachael was anything like Amy.

"Rachael's getting married in a couple of weeks. If you're still in L.A., you'll have to come to the wedding."

"I'll probably be back in Chicago by then, but thanks."

Amy waved as she hurried toward the sliding glass door. Her sister was getting married. It was easy to see how happy she was for her. Maybe it would work for Rachael. Haley had seen too many failed marriages to have any faith in the institution herself.

She looked over at Ty. "Did you get the police report?"

He shoved up the brim of his cap, exposing the sun streaks in his dark brown hair. "I got a copy." He dragged out a chair, spun it around and sat down facing her. "It's got the names of all the people the police spoke to about the art theft three years ago, but I didn't see anything that points to something that might be ongoing."

"I was hoping…you know?"

"Yeah, I do. I also got a copy of the accident report, but the truth is, it's better if your father's death was exactly what it appeared. An accident is something you can eventually get past, Haley."

"I need to be sure."

"I can't argue with that. If it was my dad, I'd want to know, too."

Hearing that made Haley feel a little better. "I took a look at Dad's laptop, but I think it must have a virus or something. Nothing was working right. I couldn't get any files or programs to open."

He frowned. "That's funny. The C drive was missing from his desktop. I figured he'd taken it in for repairs or something."

"So both his computers are down."

"Yeah."

"That's pretty coincidental."

"Yeah, and I'm not a big believer in coincidence." He got up from the chair, reached down and took hold of her hand. A little jolt ran up her arm. Ty's head came up as if he felt it, too.

"Come on," he said gruffly. "We'll go over to the office, take another look at the accident report. Maybe there's something I missed."

Haley eased her hand from his. "I'll call Betty Jean, see if Dad was having trouble with his computers." Not something she wanted to do. Just hearing the woman's voice tied her stomach in knots. But they were working together, and there was information Betty Jean had they were going to need.

"We've got his cell phone," Ty said, "or what's left of it. I'll get it to some forensic people I know, see if they can pull anything off it. It'll take a while, but they're good. They might be able to find something. Tomorrow's Saturday. On Monday, we'll go down to Allied Global, see what his coworkers have to say."

"And we should talk to the people who own boats

around Dad's slip at the marina, see if anyone saw anything out of the ordinary."

"The police talked to them." He grinned. "But it never hurts to ask twice."

Haley's insides lifted alarmingly. She ignored that wicked grin. She didn't like the attraction she was feeling for Tyler Brodie. And since she had a hunch he was feeling it, too, she was going to put a stop to it—the sooner the better.

Five

Nothing stood out in the accident report, just the date and time of the explosion, and various statements from eyewitnesses to the event.

As Haley pored over the document, reading every line, Ty felt sorry for her. It would be better if she could just let her father rest in peace. But Haley was fighting personal demons and she wouldn't be satisfied until she knew for certain what had happened.

He knew the feeling. His own father had died in a car accident while Ty was in Afghanistan. He'd read the police reports, finally accepted the fact that the truck driver who'd hit him had fallen asleep at the wheel. It was an accident. There was nothing he could do to change it.

Fortunately, at the time it had happened, his parents had been divorced for years, and though his mother had taken the news harder than he'd expected, their time apart had helped ease her grief. His own had taken longer.

Then his younger brother had been killed in Iraq,

a blow that had hit Ty even harder. Ty didn't want to think about that.

"Look at this." Haley pointed to a line on the report. "The witnesses from the marina said the boat was just easing out of the slip when it exploded. If it was a propane leak from the stove, wouldn't it have exploded the instant the engine was turned on? Dad wouldn't have time to move away from the dock."

"Maybe the boat had begun to drift away. If the lines had been cast off, that would explain it. But it could have been something else. Most boat explosions are caused by gas fumes that settle in the bilge. When the bilge pump kicks on, something sparks and the boat blows up."

"That's what the blower is for."

"When it works."

Haley looked back at the report. "Maybe if we talk to the people down at the marina, we'll have a better idea what happened."

"It's late to head down to the harbor today. There'll be a better chance of catching someone Saturday morning, anyway. What time is good for you?"

"How about eight? With the traffic, it'll take a while to get there."

"Sounds good." He looked at his watch. "It's getting on toward supper. You…umm…having dinner with your aunt?"

"No, actually. Aunt Ellie called to say she's having supper with one of her friends from the Botanical Society committee. I think Aunt Ellie is seeing someone." Haley grinned, flashing her dimples and curving those plump pink lips. Ty started getting hard.

"I've kinda been thinking that myself," he said. Ellie

had been all smiles lately, busier than usual and oddly secretive.

"I hope that's it. She deserves to be happy."

"Ellie's great. And you're right—no one deserves happiness more than she does." Ellie was the kind of woman who took people under her wing and gave them whatever help they needed. Once she called you friend, you could always count on her.

"So you…umm…want to get something to eat?" he asked, mentally kicking himself in the ass for asking. For God's sake, she was Ellie's niece!

"Thanks, but no. I've got a date with a friend."

"Old boyfriend?" he said as casually as he could, and his subconscious gave him another swift boot.

"Old girlfriend. Lane Bishop. We went to college together in Chicago. Her family moved to L.A. her second year. We used to be really close."

He relaxed a little, though he told himself he didn't give a damn how Haley Warren spent her nights.

"Have a good time, then. I'll pick you up tomorrow at eight."

Haley left his office and returned to her aunt's big house next door. Ty headed for his nearby condo, newly purchased with some of the money from the sale of his family ranch. His uncle had died last year, the last of the older Brodie clan. The money from the sale was split among him and his cousins, and there had been plenty to go around.

He had almost reached his truck when his iPhone started singing. Alabama. "If You're Gonna Play in Texas, You Gotta Have a Fiddle in the Band."

He was more an L.A. guy now, but his Texas roots ran deep, and every so often his drawl slipped out.

He held the phone to his ear. "Brodie."

"Hey, lover boy, it's Tiffany. I've missed you. I was thinking I might stop by…you know…if you aren't busy."

He tipped his head back, wishing he'd let the call go to voice mail. He wasn't in the mood for Tiffany or any other woman. He just wanted a nice quiet evening at home watching TV. Well, maybe he could warm up to a hot night in bed with Haley Warren.

He gave himself another mental ass-kicking for that.

"Listen, Tiff, it's nice to hear from you, but I've already made plans. Maybe some other time, okay?"

Tiffany ran through the next four nights and he made excuses not to see her. He hated to lie, but he didn't want to hurt her feelings, either.

"Look, honey, the truth is, I'm involved in a case and it's taking all my time."

"When will you be finished?"

"I don't know. It could go on for a couple of months. I think it would be best if you, you know, found someone else to keep you entertained."

A moment of silence on the phone. "Fine, be that way." Tiffany ended the call, and Ty gave a sigh of relief.

When Alabama started singing again, he checked the caller ID, saw it was Susan Wilson and let it go to voice mail.

Tossing his baseball cap on the dining table, he raked a hand through his hair and strolled into the kitchen in search of the leftover rigatoni he'd brought home from Marco's Italian a couple of nights ago.

He sighed. Having a lot of lady friends wasn't all it was cracked up to be. If he could be like some of his buddies, just have sex with a woman and never see her again, it would be one thing. But he just wasn't made that way.

He enjoyed sex and plenty of it. But he liked the women he took to bed, and he didn't want to hurt them.

He'd take a break, he vowed. Tonight was a start.

Ty refused to let his mind wander in the direction of Haley Warren.

Ty was waiting in the entry the next morning as Haley hurried down the hall from her bedroom in the guest wing. He was staring at his wristwatch when he looked up and spotted her. The expression on his face said, *you're late but you're a woman. I'm used to it.*

Dammit, she was only fifteen minutes late. Earlier she'd gone for a run and the time had slipped away from her. She was trying to turn over a new leaf, make some personal improvements, and punctuality was something she'd been working on.

"Sorry." She could feel those compelling hazel eyes as they moved over her, running from the blond ponytail she'd hurriedly pulled her hair into, assessing the white jeans and red-and-white-striped blouse she had tied up in front. For an instant they touched on the silver ring in her navel and seemed to shift from cool green to very warm brown.

He'd opened his mouth to say something when a country song started playing in his pocket. Ty pulled out his cell phone, checked the caller ID and let the call go to voice mail.

"Aren't you going to answer it?"

Color crept into his face. "It isn't important."

"A woman, then," she said lightly. "One you're tired of."

"It isn't like that. Well, not exactly."

But of course it was exactly like that. With a face and body like his, the man had to be swamped with girlfriends.

"You ready to go?"

"I'm ready." Ignoring an urge to see if she could make those interesting eyes change color again, she slung the strap of her purse over her shoulder and preceded him out the front door. Her aunt had already gone for the day. Ellie hadn't said where she was going, only that she would be back in time for supper. Her aunt didn't cook much, but when she did, it was usually healthy and great tasting.

Haley went around to the passenger side of Ty's pickup and opened the door. Her breathing hitched as his hands wrapped around her waist and he lifted her into the cab.

"You don't have to do that. I can get in by myself."

His gaze zeroed in on her. "I'm not trying to molest you, just helping you get in the truck."

She started to say she didn't need his help, but he was scowling already and it wasn't worth making him mad. They had a lot to do today, starting with talking to people down at the harbor.

Clearly, he liked country music; she could hear it playing low on the radio as he drove the pickup down the hill. His Texas background, she guessed.

They didn't talk much as the truck rolled toward Marina Del Rey, but as the minutes ticked past, a knot of dread began to form in her stomach. When they made the last turn and she saw all the boats bobbing in their slips, the knot tightened to the point of pain, and a wave of nausea hit her.

This was the place her father had died. It was the

last place on earth she wanted to be. And the place she needed to be most.

Ty pulled into a visitor parking space in the Village Harbor Marina lot and turned off the engine. "You okay?" he asked gently.

Haley moistened her lips, which felt strangely numb. "I just…I need a minute."

He reached over and caught her hand. "You don't have to do this, Haley. You can stay here and wait for me."

His lean fingers warmed her hand, which had gone icy cold. Some of his strength seemed to penetrate the numbness. She took a deep breath. "I need to do this, Ty. I'll be okay."

He nodded and let go. Sliding out of the truck, he made his way around to her side and opened the door. Before she had time to get out, he caught her arm and helped her climb down. This time, she just thanked him. He was clearly the protective type, and considering how jittery she felt, she was grateful.

Ty set a hand at her back as they walked toward the slip where her father's boat had been kept. She didn't ask how he knew which one it was. He was an investigator. "Knowing things" was his job.

"His slip's still empty," Ty said. "Before the recession there was a waiting list. Now there's a couple of hundred of them for rent."

They walked along the promenade till they reached the locked metal gate leading down the ramp to the dock.

"How do we get in? We don't know the combination."

Ty flicked her an unconcerned glance, then smiled at a couple who opened the gate and walked out just then.

"Mornin'," he said, stepping back out of their way.

He caught her hand and led her through the gate before it had time to close.

"I guess you're one of those people who acts first and asks permission later," she said.

"Helluva lot easier that way."

Apparently it was, because they were stepping off the ramp onto the dock and walking toward one of the vacant slips as if they had every right. There were powerboats on each side of the empty space, a thirty-foot Sea Ray and a Chris-Craft thirty-five.

A man was sanding the deck of the smaller boat. On the other, a woman in a pair of navy shorts and a pink halter top lounged in a chair reading a *People* magazine.

Ty headed for the woman, of course—long black hair, smooth skin, almond eyes, still pretty in her early forties.

"Sorry to bother you, ma'am, but I was wondering if you might be able to help us." The *ma'am* held a faint Texas drawl Haley had noticed before.

Irritation flashed across the woman's face, but the moment she looked up and saw Ty Brodie smiling down at her, her irritation faded.

"It's about the boat that blew up here a couple of months ago."

The woman stood up and walked toward them. Barefoot, her toes were painted a vibrant shade of pink, and she had a really great figure. "I'm Tara Yoshido. What can I do to help?"

Tara Yoshido. Haley remembered seeing the name on the police report as one of the people who'd been interviewed after the accident.

"Did you know James Warren?" Ty asked.

"No. I don't think— Oh, you mean Jimmy! Everyone knew Jimmy. He was a terrific guy. Terrible what happened."

"Yes, it was. My name's Ty Brodie. This is his daughter, Haley. She's trying to find out a little more about the accident. Were you here when it happened?"

"I was here earlier that day, but I left to get a sandwich. I'm really sorry, Haley. As I said, your dad was a great guy."

Haley's throat tightened. "Thank you."

"Is there anything you can tell us about that day?" Ty asked.

"Well, I wasn't here when the boat blew up, but I'd talked to Jimmy earlier. His wife went shopping with a friend, so he was going to take the *Betty Jean* out by himself for a while."

Haley swayed on her feet. Her father had named his boat after the woman he had married—gold-digging Betty Jean Simmons.

She felt Ty's arm slide around her waist, steadying her. Haley allowed herself to lean against him long enough to pull herself together, then straightened away.

"I'm sorry, Haley," Tara said. "I can only imagine how hard this must be for you."

Harder than she ever would have imagined. "Did my father say anything about the boat having problems? A leak of any kind, anything that would make you think it might be dangerous for him to take it out?"

Tara shook her head, moving her long, straight black hair. "Jimmy was a boating fanatic. He kept the *Betty Jean* in perfect condition. The boat was about ten years old, but it looked like it just came off the showroom floor."

"And yet he didn't notice a gas buildup," Haley said darkly.

Tara looked at her with sympathy. "The alarm system must have failed. I guess it was just his time."

Or someone decided it was his time. But so far nothing concrete actually pointed to that.

"Thanks, Tara," Ty said. "We really appreciate your help."

They continued walking along the dock, heading for the boat on the other side of the empty slip. Haley could barely look at the place her father's boat had been. When she did, she noticed some of the boards had been replaced and repainted, repairs after the explosion. It made her stomach churn.

"Hello there!" Ty called above the grating buzz of the sander the man was using on his deck. His skin was suntanned as brown as old oak, his features leathery and windburned. Haley would guess him to be in his early sixties.

He turned off the sander. "What can I do for you folks?"

"If you've got a minute, we'd like to talk to you about the boat that exploded here a couple of months back."

The man set the sander down on the deck. "Real bad, that. Jimmy was a good friend. We all miss him."

"I'm Ty Brodie, and this is his daughter, Haley. She was hoping you might help her understand what happened that day. Were you here?"

The man ambled to the side of the boat and climbed up on the dock. "I was here. Name's Wes Stoder." He extended a hand to Ty, and the men shook. He turned to Haley. "I'm real sorry about your dad."

She managed a nod. "Thank you."

"The explosion did some damage to the boats close by, including mine. I'm still trying to fix the last of it. Lucky no one else was hurt."

"You said you were here when it happened," Ty said. "But I didn't see your name on the police report."

"Didn't talk to them. After the boat blew, there were dozens of people milling around—cops, firemen, EMTs. It was pretty chaotic. The police talked to a lot of people. I figured they got whatever information they needed."

"What do you think happened, Wes?"

He looked over to the place the boat had once been. "Best guess—gas leak in the bilge. Spark must have ignited the fumes when the bilge pump kicked on."

"That was my thinking."

"You a boater?"

"I like the water. Never owned a boat."

Wes scratched his head. "Funny thing is, Jimmy just bought a new pump. He was real proud of it, said it had all the latest safety features."

"Then why did it explode?" Haley asked.

"I wish I knew the answer."

"What time did Jimmy get here that morning?"

"About nine, I guess."

"Before that, did you see anyone around the boat you hadn't seen before? Someone earlier that morning or maybe the night before?"

Wes frowned. "Funny you should ask. I slept on my boat that night. Sometimes I do that, you know? Just to get away from the wife and grandkids, get a little time to myself."

"What was it you saw?"

"I'm not sure. About three o'clock that morning, a noise woke me up. When I looked out the porthole, I thought I saw someone getting off the *Betty Jean*. Didn't see much more than a shadow. Still, after what happened, it kind of made me wonder."

"You tell that to the police?"

"They didn't ask."

Ty took out one of his business cards and handed it to Wes, who looked down and read the printing. "You're a private detective?"

"That's right. We're just tying up loose ends. You think of anything else, I'd really appreciate a call."

Wes stuffed the card into the pocket of his Bermuda shorts. "You got it."

"Thank you, Mr. Stoder," Haley said.

He just nodded and climbed back aboard his boat. The grating sound of the sander followed them as they walked away. They talked to a couple more people in the marina, but none had been at the harbor that day. Figuring they had done all they could for the moment, Haley let Ty guide her back to the truck.

She didn't protest when he helped her climb in. She had enough on her mind thinking about her dad.

Six

Ty drove the pickup back toward his office, his mind running over the conversations he'd had with Wes Stoder and Tara Yoshido. Nothing solid. Nothing he could take to the police. Instead of giving him answers, the information only stirred up more questions.

They were halfway back to Hollywood before Haley started talking.

"Dad had just bought a new bilge pump," she said, bringing his mind back to Wes Stoder's remarks. "It shouldn't have sparked. And Mr. Stoder said he saw someone on the boat the night before."

"Stoder said he *might* have seen someone. Or it could have been a shadow."

Haley sat up a little straighter, tightening the seat belt across her breasts and drawing his attention to their roundness and uptilting shape. They were just the size he liked, not too big, not too small. He forced his eyes back to the road.

"I called Betty Jean about the computers," Haley said. "My father never mentioned having any problems."

She turned a little to look at him, tightening the strap again, making his palms itch to cup those sweet breasts.

Don't even think about it.

"She said the laptop was only a few months old and he was always saying how much he liked it. As far as she knew the desktop was working fine, too."

"I was afraid of that."

"So if the laptop was working and dad didn't take the C drive out of the desktop, then someone else must have done it."

"That's right. And that someone would have to have been inside the house."

Her eyes widened. "You think it was someone he knew?"

"Or someone broke in, screwed with the laptop and took the C drive so no one could see what was on it. Call her back, find out when we can come by. We need to take a look, try to figure out if someone broke into the house. Dammit, we were already halfway there."

Haley took her phone out but didn't make the call. Instead she gripped it tightly in her hand.

"Dad named the boat after her, Ty. I can't believe he couldn't tell what a gold digger she is."

Ty glanced her way, careful to keep his gaze fixed on her face. Her pouty lips were thinned, her dark gold eyebrows drawn together.

"They weren't exactly living the high life, Haley. If Betty Jean was a gold digger, you'd think she'd want a whole lot more than a single family home in Torrance and clothes that came from JCPenney."

"She must have spent the money. You're an investigator. Can't you look into her bank accounts, check her spending? You could find out what she did with the money Dad got out of his retirement. He must have had several million at least when he married her."

"I'm not doing that, Haley. I don't think Betty Jean is a gold digger."

Haley seemed not to hear him. "Oh, my God—I never even thought. What if she took out some big life insurance policy on him right before he died? If she did, maybe she had something to do with the explosion."

Ty scoffed. "That's the reason she emailed you? To get you to come to California and discover she was the one responsible for his death?"

Haley slumped back in her seat. She looked tired and a little too pale. "You're right. That's crazy. I don't know what's the matter with me."

"What's the matter is you feel like your father abandoned you when he divorced your mother. You blame Betty Jean for taking him away from you. If your father was still alive, you could talk to him, figure things out, but he'd dead, so you can't."

She cast him a sideways glance. "So now you're a psychiatrist. I didn't realize I was working with Dr. Phil."

He almost smiled. "I'm a detective. Figuring people out is part of my job."

She let her head fall back against the headrest. He thought he caught the shimmer of tears. Haley sat up and stared straight ahead, her gaze on the cars rolling along in front of them. The line of vehicles was starting to slow, jamming together. Ty loved L.A., but he hated the f-ing traffic.

Haley turned her pretty blue eyes in his direction. He could read the turmoil there.

"I'm not really like this," she said softly. "Not usually. I'm sorry."

Sympathy slid through him. At least he and his dad had been friends when his dad was killed. "Was your mother really that broken up over the divorce? Clearly you were upset, but what about her?"

"My mother loved my father."

"Okay, but how did *he* feel about *her?*"

Haley closed her eyes. He wondered what it was she didn't want to see.

A slow breath whispered out. "The truth is, my mother is a difficult woman. She and my father rarely spent time together. He had his life and she had hers. Being here makes it even clearer how far apart the two of them actually were."

"I don't know what happened to cause the divorce, but I don't think Betty Jean was the only one to blame. Your father wanted a different life. He was able to find it here."

"I guess…maybe."

"Call her. Tell her we want to come by sometime tomorrow. On Monday, I'll take the laptop in to the guys who are working on his cell phone. They can probably restore the files. Maybe we'll find something there."

"And we can talk to the people in his office. See what they have to say."

"Yeah." He already had that on his agenda. He didn't need to take Haley along, but he was realizing more and more how important this was to her.

Haley made the call to set up the Sunday meeting. "All right. After church, then."

She hung up the phone, looked at him. "She and Dad went to church every Sunday."

"Nothing wrong with that."

Haley swallowed. "I didn't even know my father believed in God."

Her face looked even paler. She was struggling to come to terms with a father she hadn't really known.

Winding along Sunset, he turned up Laurel Canyon and wound his way up the hill toward his office. At the bottom of the drive, he entered the security code into a keypad, the automatic gate swung open and he pulled on up the drive.

"So you think it might not have been an accident," Haley said as he turned off the engine.

"I don't know," he said. "But we've definitely got a few too many loose ends."

Haley sat out on the deck that afternoon. She was working with her sketch pad, trying to ease a little of the tension she was feeling since their return from Marina Del Rey.

Ty had disappeared into his office down the hill. He had work to do, he'd said, previous cases to finish, calls left on his answering machine to return. There were things he needed to do to keep the business running smoothly while his partner was out of town.

"Amy helps out whenever she isn't at work," he'd told her. "She keeps us organized, kind of keeps the wheels turning."

She could tell how much he liked Johnnie's wife. Haley liked her, too.

And she was starting to like Ty Brodie. She thought of what he had said on the way back to the house. He was right about a lot of things, including the fact her parents' divorce hadn't been entirely Betty Jean's fault. Her father and mother were already having problems when he met her—big ones, she assumed, or he wouldn't have given up his family and moved away.

Haley had been twenty-one at the time, old enough

she should have been able to accept her father's choice. But she and her mother had never really been close, and losing the father who had been her dearest friend had seemed like the ultimate betrayal.

Haley still wasn't sure what had happened to his retirement money, but she figured eventually she'd find out. At the moment, finding out the truth about his death was the first order of business.

She flipped through the two drawings she had just completed on her sketch pad—Mr. Stoder and Tara Yoshido. They had known her dad. She wished she could have talked to them longer, asked them more about him.

She flipped the page, began to sketch another face. Lean, angular cheeks, straight nose, perceptive, long-lashed eyes, dark brown hair a little shaggier than it should have been. She filled in his handsome features as best she could, but as she studied the drawing, his mouth didn't look quite right.

She erased it, tried again. Still didn't like it. With a sigh, she set the sketchbook aside and wandered back into the house for a Diet Coke. Ellie was off with a *friend.* Next time she said that, Haley was going to ask her this friend's name.

Her cell phone started ringing. She ran back outside and grabbed it off the glass-topped table, pressed it against her ear.

"Hi, Haley, it's Lane."

"Hey, Lane. It was really great seeing you again."

"It really was. Listen, I had an appointment in Hollywood. I thought if you weren't busy, I might stop by before I went back to the studio."

"Absolutely." She gave her friend directions and hung up the phone. Over supper, they'd had a great time reminiscing about their college days. Haley had hated to see the evening end. When the intercom buzzed, she went over and punched in the code, setting the gate at the bottom of the drive in motion.

A few minutes later, she opened the door and Lane Bishop walked into the foyer. She was far prettier now than she had been in college, her features stronger, more confident. With her shoulder-length auburn hair and high cheekbones, long legs and slender figure, she was stunningly beautiful.

"God, it's good to have you back," Lane said, leaning over to hug her. "Someone I can really talk to."

"I know what you mean. Last night felt like we'd been together just last week instead of six years ago." Though Lane was a year older, they'd both been sophomores in college when Lane's mother had been diagnosed with breast cancer. Lane had moved to L.A. to take care of her. Haley had never had another friend she could talk to the way she could Lane.

It seemed that hadn't changed.

They popped a couple cans of Diet Coke, poured them over ice and wandered back out on the deck.

"Gorgeous house," Lane said. "I love the view."

"Me, too. My aunt isn't home, but she's really great. I'd love for you to meet her."

"That'd be great. Maybe we can all go to dinner sometime." She took a sip of her soda. "So, what's the latest on your investigation?"

"Lots of loose ends. That's what Ty says. And too many coincidences."

"Ty Brodie—the young detective. You said he was really good-looking." Lane spotted the half-finished sketch on the chaise lounge, walked over and picked it up.

"You're still drawing?"

She shrugged. "Just for fun. How about you? You still painting?"

Lane shrugged. "I decided I'd rather be a working designer than an unemployed artist. The pay is definitely better."

Haley laughed. It was never easy to follow your dreams.

Lane looked down at the picture. "I've got a feeling this is Mr. Macho, former Marine and definite hottie."

"That's him. He's actually better-looking. I haven't been able to get it quite right. I'm not that good an artist."

"You're not that bad, either, and he looks damn good to me." She set the sketch pad back on the chaise and they wandered over to the table and sat down. "So when do I get to meet him?"

Haley's stomach tightened. Lane was beautiful, poised and intelligent. In college, the boys used to fall at her feet. She knew just how to handle them, how to keep a guy dangling. Haley was never that good with men.

Back then it bothered her. Now that she was older, she didn't really care. She might be attracted to Ty Brodie, but she knew if she tried for any kind of relationship, even just a few nights in bed, she would only be disappointed.

"His office is right next door," Haley said, trying to sound nonchalant. "You'll probably run into him sooner or later."

Lane set her Coke down on the table. "How about sooner? How about right now?"

Haley felt a jolt of panic. "He's working. He wouldn't want to be disturbed."

Lane fell back in her chair, laughing. "I knew it! You can tell me you aren't the least bit interested, but I've known you too long. If he looks as hot as your sketch, I think you ought to take him out for a spin."

Haley felt a trickle of relief that Lane respected their friendship and wasn't interested in Ty, which was ridiculous under the circumstances.

"No, thanks. I have enough things to worry about right now."

Lane's smile instantly faded. "I know you do. I remember how you always worshipped your dad. But maybe having a little fling with Brodie would help ease some of the pain."

But it wouldn't, Haley knew. "It would only make working together a lot harder. Maybe impossible." And afterward, she would feel the same emptiness and dissatisfaction.

"Tell me about Modern Design," Haley said to end the subject, and Lane launched into a long conversation about the interior design studio she had opened several years back.

"You know, Haley, you've always had such a wonderful artistic eye. If you stayed in L.A., maybe we could combine your art background with my design work. You know—I do the plan for the refurbishment of a home and you help the owner choose the art. We could be really great together."

Haley shook her head. "My life is in Chicago. As soon as this is resolved, I'm going home."

Lane wiggled her russet eyebrows. "So I guess Studly Do-Right is out of luck."

Haley laughed. "Absolutely. By the way, how's *your* love life? I can't believe you haven't got a hottie of your own?"

Lane smiled. "I'm on the wagon. I was dating this guy for a while, but he turned out to be a major creep.

Started calling me all the time, following me around. At the moment, he's in jail for assault. Beat some poor guy up after a Lakers game."

"Sounds like you were way off on that one."

"He was good-looking and smart. We only went out a couple of times before I figured out he was also really weird."

"No wonder you're on the wagon."

Lane smiled. "Hey, you want to go windsurfing sometime? Remember how much fun we used to have out on the lake? You used to be really good."

"I'd love to go, once all of this is settled. I'm a little rusty, since I kind of took up paragliding instead. But I don't think it would take me long to get back in the swing."

"Great, we'll make a date."

"I'll keep you posted on what's happening with… you know…the accident."

Lane reached over and caught her hand, gave it a re-assuring squeeze. "You want to talk, call me anytime." She got up from her chair. "I better get going. You sure about Mr. Hot?"

"I'm sure." But as she thought of Ty and the little zing she felt whenever he touched her, she couldn't help a pang of regret that she wasn't more like Lane when it came to men.

Seven

"Come on in, you two." Still wearing her church clothes, a soft yellow pantsuit and pearls, Betty Jean smiled her usual warm greeting. "I just got home. There was a church meeting after the service that ran a little late. I haven't had time to change."

"That's all right," Ty said. "We don't mind waiting if you want to put on something more comfortable."

Betty Jean looked at Haley, standing quietly next to him. "Are you sure? If you're in a hurry—"

"No, it's fine," Haley said.

"Well, if you have the time, I think I will."

Ty gave her a smile. And while she was gone, he could take a look around, see if there was any sign of a break-in.

"I'll be right back." Betty Jean looked at Haley, the soft yearning in her face Ty had seen before. She wanted the daughter of the man she'd loved to like her. Maybe wanted her to understand that he had been happy.

Betty Jean hurried off down the hall to the bedroom,

and Ty led Haley into the kitchen. "Let's take a look, see if there's any indication of a break-in."

"There's an alarm system," Haley said. "I saw the sticker on the window."

"I saw the keypad by the kitchen door when we were here before. Not much of a system. An amateur could get in without setting it off."

One of her eyebrows went up. "I guess that means you could do it."

He grinned. "Piece of cake."

Haley flashed him a look, but the corner of her mouth kicked up and one of her dimples appeared. Ty felt an instant shot of lust.

Not good. His resistance to the pull of those dimples was dwindling, and he couldn't afford to let that happen.

Her smile slowly faded. It didn't show up that often. He had a feeling she felt guilty about enjoying herself so soon after her father had passed.

Ty started moving around the kitchen, checking the back door for marks on the jamb, checking the window over the sink and the one in the breakfast nook for any hint that either had been forced open. When nothing turned up, he headed for the study which, like the kitchen and master bedroom, faced the backyard.

The window wasn't locked, he saw. Pushed tightly closed, but not locked. He caught Haley's hand, felt her knee-jerk effort to pull free, then she relaxed and let him lead her back into the kitchen and out the back door.

Moving along the outside wall, he paused when he reached the study window.

"See this?" He pointed to a mark on the aluminum frame.

"I don't see anything." He took out his flashlight and shined it on the bottom of the frame, illuminating the indentation he had spotted from inside the house. "Someone used something to pry open the window," she said.

"Weather's been warm. Your dad probably opened it to let in some air. He might have shut it, but he didn't lock it. Whoever was looking for a way to get in found an easy avenue."

"What about the alarm?"

"Disabled it before they started searching for a way inside. We need to check for prints."

"Fingerprints? How do we do that?"

"I've got a kit in the truck. I'll be right back." When he returned, Haley was in the kitchen having a somewhat stilted conversation with Betty Jean. At least they were talking.

The older woman looked up at him. "Haley says you think someone may have broken into the house." She'd changed from the pantsuit into jeans and a purple flowered top.

"Unless at some time you climbed into the house through the study window, I'd say there's a distinct possibility."

Her lips faintly curved. "No, I don't think I could do that on my best day."

"Ty thinks whoever did it came in to destroy the computers. He may have found something on the C drive. Instead of trying to erase it, he just stole it."

"Oh, my heavens!"

"You need a better alarm system, Betty Jean. I can recommend someone if you want."

"Yes, all right."

Ty jotted down the names of two security companies he knew were good, then went back outside, used a brush and powder to check for prints on the sill, but didn't find any.

Back in the study, he found a couple of prints, used tape to lift them, then bagged the tape. He'd take the tape to the forensic lab, but from the position they were in, he had a hunch they belonged to James Warren.

The women were quiet when he returned to the kitchen. "Either the intruder wiped the place down or he was wearing gloves. I got a couple of prints, but I have a hunch they belong to…umm…Jimmy."

Haley frowned and Betty Jean bit her lip.

"Was your husband working a current case that might have been reason enough for someone to want him out of the way?"

Betty Jean shook her head. "I don't think so. There was a burglary at a small boutique, but not that much was taken. Jimmy said the claim checked out. A couple of weeks later, he mentioned the old art theft again. Jimmy said he might have stumbled across something that could lead him to the people involved. He never stopped looking for them."

"A Titian and a Caravaggio," Haley recalled. "The originals would have been priceless."

"Even on the black market, they could have sold for tens of millions."

"If Jimmy was close," Betty Jean said, "if he had picked up information that could bring the thieves to justice, they might have been willing to kill him to keep him from sending them to prison."

Ty reached over and squeezed her hand. "We'll stay on this. We'll figure it out, okay?"

"We won't quit until we find out the truth," Haley promised.

Betty Jean looked at Ty and her lips trembled. "Thank you." She turned to Haley. "You remind me of your father. So strong and determined. No wonder he loved you so much."

Moisture flashed in Haley's eyes, then it was gone. Turning, she headed for the front door, pulled it open and walked outside.

Betty Jean sighed. "I don't suppose she'll ever forgive me."

"From what I've seen, Haley's smart and she's no fool. Sooner or later she'll figure things out. You just need to be patient."

Betty Jean wiped a tear from her cheek. "You're a good man, Ty Brodie. I'm glad you're helping her."

"I'm helping both of you. That's what I do. I'll keep you in the loop."

She nodded as he turned and walked out of the house. Haley was waiting beside the pickup when he pushed the electronic key and the locks clicked open. She didn't protest when he helped her climb into the seat.

Ty took it as a good sign.

The Sunday traffic was worse on the way back to the office. Living in downtown Chicago made things easier, Haley thought. She could walk or cab anywhere she needed to go.

"I've got some business to take care of," Ty said as they finally drove into the parking area and he turned off the engine. "And I'd like to take another look at that laptop before I take it into the lab in the morning."

"We're also going to my father's office, right? Talk to people at Allied Global who worked with him?"

"That's right. Maybe we can get a look at the computer he was using."

"Good idea." Haley left him there and headed up the hill to retrieve the laptop. She didn't really think he'd get the computer to work any better than she had, which was not at all, but it was worth a try. She went inside and got it out of her bedroom, walked back down to Ty's office, rapped on the door and walked inside.

Ty flicked her a glance, but his attention remained on the computer screen in front of him. "Why don't you set it up on the spare desk over there?"

The office was roomy, maybe two thousand square feet, the lower floor of the former guesthouse upstairs, with an entrance from above, and one Ty and his partner had added that led to the parking lot.

Like the upstairs level, a wall of windows looked out over the valley, a similar view to the one her aunt had in the big house up the hill. There were two separate work areas and an extra desk. A line of hot car photos decorated the walls: a '57 Chevy, a couple of tricked-out Mustangs, a rebuilt El Camino pickup.

The only thing unusual about the office was the gym set up in the corner, complete with five-inch rubber mats. Clearly, John Riggs and Ty Brodie liked to stay in shape.

A thought that had her gaze swinging toward him. She had sketched his face fairly well, gotten the right shape to his ears, nose and eyebrows. It was his mouth she couldn't quite capture.

She found herself staring at it, trying to memorize the curve of his upper lip, the fullness, the way the bottom and top lips connected at the corners, the way they looked firm but at the same time soft. Though he was handsome, there was nothing soft about his features except maybe for those lips. She couldn't seem to take her eyes off them.

She hadn't realized he had turned and was watching her just as she watched him. Not until she heard the sound of his chair sliding back, the heavy thud of his worn cowboy boots as he strode toward her.

"You're staring at me," he said.

Her gaze jerked up. Those changeable eyes were a hot molten brown. "I'm…I'm sorry. I just… I did a sketch of you. Charcoal drawing's a hobby of mine." He was standing right in front of her. Six-foot-two inches of rock-solid male. For an instant, she thought of what Lane had said. But having a fling with Ty Brodie wouldn't work.

Just like it had never worked before. "I was trying to get your mouth just right," she said.

Those elusive lips quirked up. "Maybe if I kiss you, it'll help."

She swallowed. "That's not a good idea."

Ty moved closer. "Why not?"

She could smell his aftershave, something a little spicy. "Because I'm not…not good with men. In fact, lately, I've been wondering if I might be more comfortable in a…umm…woman-woman relationship."

His eyes widened. "Wow, I didn't see that one coming. So you and your friend, Lane—you're lesbians?"

"No!"

"Not that I have anything against that kind of thing. Each to his own, and all that. But you just don't seem—"

"I—I've never tried it or anything. I just thought that maybe it would explain my failure in the area of… umm…sex."

"So you've never tried it, but you're attracted to women?"

"No! I mean, I don't know." *Oh, God!*

One of his dark eyebrows went up. "You're not a virgin, are you?"

"No, of course not. It's just…with men, it's always been disappointing, so I figured, maybe—"

"Disappointing, huh?" Something shifted in his features, changed to a look of determination. "Why don't we see?"

Catching her shoulders so she couldn't escape, Ty pulled her closer, lowered his head and caught her mouth in a ravishing kiss. He didn't give her time to think, time to stop him, just settled in and started kissing her. Those firm/soft lips simply took over, framing hers, melding, taking, coaxing, then taking charge again.

Liquid warmth spread through her. Butterflies floated up beneath her ribs, her skin tingled and suddenly she felt light-headed.

Ty didn't stop, just kept kissing her, teasing her lips apart, then sliding his tongue inside. A rush of heat roared through her and she started to tremble. Her legs went weak, threatening to buckle beneath her, and he pulled her into his arms. If he hadn't been holding her up, she might have melted into a puddle at his feet.

Ty was leisurely now, kissing her without the slightest hurry, the way he seemed to do everything else. Nibbling the corner of her mouth, nipping an ear, then taking her lips again. She couldn't remember when she slid her arms around his neck, didn't know when she'd leaned into him and started kissing him back.

She only knew she felt like butter in the sun, her stomach flipping, her knees shaking, her head spinning. She wanted him to kiss her forever. A little whimper escaped the instant before he lifted his head to look down at her.

"Wow" was all he said.

Haley wheezed in a breath. "I can't...can't breathe. I think I'm going to faint."

Ty grinned and eased her over to the chair at his desk. "Not a lesbian, I don't think."

"What did...did you do to me?"

His grin widened. "I just kissed you, darlin'. Sometimes it works. Sometimes it doesn't." His smile slipped a bit. "I had a hunch this was going to work a little too well."

Haley reached up and touched her lips, ran her tongue over them, tasted him there. "Oh, my God."

"I want to take you to bed, honey, show you just how good it can be, but, Jesus, you're Ellie's niece."

She looked up at him, tried not to focus on that amazing mouth and bring her pounding heart under control. "It...it probably wouldn't be any good anyway. It never has been the times I tried before."

"I have a hunch there weren't that many times, and maybe the chemistry just wasn't there. It's there in spades with us, sweetheart."

She shook her head, which made her feel dizzy again. "We're working together."

He stepped back, raked a hand through his hair. "Yeah, and besides, Ellie's your aunt and my friend. It wouldn't be right to take advantage."

But Haley wondered if it wouldn't be the other way around, since she had already considered sleeping with Ty.

"I'd better go." She tipped her head toward the laptop. "I didn't get it hooked up, but it's there if you want to take a look." She started walking, forced her wobbly legs to move toward the door. "I'll see you in the morning."

Ty just stood there, his eyes still hot, hands propped on lean hips as he watched her leave.

Haley didn't sleep well that night. At three in the morning she awakened in the throes of the hottest sexual fantasy she'd ever experienced. Ty Brodie's hard body was on top of her, his erection moving inside her. His hands were fisted in her hair, holding her in place as he ravished her mouth in a kiss even more erotic than the one that afternoon.

Teetering on the edge of climax, she gasped as she jerked awake, her body drenched in perspiration and shaking all over.

Frustration gripped her, followed by the hollow ache of disappointment. With a sigh, Haley let her head fall back against the pillow. It had been that way since the first time she'd had sex. Mark Winters had been her high school sweetheart, the star quarterback. She had given him her virginity in the back of his father's Cadillac Seville and been surprised to discover what a nothing experience it was.

No stars bursting, no flashes of lightning behind her eyes. In fact it had been over too fast for her to get any real sense of what sex was like. The times after that weren't much better. Not for her and not really for Mark. They'd broken up when they were accepted at different colleges.

She had dated Richard Marshall, an art student and aspiring artist, her last year of college. Being more friends than lovers, they were unable to create much passion. The relationship had ended and neither had been particularly upset about it.

She had tried a one-night stand, but it had left her

even more dissatisfied, and she had realized she wasn't cut out for that kind of thing.

Punching her pillow, she turned onto her side and tried to go back to sleep. At 6:00 a.m., she gave up and rolled out of bed, pulled on her running shorts and took off up the hill, taking a lap around the dirt track that ran along the perimeter fence surrounding the property.

She felt better when she got home, ready to face the day ahead. Determined not to think about kissing Tyler Brodie.

Eight

It was blue skies and California sunshine, a light breeze in off the ocean as Ty headed for the parking lot the next morning, Haley walking beside him. She hadn't said three words since she'd arrived at the office. He figured she was trying not to think of the hot kiss they'd shared, same as he was. He wished he could wipe it completely from his memory, but so far it hadn't worked.

His cell phone started playing before they reached his pickup. He pulled it out of his pocket, checked the number, saw it was Susan Wilson and shoved it back into his jeans.

"Same girl?" Haley asked, her pretty blue eyes on his face.

Ty just nodded. Susan had always been persistent.

"Did you call her last night after I left?"

His head snapped up. "Hell, no. I don't work that way." He'd thought about it, though, which was bad enough. Haley had left him so hard and aching he'd considered making a booty call. Not his usual style. He was single-minded when he wanted a lady.

Unfortunately, the lady he wanted was pretty much off-limits.

"Why not?"

She wasn't going to let it drop. Since he wasn't much good at lying, he might as well tell her the truth. "Because you were the woman I wanted. I wasn't in the mood for someone else."

Her cheeks colored faintly. "Oh."

He stopped beside the passenger door of the truck. "Look, Haley. I get that this attraction between us isn't going anywhere, so you don't have to worry. I'm not going to push you into doing something you don't want to do."

Not that it wasn't tempting.

She was so damned cute with her hair pulled into the same blond ponytail she'd worn to the harbor. It made her look like a high school student, which, considering his thoughts, should have made him feel like a pervert.

But Haley was twenty-six years old, and though she might be a little naive, he had a feeling they'd be dynamite together in bed.

They drove mostly in silence. He tried to keep his mind on business, but every time he looked at her, his gaze fixed on her mouth. He remembered the exact shape and softness of those pouty lips, the way they fit so perfectly with his, and inside his jeans, he went hard.

With a silent curse, he pulled off the freeway. They had a stop to make on their way to her father's office at Allied Global. On the south side of Santa Monica, Ty drove into the parking lot of Forensic Services, Inc, the private lab he and Johnnie used for DNA and fingerprint work.

The fee wasn't cheap, but the client was usually willing to pay a premium to speed up the investigation. And the lab was full service, with tech guys who were geniuses at recovering computer and cell phone information from damaged equipment.

Ty dropped the bagged fingerprint samples off at one end of the lab, then headed down the hall with the laptop in search of Ian Whitlow, one of the computer techs. Haley's long strides kept pace as they approached the counter where Ian stood. He was wearing a satisfied grin that could only come from morning sex. It made Ty think of Haley and curse his bad luck.

"Haley Warren meet Ian Whitlow," he said.

"Nice to meet you, Haley." Ian was the same age as Ty, blond and good-looking. They'd been friends since Ty had fixed him up with a little brunette named Sadie Perkins he had met on a case. Since Ian had fallen hard for Sadie and they were getting married, Ty figured his friend owed him big-time.

"Find anything on the iPhone?" Ty asked.

"Still working on it," Ian said. "Phone was in bad condition. Melted and waterlogged. Heat must have been incredible."

Haley's face went a little pale as she absorbed the implication. Ty flicked his friend a glance, warning him to watch his words.

"This is his laptop." Ty lifted the case up on the counter. "Looks like someone tried to wipe it. I gave it a shot. So did Haley. We couldn't get squat."

"I'll take a look." Ian flashed her a sympathetic glance. "Sorry about your dad."

"Thanks."

"Let me know if anything turns up," Ty said.

"Will do."

They headed out the door and continued to the Allied Global office on the ninth floor of a high-rise building on Admiralty Way. A stout receptionist with mouse-brown hair smiled a greeting as he and Haley walked up.

"Good morning, Ms...." Ty read her tag. "Mrs. Steinman." He returned her smile. "My name's Tyler Brodie. This is Haley Warren, James Warren's daughter. We'd like to speak to Mr. Warren's boss."

Mrs. Steinman cast a sympathetic glance at Haley. "Your father mentioned he had a daughter. It's nice to meet you. Everyone loved your dad. We called him, Jimmy, though. We really miss him around here."

Haley managed a smile. "That's kind of you to say."

"I'll call Mr. Potter. He was Jimmy's direct superior. I'm sure he'll be happy to speak to you."

Ten minutes later, they were sitting across the desk from a man in his forties in a navy blue suit and red power tie. He had thick, sandy-brown hair.

"I can only imagine how difficult your father's death must be for you," Potter said to Haley. "If there's anything at all we here at Allied Global can do for you, you only have to ask."

"I'd like to know a little about what he'd been working on before he was killed," Haley said, leading the conversation in the right direction.

"Like most of our investigators, he was working a number of different cases. Your father was in the SIU. That's our Special Investigations Unit. He was one of our top people so he was always busy."

"Was there anything specific?" Ty asked. "Something important enough that his life might have been in danger?"

Surprise registered on Potter's round face. He leaned back in his chair. "Surely you don't think the explosion was more than an accident?"

"We don't know. I'm a private investigator working for Ms. Warren. Haley just wants to be sure all the loose ends are tied up."

Potter relaxed a little. "Yes, I can understand that. As I said, Jimmy had a fairly heavy caseload. He was working a possible arson fire on a home-owner's garage, as well as a suspicious burglary at a local Food Mart. Both of those matters have been settled. He was working a robbery/vandalism at a little boutique, but there wasn't a lot of money involved."

"I'd like to have a list of the cases."

Potter shook his head. "I'm afraid it would be against company policy to give out the specifics of any given claim, but as far as I know, there was nothing out of the ordinary. Certainly nothing that would be motive enough for murder."

"How about enemies? Someone from an old case who had a bone to pick with him?"

Potter shook his head. "Honestly, I can't imagine that happening. Jimmy was always very thorough, but once he got the facts, the case was handed on to another agent for settlement."

So no enemies, nothing current that stood out. Which led them back to the art fraud case.

"There was an old case my father was interested in," Haley said, picking up Ty's train of thought. "It had to do with the theft of some very valuable paintings."

Potter chuckled. "Your father was a real bulldog when it came to solving a mystery. Even three years later, he was convinced eventually he would find the culprits who stole those priceless works of art."

"Then maybe he stumbled onto something," Ty suggested. "Is there a chance we could take a look at his computer? I'd like to see if there's anything new in his files regarding that case."

Potter pondered the notion. "I shouldn't allow it. But since the case is no longer active, I suppose it wouldn't hurt. Currently Jimmy's computer is being used by the woman we hired to replace him—not an easy thing to do, I assure you. Stella's in the office. Let me talk to her, see if she has any objections."

"Thanks." Sitting next to Haley in front of Potter's desk, Ty waited while the man went down the hall to speak to Warren's replacement.

Haley looked both anxious and fiercely determined. The lady was a bit of a bulldog herself.

Potter returned a few minutes later. "Stella's going to take a break while you look at her computer."

"Thank you."

"Try not to take too long." Potter led them down the hall into one of the private offices. A window looked out over the blue Pacific.

"He must have been good at his job," Ty said, taking in the spectacular view of harbor and ocean.

"Dad was good at anything he set his mind to. That's the way he was about art. When he and my mother got married, my mother was the one who was interested in art, but Dad knew how important it was to her so he made a real effort to understand the subject. He never came to like modern art, but he really enjoyed the old masters."

"Probably part of the reason he was so interested in the case."

Ty walked over to the computer. It was already turned on when he sat down. A couple of clicks and the menu popped up on the C drive, files that went back several years. He started checking dates, beginning a year ago and moving forward to around the time James Warren had died. One file snagged his attention.

Old Masters February 2, 2012. A week before he'd been killed. Ty clicked open the file.

"What is it?" Haley peered over his shoulder, standing so close he could smell her soft perfume. He clamped his jaw against a rush of heat headed straight for his groin.

He looked at the screen. "The art theft file. All the information your dad uncovered on the original theft is in here. Names, dates, people he talked to, places he went trying to come up with a lead." He reached over and hit the print button, heard the printer click into gear.

"I guess we're still acting first and asking permission later."

"We're not asking at all. Stick those papers in your purse."

He thought she might hesitate, but she just reached over and grabbed them out of the printer, shoved them into her leather handbag. She went back to studying the monitor from behind him, standing close and driving him crazy.

"Is there any information in the file that looks new?" she asked.

"Hard to know for sure without reading it all the way through. We'll do that when we get back. From what I can tell, it appears to be just the information he'd gathered for the original investigation." Ty looked at her over his shoulder. "The interesting thing is the date."

Ty moved the cursor so the date of the last viewing showed up.

"February second of this year," Haley said. "But the case was three years old." Her eyes locked with his. "Dad was reviewing the file just before he was killed."

Nine

They spent the afternoon and early evening perusing the file, jotting down pertinent information. All of the entries would have to be gone over, calls made to the people involved, some of them interviewed. It was a big job, one that would take hours of labor.

Haley wouldn't have been able to afford the cost, but Ty was working for free. It was a lot to ask a man she had only just met. And yet, she wouldn't refuse his offer of assistance. She owed it to her father to find out the truth.

As the evening settled in, Ty ordered Chinese take-out, and they carried it up to the big house to share with Ellie. Her aunt supplied plates and they all sat down at the kitchen table. Even the nook in the kitchen had a gorgeous view, the lights of the city beginning to flicker on in the valley below.

Using chopsticks at Ellie's insistence, Ty forked in a mouthful of chow mein with amazing expertise, washed it down with a sip of hot green tea. "So Jimmy—sorry,

I mean James—was working on the cold case art heist, or at least looking into it, right before he was killed."

"You might as well call him Jimmy," Haley said with a sigh. "Everyone else does."

His mouth edged up as if he approved, then he shoved in a big lump of sweet-and-sour pork and Haley had to tear her gaze away from his lips as he chewed. Ruthlessly, she tamped down the memory of the sexiest kiss she'd ever had, and took a mouthful of fried rice.

"So you're starting to believe it wasn't an accident," Ellie said to Ty.

"When you put it all together, it's a definite maybe-not. Betty Jean says he mentioned he might have found a new lead on the cold case. The computer in his office at work verifies he'd been looking into the file the week before he was killed. The C drive in his desktop is gone, and the files on his laptop have been corrupted. Add to that, the coincidence that none of the alarms on his boat were working and his brand-new bilge pump just happened to spark that same morning."

"And don't forget Mr. Stoder," Haley added. "He thinks there may have been someone aboard Dad's boat the night before it blew up."

"Wouldn't the police have found some sign of a bomb or other explosive device when they investigated the in-cident?" Ellie asked.

"Probably. But there are other, more subtle ways to cause an explosion."

"Such as?" Haley asked.

"The gas leak theory might be right on. The question is why was it leaking in the first place and why were the sensors not working?"

Ellie took a sip of her tea. "Still…you'd think the

police would have run across something that would indicate foul play."

"The cops had no reason to suspect the accident was anything other than what it seemed—a powerboat explosion resulting in loss of life. The arson squad would have been called in, but under the circumstances, they wouldn't have been looking too hard for evidence of murder."

The word made Haley's stomach tighten. She forced herself to swallow the bite of chow mein she'd just taken. "Would they have kept whatever was recovered from the water after the explosion?"

"Good question. There may be something in the boat salvage yard. I've got some friends. If there's anything there, I can probably get in to see it."

Haley thought of the *Betty Jean,* bobbing peacefully in the water one moment, exploding into a ball of red-hot flames the next. The knot in her stomach went tighter. No longer hungry, she pushed her plate away.

Ty's hand settled gently on her shoulder. "We can stop anytime you say. We can let your father rest in peace."

But he wasn't in peace. Not if he had been murdered. If she had been the victim, he would have searched till the day he died to find her killer. "If he was murdered, someone's going to pay."

Ty squeezed her shoulder as if he'd expected that answer. "Then we'll figure it out." For an instant their eyes caught, and the air between them seemed to sizzle with sexual heat. She thought of that mind-blowing kiss and her breathing went faster. She had to drag her gaze away.

They finished the meal. Ty shoved back his chair and began to gather up empty cartons.

"I'll do that," Ellie said, carrying her plate over to the sink.

"I'll take care of it," said Haley.

Ty grinned and stepped back out of the way. "The old Tom Sawyer trick. Works every time."

Haley arched an eyebrow in question.

"Make it look like fun," Ty said, "so everyone wants to do it and you're off the hook."

She smiled. "You're a Mark Twain fan?"

"I loved his books as a kid. I used to read them to my little brother." His smile slowly faded. "I'd forgotten that. Funny how time slips away."

"So the two of you are close?"

"Were, till he joined the army. Davy was killed in Iraq."

"Oh, Ty, I'm so sorry."

He glanced away. "After it happened, I made it my personal mission to avenge his death. I re-upped and went Force Recon."

Ellie looked at Haley. "That's the Marine version of the Navy SEALs, dear."

Haley's gaze shot back to Ty, but he was staring out the window. From the start, she had sensed some inner toughness, a core of steel that belied his easygoing manner. Now she knew what it was.

She carried the empty tea mugs over and set them down on the counter. "Go ahead and go. I'm sure you have something better to do than dishes."

His smile was back in place. "Actually, I do."

"Late date?" she couldn't help asking.

"Date with an old case file. Couple more things I want to check. If I find anything, I'll let you know in the morning."

Not a woman. She shouldn't have been so relieved. "Good night, then."

"Good night. Night, Ellie. Thanks."

Her aunt chuckled. "You're the one who brought supper."

Ty just waved and headed for the door. Haley watched his lanky frame disappear outside, heard the door close softly behind him.

When she looked up, her aunt's pale blue eyes were watching with far too much perception. "So now that you two have been working together, what do you think?"

Haley shrugged, tried to act nonchalant. "He definitely seems capable. He's nice enough."

Those sleek silver eyebrows went up. "He's nice? That's the best you can do? Please. I may be old but I'm not dead yet."

Haley laughed. "All right, I like him. He's honest, and I feel like I can trust him to do a good job."

"And?"

"And he's very good-looking."

"You mean he's hot."

Her cheeks flushed. "Well…yes."

"So why don't you go out with him? I know he must have asked."

"Actually, he hasn't." Not exactly. He'd said he wanted to take her to bed. Big difference.

Ellie frowned. "The way the two of you look at each other, I thought by now—"

"Wait a minute. We hardly look at each other at all."

"Exactly. Which means you find each other attractive and you're trying to ignore it. What I don't understand is why."

Several reasons, one being her aunt's friendship

with Ty. Haley sighed, gave her the easy answer. "The truth is, I'm really bad with men and Ty is really good with women. He has a legion following him around, and I don't want to be one of them."

Her aunt nodded. "Ty likes women and they like him. But he isn't really a playboy. Not in the usual sense. I think if he met the right woman, he'd be completely faithful."

"Maybe so, but I'm still not interested."

"Why not?"

"I told you, I'm not good with men. Until recently, I actually thought maybe I might be…you know, gay."

Ellie burst out laughing. "I'm a pretty good judge of people, honey, and the way you look at Ty makes your sexual orientation more than clear."

There was no longer any doubt of that. She hadn't been able to keep her mind off Ty Brodie since he'd set his mouth over hers and proceeded to demonstrate very thoroughly how entirely heterosexual a female she was, one who was putty in the hands of a certain type of male.

"Even acknowledging the attraction, I'd rather not get involved with someone I'm working with on something as important as this."

"And Ty feels the same?"

Haley glanced away. If it weren't for his friendship with her aunt, she didn't think he would hesitate to seduce her. But if things didn't work out—which they wouldn't—he didn't want Ellie thinking badly of him.

She understood his reasoning, since she felt exactly the same, but she almost wished things were different.

Almost.

"I think I'm going to my room and read a little before I go to bed. Good night, Aunt Ellie."

"Good night, honey."

Haley yawned as she headed down the hall. She hoped she'd be able to sleep without having another erotic dream about Tyler Brodie.

As the hours slipped by, she drifted off more easily than she'd imagined. It wasn't until three in the morning that she jolted awake covered in perspiration, her heart trying to pound its way through her chest.

But she hadn't been dreaming of Ty. She'd been racing toward the harbor, shouting her father's name, trying desperately to warn him, silently screaming in horror as his boat exploded into a thousand pieces and burst into brilliant orange flames.

Curled on her side in bed, Betty Jean stirred, a faint noise penetrating the depths of her dreamless sleep. She tried to fight the intrusion, remain in that pain-free place where she could dream of Jimmy, but her eyes slowly opened. It was dark in the bedroom, the windows closed and the shades drawn.

Another noise sounded, distant, muffled. Ears straining, she listened for the source. She told herself there was nothing to be afraid of. She had lived in the house since before she'd met her beloved husband. She knew every shift and groan of the hardwood floors, knew the sound of the wind whistling through the eaves, the scratching of the mulberry bush beneath the bedroom window.

The floor creaked in the kitchen, and her breathing quickened. It was a sound she knew, the faint tread of a footfall. Jimmy's had been heavier, familiar.

She listened again, heard nothing. Told herself she had merely been dreaming and imagined the sounds. She closed her eyes and decided that tomorrow she would do as Tyler Brodie had insisted and get herself a better security alarm.

The sound came again, closer now, moving along the hallway toward her bedroom. Her heart jerked, started pounding. Not a dream. Someone was there, inside the house. Reaching toward the nightstand, she groped for the phone. Her fingers closed around the receiver and she lifted it off, carried it to her ear with a hand that trembled, leaned over to punch in 911.

A scream clawed its way up her throat as the door crashed open and two men in ski masks and dressed completely in black stormed into the room. The first man, big, with a thick neck and shoulders, grabbed the phone out of her hand, jerked the cord out of the wall and tossed it away. The other man, smaller, with little pig eyes she could see through the mask, grabbed the front of her nightgown, hauled her out of bed and shoved her into the chair next to the window.

"Take…take what you want and leave," she gasped. "There's money in my purse. It's…it's on the dresser."

The bigger man scoffed. "We aren't here to rob you, lady. We're here to deliver a message."

She swallowed, forced herself to breathe. "Message? Wh-what message?"

He slapped her, not hard, just enough to shock her into paying attention. "You want to stay alive, you stay out of your dead husband's affairs. You and the girl. You tell the daughter you were wrong. It was nothing but an accident. Tell her you just want to put this all behind you. You want to get past your husband's death and get on with your life. Tell her to go back to Chicago and start thinking about her future."

"You killed him," Betty Jean whispered. "It was murder. I knew it."

The smaller man stepped up and smashed a fist into her face. Pain shot into her jaw and tore through her skull. She fell back in the chair with a moan.

"You don't know anything," the man with the pig eyes said, "and that's the way it's going to stay."

She was shaking all over. Blood oozed from the corner of her mouth and dripped onto the front of her nightgown. "She won't...won't listen to me. She believes her father was murdered. She won't stop until she finds the men who did it."

The big man slapped her again, harder this time, making her ears ring. "Then you'd better convince her. You get her to stop or she ends up as dead as he is."

A fresh wave of fear rolled through her. Haley was in danger. All of them were. She had to do something, had to find a way to protect them. This was her fault. She was the one who was to blame.

Betty Jean summoned her courage, straightened a little in the chair. "Get out of my house. Get out before one of my neighbors calls the police."

The big man's dark eyes narrowed. "You bring in the cops, she's dead. You do anything to make the police suspicious, she's dead. You got it?" He slapped her. "You got it?"

"Y-yes..."

The smaller man punched her again, so hard the chair toppled over backward and her head slammed against the corner of the dresser. Her vision blurred and a wave of nausea hit her.

"You stupid fuck," the big man said to his partner. "Now look what you've done."

"She'll be all right. And when she wakes up, you can be sure your message will get delivered."

Through a haze of pain, Betty Jean watched the men

move toward the door. She had to reach Haley, had to warn her. She fought to stay conscious but her vision was narrowing, fading in and out. "Haley…" she whispered. "Haley…." Then her eyes rolled back in her head, and the world spun into darkness.

Ten

Ty stood in Ellie's fancy kitchen drinking a cup of coffee as he waited for Haley the next morning.

"She'll only be a few minutes more," Ellie said when she caught him checking the time on his wristwatch. It was eight-fifteen. They'd agreed on 8:00 a.m. Why was it a woman always tacked on a few extra minutes? Just to keep a man guessing, he supposed.

She hurried in, looking a little flustered in a pair of jeans and a T-shirt that read Old Artists Don't Die. They Just Paint Away. Ty bit back a grin.

"Sorry. I went for a run this morning to clear my head. I guess I need to start getting up a little earlier."

"You run?" Ty asked, forgetting her tardiness.

Haley nodded. "I try for three to five miles, at least three times a week. Gets me going in the mornings."

"I wouldn't have pegged you for the athletic type." Although if he had seen her in a pair of shorts, he might have noticed the muscles in those long, sexy legs. He'd been too busy looking at her navel.

"In the winter, I ski as much as I can," she said. "In

the summer, I windsurf on the lake. If I could choose a favorite, I'd pick paragliding."

He felt his eyebrows creeping up. "You paraglide?"

"I started year before last when I came out to visit a friend in San Diego. She introduced me to the wing, and I was hooked."

A woman who liked sports. He wasn't usually attracted to the athletic type. He was good at sports, but mostly he enjoyed them with other guys. He would definitely be willing to make an exception in Haley's case.

"Malibu's a good spot. I go up whenever I can find the time. We'll have to make it happen while you're here."

"Maybe," she said warily. "But I plan on heading back home as soon as we're finished."

Disappointment filtered through him. *Better that way,* he told himself as he flicked a glance at Ellie. He wondered what the older woman would say if she found out he'd had erotic dreams about her niece. Probably take that old shotgun of her late husband's, fill it with buckshot and shoot him.

"Listen, I was going through that cold case file of your father's last night and it got me thinking. After the fire at the Scarsdale Center, they discovered two of the damaged paintings were forgeries. But the forgeries might never have been found if it hadn't been for the fire. Which tells me they had to be damned good copies."

"That's right," Ellie said. "For the museum staff not to notice something wrong with the paintings, they had to be very good."

"There can't be many people who could reproduce that caliber of work," Haley added.

"Your dad was pursuing that angle. He mentioned

talking to a guy named Jules Weaver, but the lead didn't pan out. I checked on Weaver this morning. Painted in France after high school, studied the old masters there. But he never made it as an artist and I guess he got desperate for money. Sold some forgeries to a gallery in San Francisco, got caught and went to jail."

"Is he still there?"

"Got out three years ago, a few months after the forgeries at the Scarsdale were discovered."

"They don't know when they were originally painted. Maybe Weaver did them."

"That's probably the reason your father talked to him. But Weaver was back at it again a year after he got out. Sold some forgeries to a gallery in Santa Barbara and got caught a second time. He's serving seven years in San Luis State Prison."

"Not a very successful criminal," Haley said.

"Not very. Which, according to the notes in the file, is one of the reasons your father didn't think he was the guy."

"He just wasn't good enough," Haley said.

"There's another angle to consider," Ellie said. "Not only would the paintings have to be as good as the originals, but they would have to be aged to look as if they were done in the correct time period."

Ty nodded. "That's definitely a factor. But someone managed to do it, and Weaver might know who that someone is."

"And San Luis isn't that far away," Haley said. She glanced up at the clock on the kitchen wall. "We could be there by this afternoon."

"I checked visiting hours," Ty said. "Ten to four. We can make it if we get on the road."

"Then let's get going." Haley grabbed the strap of

her leather bag, slung it over her shoulder. "See you tonight, Aunt Ellie."

"Drive carefully, you two." She flicked Ty a glance. "I'll understand if you get stuck there overnight."

Ty's eyes widened. He felt a jolt of heat and bit back a groan. He couldn't think of anything he'd rather do than spend the night in bed with Haley Warren.

Not gonna happen, dumb-ass. Ellie's trust just made it worse.

Haley's phone started ringing before they reached the door. She pulled it out of her pocket and pressed it against her ear.

He couldn't hear what was being said, but the blood was slowly draining from her face. He caught her as she started to tremble, eased her into one of the kitchen chairs.

"When did it happen?" she asked.

She looked up at him, mouthed the words, *Betty Jean.* "Where is she? Torrance Community Hospital," she repeated, her fingers tightening around the phone. "Okay, we'll be there as quickly as we can." She ended the call and looked up at him.

"What happened?" Ty asked.

"That was Detective Cogan. There was a break-in at Betty Jean's last night, a home invasion, they think. The neighbor found her this morning, unconscious on the bedroom floor." Haley took a deep breath. "Apparently, she'd mentioned me to the neighbor and the woman told the police. They found my number on her cell phone."

Haley swallowed and her eyes filled. "She's in a coma, Ty. They don't know yet how bad it is."

"Oh, dear God," Ellie said.

"I need to get down there." Haley brushed the tears

from her cheeks. "Whatever my issues with her are, my father loved her. He can't be there for her, but I can."

Ty felt a rush of respect for Haley Warren. She might be fighting her own demons, but she wasn't letting another person suffer because of them. And she was smart enough to understand the way her father had felt about the woman he had married.

"I'll drive you down," he said.

"I'm going with you," said Ellie. "We can take the Mercedes."

Under different circumstances, he might have smiled. Silver Mercedes S550. He loved his pickup, but it wasn't a Mercedes. "Let's go."

With the traffic, it seemed to take forever to reach the hospital. Ignoring the smells in the lobby that reminded him how lucky he was to come home from the war in one piece, reminded him of the brother who hadn't, he escorted the women to the information desk, then into the elevator. He pushed the button for the fifth floor, led them out and down the hall.

A white-coated, silver-haired doctor walked toward them, a pair of half-glasses perched on his nose. "I'm Dr. Rodriquez. Are you part of Mrs. Warren's family?"

Haley's shoulders straightened. "I'm Haley Warren. Do you know what happened?"

Dr. Rodriquez removed his glasses. "She was brought in this morning. She was assaulted and badly beaten. From the gash on the side of her head, it looks like she fell or was pushed and hit her head."

"How…how is she?"

"She has a serious concussion, which means there's

some swelling of the brain. We may have to operate to relieve the pressure. We won't know for a couple more hours. We're hoping the swelling subsides on its own."

The doctor glanced toward the door to the ICU. "You can go in and see her for a moment if you'd like."

Haley nodded. "Yes. Thank you."

As the doctor led her away, Ty felt oddly proud of her. He had an overwhelming urge to go with her, make sure she was okay. Since he wasn't family, he forced himself to stay where he was.

"She's a good girl," Ellie said, watching Haley and the doctor disappear through the swinging door. "Her father would have been proud of her."

"Yeah, I think he would."

They stood quietly, waiting for her return, watching nurses in scrubs hurrying down the corridor, worried family and friends of other patients pacing up and down outside the ICU.

Ty did his best to close out memories of his Marine buddies lying in the hospital wounded, limbs gone, their families' hearts broken. At least they'd come home, he thought, not like his kid brother.

He released a slow breath, chasing away the memories, looked up to see Haley push through the ICU door. Her face was pale and her eyes glistened.

"How is she?" Ty asked softly.

Haley looked back toward the swinging doors. "She looks awful, Ty." She clamped down on her bottom lip to keep it from trembling. "Her face is black-and-blue, and unbelievably swollen. There's a white bandage around her head and she's got tubes in both arms. God, Ty, who would do something like that?"

He clenched his jaw. There were scumbags everywhere. It was just a matter of figuring out which ones had assaulted Betty Jean.

And just as importantly, why?

Haley felt shaken to the core. She was determined not to like Betty Jean Warren, but no one deserved to be beaten as viciously as her stepmother had been. No one deserved to be left helpless and hurting, perhaps left to die.

She clamped down on her emotions. Betty Jean was alive, and the doctors were taking good care of her. She had to stay positive, had to believe the woman would be all right.

"You okay?" Ty asked, and she realized she was grateful he was there.

"I'm all right. I just…I feel so sorry for her."

"She's gonna be okay. You just keep telling yourself that. It's all you can do."

There was something in his words, as if he had said them before. And suddenly she knew. "That's what you told yourself when your brother joined the army. That he would be okay."

Pain flashed for a moment in his eyes. "That's right. I tried to convince myself, but I was wrong. The reconnaissance vehicle he was in hit an IED. He and another soldier were killed."

"I can't imagine how terrible it must have been for you."

"I think I was the reason Davy enlisted. He always looked up to me."

She settled a hand on his arm, felt the warmth and strength. "That's what big brothers are for. He looked up to you and wanted to be like you. That's the best compliment he could have paid you."

Ty's jaw flexed. "It's not going to be that way with Betty Jean."

Ellie walked up just then. "No it isn't," she said firmly. "We'll see Betty Jean gets the best treatment available. And we'll pray for her. God's the best friend she has right now."

Haley looked from Ty to her aunt, and the pressure on her chest began to ease. Betty Jean wasn't alone in this. They were all there to help her. For an instant, she felt as if her father was up there, smiling his approval. *I won't let her down, Dad,* she thought.

Movement caught her eye, and she looked past her aunt and Ty to see two men in suits striding toward them. One in his early thirties was blond and strikingly handsome. The other had thinning brown hair, dark eyes and a slight paunch. He was late fifties, early sixties.

"Haley Warren?" the older man asked.

"That's right."

"I'm Detective Charles Cogan. We spoke on the phone. This is my partner, Detective Matthew Rollins."

"Detective Cogan." She turned, nodded her head in the blond man's direction. "Detective Rollins." Rollins gave her a smile that somehow went beyond professional, his gaze drifting over her, head to foot. Haley ignored the inspection that bordered on rude. "This is my aunt, Eleanor Stiles, and this is—"

"Hello, Charlie." Ty extended a hand, which the older detective shook. Ty cast the younger man a glance. "Rollins." But the respect he'd shown Cogan was no longer there. Haley wondered why.

"Surprised to see you here," Cogan said to Ty.

"Surprised to be here," said Ty.

"How do you two know each other?" Haley asked.

"Charlie works robbery/homicide," Ty said. "Occasionally I do private retrieval of stolen merchandise."

"A '56 Lamborghini, last time," Cogan said. "Besides being worth a fortune, the car had sentimental value to its owner, who reluctantly gave it up at gunpoint."

"And you found it?" Haley asked.

"Along with a half dozen other stolen vehicles," Cogan answered.

"Couple years back, I worked with a guy named Dev Raines to uncover a car theft ring. Some of the names popped up again when I was looking for the Lamborghini."

Cogan smiled. "Ty's got a nose like a bloodhound."

"So what are you doing here, Brodie?" the blond detective asked. "I doubt Betty Jean Warren owned anything as valuable as a race car. Seems to me, you prefer high-end cases." His gaze skimmed over Haley. "Unless you're getting another kind of payment."

"Watch your mouth, Rollins."

"Take it easy, Brodie. Just wondering what you're doing here."

"I work for Ms. Warren and Mrs. Stiles. We're looking into the death of Haley's father."

Rollins's lip curled into a sneer. Haley didn't like the way the testosterone level was ratcheting up. Clearly, Ty and Matthew Rollins were acquainted and they didn't like each other.

She fixed her attention on the older detective. "Can you tell me a little more about what happened to my… umm…stepmother?"

"As I said on the phone, it looks like a home invasion. Evidence points to two men. Came in through the back door and rushed the victim while she was in bed. The phone cord was pulled out of the wall. She must have put up a fight, maybe tried to stop them from taking something she valued. We won't know for sure until she wakes up."

"What about the alarm system?" Ellie asked, speaking up for the first time. "Ty said she had one. He wanted her to get a new one."

"She had one, all right. Must have forgotten to set it that night. None of the neighbors heard it go off, and it wasn't armed when we got there."

"What did they take?" Ty asked.

"They rifled through her purse, dumped the contents. Took whatever money was in her wallet. Took the jewelry in her jewelry box. They vandalized the house, presumably looking for something they could sell. Mrs. Warren will have to tell us exactly what's missing."

Haley's stomach knotted. What if Betty Jean never woke up? What if she died from the assault? She glanced over at Ty. "Do you think this is connected to my father's murder?"

Cogan's dark eyes swung in her direction. "Unless you know something we don't, this was a clear-cut robbery/assault."

"Or maybe not," Ty said. "We don't have much on Warren's death, but there're enough unanswered questions to make things interesting. Now Mrs. Warren's in a coma. You have to wonder why that is."

"You have to wonder," Cogan drawled, "why some people can't accept the facts—which say Warren's death was an accident and completely unrelated to what happened at the house."

Ellie spoke up just then. "It might be best if we heard what Mrs. Warren has to say first."

Cogan just grunted. He returned his attention to Ty. "Anything else you want to add?"

"Not at this time."

"How about you?" he asked Haley.

"No." Haley watched the men head off down the hall, Cogan's step a little slow, Rollins's almost cocky. When they disappeared behind the closing elevator doors, she turned to Ty. "You're not happy with Cogan and you don't like Rollins at all. Why is that?"

He shrugged. "Cogan's a good cop, but he's just marking time until he retires."

"And Rollins?"

"I don't like the way he treats women."

She arched a brow. "In general or someone you know?"

"In general. He's the kind of guy who gives men a bad name."

"He's abusive?"

"Just dishonest. In a way that's damn near as bad."

In a way it was. A man who would lie about his feelings to get a woman in bed. It had happened to her once. Fortunately, it was one of those relationships that never really got off the ground.

They started toward the elevators, Ty walking between her and Ellie.

"Do you think it's possible whoever killed my father thought Betty Jean knew something about the art theft and didn't want her to tell?"

"If they wanted to silence her, they could have killed her."

"Or maybe it was a home invasion," Ellie said as they stepped into the elevator. "Just like the police believe. Maybe it was only a coincidence that the house they picked belonged to Betty Jean."

The doors opened on the ground floor level and Haley picked up her pace as they headed for the glass exit doors. "Or maybe whoever did it read about the accident in the papers or saw my father's obituary and knew Betty Jean was living alone. I've heard criminals do that."

Ty's eyes went from green to a dark, turbulent brown. "Anything's possible."

"But you don't believe it," Ellie said.

"I don't believe Betty Jean forgot to set the alarm. I think whoever went into the house knew how to disarm it, same as before."

Haley's mouth went dry. "So what were they after this time?"

"I wish I knew."

"I wonder if they found it," Ellie said as she shoved through the doors and stepped out into the sunlight.

"Maybe we should take another look," Haley suggested following her out.

"Oh, yeah," Ty said as he walked out behind her. "We're gonna look. And tomorrow, I'm going to San Luis to talk to Jules Weaver."

Ellie's gaze fixed on Ty's face. "So you really think James was murdered."

"I think Betty Jean may be lucky she's still breathing."

Eleven

❧❧❧❧

Ty drove the Mercedes back to Ellie's house, left the women there and walked down the hill to his office. He was sitting at his desk when Amy Riggs came down the inside stairs, Johnnie pounding along beside her.

Ty shoved back from his desk and stood up smiling. "You're home. Good to see you, partner." John Riggs was six feet tall, barrel-chested, with powerful arms and legs. He had very dark hair, dark eyes and a punch that could send a man to his knees. A former Army Ranger, his specialty was digging up information, knowing everything that happened in the L.A. underworld.

"Good to be back," Johnnie said, a thick arm resting possessively around his tiny wife's waist.

Ty fought a grin. His friend had been a dedicated bachelor until he'd seen Amy one night at the Kitty Cat Club, a local strip joint where Johnnie had gone to catch a bail skip. That night he'd run into Angel Fontaine, a sexy little blond pole dancer who was searching for her missing sister.

Unfortunately for Johnnie—or, fortunately, as the

case turned out—she wasn't a stripper and she wasn't Angel Fontaine. Amy Brewer was a kindergarten teacher. The woman John Riggs had fallen for, married and was still crazy in love with.

"How's Mrs. Warren?" Johnnie asked. "Amy's been talking to Ellie," he explained when Ty flashed him a how'd-you-know look. "She's been keeping me filled in on the case."

"Betty Jean's still in ICU. They're hoping to know more by tonight."

"Haley's really had a lot to cope with lately," Amy said.

"Yeah, and it's beginning to look like it's all connected."

"So you think Warren was murdered," Johnnie said.

"Looks that way."

"What do the cops have to say?"

Ty scoffed. "Cogan's working the case. He and Matt Rollins."

Johnnie frowned. "Cogan's a short-timer, and all Rollins cares about is getting laid."

And he didn't care what bullshit story he told to make it happen.

"Cogan's determined to take the low road. Says we don't have anything but a bunch of unlikely coincidences. No real reason to suspect foul play."

"Any chance he's right?"

"I wish. Unfortunately, I don't think so."

"What's your next move?"

"Couple of things. I want to see what's left of the wreckage from the boat. It's probably piled up in a salvage yard somewhere."

"I'll call Vega, see if he can find out where it is." Rick Vega was a homicide detective, a longtime friend of Johnnie's, the man planning to marry Amy's sister, Rachael.

"Thanks. And I need to go back to the Warren house, see if the men broke in to find something, try to figure out if they found it, maybe get lucky and find it myself."

"There's another possibility, you know."

He sighed. "Yeah, I know. It could have been a warning."

"That's right. If Warren was murdered, whoever did it might have been warning his wife to back away."

"Could be. I'm hoping she can tell us when she wakes up."

"What about Haley?"

"You're thinking if we keep digging, they might come after her, too? It's crossed my mind."

"You're just the hired gun. Haley's his daughter."

Ty looked at his friend, afraid he might be right. "How long before you have to go back to San Diego?"

"Not for a few more days. I'll keep an eye on things here until then, make sure no one shows up who isn't invited. If you need me, I'll cancel the trip."

"Let's see how it goes. Ellie's got the best alarm system money can buy so getting in won't be the cakewalk it was at Betty Jean's. In the meantime, I'm hoping she'll come out of her coma and we'll find out what really happened."

"What else?"

"Besides going back to the house, I'll be heading to San Luis to follow up on a lead from an old cold case that might be the motive for Warren's murder."

Ty filled Johnnie in on the latest details of the heist from the Scarsdale Center and the two priceless paintings that were never recovered.

"They're worth millions," Ty said. "Maybe as much as twenty or thirty apiece."

Johnnie grunted. "Plenty of motive for murder."

"Yeah."

"Keep me in the loop," Johnnie said. He leaned down and whispered something in his pretty wife's ear and she blushed. "See you later." Johnnie urged Amy toward the stairs for an intimate reunion of the kind that made Ty think of sex with Haley, and sent the blood rushing into his groin.

Dammit. He forced his mind back to the file and didn't look up until he heard a knock at the outside door. He straightened as Ellie walked into the office.

"Is it Betty Jean?" he asked, coming out of his chair.

She shook her head. "Nothing new there." She was wearing a navy blue jogging suit and a pair of sneakers, her favorite casual attire. "But there is something I want to talk to you about."

She sat down in the chair next to his desk and he returned to his seat. "Something about the case?"

She smiled. "Something about you and Haley."

Oh, Jesus. Now she was a mind reader, as well as the most perceptive woman he'd ever known. "So… umm…what is it?"

"You like her, right? You're sexually attracted to her?"

"For God's sake, Ellie, you're talking about your niece."

"I realize that. I have a feeling that's the problem."

"What the hell are you talking about?"

"You'd like to ask her out, right?"

"We're working a case. We don't have time to go on a date."

"But you'd like to. You'd like to take her to bed."

"Ellie!"

"Right or wrong? You're interested in taking Haley to bed or you're not."

Ty gritted his teeth. "This is not a conversation we should be having."

Ellie arched a silver eyebrow.

"Okay. She's pretty and she's sexy and I like her. I'd love to take her to bed, but I won't do it. I give you my word, okay?"

"You're missing the point, Tyler. You want Haley and she wants you. I think having an affair would be good for both of you."

"What!"

"Haley's a sweet girl and very pretty, so of course men are attracted to her. But she's never had much luck with the opposite sex, and she lacks confidence. I think you could give her the confidence she needs."

"Wait a minute—you *want* me to take her to bed?"

"Well, not unless she wants that, too, of course. But I'm fairly certain she does. I've seen the way the two of you look at each other."

"I've been doing my best not to look at her at all."

"Yes, well, it doesn't really matter. The thing is, I've known you long enough to know how you treat a woman. You stay friends with them long after the relationship is over. Most men don't understand how to do that, but you do. I know if things didn't work out, you'd do everything in your power not to hurt her."

"I don't believe we're having this conversation."

Ellie rose from her chair. "I just wanted you to know it would be all right with me."

Ty stood up, too. "You're giving me permission to seduce your niece."

"As I said, I think it would be good for both of you.

Think about it, Tyler. Just make sure it's what Haley wants, as well."

Ellie walked out the door, and Ty just stood there staring after her. *Jesus.* Ellie wasn't going to shoot him. She was going to give him a merit badge for taking her pretty blonde niece to bed.

He started grinning. He could only imagine what Haley would say if she knew.

On the other hand, maybe it wasn't such a bad idea. Ty had no doubt they'd be dynamite together in bed.

His smile slowly faded. Unfortunately, at the moment, she was worried about her stepmother, who was lying in a coma in the hospital. Not the best circumstances for seduction.

And if the attack had been meant as a warning, Haley might also be in danger.

The arousal he'd felt while thinking about her slowly disappeared. With a sigh he sat back down at his desk and started sifting through James Warren's cold case file again.

Haley walked down to Ty's office the next morning. By midnight last night, Betty Jean's condition had improved enough she wouldn't need surgery. Though she hadn't come out of her coma, the swelling in her brain had gone down and the doctors were optimistic. Maybe the prayers Haley and her aunt had said had helped in some way.

As she pushed through the office door, she spotted Ty working out in the gym in the corner. Apparently he took advantage of the weights she had noticed before.

Bare-chested, in a pair of running shorts, he lay on a padded bench, lifting a bar loaded with weights. Tall and lean, his body drenched in sweat, he was solid muscle, his shoulders wide, his chest banded in sinew, a ladder of muscle across his ribs.

For a moment, Haley couldn't breathe.

"What are you doing here?" he said, his impressive biceps bulging as he set the weight bar back on the rack above his head and rolled to his feet. For the first time, she noticed his tattoo. A strand of barbed wire circled his upper right arm, just high enough not to show beneath the sleeve of a T-shirt.

He grabbed his towel off a hook and started mopping his face and chest. "I thought you were going to the hospital."

Haley fixed her eyes on his and worked to keep them there. "Betty Jean's…umm…improving, but she isn't awake yet. You said you were going to the salvage yard. If you are, I…umm…want to go with you."

He nodded, mopped his face a little more and slung the towel around his neck. "Rick Vega fixed it up. He's a homicide dick, a friend of Johnnie's. He's engaged to Amy's sister."

"Handy guy to know."

"Rick's great. Perfect for Rachael."

"I…umm…look forward to meeting her."

"Listen, I need to jump in the shower. I'll be out in a minute." He walked to the door of the office bathroom, opened the door and disappeared inside.

She heard the water go on and tried not to imagine that hard body naked, water sloshing over all those beautiful muscles. She tried not to imagine what the male part of him looked like, closed her eyes against the unwanted image she couldn't quite block and inwardly moaned. How she could ever have thought she was anything but heterosexual she would never know.

Ten minutes later, Ty emerged from the bathroom

dressed in his usual jeans and T-shirt, this one with the L.A. Kings crown logo on the front. His damp hair curled against the nape of his neck, and the T-shirt stuck to several damp spots on his skin, outlining the six-pack muscles across his stomach.

Haley forced herself to concentrate. "So...umm... can I go with you to the boatyard?"

"Be better if you kept a low profile till we find out what actually happened to Betty Jean."

A chill slipped through her. "You're thinking the men who attacked her might come after me."

He shrugged those wide shoulders. "You're asking questions about a possible murder. Someone might want you to stop."

"Is that what you believe happened? They wanted Betty Jean to stop digging into my father's death?"

"She went to see Cogan, told him she thought her husband was murdered. She talked to us, probably told other people. Like I said, anything's possible."

Worry filtered through her. She looked over at Ty. He was amazingly handsome, but under the lazy grins and easygoing manner, his strength and confidence had a way of seeping through.

Haley smiled. "Then it's a good thing you're here to protect me."

His eyes drifted over her, from the blond hair she'd pulled up in a ponytail to the swell of her breasts beneath the blue scoop-neck top she was wearing. She felt a little curl of heat as his mouth edged up.

"The thing you need to ask yourself is, who's gonna protect you from me?"

Desire slipped through her, settled low in her belly. Those changeable eyes had turned from cool green to hot brown and there was no doubt what he was thinking.

"I thought...thought we'd decided it wasn't a good idea to get involved."

"Situations change." He took her completely by surprise when he closed the distance between them, hauled her into his arms and his mouth came down over hers. The kiss was hot and wild, deep and erotic, and it set her on fire. Just when she was about to combust, he slowed, started nibbling and tasting as if he had all the time in the world.

Haley whimpered. She didn't remember locking her arms around his neck, didn't remember sliding her fingers into the hair curling at the nape of his neck. She could feel those rock-hard muscles beneath his T-shirt, remembered the sexy way they looked, and it was all she could do not to yank the shirt over his head.

Instead, she just kept kissing him. She could feel his erection, thick and hard, pressing against the front of his jeans. It should have been a warning, but it only made her want him more.

With a groan, Ty eased away, and Haley swayed against him. For a moment the hard arm wrapped around her waist was the only thing holding her up.

He stepped back, raked a hand through his hair. "Jesus, Mary and Joseph."

Haley touched her kiss-swollen lips. "Good heavens, where did you learn to kiss like that?"

He only shook his head. "Damn."

She released a shaky breath. The blood was returning to her head, thank God, and she was finally able to think. "Whatever just happened, we can't...can't afford to get sidetracked."

"I know. I just... I wanted to see if maybe I was wrong."

"Were you?"

He grinned. "No way."

That grin, combined with the memory of a second steamy kiss, made her stomach float up beneath her ribs. Even if she wanted to find out if sex would be different with Ty, now wasn't the time.

"We...umm...need to get going."

He gave her a last slow perusal, picked up his ball cap and settled it on his head, ambled over to the door and pulled it open. "After you, darlin'."

Haley ignored a flutter in her stomach and walked past him out the door.

Just as Ty stuck the key into the ignition, a fiddle started playing, telling him a call was coming in on his cell phone. He dragged the phone out of the pocket of his jeans and checked the caller ID. Lisa Johnson, a girl he had dated a few months back. He didn't want to talk to her, especially when he was still trying to recover from that mind-blowing kiss with Haley.

But Lisa was a friend of Ian and Sadie's, a blind date that had gone from tepid to hot in forty-eight hours. The relationship had lasted just about that much longer.

Still, she was a nice girl and he didn't want to hurt her feelings. He let the phone go to voice mail and made a mental note to call her back later.

"Same girl?" Haley asked with the lift of an eyebrow.

He shoved the phone back into his pocket and shook his head. "Old friend."

"Old *girl*friend, right?"

He shrugged. "Lisa and I went out a couple of times. It didn't work out."

"Does it ever?"

Ty flicked her a glance. "Couple of years back, I was involved with someone. We went together for about ten months. I expected the relationship to be exclusive. Lindsey wasn't ready to settle down. We parted friends."

"Were you in love with her?"

"I thought I was. As I look back on it, I figure it didn't hurt enough when it was over to be the real thing." He studied her face. "How about you? You said you weren't good with men. Does that mean you've never been in love?"

Haley sighed and leaned back in the seat. "I'm not sure I even believe in love. My parents were married. My mother loved my father, but he didn't love her back. They fought all the time. Half my friends' parents are divorced. I don't know anyone who's truly happily married."

"What about your aunt? She and her husband had a really solid marriage. At least that's the way she tells it."

"Harry's been dead for years. Maybe she remembers it different than it really was."

"Maybe. My parents got divorced. Doesn't mean I don't believe in marriage. Johnnie and his wife are over-the-top happy. I think if it's right between two people it can work."

"I'm not convinced."

Before he could reply, Ty's cell interrupted again, this time chiming the arrival of a text. He pulled out the phone and checked the message that ran across the bottom of the screen.

got something 4 u ian

Ty jammed the phone back in his pocket. "That was Ian Whitlow at the lab." He cranked the engine on the truck. "We need to get down there. The boatyard's in San Pedro, so the lab's kind of on the way."

"I hope it's something we can use."

"So do I."

They needed a lead. They needed to get a line on what was happening before someone else got hurt.

Twelve

By the time they got on the road, the early-morning traffic on Sunset had thinned to a slow but steady roll. They crawled a little on Santa Monica Boulevard, but picked up speed west of the 405 Freeway.

Ty's hopes ran high as he pulled the Silverado into the Forensic Services parking lot, got out and walked around to help Haley down. He definitely needed to install a step rail. The truck rode high off the ground, and the big chrome wheels lifted it a few more inches. Getting in and out was a problem for anyone who wasn't that tall.

Inwardly he grinned. On the other hand, every time he lifted Haley down, that electricity crackled between them. He'd hate to give that up.

They made their way into the lab. Ian met them at the counter and led them back down the hall into his office and over to his desk. He was wearing his white lab coat, his weekend tan starting to fade. He worked long hours. Ty hoped they'd paid off.

"You were right about the fingerprints you found in Warren's study," Ian said. "They belonged to him."

"I figured."

"We had better luck with the laptop. Got a partial email and a portion of Warren's reply."

Interest jolted through him. "You get the sender's address?"

"Unfortunately not. We transferred the messages onto a flash drive and printed them." Ian handed him the page with the emails and Ty read the words.

"'…11:00 p.m. Tuesday. Blue Oyster.' Your father replied, 'I'll be there.'" Ty looked over at Ian. "Any way to know how old this is?"

"Can't be that old. The laptop's fairly new."

"Betty Jean said my father bought it a month before he died," Haley reminded him.

"That's right. Could be the meeting had something to do with the stolen paintings."

"We need to find the Blue Oyster."

Ty took out his iPhone and plugged in the name. "It's a bar in El Segundo not far from the airport. The Blue Oyster Lounge. I'll go down there tonight, ask a few questions."

"I want to go with you."

Ty shook his head. "It's a bar, so not this time."

"It's a bar. So what? You think I've never been in a bar?"

"Look, that area's pretty mixed. Might not be the best neighborhood. I'm not taking any chances."

Haley's lips tightened but she made no reply.

Ty turned back to Ian. "What about the phone?"

"Got a couple of partial numbers. They won't do you any good unless you come up with something to cross-reference." Ian handed him another piece of paper. "No area code. Just the last six digits of each." 12-4356 and 63-7764.

Ty handed the papers to Haley. "We'll show this stuff to Betty Jean, see if anything looks familiar."

"I wonder how she's doing," Haley said.

"Why don't you call the hospital and find out?"

Haley nodded. Pulling out her cell, she walked over to the corner to make the call, leaving them to finish their conversation.

"Pretty girl," Ian said, ever the matchmaker, his eyes assessing Haley.

"Yes, she is. Say hello to Sadie."

"Will do. Good luck."

Haley joined him as he headed for the door.

"What's the update on Betty Jean?" he asked.

"The nurse says she's responding very well. They think it's only a matter of time till she wakes up."

"That's good news. We'll stop by the hospital after we go to the salvage yard."

"That'd be great."

They headed back down the hall to the front door, Haley holding the printouts in her hand. There wasn't much to go on, but little by little they were assembling information. Sooner or later, something would turn into a solid lead. Maybe they would find it at the boatyard.

Harbor Marine Salvage was a privately owned salvage yard in the L.A. Harbor near San Pedro. Haley walked next to Ty through a jungle of wreckage, derelict ships, recovered sunken boats of every design and size and all their miscellaneous pieces and parts. It bothered her to imagine her father's prized *Betty Jean* discarded among the mountains of debris.

Her chest tightened. She was glad she'd never been

aboard. Glad she had no memories of her dad smiling as he steered the boat through the harbor. Only those she conjured in her imagination.

Still, she couldn't block images of what it must have been like to see a man and his boat explode into thousands of burning pieces.

She shuddered.

"You sure you don't want to wait in the truck?" Ty asked gently.

"I'm okay." She wasn't, but she needed to be there, had to see this through along with everything else.

A small wiry man with a short-cropped white beard and neatly trimmed white hair walked toward them. "Can I help you?"

"I'm Tyler Brodie. This is Haley Warren. Rick Vega with the LAPD called. We'd like to see what's left of the boat that exploded down at Marina del Rey a couple months back."

The little man scratched his beard. "I talked to Vega. That was the *Betty Jean*. Twenty-six-foot Pacific Flyer. Got some good salvage off her—what was left of her we were able to recover, that is."

"Could we see it?"

"Sold some of it. People need parts for repair, you know. What's left is back here." The old man wove his way through stacks of rusted sheets of metal, old wooden hulls, propellers of every size, anchor chain, torn sails and miscellaneous parts, to a pile of wood and debris that was unrecognizable as a boat.

"Look all you like. Let me know if you're after anything in particular."

"Thanks." Ty turned in Haley's direction. "I'm gonna take a look, just wander a little, see if there's anything interesting."

She nodded, then started prowling herself. She didn't know exactly what she was looking for but something might catch her eye.

They dug among the debris for nearly an hour, the sun beating down, the days getting warmer as May marched toward June. In Chicago she would be gearing up for the tourist season, working with various artists, setting the dates for summer shows in the Seymour Gallery.

She missed her job a little, missed seeing her friends. But what she and Ty were doing was more important. She owed it to her father. And if the terrible beating Betty Jean had suffered was connected to her father's death, she owed it to the woman he had married.

Haley looked over a four-foot stack of rubbish to see Ty lifting off a chunk of what appeared to be decking and setting it aside. Haley returned to the task at hand, bending down to pick up a piece of metal that turned out to be a burner off the galley stove. There was nothing unusual about it. So far, there'd been nothing unusual about any of it.

Haley tossed the burner away and moved on, picking up smaller pieces of wood and metal, looking for burn marks, anything that might indicate what had caused the explosion.

She shoved aside a couple of pieces of padded blue vinyl attached to plywood, part of the banquette seating in the dining area, and a piece of metal glinted in the sunlight. Next to it, a length of rubber tubing was wedged between two pieces of wood. If she hadn't moved the banquette, she would have missed it.

Ty walked up just then. "I didn't find a damned thing. How about you?"

"I'm not sure." She pointed to the length of thick rubber tubing. "I think that might be part of the fuel line. What do you think?"

Ty studied the piece of rubber that had been roughly severed at both ends during the explosion. "Yeah, I think it is." Ty helped her work the two-foot section loose from where it was stuck between the boards.

"This is what caught my eye." She pointed to a perfectly circular spot about a quarter inch in diameter. "Look at that hole. It doesn't look like it was punctured. It's too perfectly round. It looks like it was drilled."

Ty took the tube from her hand and examined it closely. "It was drilled, all right. I can see the marks the drill bit left behind." He glanced out at the blue water sparkling in the harbor. "There was definitely a leak in the gas line. But it didn't happen by accident. Somebody wanted that boat to explode."

The two-foot length of fuel line torn from the boat in the explosion cost Ty a dollar and fifty cents. The old man at the salvage yard seemed happy with the sale.

"What do we do with it?" Haley asked as they walked toward the truck. "Take it to the police?"

"We could tell Cogan what we found, but there's no way to prove it actually came from your father's boat. The salvage yard isn't part of the crime scene."

"I thought of that, but the evidence is starting to stack up. Pretty soon they won't be able to ignore the truth any longer." As they reached the truck, he heard Haley's cell phone ringing in the purse she'd left locked inside.

Ty hit the auto locks and opened the door. Haley grabbed her purse, pulled out her smartphone and pressed it against her ear.

"This is Haley." She looked up at him, listened and started nodding. "We're on our way."

"What is it?"

"The hospital's been calling. Betty Jean woke up an hour ago. She's been asking for me."

"Let's go."

It took a while to get from San Pedro to the Community Hospital in Torrance. Ty checked in at the nurses' station, learned that Betty Jean was doing well and had been moved to a private room. He wondered if Ellie Stiles had been behind the upgrade.

The halls were a little less crowded on the eleventh floor, but the smells were just the same, irritatingly pungent and filled with unpleasant memories. He could hear the soft squish of a nurse's shoes, the rattle of a medicine cart as it rolled along.

He pushed open the door to room 1108, waited for Haley to walk inside, then let the door close slowly behind them.

"She's sleeping," Haley said softly, but the sound of her voice was enough for Betty Jean's eyes to crack open. They were black-and-blue, puffed nearly closed. Her short, curly blond hair was matted and her skin looked pale. Fluids still ran through tubes into her veins, but there was no oxygen flowing into her nose.

Haley walked over and sat down in the chair beside the bed. She managed to smile. "We've all been so worried. I'm glad you're doing better."

Betty Jean swallowed. She flicked a glance at Ty, but kept her attention on Haley, seemed to be struggling to find the right words.

"I'm glad…to see you. They said…you'd come down to the hospital and that…you'd been calling…to find out how I was."

"That's right. It was terrible what happened to you. We've all been worried sick."

Betty Jean reached over and took hold of Haley's hand. "I appreciate…you coming. I appreciate a lot of things. While I've been lying here…I've had time to think about all of this…make some decisions. Life is precious, Haley. Too precious to spend…worrying about the past. I think your father would want you…to accept what happened and get on with your life."

"I know you're hurting, Betty Jean, but Ty and I are certain my father was murdered. We're getting close to proving it. I have to find the men who did it."

Ty moved toward the bed. "Can you tell us what happened the night you were attacked, Betty Jean?"

She bit her lip, which was cracked and swollen. She took a breath, let it ease out. "I was sleeping. Two men… They broke into the house. They…wanted money. I told them to take my purse and go, but I guess…there wasn't enough in it." She cut her eyes toward the window. Her voice was rising. Ty rested a hand on her shoulder.

"Take it easy. There's no rush."

She nodded, eased out a slow breath. "The men… they shoved me into the chair next to the bed and hit me a couple of times. The last time…the chair went over backward, and I hit my head on the corner of the dresser. That's all I…remember."

Ty believed that was part of what happened. But Betty Jean wasn't a very good liar. "Did the men mention your husband?"

She blinked and a frightened look crept into her eyes. "No. This…this wasn't about Jimmy. I told you, they just wanted money. Probably to…to buy drugs or something."

"Have you talked to the police?"

"Not yet. I imagine they'll want to speak to me… sooner or later."

"And you won't tell them they threatened you? You won't say they warned you to drop your investigation into your husband's murder?"

"No!" She reached out and caught his hand, and he could feel her desperation. "Please, Ty. I can't deal with this any longer. I just…I want it all to be over. I want Haley to go home to Chicago and leave all of this behind."

"We found something today," he said, watching her closely. "We found a section of fuel line off the boat. A hole had been drilled into it. There was definitely a gas leak, but it wasn't from faulty equipment."

"Oh, dear God."

"We're collecting evidence," Haley said. "Pretty soon we'll have enough to convince the police."

"No police!" Betty Jean came up from the bed, rattling the equipment she was attached to, panic clear in her face.

"Easy…"

Her nails dug into his hand as he eased her back down. She looked at him and her eyes filled with tears. "They'll kill her, Ty. They'll find out and they'll kill her. Promise me you won't involve the police. Promise me!"

He gave her hand a gentle squeeze. "I won't let them hurt her."

"No police," she said again. "Promise me."

"All right. No police." Without Betty Jean's statement, they wouldn't have enough evidence to convince them, anyway. "You have my word."

Betty Jean slumped back against the pillow. A nurse shoved through the door, and seeing her patient's pale face and the heart monitor wildly beeping, cast them a disapproving glance.

"You've tired Mrs. Warren enough. She needs to

rest and recover. The doctor said no more visitors until tomorrow."

Haley reached down and squeezed Betty Jean's hand. "Get some rest, okay? Everything's going to be all right."

Betty Jean looked up at Ty, her battered features beseeching. "Keep her safe," she implored.

Ty's jaw hardened. "Count on it."

"I'm not stopping," Haley said, once they were back in the truck. "Not now."

"You saw what happened to Betty Jean. Are you sure you want to take that kind of risk?"

"He was my father, Ty. He wasn't some drug dealer who was killed selling cocaine on the street. He was a good man trying to do what was right."

"I know that. Doesn't change the situation. These men are dangerous, Haley. They've killed once. Could have wound up killing Betty Jean. You keep pressing, there's a good chance they'll come after you."

Haley looked up at Ty and wondered how much she could count on him. "What about you? You're involved in this, too. What if they come after you?"

"I'm just a hired hand. You stop digging and they figure I won't have any reason to keep looking. You're the one who's in danger."

"Can't you protect me?"

Something shifted in his features, made him look like the hard man she was beginning to understand he was. "I'll do everything in my power to keep you safe."

He meant it, she realized. He would protect her no matter the cost. She didn't doubt he could handle the job.

She straightened. "Then we keep digging."

Ty just nodded. He started the truck, shoved it into gear, and they drove out of the hospital parking lot.

"What about the Blue Oyster?" she asked.

"I told you. I'm going there tonight."

"I still want to go."

"And I'm still not taking you."

She sat back in the seat, crossed her arms over her chest. "Fine."

But she didn't need Ty Brodie's permission. She would get directions from Google Maps. There were questions that needed to be asked, answers she needed to hear, and there were certain things a woman could just flat-out do better than a man. If things checked out, she was going to the Blue Oyster Lounge tonight.

Thirteen

Haley did her homework. The Blue Oyster was a blue-collar bar with a poolroom in the back. According to their website, they served pizza and burgers in a room off to one side and were famous for their oyster shots and tropical drinks. The area wasn't great, but it wasn't that bad, either.

Hey, she lived in downtown Chicago. As long as you were careful, you were safe.

Haley smiled as she pulled into the parking lot in the red, '72 Triumph GT-6 her aunt had been letting her drive. It was the fastback version of the little British sports car, not as popular, but wow, the car could really move. Ellie said it had been Harry's favorite and she just couldn't part with it.

Haley thought of the power beneath the hood and grinned, understanding the movie mogul's preference over the other two cars he had owned, which now sat, along with Ellie's silver Mercedes, in the four-car garage at Ellie's house.

She parked the Triumph under a streetlight and

turned off the engine, checked her makeup in the mirror one last time. The bar was a single-story building with tiki torches burning on each side of the carved wooden front doors.

The clientele looked average enough, women and men twenty to fifty out to have a good time. Some of the younger women wore high heels and very short skirts, the same outfit she had chosen tonight, while the men were mostly in chinos and short-sleeved shirts, or T-shirts and jeans.

She looked around, but didn't see Ty's Silverado pickup. Good. She had hoped to get there before he arrived, see what she could find out before he pitched a fit and insisted she go home.

It was dark inside, lit with neon beer signs over the bar. A row of palm fronds formed a roof above a row of round cocktail tables where patrons sat drinking pitchers of beer or fancy Hawaiian drinks with little umbrellas.

A digital jukebox was playing in the corner, next to a small stage area that was empty tonight. Her eyes began to adjust as she made her way toward the bar, surveying the customers, trying to figure which ones, aside from the bartender, might be the most helpful.

She took her time crossing the room and finally sat down on the only empty bar stool between an older couple and a bald-headed man watching sports on a muted TV screen.

Haley smiled at the bartender—early thirties, short, dark, Hispanic and good-looking. She read the drinks menu, just to have something to do.

"I'll have one of those mai tais you guys are famous for."

He gave her a flashy smile. "You got it, sweetheart."

He turned to the task, and she tucked away the name on his shirt pocket, Raphael, for later. Her drink arrived in one of those big glass buckets, the contents the color of a pink-and-orange sunset. It really did look good. But she was there on business, not to party.

She scanned her surroundings, noticed the place was a little more than half-full. Since the bartender was busy, she turned to the bald guy next to her. "I'm in from out of town," she said with a smile. "I'm looking for a friend of mine. His name is Jimmy Warren. Any chance you know him?"

The bald man shook his head, kept his attention on the screen. "'Fraid not."

No help there.

She turned to the bartender, who was mopping the bar with a towel in front of her during a lull in the drink ordering. "How about you, Raphael? I bet you know everyone who comes in here."

"What's the guy's name?"

"Jimmy Warren. Some people call him James."

Raphael shook his head. "Name doesn't ring any bells."

"Jimmy's my uncle, my mother's brother. Ever since I got to L.A., she's been after me to track him down." She pulled out a copy of the photo she and Ty had taken from Betty Jean's.

The bartender took the picture, studied it and shook his head. He handed it back across the bar. "Sorry."

She sipped her drink, laughed at something she overheard the couple next to her say. "So I guess you come in here a lot," she said to start a conversation.

The woman, black-haired, late-forties, was drinking a martini. "We come in quite a bit. It's close to home. Good place to relax and forget your troubles, you know?"

"Looks like a nice bunch of people."

The woman glanced around. A couple of guys in leathers had just walked in. They were laughing too loud, using foul language. "Mostly."

Haley gave the couple the same spiel she had given the bartender.

The woman took the photo, and she and her husband both studied it. "Sorry, I've never seen him."

Haley shrugged, smiled. "Thanks anyway."

She took her drink and moved down the bar, showed the photo to a couple of different people. Got the same shake of their heads.

Another seat opened up, this one next to a guy she'd noticed when she walked in. Mid-thirties, brown hair, not bad-looking. In the past twenty minutes, he'd talked to half a dozen people. He was obviously a regular, drinking straight shots of whiskey, old enough to know better and still too young to care.

She had left her mai tai unfinished at the other end of the bar, but since she still didn't have the information she'd come for, she ordered another as she climbed up on the bar stool next to the brown-haired guy.

He turned toward her, gave her a little-too-familiar once-over that told her he was well on his way to drunk. Which might be good.

"Put that on my tab," he said to Raphael, flashing Haley a friendly smile.

"Thanks." She stuck out her hand. "I'm Haley, and you are..."

"I'm Bill."

"Hi, Bill, nice to meet you."

He lifted his whiskey glass in toast. "To new friends."

Haley lifted her mai tai glass and clinked it against his. "New friends." But she didn't like the way Whiskey Bill was looking at her, and for the first time she glanced toward the door almost hoping she'd see Ty walking into the bar.

Almost.

But she needed to find the man her father had met at the Blue Oyster, and she wasn't ready to give up yet.

Ty stood in the shadows, trying to hang on to his temper. The minute he had seen Ellie's red Triumph parked in the lot, he had known Haley had ignored his warning and was inside the bar. He'd wanted to storm the place, haul her out, bend her over his knee and land a couple of swats on her sweet little behind.

Didn't she get how dangerous this was?

But he knew Haley was anything but stupid, so he'd calmed down, slipped quietly inside and stood in the background watching her.

She looked sexy as hell in a tight white skirt so short his heart stopped every time he watched her shift on the bar stool then tug it back into place. So far she'd been quietly moving around the bar, talking to people, but not stirring up undo attention.

Which was a miracle, considering how luscious she looked.

But the guy she was talking to now was trouble. Ty could see it in his eyes, in the twist of his lips as he watched her. This guy wanted her, and Ty had a hunch he'd be willing to do whatever it took to have her.

Fresh anger trickled through him. He took a drink of the Bud Light he'd been sipping, set the bottle down on the table and started making his way though the shadows closer to the bar.

He could hear them talking now, saw the guy—*Bill,*

Haley called him—reach over and pluck the photo of James Warren from her hand.

"Yeah…I might have seen your uncle in here a couple of times."

Haley straightened. In the light of the neon beer sign over the bar he could read her excitement. "Really?" She flashed a winning smile. "I'd be in my mom's good graces forever if I could find him."

Bill handed back the photo. "I haven't seen him lately. Not for quite a while. The couple of times I saw him, he was in here with another guy."

"Same guy each time?"

He nodded. "Like I said, I only saw them maybe twice. I wouldn't remember except the guy with your uncle had part of an ear missing and a scar on the back of his neck. He looked like a real bad-ass."

"But you don't know his name or where I can find him."

He caught her hand, turned it over and kissed the palm. "What do you say we get out of here, gorgeous? I might remember a little better if we went back to my place. Come on, what do you say?"

Ty felt his hackles rising. In another minute he was going to be in the guy's face in a very big way. Haley eased her hand free.

"Listen, Bill, I appreciate the drink, but I've got to get going." She climbed down from the bar stool, nudging up her skirt a little in the process, giving Ty a view of those long, shapely legs. Giving the SOB next to her the same view he'd gotten and pissing him off again.

As she headed for the door, Bill came down off his stool, tossed some money on the bar and started after her. Ty fell in behind them.

Haley stopped just outside the front door, the flames

of the tiki torches illuminating her pretty face. Ty held back, fighting his temper, hoping to avoid any trouble.

"Listen, Bill. I'm not going home with you, and I'd appreciate it if you'd leave me alone."

"That's a bunch of crap. You let me buy you drinks."

"One drink."

"Well, I want something in return." He grabbed her, jerked her against him and bent his head to kiss her. Haley ducked the kiss and shoved, but Bill grabbed her again and started pushing her into the shadows.

"Let me go, dammit!" But Bill was bigger than he'd looked in the bar and not nearly as drunk, and he was all over her.

Ty's temper snapped. Striding into the shadows at the edge of the lot, he grabbed the back of the guy's flowered shirt, whirled him around and hit him. As much as he tried to pull his punch, good old Bill went sprawling.

"Don't get up," Ty warned, his fists still clenched, the fury in his eyes enough to keep the bastard where he'd fallen.

He turned his wrath on Haley. "I told you not to come here."

She was trembling, but she didn't back down. "Since when do I take orders from you?"

"Since you put on a skirt that barely covers your ass and got that crazy bastard so hot and bothered he might have hurt you!"

"That's ridiculous! I could have handled him. I was doing just fine on my own!"

"Bullshit! You were damned glad to see me walking out that door."

She looked down at the guy on the ground, now crawling on his hands and knees back toward the bar. A tiny smile tugged up the corners of her lips.

"All right, I was glad to see you. But it was worth it. I got us some information."

His own mouth edged up. "Yeah, I heard. Maybe you did." And then he was moving, sliding his hands into that tangle of honey-gold hair and hauling her against him, kissing her like he couldn't get enough. His tongue was in her mouth and hers was in his. His hands were cupping that sweet little ass, and all he could think of was being inside her.

"Let's…let's go to your house," Haley breathed as she pulled away, reminding him they stood in the parking lot and people where beginning to pay attention. At least the guy he'd punched had managed to get to his feet and disappear back into the bar.

"It's too damned far. I want you now. Besides, you might change your mind." On the other hand, they needed to get the hell out of there before someone called the police.

"I'll follow you, and I won't change my mind. I have to know if it's as good as you think it'll be."

Ty looked at Haley, thought how much he wanted her and grinned. He'd always loved a challenge.

Haley followed Ty's pickup all the way back to Hollywood. He had given her his address in case she got lost, but kept her in sight all the way, and there wasn't much traffic. As Ty pulled into the single-car garage next to his condo on Fareholm on the north side of Hollywood Boulevard, Haley pulled up in front and turned off the engine.

The area was hilly, with a lot of open space, like the neighborhood Aunt Ellie lived in and not too far away. She started up the walk, and Ty met her at the front door, hauled her inside and started kissing her again.

Haley sank into it, let the heat wash over her. He had almost been right about changing her mind. They were working together. Making love with Ty was a crazy thing to do.

On the other hand, no man had ever turned her on the way he did. She wanted to know if sex could really be as good as he promised, as good as Lane and some of her other girlfriends had said it was for them.

She wanted to know, and she wanted to find out with Ty Brodie.

He paused long enough to lock the front door behind them, and she caught a glimpse of the inside of his condo, saw that it was neat and masculine—a brown plaid sofa and chairs, oak tables, athletic trophies on the bookshelf, a huge flat-screen TV.

Then he was kissing her again, his hands sliding beneath the blue sleeveless knit top she'd been wearing with her white miniskirt, unfastening her white lace bra, reaching around to cup her breasts. Ty groaned as his thumbs ran over her nipples, and her breath caught. He pulled off the top and bra, and stripped off his T-shirt, drew her back against him for another scorching kiss.

Hard muscle cradled her breasts, made her nipples ache and tighten. His body was as smooth and hard as sun-warmed granite, his tongue slick and hot as he explored the inside of her mouth.

She was wet. Incredibly hot and wet, her breathing so shallow she felt light-headed.

"Easy," he said, pressing his mouth to the side of her neck, gently biting an earlobe. "We've got all the time in the world."

But Haley didn't want more time. At least part of her didn't. Her body wanted what every hot kiss promised, wanted the elusive pleasure that loomed just out of reach.

Bending his head, Ty took her breast into his mouth and began to suckle, gently at first, then harder, making her stomach quiver. Her insides turned to jelly and her knees went weak. She didn't want him to stop touching her and at the same time she wanted a whole lot more.

"Let's…let's go to bed."

He cupped her face in his hands and kissed her. "That's exactly where we're headed, honey. Just not quite yet."

Haley whimpered as he took her breasts again, first one and then the other, a leisurely exploration that had her trembling all over, the muscles across her stomach stretched taut. Just when she was sure she couldn't stand a moment more, Ty scooped her up in his arms and started up the stairs.

Haley slid her arms around his neck and just hung on. At the top of the landing, he turned into the master bedroom, settled her in his king-size bed. The next thing she knew, her skirt and high heels were gone and all she was wearing was her skimpy white lace thong.

Ty stepped back and just stared. "You are one hot lady." His mouth edged up. "I'd like to tear those off with my teeth."

She laughed. It was the last thing she'd expected. That sex and laughter could go together. The laughter slipped away as he shed his boots and jeans and started walking naked toward the bed. She had never seen a body so powerfully muscled, so lean, so physically fit. Below those wide shoulders, thick pectoral muscles bunched across his chest, which tapered to a six-pack stomach, narrow hips and long legs.

She was still staring when he came down on the

bed and started kissing her again, settled himself between her legs. Hard muscle warmed her everywhere. The dark hair on his chest grazed her nipples. Heat and need radiated out through her limbs as she moved restlessly beneath him.

"I want you," he said. "So damned much."

She didn't want to think how many times he'd said those words, but the thought must have shown in her face.

His hand came up to her cheek. "It isn't like that, Haley. It's just the two of us in this room. No shadows. No one else. You're the only woman I want. I have since the minute you walked through my office door."

And then he was kissing her again, stroking between her legs, touching her exactly where she needed to be touched, making her ache and squirm. He suckled her breasts, wound his tongue around her navel, lapped at her belly-button ring.

She was hot and wet and ready. It seemed the most natural thing in the world when he peeled off her thong, sheathed himself and slid his heavy erection deep inside. Exactly right when he started to move.

Then her mind shut down and her body took over, arching, taking him deeper, responding to the fierce, penetrating thrusts that pushed her toward climax.

In and out. In and out. Powerful. Relentless. She came once. Hard. Her body quaking, her nails digging into the bands of muscle across his shoulders. Dense, saturating pleasure washed through her, sucked her back under. Ty's muscles tightened, but he didn't stop, just shifted a little, driving into her from a slightly different angle and pushing her to a second shattering climax.

When she sobbed his name, he followed her to release, his whole body tightening, his head thrown back, his jaw clenched against the rush of pleasure.

For several moments, he held himself above her. Then with a sigh, he settled himself beside her and eased her into his arms. She thought he'd say something, make light of the moment and the feelings still washing through her, rising and falling like a tide that had crested and now washed back to sea.

Instead, he gently kissed her one last time and didn't say a word.

Fourteen

The red numbers on the digital clock beside the bed glowed in the darkness, ticking off the seconds, then minutes that passed. Ty was still trying to get his bearings after the most earth-shattering climax he could recall. He'd been right about the chemistry between them. More than right.

He told himself that's all it was.

"You need to call your aunt," he finally said, the last thing he wanted to think about at the moment. "She'll be worried."

Haley shoved back her heavy blond hair. "I told her I'd probably be late, but I'd better go home."

He caught her wrist as she tried to get up and brought her down on his chest. "I want you to stay."

Haley shook her head. "I don't think so. Not tonight."

"Disappointed?"

A quick flash of moisture appeared in her pretty blue eyes. "No. It was wonderful. You were wonderful. I've never felt anything like it."

"We were good. I knew we would be."

Haley started to rise, but he pulled her back down in bed and came up over her. When he kissed her, she didn't resist, just started kissing him back, squirming beneath him, and he was once more sheathed and buried deep inside her.

He tried to pace himself, to go as slowly as he could. He prided himself on his skill at pleasing a woman, but he'd wanted Haley badly, and it took more willpower than it should have. As soon as she reached release, he followed, pounding into her and riding out the pleasure.

He felt her hands sliding over his back as he eased himself off her, took care of the condom and settled himself beside her, waited for their heartbeats to slow.

She ran a finger through the curly dark hair on his chest. "You make sex seem so easy."

He just shrugged. "When it's right, it's right. There's nothing hard about it."

She grinned, dimples digging into her cheeks. "Oh, I think maybe there is."

His mouth edged up. He was getting hard again just thinking about it.

Haley scooted backward until she came up against the headboard. Ty was grateful she had pulled the sheet up, covering her luscious curves.

"So…who do you think my dad was talking to in the bar? Bill said the guy had part of an ear missing and a scar that made him look like a bad-ass. Why would my dad be meeting a guy like that?"

Ty settled himself beside her. "The Blue Oyster's the kind of place I'd pick if I wanted to have a conversation that would go unnoticed but still feel fairly safe. Nondescript neighborhood. Dim lighting. Semicrowded. Music loud enough to muffle whatever was being said.

Your dad was an investigator. I think he was talking to an informant."

Her eyebrows went up. "You think it could have been someone who knew something about the art theft?"

"Hard to say. He was working other cases, and that one's three years old. Maybe something new came up."

"You think we can find him?"

"I'll do some digging. And Johnnie's still in town. With those physical scars, if the guy's an informant, Johnnie might know him or someone who can find him."

Haley swung her legs to the side of the bed. "I really have to go."

He didn't want her to leave. He hadn't had enough of her. Not even close. "You sure?"

She spotted his bathrobe draped over the back of a chair, grabbed it and slipped it on. She freed her hair and rose from the bed, the robe trailing on the floor as she grabbed her skirt and sexy little white thong.

"We're still working together," she said. "That needs to come first." Haley headed out of the bedroom to collect the rest of her clothes. As Ty pulled on his jeans, he could hear her in the bathroom downstairs.

She was dressed when he reached the living room. He figured her thong was back in place, tried not to imagine grabbing it with his teeth and told himself he was a dumb-ass for wanting her again so soon.

"There's one more thing," he said, and she flashed him an uncertain glance. "When you went off by yourself earlier, you could have been followed. You could have wound up like Betty Jean—or worse."

Her gaze locked with his. "You can't think they're watching Ellie's house."

"I think it's possible. I promised Betty Jean I'd take

care of you. To say nothing of what your aunt would do to me if I let you get hurt."

"I suppose you're right."

"Don't do something like that again."

She just nodded. "I'll be more careful," she said softly.

Not exactly the answer he wanted, but he could see it would have to do. Bending his head, he kissed her. "I'll follow you home."

"You don't have to do that. It's late, and it isn't that far."

He gave her the look, the one that had kept good ol' Bill on the ground, and wisely, she let the subject drop.

Ellie was asleep when Haley got back to the house. When she finally dragged herself out of bed the next morning, her aunt was already up and about. Haley found her puttering around in the big, ultramodern kitchen.

"Dolores has coffee brewed," Ellie said. Ellie's petite housekeeper was like a ghost moving around the house—there, but rarely seen.

"Smells great." Inhaling the aroma, Haley padded over to pour herself a cup, adding a little milk but leaving it strong enough to get a jump on her addiction.

"How did it go last night?" Aunt Ellie asked, sipping a cup from her place at the kitchen table. "Were you able to come up with any new information?"

"Actually, I did learn something." As she wandered over to the table, she told her aunt about her conversation with Bill at the Blue Oyster, leaving out the part where Ty had knocked the sleazebag on his insufferable ass.

She thought of her drive to the bar and wondered if,

as Ty had said, someone could be watching the house. Maybe parked at the bottom of the hill, waiting for her to drive out. The attack on Betty Jean had been a warning. She wasn't a fool. Next time she'd be more careful, make sure it was safe.

Inwardly she grinned. Next time she'd have to work harder at talking Ty into taking her along.

"Ty thinks the guy Dad was meeting might have been an informant. He's hoping Johnnie will be able to help him track this guy down."

Ellie sipped her coffee. "You and Tyler seem to be working well together."

Haley could feel her face heating up. If that was work, she was putting in for overtime.

"We've got a couple of leads to follow. We still need to go down to San Luis and talk to Jules Weaver—he's the forger Dad mentioned in his old case file. Right now I need to call the hospital and check on Betty Jean."

"That reminds me. Detective Cogan called while you were sleeping. He says they've released the crime scene. He thought you'd want to know."

She nodded. "That's good. We need to take another look around the house, see if we missed something the first time."

Retrieving her cell, she found the hospital number in her recent calls and hit the send button. She checked on Betty Jean's condition and was surprised to discover she was being released tomorrow morning. The nurse told her a friend, the neighbor who had found her, was picking her up and taking her home. Then the call went to room 1108.

"I hear you're getting out tomorrow," Haley said, forcing a note of cheer into her voice.

"Yes, and thank heavens for that. I'm feeling much

better, though I still look like something out of a Stephen King novel."

Haley chuckled. "Don't worry about the house, okay? We're going to take care of it."

"You don't have to do that, Haley."

"Yes, I do." She still had mixed feelings about the woman her father had married, but Betty Jean was his widow, and by digging for answers about the explosion, Haley was in some way responsible for what had happened to her.

She badgered Betty Jean into giving her the alarm code, though Ty could get in without it. "Thanks. We'll reset it when we leave."

"Have you thought about what I said?" Betty Jean's voice sounded tired and worried. "I really want you to stop, Haley, before you or Ty get hurt."

"We're being careful, Betty Jean. I promise." But the thought of what could happen scared her. She ended the call and looked up to see her aunt watching her closely.

"She wants you to stop investigating, doesn't she?"

Haley nodded. "She's afraid someone else will get hurt."

"Namely you, I imagine. Are you sure it's worth it, dear?"

"I'm doing what's right, Aunt Ellie. That's what my father always taught me."

"Doing what's right may be what got him killed."

She lifted her chin. "I'm not stopping."

Ellie shook her head. "I shouldn't have let you go out last night by yourself. It never occurred to me it could be dangerous."

"Ty was there. We just didn't go together."

"He didn't want you to go, did he?"

"Not at first. But he changed his mind after I got the information." *Well, sort of.*

"Promise me you'll do what he says from now on."

"Of course I will." Within reason. "But I have a life, too. I'm not going to sit around waiting for him to play bodyguard when I have things to do."

Ellie tapped a finger against the side of her coffee cup, then her head came up. "For heaven's sake—why didn't I think of it? I'll call Kurt Stryker. He used to work for Harry. He's a chauffeur and bodyguard. He can protect you when Ty is busy doing something else."

"I can't afford—"

"Don't be silly. I can certainly afford to make sure my niece is safe, and it won't be forever. Just until this mess gets straightened out."

It was an interesting idea. Ty was extremely protective of her, but there were things he needed to do besides help her. Haley had a brain of her own, and she intended to use it.

She walked over to the window just as Ty's pickup pulled into the lot next to his office and watched him go inside, instead of come up to the house.

Haley wondered if last night had been nothing more to him than a one-night stand, but it was hard to imagine Ty being the kind of guy who was strictly into the conquest.

Then again, she'd been wrong about men before.

Ty found Johnnie at his desk in the office working on a case file.

"There's coffee," Johnnie said, his dark eyes glued to the screen.

"Thanks." Ty meandered toward the aroma coming

from the pot on the counter, and poured a cupful of the thick dark brew.

"Amy talked to Ellie this morning," Johnnie said. "I guess you and Haley went to the Blue Oyster last night."

"I went. Haley was already there. I told her to stay home, but she can be pretty mule-headed."

Johnnie chuckled. "Can't they all?"

Ty found himself smiling. Though it was a dangerous thing to do, he couldn't help feeling proud of the way she'd handled herself. Well, up until good ol' Bill decided he ought to get a piece of tail in exchange for the mai tai he'd bought her.

"She managed to find out something about who Warren met at the bar."

Johnnie looked up. "Good for her. She get a name?"

"No, but the guy's a real standout. Piece of his ear missing. Scar on the back of his neck. Ring any bells?"

Johnnie thought it over, shook his head. "I can't place him, but I can ask around, see if I can get a name. A guy like that leaves an impression."

"I've got some people who might know something. I'll talk to them." Ty looked up as Haley knocked on the door then walked into the office.

Her gaze slid over Johnnie, then sliced to Ty. "I hope I'm not interrupting."

Ty set his coffee mug down on the counter. "Haley, this is my partner, John Riggs." Johnnie gave her a once-over, taking Haley's measure. She looked sweet as sin in jeans and an orange tank top, her blond ponytail swinging with every move.

Johnnie's gaze went back to Ty, and his lips twitched. Clearly, he'd assumed Haley was more than just a client. How much more remained to be seen, but after last night, he definitely wanted to find out.

"Nice to meet you. My wife has said good things."

"That's nice to hear. I really like her."

Johnnie grinned. "Yeah, me too."

Haley looked at Ty, and his mind shot straight back to the bedroom and how she felt moving beneath him. Arousal burned through him and he fought not to get hard.

As if she read his thoughts, her cheeks went pink and she glanced away.

"Johnnie's going to do some digging," Ty said, hoping to get them both off the hook. "Maybe we can find your father's mystery man."

"That's good. I…umm…just came over to tell you Detective Cogan called. The crime scene has been released."

"About damned time."

"Betty Jean's getting out of the hospital tomorrow so Aunt Ellie and I are going over to clean up her place. If you want to take another look around, now would be a good time."

"All right. I had a couple of things to do, but they can wait till I bring you back."

"You could meet us there. Aunt Ellie called a friend of Uncle Harry's. His name's Kurt Stryker. He was Harry's chauffeur and bodyguard. He's going to fill in when you're too busy. He can drive us down."

Ty gritted his teeth. He knew Stryker by reputation. Word was the guy was big, bad and capable. Ty didn't like the idea of him with Haley.

"You don't need Stryker. I'll take you to the house."

"Are you sure? I think Aunt Ellie's put him on some kind of retainer."

He clenched a muscle in his jaw. "I said I'd take you." He sliced a glance at Johnnie, who was wisely keeping his mouth shut. Ty didn't miss the faint grin tugging at his lips.

"Okay, I'll tell Aunt Ellie," Haley said. "What time do you want to go?"

"The sooner the better."

"We can take the Mercedes, if you want."

The words defused some of his temper. The Mercedes. Yes! "All right. Let's hit the road."

Fifteen

Betty Jean's house wasn't as badly torn up as the police had led Ty to believe—which told him the intruders weren't really searching for anything. Ty thought of the woman battered and lying in a hospital bed, thought of Haley and what might happen to her.

Message received loud and clear.

While Ellie and Haley straightened up the house, vacuumed and put things back in order, Ty rummaged through closets and drawers, checking for anything James Warren might have hidden or something they might have overlooked the first time they were in the house. Ty didn't find anything unusual until he went into the garage.

Betty Jean's blue Toyota Corolla was parked on one side, the Jeep Cherokee James Warren drove on the other. Warren had driven the Cherokee to the harbor the morning he was killed. Ty had sorted through the stuff in the back, mostly boating equipment, some tools, a life jacket and a couple of old floats.

The front of the car had been empty except for the

garage door opener and the items in his glove compartment: maps, LifeSavers and Chapstick.

At the time, he still wasn't convinced the accident had been any more than that. Today, Ty made a more thorough inspection. And sure enough, there was something he had missed.

Wedged between the seats where it had slipped down out of sight, was Jimmy Warren's iPad. Betty Jean had assumed it was destroyed in the explosion, but apparently he'd left it in the car instead of taking it aboard the boat. Ty felt a rush of adrenaline as he pulled it from between the seats.

He looked up at the sound of the door into the house swinging open. Haley stuck her head out. "We're just about finished. Did you find anything?"

He closed the driver-side door and held up the iPad. "Whoever broke into the house and took the computers missed this. Maybe we'll get lucky."

"Oh, my God!" Haley ran down the steps and when she reached him, he grabbed her and hauled her into his arms.

A quick hard kiss and he let her go. "I've been wanting to do that all morning."

Haley glanced away. "I thought maybe you'd… umm…forgotten."

Ty grinned. "Honey, last night wasn't something I'm gonna forget anytime in the near future."

She smiled up at him, a little relieved. "Me, either."

He dipped his head and kissed her again, then remembered Ellie Stiles was in the kitchen. "Let's go inside and take a look, see what's on this thing."

Haley nodded and hurried ahead of him into the house.

"At least Betty Jean won't have to come home to a

mess," Ellie said, putting the broom and vacuum cleaner back in their place in the utility room.

Haley turned to Ty. "Do you think she's still in danger?"

"Probably not. She's not the one still asking questions. But I think it might be a good idea for her to take a little vacation for a while, just to play it safe."

"That's a good idea. I hope we can convince her."

"We'll convince her," Ty said and meant it.

Haley must have believed him. "Okay." He thought she was coming to trust him a little more every day.

Haley grabbed a dustpan and put it up on the shelf. "Ty found Dad's iPad in the car, Aunt Ellie. We're going to take a look, see what's on it."

"Well, that sounds promising," Ellie said, but her canny eyes shifted between the two of them, and he thought she had a good idea what was going on.

They huddled around the kitchen table as he turned on the device and waited for it to start. The screen lit up. Ty went into the menu and scanned the names of the files, but there was nothing obviously pertaining to the art theft.

"I don't see anything right off. Looks like he mostly used it on the road. I need to go deeper, see if there's something in one of the files. That'll take a little time."

Haley sighed glumly. She was getting discouraged, but Ty had been on the job long enough to know they were making progress even if it didn't seem like it.

"We're moving forward, Haley. One step at a time. It just takes a while."

Ellie squeezed Haley's hand. "Ty will figure all of this out, dear. You just have to have faith."

She released a slow breath, summoned a smile. "You're right. We just have to keep searching."

Which meant he needed to get Haley back to the house where she would be safe and he could get to work.

At least with Stryker on the job, he wouldn't be as worried about her.

He shook his head. The hell he wouldn't.

Kurt Stryker arrived at Ellie's house later that afternoon.

"Hello, Kurt, it's nice to see you," Ellie said.

He gave a quick nod of his head. "Mrs. Stiles. Good to see you, too. It's been a while."

"This is my niece, Haley Warren. As I told you on the phone, Tyler Brodie is handling her personal protection, but I'd like you to help him look after Haley whenever he's busy."

"We've never met, but Brodie's got a solid reputation. I'm happy to work with him."

Stryker was taller than Ty, about six-five, and maybe thirty pounds heavier. He sported a shaved head, a Fu Manchu mustache that ran beneath his nose and curved down to his chin and a silver earring in each ear. He looked like he ate nails for breakfast, but in a hard sort of way, he was the kind of man women found attractive.

Haley also noticed the slight bulge beneath the brown leather sport coat Stryker was wearing, obviously a weapon of some sort.

"Ty's busy working on something this afternoon," Haley said. "I need to get out of the house for a couple of hours."

She was climbing the walls waiting for him to get home. He was looking for the man who was missing part of his ear. He'd said that in the places he'd be going, she'd be more hindrance than help.

For once, she agreed with him.

After Ty had left, she'd searched through the iPad but nothing useful jumped out at her. Ty would be going through it again when he got back to the office. In the meantime, she couldn't just sit and wait. "I'd like you to drive me over to see a friend."

It was after three in the afternoon. Lane was meeting her at four, taking off work a little early, since she had finished her appointments for the day. Haley needed a little girl-talk, and Lane was perfect for the job.

"No problem," Kurt said.

"You can use the Bentley." Ellie smiled wistfully. "You're used to driving it. You took Harry and me to dozens of premieres in that car."

Beneath his mustache, Stryker's mouth edged up. "I always liked your husband. He was one in a million."

"Yes, he was." Ellie walked over and handed him a set of keys. "The key to the garage is on there, too."

Stryker tossed the keys into the air and caught them. "I'll get the car and bring it around." He started to walk away, then turned back. "Anything in particular I need to be aware of in regard to Ms. Warren's protection?"

Ellie hesitated only a moment. "Haley's father was killed about three months ago. The police think it was an accident, but it may have been murder. Haley's been asking questions. We're just taking a few extra precautions."

Stryker drew back the leather sport coat he was wearing, revealing the automatic weapon holstered at his waist. Haley suppressed a shiver.

"Be right back," he said.

As soon as he was gone, Haley's attention swung to her aunt. "Are you sure about this guy?"

One of Ellie's silver eyebrows went up. "You don't think he can handle the job?"

"I think he could tear someone apart limb by limb, but I don't want that someone to include me."

Ellie laughed. "You're not afraid of him, are you? A lot of women find Kurt attractive. I thought you might feel that way, too."

But all Haley felt was an unease she hadn't expected. "You know him far better than I do. If you trust him, I'm sure he's fine."

They left the house in Harry Stiles's dark green Bentley, a beautiful car but showy, with Stryker in the driver's seat, Haley in the back. She had to admit, the man seemed the consummate professional, handling the car with ease and not saying a word.

At Lane's small Spanish-style house in Beverly Hills, he waited in the living room while Haley and Lane sat out on the patio at the rear of the house.

The house itself was not at all what Haley had expected from her vibrant friend, but it was amazingly homey. The interior, decorated with heavy Spanish accents, had cream sofas with autumn-toned throw pillows, gilt mirrors and California Impressionist paintings on the walls. It was a combination of old and new that was unique and somehow perfectly Lane. Clearly her friend was a very talented interior designer.

Another surprise was the huge dog that ran up to greet them when she and Lane walked outside.

"Oh, my God!"

Lane just laughed as the dog loped up beside her, and stuck his head beneath her hand for a scratch. "This is Finnegan." She rubbed his coarse fur. "He's an Irish wolfhound. A male usually weighs about a hundred and twenty pounds, but Finn was the runt of the litter. He only weighs a hundred."

Haley's eyebrows went up. "Only? You're the last person on earth I would have figured to own a dog."

Lane smiled and stroked Finn's head, got an adoring look from his big brown eyes. "A friend of mine went to the animal shelter to get a puppy for her little boy. I was just supposed to keep her company, but there was Finn. If no one took him, they were going to put him down. He was just so cute. What else could I do but take him home?"

The dog stood placidly as Haley walked over and ran a hand over his rough coat.

"He seems very well mannered," Haley said. "Aren't you, Finn?"

As if in answer, the dog trotted over to his bed on the far end of the patio, lay down and closed his eyes.

"He's big, but he's a real sweetheart," Lane said. "He's been wonderful company for me."

"How about a male with a little less fur? You mentioned the weirdo, but what about someone else?"

Lane poured two glasses of white wine from the chilled bottle she'd brought outside, and they sat down at the heavy, wood-and-wrought-iron table beneath the covered patio.

"I date. Just not all that much. I know it's crazy, but every time I get close to having a relationship, I feel like I'm betraying Jason."

Lane had told Haley about her fiancé, Jason Russell, who had died three years ago in a motorcycle accident. Apparently, she had never really gotten over his death.

"Have you heard anything from the guy who went to prison?" Haley asked.

"No, thank God. He's in there for at least six more

months. Hopefully, by the time he gets out, he'll have forgotten all about me."

"Obviously, he wasn't *the one,* but someday you'll meet someone who can make you think of the future instead of the past."

Lane made no reply, which was a reply in itself. She tipped her head toward the living room. "I can't believe your aunt hired a bodyguard."

"If you'd seen Betty Jean Warren, you'd understand."

Lane lifted her wineglass. "Well, he certainly looks like he can do the job."

Haley thought of the hulking giant who was in charge of her safety. "Do you...umm...find him attractive?"

Lane shrugged, took a sip. "I can see where some women might. He's certainly masculine, but no, he's not my type."

"Mine, either."

Lane lifted her glass, eyed her over the rim. "There's something different about you today. I'm not quite sure what it is."

Haley thought of last night, the deep, erotic kisses, the feel of Ty's hard-muscled body moving over her, inside her, driving her to climax. She tried to will the memory away, but faint color crept into her cheeks.

"Oh, my God, you got laid! It was Studly Do-Right, wasn't it?" Lane laughed. "I knew you were hot for him."

Haley sipped her wine, tried to act nonchalant. "It just happened, you know? I didn't plan it or anything."

"So how was he? I got the impression most of the guys you've known have been more into themselves than you."

An interesting thought. Haley wondered if it might not be true. She leaned back in her chair and couldn't keep a slow smile from creeping across her face. "It was amazing. *He* was amazing."

Lane started nodding. "I had a feeling. That sketch you did of him seemed…I don't know…somehow revealing. Like he was more than just a pretty face."

"Ty has this underlying strength, you know? I can't exactly explain it. It's so much a part of him I don't think he'd be who he is without it." She ran a finger through the condensation on her glass. "And there's this danger. Like a leopard asleep in the shade. On the surface he looks sweet and mild-tempered, but underneath—"

Lane laughed. "Kind of your own personal Clark Kent?"

Haley smiled. "Yeah, I guess so. You should have seen him at the Blue Oyster last night. This guy in the bar was giving me a pretty hard time. He followed me out of the club, started pushing me around. I'm not sure what would have happened if Ty hadn't shown up when he did. He grabbed the guy and spun him around, hit him once— and *pow!* It was over."

"How bad did he hurt the guy?"

"Oh, he was fine. I think Ty held back. He seems to have a great deal of self-control."

Lane grinned. "I think I'm going to like him."

Haley looked at her beautiful friend and alarm bells went off in her head. Lane must have sensed it. She leaned over and caught Haley's hand. "If this guy is as good as you said, odds are he's really into you. He's not going to be putting the moves on one of your friends."

Haley sighed. "He gets calls from women all the time. It's like he's the pied piper of women."

Lane's russet eyebrows went up. "You think he's just notching his bedpost?"

"Oddly enough, I don't. I trust him. I probably shouldn't, but I do."

Lane relaxed. "My advice is to follow your instincts. I have a feeling you've got good ones."

"I don't know—they haven't been great in the past."

"You're older now and wiser."

"Maybe, but I'm not about to get in too deep, and Ty probably doesn't want that, either. In the meantime, I've got more important things to worry about."

Lane flicked a glance toward the living room. "Like staying safe."

Haley nodded. "And finding my father's killer."

Aguri Tanaka tore his gaze away from the sight that never failed to move him. The painting, with a beam of light from a hidden track light in the ceiling seemed to shine with an inward glow. Ethereal. Timeless.

He'd purchased the painting six months ago, a priceless work by an artist he had admired since he was a boy. His grandfather had been his inspiration, a man who had come to America from Japan before the war, a patriot, and yet he had wound up in an internment camp until the war was over.

His father had been a successful businessman, a small-time art collector, but he had never amassed the level of wealth that Aguri had. His grandfather and father were gone now and with them, their stifling, antiquated beliefs in a code of honor no one else bothered to follow anymore.

Aguri had made billions in the electronics industry. He loved fine art and sculpture, collected beautiful pieces from all over the world. After a particularly good year, he had rewarded himself with the purchase of this piece.

He had hung it on his study wall with great pride, where everyone could see it.

Many of his guests had admired the portrait. Not one soul had asked where he had acquired it. Several times, Aguri had explained that he had purchased the beautiful copy in a gallery in New York, that he had admired the artist's ability to capture so closely Rembrandt's glorious work.

It was a total fabrication, of course. The painting itself was the original. Any fool could see that. No one else could achieve the perfect balance of light and shadow, the way the subtle shades of taupe and fawn, the faint hints of amber, captured the aging pallor of the old man's face. Nothing could compare with the dark, flowing lines of his robe, the texture and rich scarlet hues of the sash at his waist.

But to the rest of the world, the seventeenth-century painting hung in a place of honor on a wall of the Fizer Foundation. Hundreds of tourists and school children admired the fake every day.

Aguri smiled. People were so easily duped.

And yet there were always those whose agenda might lead them here, who wanted to ask difficult questions. Someone was digging into an old art-theft file. Names were turning up, people who knew people. People who might be dangerous to Aguri.

But it was nothing to worry about. It was being taken care of. All would be well very soon.

Sixteen

Ty spent all day and night, until after the bars closed, talking to people he worked with, people he paid to come up with information. Pimps and hookers, down-and-outers, drunks and drug dealers. None of them knew anything about the man missing a chunk of his ear.

He went home tired and restless, frustrated in more ways than one. He sat up watching an old John Wayne Western until he finally fell asleep. He'd awakened with a hard-on, faintly recalled he'd been dreaming of Haley, dragged himself out of bed, showered and dressed and headed over to the office.

Fortunately, his partner's luck had been better.

"I found him," Johnnie said when Ty walked in, yawning and still half-asleep, trying not to think how good he'd felt the morning before, after his hot night with Haley.

"That's great!" Ty padded over to pour himself a cup of coffee. "Who is he?"

"Name's Ray Farrell. Lowlife who used to run a bar

called the Dandelion till he drank up the profits and wound up on the street."

Ty inhaled the robust smell of the rich brew. "How do I get to him?"

"Farrell's down on his luck. Way down. I waved a Benjamin in his face, promised him a couple more if he showed, and he agreed to meet you."

"Where?"

Johnnie grinned. "Kitty Cat Club. Someone's always got your back when you're in there."

That was the truth. Since Johnnie's wife, Amy, had worked the club while she searched for her missing sister, the employees—the dancers, the huge Asian bouncer, Bo Jing, and Tate Watters, the owner—had become Johnnie and Amy's friends. Which meant they were Ty's friends, too.

"Good choice. When?"

"Tonight. Eleven o'clock. Should be good and noisy in there by then. You want me to go with you?"

"Might be less intimidating if I go by myself."

Johnnie chuckled.

Sometimes Ty's laid-back, easygoing manner got him further than Johnnie's dark, overbearing presence. Sometimes it worked better the other way around.

"Call me if you need me," Johnnie said.

"Will do." Ty checked his watch, yawned again. It was a little past ten, late enough to make a house call. He'd phoned Haley last night, just to check on her, make sure she was okay. Make sure she wasn't off somewhere with Kurt Stryker.

He wondered if Stryker was Haley's type. He couldn't really see it, but as much as he thought he knew about women, they continued to surprise him.

He finished his coffee, set the mug on the counter

and glanced out the window toward the big house up the hill. "I need to talk to Haley, see if she found anything on Warren's iPad. I'll see you later."

Johnnie just nodded. As Ty headed out the door and started up the hill, he spotted a shiny new, canary-yellow Camaro parked out front of Ellie's. First guess, Kurt Stryker.

He climbed the porch steps and rapped on the door, smiled when Haley pulled it open.

"Hi," she said, smiling.

"Hi, yourself." He kissed her, taking a little longer than he should have. With any luck, Stryker would be looking out the window.

Haley stepped back. "Come on in. I just got off the phone with Betty Jean. She should be going home late this morning. I told her you thought it was best if she left town for a while. She wasn't that hard to convince."

"Amazing what a stint in the hospital will do to clear your head."

"She says she's been wanting to visit her sister in Michigan anyway. She's got enough air miles she can fly for free. She's leaving tomorrow, so we won't have to worry about her."

"Smart lady."

"I also asked her about the partial phone numbers, and the Blue Oyster Lounge. She said neither the numbers nor the bar sounded familiar."

He'd expected that. He had a feeling Jimmy Warren kept his work pretty much separate from his home life. He liked the cozy nest his wife made for him. He didn't want anything to intrude. "What else did she say?"

As they walked across the marble-floored entry, Haley hesitated. When he leveled a stare at her, she sighed.

"She begged me again to give up the investigation, okay? I told her I couldn't do that."

"Be the wisest thing to do."

"I know."

"But you aren't going to stop."

"No."

He'd known she would say that. She was just as mule-headed as he'd told Johnnie she was. Why he liked that about her, he had no idea.

"Johnnie found our man. Name's Ray Farrell. I'm meeting him tonight."

"I want to go with you."

Ty shook his head. "Not a chance. We're meeting at the Kitty Cat Club. It's a strip joint. I'm not about to take you there."

She looked like she wanted to argue, but didn't. Maybe she was learning to pick her fights.

"Did you find anything on the iPad?" he asked, hoping to deflect the conversation.

"There wasn't much on it, period, and nothing about the stolen art. But I think you should take a look in case I missed something."

"All right. Where is it?"

"In my bedroom."

Ty grinned. "Too bad Stryker and your aunt are in the house." His gaze traveled over the snug jeans and yellow midriff top. He remembered the metallic taste of her belly-button ring against his tongue, and heat slid into his groin.

As if she read his thoughts, a flush rose in her cheeks.

"How about an early dinner at my place?" he said. "Before I head down to meet Farrell." The Kitty Cat Club was on Sunset, not far from the office or his condo.

He'd have enough time to continue what they'd started the other night and still make his meeting.

Stryker walked into the hall before she had time to answer, a mountain of a man Ty had heard of but never worked with before. But Ellie vouched for him, and he had a reputation for being good at his job.

The only things that should have mattered.

"Stryker."

"Brodie."

Ty extended a hand and the two men shook. Stryker didn't pull the old power squeeze, just kept the meeting friendly.

Stryker turned to speak to Haley. "Looks like you won't be needing me today."

"Not today," Haley said, her lips curved in what didn't quite pass for a smile. She had moved a couple of inches closer to Ty as she talked to Kurt. A natural female reaction, he figured, to a man who could break a woman in two. Ty didn't like the notion.

"Why don't you go get the iPad?" he told her, giving her a gentle nudge toward the guest wing. She glanced from one of them to the other, turned and hurried away.

Ty tipped his head to where Haley disappeared down the hall. "She's hands-off, you understand? She belongs to me. Anything happens to her, you and I are going to have a problem."

Stryker's bald head and silver earrings gleamed beneath the modern, beveled-glass light fixture in the foyer. His mouth edged up as if he couldn't believe what he was hearing. Then he looked into Ty's face, read the threat and just nodded. "No worries."

"Good. Then we'll get along just fine."

Stryker's dark eyes remained on his face. "I heard you were Force Recon. That true?"

"Been a while."

Stryker nodded, getting the picture. "I'll keep that in mind."

"Has Ellie got you staying here at the house?"

"I'm in the apartment over the garage."

"Good."

Stryker handed him a business card with his numbers on it. Ty dug one of his out of his wallet and did the same.

"Let me know if you need me for anything." Stryker turned, strode toward the door.

Ellie walked out of the kitchen. "Everything okay?"

"Peachy," Ty said, thinking of Haley and staring at Stryker's broad back.

"Good. I've got to get going. I've got a busy day." Ellie waved as she hurried off toward her bedroom at the other end of the house.

Ty waited another minute for Haley to return. When she didn't, he started down the hall into the guest wing. Ellie had given her consent to a relationship, however brief, between him and Haley, but he didn't think she would appreciate him taking her niece right there in the house.

He grinned. He didn't have to think twice to know how shocked Haley would be at the thought. Still, it was tempting.

Her bedroom door stood partially open. He nudged it the rest of the way with his boot and found Haley bent over a small table against the wall, studying her computer screen. His gaze ran over her perfect ass, and it was all he could do not to drag those jeans down over her hips and take her from behind.

Inwardly, he groaned. Now, every time he looked at her, he'd fantasize about doing just that.

Haley straightened, turned toward him and smiled.

"Come and take a look." She moved aside so he could see the screen.

Ty ignored the hard-on throbbing beneath his jeans and managed to return her smile. "All right, let's see what we've got."

"About dinner tonight…" Haley said, returning his thoughts to the dangerous place they had been before. "Why don't I come over and…umm…cook for you? I'm a really good cook, and afterward we can go to the Kitty Cat Club together."

It was bribery, pure and simple. He thought about bending her over the arm of the sofa in his living room. It would almost be worth it.

"Sorry, darlin', as tempting as that offer might be, I'm not taking you to a strip club. Your aunt would have my head."

Haley just shrugged and looked embarrassed. She was new at this game they were playing. He had a feeling it wouldn't take her long to figure out the womanly advantage she held over him. He pulled her into his arms. Kissed her long and deep.

He was starting to weaken, thinking maybe it wouldn't be so bad if she went to the club with him when his cell phone started fiddling, snapping him back to his senses.

Ty pulled it out of his pocket, recognized the number that belonged to his ex-girlfriend, Lindsey Rosemund, and swore a silent oath. Ty let the call go to voice mail. At least his big head was functioning again. He wasn't sure whether it was a blessing or a curse.

Haley knew without asking that the phone call had come from a woman. "Who was it? Old flame number one or forty-two?"

Ty flashed her a look. "It was Lindsey, the girl I told you about. I haven't talked to her since we broke up, actually. That's been more than two years."

At least he didn't dodge the question. That was a plus.

"Sorry, it's really none of my business."

"It's your business. I'm not interested in anyone but you, and as long as we both feel that way, it's important to be honest."

The pressure in her chest eased. She couldn't believe she'd tried to proposition him into taking her to the club. How brazen could she be? She wanted to go, of course, but the real truth was, she wanted more of Tyler Brodie. She wanted him to give her the same amazing pleasure as before.

"You feel that way, right?" he asked, his gaze on her face. "You're not interested in Stryker or some other guy?"

Her eyebrows shot up. "Stryker? Are you kidding? And, no, there isn't anyone else."

He bent and softly kissed her. "Let's take a look at the iPad." Then he grinned. "Unless you want to *cook* for me right now?"

Haley laughed. He had a way of doing that, lifting her mood and making her smile. "I'm not *cooking* in here. Aunt Ellie's in the other room."

Ty reached for her, eased her back into his arms. "I want more of you, honey. A lot more. But a strip club can be dangerous, and I don't want you getting hurt."

Haley slid her arms around his neck, went up on her toes and kissed him. "No wonder all those women keep calling."

"I'm not interested in them. I'm interested in you.

Now, we had better get to work before your aunt has to come in and play chaperone."

She smiled as Ty turned back to the computer and started searching the *Pages* files, the word processing part of the tablet.

"You went through all these?" he asked, opening each file and scanning the contents.

"I didn't see anything that had to do with the art theft." But maybe Ty would see something she missed. As he continued checking the files, her cell phone started to ring. Recognizing the caller ID, she pressed the phone against her ear and heard her mother's voice.

"Hello, Mother."

"Hello, darling. How are you, sweetheart? I expected to hear from you by now."

"I've…umm…been busy." *Trying to find a killer and having incredible sex.*

"When are you coming home, darling? People are starting to wonder where you've gone. You've missed some wonderful parties. The Stanfields and the O'Conners, the Brighton girl's wedding. There's a big benefit at the country club in two weeks. Michael Stanfield is gong to be there. You remember him—Avery's son? He's a couple of years older, graduated from Harvard. He'd be perfect for you, darling."

Haley looked at Ty, who was still searching through files, so masculine and handsome it made her heart beat faster just to look at him. "I'm not finished here, Mother."

Her mother's voice sharpened. "I'm trying to be patient, Haley. I realize you and your father were close at one time. But James ran off with some little tramp and left us. You don't owe him anything."

She thought of Betty Jean, beaten and lying in a

hospital bed. "What happened to the money from his retirement, Mother? I always thought Betty Jean married Dad for his money, but I don't think that's true."

Silence fell on the phone. "I'm not discussing this with you now. Not over the phone. When you get back, we can talk about anything you like. Now, I'll be happy to send you a plane ticket. I think sooner would be better than later. We'll need time to shop for the summer season."

Haley's hand tightened around the phone. "I'm not coming back yet, Mother. Not until I find out who killed Daddy."

Her mother made a scoffing sound on the other end of the phone and the line went dead. Haley felt the same sense of defeat she had always felt when she talked to Allison Warren. Or mostly just listened.

She felt Ty's arms go around her, easing her back against his chest. "Your mom?"

She nodded.

"I take it she isn't happy you're here."

She turned in his arms, tried to smile. "She wants me to come back in time for the summer season. Parties at the country club, tennis with all her wealthy friends and all their eligible bachelor—totally boring—sons."

His hold tightened. "But you're staying, right?"

She sighed. "I'm not leaving. Not until all of this is over."

Ty searched her face, then let her go, and went back to working on the iPad.

"Any luck?" she asked.

"Not so far." He clicked around a little, then went back to the desktop. There was an icon in one of the rows she hadn't noticed. Ty clicked it up.

"What's that?"

"Notepad app. Penultimate. You can make notes on

it with your finger, write messages when you're in a hurry." Using the tip of his index finger, he drew a couple of lines that indicated a curvy figure, wrote the name Haley at the top and the word *hot* at the bottom.

Haley laughed. "That's great. I haven't seen that app before."

Ty moved through the few pages her father had scribbled messages on. Some were neat enough to read. A note reminding him to bring home a quart of milk. One that read, *Appointment 1:30.* Another page had what appeared to be three names scribbled down in a hurry.

"That's Dad's handwriting," Haley said. "It was always impossible to read."

"The letters all run together," Ty said. "What's it look like to you?"

Haley frowned as she studied the letters in the first name. "I can't tell if it's *Tanker* or *Tandem* or…maybe it's *Tamara.*"

"*Carlton* and *Silverman* are easy enough to read, but there're no first names to go with them."

"I wonder who they are."

"Someone your father crossed paths with. We'll try to find out why he wrote down their names."

"We should call Dad's boss, Mr. Potter, see if they were part of a case my father was working."

"Yeah, we'll do that."

"We haven't talked to Jules Weaver yet. The morning's pretty much shot. Are we still going up to the prison?"

"I'd planned to, but I can't afford to miss that meeting with Farrell tonight, and if we go all the way to San Luis, we might hit traffic and not get back in time."

"So we'll go tomorrow. What do we do this afternoon?"

His mouth edged up. "What I'd like to do is take you back to my house and *cook,* but since that's probably not an option, I've got some work to do in the office."

Amusement slipped through her. "On the case?"

He nodded. "We need to call Potter, and I've got some other calls to make—people in the old art-theft file. I may need to see some of them in person."

"Can I help?"

"Sure, you can make some of the calls. I'll show you how it's done, the kind of questions you need to ask."

"All right."

Ty took the iPad, then waited for Haley to walk out of the bedroom and fell in behind her.

She cast him a look over her shoulder, admired the sexy way he moved. Unfortunately, for the moment at least, *cooking* was out of the question.

Seventeen

Darkness engulfed the city, but the lights on the Sunset Strip turned night into day. Traffic crawled along the street, music blasted from a string of restaurants and bars, and pedestrians in leather and spandex, tattoos and piercings, meandered the sidewalks in full party mode.

The Kitty Cat Club was already noisy and crowded when Ty walked in. He was an hour early for his meeting with Ray Farrell. He wanted to check things out, find a place in the back of the room where it was dark and a little more private.

People talked more freely when they could hide in the shadows.

It was dim inside the club, except for the neon signs behind the bar and the glow of lights over gilt-framed photos of 1950s strippers that hung on the walls. The Kitty Cat, one of the more upscale strip clubs on Sunset, was always busy. The owner, Tate Watters, was cop-friendly and ran the kind of place where out-of-town businessmen could have a little fun and not get into too much trouble.

Ty glanced toward the stage at the opposite end of the room. A hot little redheaded pole dancer strutted her stuff in the colored spotlight. Ty watched her limber movements; she was naked except for the red pasties she wore over her nipples and the red thong cutting up the crack of her ass.

Too much makeup and too well used to interest Ty, but the thong reminded him of the little white scrap of lace Haley had been wearing. Damn, the lady had gotten under his skin, that was for sure. He didn't quite know what he planned to do about it, but he was sure he wanted more.

"Well, if it isn't Mr. Tall-Dark-and-Handsome."

Ty grinned at the cocktail waitress approaching his table. "Hey, Babs, how's it going?" Babs McClure was taller than average, with a curvy figure and chin-length dark brown hair. Tonight she wore it shoved up beneath a hot pink wig. She had been Amy's roommate when she had worked the club.

"It's pretty much same ol', same ol'." She held her tray up and cocked a hip. "How's Amy? Haven't seen her in a while."

"Still married, still in love with Johnnie and vice versa, from what I can tell."

"Good for her. I got a guy I been seeing lately. Tell her he's real nice, will you? Tell her I might even marry him."

Ty smiled. "She'll be happy to hear it."

"So what can I get you, hot stuff?"

"Bud Light'll do. And tell Dante where I'm sitting." Dante was the bartender, second in line to Watters. "I'm expecting someone. He'll be looking for me."

"You got it, cowboy. Be right back."

Babs brought his beer a few minutes later and took off to another table. Ty leaned back in his chair, settled in to wait, ignored the smell of stale beer and the sound of heavy breathing. Around him, men sat at small round tables sipping whiskey or nursing a brew, grinning at the redhead up on stage.

The bottle was cold in his hand as he took a drink. After he'd found the names on Warren's iPad, he and Haley had spent the afternoon making calls, one to Warren's boss, Fred Potter, but Potter didn't recognize the names.

Late in the afternoon, they had driven downtown to the Scarsdale Center to talk to some of the people who were working there when the paintings were stolen. Some of the employees had quit and moved on to other jobs, some were new and had only heard about the incident. No one they talked to had any suspicions before the fire that the paintings had been stolen and replaced with forgeries.

No one recognized the names on the iPad.

Or at least that's what they'd said.

In the end, it was too late by the time they got back to the office for Haley to come to his house for supper. As much as he would have enjoyed a quickie, he wanted to take his time, make it good for both of them.

Ty leaned back in his chair and nursed his beer, kept an eye on the front door. At a quarter to eleven, it opened for the umpteenth time and in the brief flash of light coming in off the street, a lone man walked into the club.

Ty watched him move toward the bar. The man ordered a beer. Dante slid it over to him and pointed in Ty's direction.

Ray Farrell was about six feet tall, medium build and brown hair. As he wove his way across the crowded room, Ty shoved a chair out with his boot. Farrell grabbed it and sat down. Even in the dim light, Ty could tell the bottom part of his ear was missing.

"You Brodie?"

"That's right. I appreciate your coming."

Farrell took a drink of beer. "So what do you want?"

"Same thing everyone else wants. Information." Ty drew a hundred-dollar bill out of his shirt pocket and slid it across the table. "I want to know why you were meeting Jimmy Warren."

Farrell tipped up his beer, took a long draw. "I worked with Warren for a couple of years. He came to me for information. He paid well, so I did my best to give it to him."

"When was the last time you saw him?"

"About a week before he died."

"At the Blue Oyster Lounge?"

"That's right. We met there a couple of times."

"What information did you give him?" When Farrell didn't answer, Ty slid another hundred across the table.

"A few years back, a couple of valuable paintings went missing from the Scarsdale Center. Warren was on the case. He asked me to dig around, see what I could find, but I never came up with anything. Warren refused to quit. He told me if I ever heard anything to give him a call. A few months back, I heard some rumors. I needed money, so I called. Warren set up the meets at the Blue Oyster."

"So you came up with new information just before he died."

"That's right."

Ty slid another hundred. "What was it?"

Farrell fingered the bill, set it neatly on top of the others. "There was another heist. Happened a few months before I heard about it."

Ty straightened in his chair. He hadn't expected that one. "Puts it back about six months ago."

"That's right. Rumor on the street was the second heist was even bigger than the first. Three paintings this time, all of them priceless."

"From the Scarsdale Center?"

"I don't know, but I don't think so."

Ty pointed toward the hundreds lying on top of the table. "I can make that stack grow if you can give me names."

Farrell released a slow breath, took a long draw on his beer. "I know there was big money involved—real big. But I don't know who stole them. After what happened to Warren, I can't say I'd want to know." He finished the beer in a couple of long swallows, picked up the hundreds and got up from the table. "See you around."

Ty watched him leave. Another burglary. More forgeries substituted for original art? Three paintings of the caliber that had been stolen before could mean tens of millions. Maybe more.

Ty's thoughts went from Jimmy Warren's death to Haley, and unease filtered through him. Instead of going back to his condo, he found himself driving toward the office. He wanted to check out the house, make sure it was secure.

He phoned Kurt Stryker along the way, told him he was coming in. Told him to take a look around, make sure everything was locked up tight.

But he didn't know Stryker, and though Ellie trusted him, he wouldn't be able to sleep without checking things out for himself.

And the thick rubber gym mat on the floor in the office made a pretty decent bed.

* * *

Haley woke up at the crack of dawn. She hadn't slept well. She wished Ty had called. She didn't care if it was late. She wanted to know how his meeting with Ray Farrell had gone.

She was edgy and out of sorts, frustrated that the investigation hadn't progressed any further. She needed to get rid of some tension. Running always settled her down, and she hadn't done it in days.

Slipping into a pair of jogging shorts, a tank top and a pair of Reeboks, she headed out the back door. Calling Stryker crossed her mind, but she was afraid he would want to come along and she needed some time to herself. Besides, the property was fenced, and there was a perimeter alarm so she should be safe enough.

Haley took a couple of deep breaths, stretched and ran in place, then set off for the top of the slope north and east of the house. Since Ellie liked to jog, a trail had been cleared around the perimeter, ten acres of dirt, rock and scrub that made for a fairly difficult run.

The morning was crisp and clear, the dirt path hard beneath her shoes. Birds scampered into the scrub brush along the trail in front of her, and a hawk soared high overhead.

Haley smiled. She'd forgotten how good it felt to fill her lungs with fresh air, to exercise her muscles, stretch her legs and fly. She increased her pace, settled into a rhythm. Little by little, her mind began to clear, her thoughts to focus.

The mountains around her were scarred with ravines and dry streambeds, covered with prickly pear cactus, but the sky was a bright azure blue. For the first time in days, she was able to forget the guilt she had been carrying, the regret that she hadn't mended the rift with her father before it was too late.

She had failed him before but she wouldn't fail him again. She was doing the right thing in finding out who killed him. As she thought of the mounting evidence, she believed they were getting closer all the time.

Haley rounded the path at the top of the slope and started the loop back down. A pair of mourning doves crossed the trail ahead of her, then fluttered their wings and lifted into the air. Haley smiled.

As she jogged down into a low spot and ran up the far side, something flashed in the sunlight on the other side of the fence, up at the top of the mountain. She couldn't tell what it was, saw it again and an instant later heard the loud, sharp crack of a gunshot.

She cried out at the sting on the side of her face as a chip flew off a big granite boulder just inches from her head.

Haley bolted down the trail, flying full tilt toward the house. Another shot rang out, this one just ahead of her. The gunman was marking her path and if she kept going straight, he wouldn't miss again.

Swerving off the path, she ran into the rocky landscape, her heart hammering, her adrenaline pumping, her senses on high alert. Keeping low, she darted from boulder to boulder through the uneven terrain, dodging cactus and sagebrush, never moving in a straight line, racing downhill toward the house.

Praying Kurt Stryker or someone else had heard the shots and was on his way to help her.

At the sound of gunfire, Ty dropped the towel he was using to dry his hair and shot out of the bathroom. He grabbed his pistol, an M-9 Beretta, from the drawer beside his desk and raced out the door. Wearing only the jeans and boots he'd had on the night before, his chest bare and his hair still wet, he raced up the hill to the house.

He spotted Haley on the jogging path, heard the echo of another shot, and his heart slammed hard against his ribs. As he bolted past the back of the garage, Kurt Stryker ran out of the second-story apartment and charged down the stairs, but Ty was leaner and faster, and in seconds, he'd left Stryker behind.

Up the hill, Haley had darted off the path along the fence into the rocky landscape. She was running a zig-zag pattern, heading downhill, crouching low, racing toward safety.

His chest tightened. *Baby, I'm on my way.*

Another shot rang out and he caught the glint of a rifle barrel near the top of the mountain. Ty fired three cover shots, saw Haley duck behind a boulder, fired off another three rounds.

"Stay down!" he commanded as he reached her, diving on top of her, pressing her into the dirt. He could feel Haley trembling beneath him, hoped like hell he hadn't hurt her.

"Easy, baby," he said, searching the rocks and out-croppings above them for any sign of the shooter. He eased himself off her, drew her up behind his body, shielding them both behind the boulder. In the distance, he could hear the scream of sirens racing up Laurel Canyon Boulevard, turning up the road that wound toward the front gate and the drive up to Ellie's house.

"You okay?" he asked, still standing in front of her. When she didn't answer, he turned, saw the blood streaming down the side of her face.

The muscles across his stomach contracted. "Jesus!"

"I'm…I'm okay. A piece of granite flew off a rock and hit me. It's really not…not that bad."

He pushed her back a little farther, saw Kurt Stryker running up the hill, a .45 semiautomatic in his beefy hand. He was breathing hard by the time he reached them.

"Cops are on the way." Stryker handed him the binoculars he had been using. "Looks like our shooter's gone."

If he's smart, Ty thought, fighting to control the fury burning through him, feeling Haley tremble again.

Ty fitted the binoculars against his eyes, scanned the mountainside, checked the cluster of boulders where the shots had come from. Saw nothing and lowered his pistol.

He eased Haley out from behind the boulder. "Can you make it?"

She was shaking, but she nodded. "I'm okay."

"Let's get out of here. We need to see how bad you're hurt." With a last glance up the hill, he wrapped an arm around her shoulders and started guiding her back to the trail leading down to the house. Haley leaned into him, seeking his protection, and Ty softly cursed. He should have been there, should have figured something like this could happen.

When they got to the house, Ellie was standing just inside the back door. She caught Haley's arm. "Oh, my Lord, you're hurt."

Haley touched the gash on the side of her head, came away with bloody fingers. "It was only a rock chip. I'm a little shook up, but I'm okay."

"Come inside, and we'll take a look."

Ty stuck his pistol into the waistband of his jeans and stepped back as Ellie led Haley into the kitchen.

His adrenaline was still pumping, his blood rushing. Unconsciously, his hand balled into a fist.

He told himself to stand down, that the battle was over—at least for now. But his years of training kept him on high alert, made him far too conscious that things could have gone the other way. That Haley could have been killed.

He turned to see Johnnie striding toward the back door, shoving his pistol in the shoulder holster he wore over a black T-shirt. Dust puffed from the bottom of his heavy leather boots.

"Shooter hightailed it. I picked this up from his location." Johnnie handed Ty a shell casing.

Ty fingered it, felt the heat of the sun-warmed brass. "Winchester thirty-ought-six. Deer rifle. I would have figured maybe a .308."

"Not a sniper rifle, but plenty of power to do the job."

"Yeah."

"I saw some footprints next to a rock in the open space farther up the mountain, maybe a couple of hundred yards out, some dry grass matted down where he'd been watching the house. Tracked him to the road up above, but he was long gone."

Ty released a slow breath, raked back his damp hair. "I was afraid they might be watching the house, waiting for one of us to drive out, but I didn't figure them for a direct assault."

"You can't figure everything."

Amy opened the back door and rushed in, long blond hair flying around her. She hurried over and handed Ty a clean white T-shirt. "I saw you out the window. Johnnie told me not to move until it was over." She managed to smile. "I've learned to trust what he says."

"Thanks." Ty pulled the T-shirt over his head, his

gaze going to Haley, sitting in one of the kitchen chairs while her aunt cleaned the gash on the side of her face near her temple.

Ty walked over and pressed the button that opened the gate at the bottom of the drive and police cars swarmed up the hill. Johnnie had called them and updated them on the situation, told them the threat had lessened and that three of them were legally armed. He also told them the perp had escaped. Unless a patrol car in the area made a lucky stop, the shooter had gotten away clean.

Ty's stomach churned. Since he'd driven out of the parking lot of the Kitty Cat Club, his instincts had been screaming. He'd slept in the office last night so he could be close, but it hadn't been enough.

He went over to Haley. "I had a bad feeling something was off. I should have told you not to go out."

"There's no way you could have known. I thought as long as I stayed inside the fence, I'd be okay."

He worked a muscle in his jaw. "You'll be okay from now on—I promise you."

Stryker walked through the back door, big, brawny and powerful. "Sorry, brother. I should have been paying closer attention."

"We both should have."

Stryker looked at the blood on the rag Ellie was using to clean the wound near Haley's temple. His gaze zeroed in on Ty. "I think maybe it's time you filled me in."

Ty studied the man with the shaved head and earrings, a man who could kill Haley with his bare hands. But then Ty was capable of that same thing. He reminded himself that Ellie trusted Stryker and that two of them guarding Haley were better than one.

The intercom buzzed. While Ellie went to the door

to welcome the police, Ty filled Kurt Stryker in on the case he and Haley had been working.

An investigation that involved a fortune in stolen art, murder and a deadly attempt on Haley's life.

Eighteen

~∽⟋⟋⟍⟍∽~

Haley looked up at the sound of footsteps, saw the familiar, slightly overweight man with thinning brown hair and dark eyes walking into the kitchen. Detective Charles Cogan. His partner, overly cocky and a little too handsome, Matt Rollins, sauntered in behind him.

"Detective Cogan," Aunt Ellie said. "You remember my niece, Haley, and our investigator, Tyler Brodie?"

He tipped his head. "Ms. Warren. Brodie."

"We're very glad to see you." Ellie turned to the younger blond man. "You, as well, Detective Rollins. As you know, we had quite a serious situation here this morning."

Cogan's gaze lingered for a moment on her aunt, and it occurred to Haley that with her silver hair and trim figure, Ellie was still a very attractive woman.

The detective's attention slid to the dark, barrel-chested man standing next to Amy near the window. "Riggs," he grunted. "I should have figured you'd be in the middle of this."

"I live here, Cogan. Pretty hard not to be."

Cogan returned his attention to Haley, his gaze skimming over the blood on her tank top and the wide Band-Aid near her temple. "You want to tell me what happened?"

Ty answered for her. "Someone tried to kill her—that's what happened. Probably the same someone who murdered her father." He was still wound up, Haley could tell, his adrenaline still pumping. She felt some of that same edginess racing through her, as well.

"You don't know that," Rollins said defensively. "You haven't got a damn bit of evidence."

"Bullshit!"

Cogan ignored them both. "Why don't you start from the beginning, Ms. Warren? It's early. What were you doing out this time of the morning?"

Haley took a deep breath and started in, beginning with the idea of going for a morning run. Over the next few minutes, she told her story, start to finish, then turned to Ty, who picked up the tale from the moment he'd heard the gunshots and come racing up the hill.

Johnnie added his point of view, and Stryker came in from outside to fill out the picture.

"Before we go any further," Cogan said, "we need to take a look at the crime scene."

"Unless you've managed to destroy it," Rollins muttered.

Ty's jaw hardened.

"When we get back," Cogan continued, "I'll need statements from all of you, including Mrs. Stiles and Mrs. Riggs."

"I'll drive you up there," Johnnie offered. "It's rough terrain, a couple hundred yards up the hill. Easier to walk down from the street. Nothing's been touched."

Rollins scoffed. "Hard to believe if you were up there stomping around."

Johnnie bristled, got right in his face. "You'd better shut it, Rollins, or you're gonna wish you had."

"Is that a threat?"

"Knock it off, Matt." Cogan turned to Johnnie. "Lead the way." He glanced at Ty. "Brodie, I need you to show me where you and Ms. Warren were positioned during the shooting. Let's start there."

Ty nodded, flicked Haley a glance and fell in behind Johnnie. The men disappeared outside, Ty closing the door behind them.

In the silence that followed, Haley took her first deep breath since she had reached the top of the slope and heard the echo of gunfire.

Ty stood next to Johnnie, watching Cogan and Rollins descend from the upper road to the spot where Johnnie had retrieved the shell casing. The morning was slipping past, the sun beating down, doing nothing to cool the fury still pumping through his veins.

Sometimes after a mission he'd been like this for hours, the adrenaline still flowing, his mind going over every detail of what had happened, sifting and sorting, looking for mistakes, filing the information away in case he needed it again. He closed his fist, remembering the pressure of the pistol against his palm, though it now rode beneath his T-shirt in the waistband of his jeans.

Cogan and Rollins examined the site then turned and started back up the hill, Cogan carrying the rest of the shell casings in an evidence bag. All but the one Johnnie had retrieved.

The detectives stopped when they reached the two

men. Rollins jiggled the bag. "Thirty-ought-six casings. Hunting rifle. Good chance the guy was a poacher."

Ty's blood pressure shot up. "Have you lost your fucking mind?"

"Take it easy, Brodie," Cogan warned.

"Lots of deer in the area," Rollins said. "They wander around in the open space at the top of the mountain, meander down the hill. Guy probably saw something, got buck fever and took a couple of shots, missed the target and came close to Ms. Warren."

"This guy was no deer hunter," Johnnie said darkly, "and both of you know it. What the hell's going on?"

Ty turned the possibilities over in his head, shot a glare at Cogan. "I get it. You blew the original investigation into Warren's death, and you haven't done squat about his wife's assault. That could look real bad for you, and you don't want it to go into your file."

"Look," Cogan said. "I've only got a couple of weeks and I'll be out of there. Whoever was up at the top of the hill is gone. We can beef up our patrols in the area. That ought to keep anyone from getting near the house. That's the best we can do."

"That isn't enough," Ty said. "Haley could have been killed out here this morning."

Rollins's lip curled. "She's paying you to protect her, right? You and Stryker? Just do your jobs and she'll be fine."

"Why don't you do your job and find the guy who killed her father?"

"That case is over and done," Cogan said flatly. "Haley needs to go back to Chicago and forget all this. Put it all behind her."

"Why, so you can retire with a perfect record?"

Cogan stiffened. "Watch it, Brodie, or I'll haul your ass in for interfering with a police investigation."

"There is no police investigation," Ty said. "That's the problem."

He felt Johnnie's hand on his shoulder. "Take it easy, partner. These guys are busy. Let's let them get back to work."

Fuck them, Ty thought but didn't say it. Turning, he started back to the road at the top of the mountain, heard Johnnie's heavy boots plodding along behind him.

Clearly, they were on their own.

But then, they had been since all of this started.

The police were finally gone. Johnnie and Amy had returned home, Stryker was somewhere outside and Ty sat brooding on one of the stools at the breakfast bar. Aunt Ellie had brewed a pot of coffee. Haley took a sip from the mug in her hands, but the coffee had gone cold.

At least she'd had time to change out of her bloody clothes into jeans and a pink scoop-neck top. The Band-Aid was annoying against the side of her face.

"There's a clinic just down the hill," Aunt Ellie said as Haley absently reached up to touch it. "Are you sure you don't want to have the doctor take a look?"

"I'm not going to the doctor. Not for something as insignificant as this. I've had worse scrapes out hiking."

Ellie looked over at Ty and shook her head. Haley glanced in his direction, images returning of the man who had raced up the hill half-naked, every muscle tense, firing a steady stream of bullets at the assassin trying to kill her.

As he sat on the stool, any trace of the smiling, easygoing Texan who'd been in the kitchen yesterday was gone. There was no smile today. Instead the muscle in his jaw was clenched so tight it looked painful. His dark brows drew into a scowl, and his mouth was a thin, angry line.

This was no soft-spoken country boy. This was a Marine, a hard, capable man who, like the sleeping leopard, had just been awakened.

"You did good out there today," he finally said. "You did just what you should have—ran a zigzag pattern, kept your head down, stayed focused."

She managed a smile but it didn't feel quite right. "I've watched a lot of old Stallone movies."

His eyes were dark and stormy. "The only thing you did wrong was to go out there in the first place."

She stiffened. "I told you, I thought—"

"I know." He sighed. "It wasn't your fault." He glanced out the window then back. "It's just…you really scared me."

She had seen it in his face as he ran toward her, seen his fear for her, along with his determination to protect her.

Something pulled at her insides. She was coming to care for Tyler Brodie in a way she had never expected. Considering the different lives they led, the different people they were, it was dangerous. Perhaps more dangerous than searching for her father's killer.

Ty got up from the stool and began to move restlessly. She could feel the edginess, the brittle anger he fought to keep under control.

He paced over to where she sat at the table. "Stryker's outside. I've got some things I need to do. You'll be safe in the house, and I won't be gone long."

She frowned, read his intent and came up out of her chair. "Wait a minute. You aren't thinking I'm just going to sit in here and do nothing until you catch these guys?"

"Like I said, you'll be safe here. You leave, you'll be in danger. It's as simple as that."

"Well, I'm not just going to sit here. I'll go crazy. I need to get out of the house, and that's exactly what I'm going to do. You can take me with you or I'll have Stryker drive me."

"No way."

She jerked up her chin, clamped her hands on her hips. "Take me or I'll go with Stryker. What's it going to be?"

A muscle flexed in his jaw. The hard, dangerous look he'd worn since the shooting remained. It changed his features so completely she had to force herself not to back away.

"You need to think about this, Haley. Very carefully. Someone tried to kill you. You keep digging, they're going to try again."

"I'm in this until it's over. Are you taking me with you, or not?"

She could read his frustration in the rigid set of his shoulders. He wanted her safe, but he didn't completely trust leaving her with Stryker. "Fine. I'll take you wherever you want to go."

Her heart started pounding. There was only one place she wanted to be. "Let me get my purse."

She returned a few minutes later, found him restlessly pacing the floor in the entry, his features set in the same fierce expression he'd worn before.

After the police had gone, he had changed into a pair of low-topped leather boots—better traction, she figured, than his slick-soled cowboy boots in case he had to move in a hurry. He had also retrieved his holster, and now wore his pistol clipped to the belt on his jeans.

"Stay inside. I'll get the truck." He went out the door

first, used the binoculars to scan the area just to be safe, then took off down the hill to the parking lot.

He was back a few minutes later, left the truck running and came in to get her. As she started to climb into the passenger seat, she felt his hand on her bottom, giving her a not so gentle shove, then he slammed the door, walked around and slid behind the wheel.

As he drove the truck around the drive and headed back down the hill toward the gate, he flicked her a sideways glance. "So where do you want to go?"

Haley looked at him, her pounding heart rocketing up again. "Your house. That's where I want to go."

Ty's features hardened even more. "We go there— you know what's going to happen. You don't want me to touch you—not when I'm like this."

"Yes, I do."

He shook his head. "I'm still running on adrenaline. I'm pissed, and at the moment, I'm not the nice guy you were in bed with before. If I take you now, it won't be making love. It'll be hot, hard fucking. Is that what you want?"

Heat and need rolled through her. She understood what he was feeling. The restlessness, the tension, the leftover fear. She looked up at him. "That's exactly what I want."

Ty stepped on the gas.

Nineteen

The truck fishtailed around a corner. Ty looked in the mirror, expecting red lights and sirens any minute. He almost wished the cops would stop him. He didn't trust himself with Haley. Not when he was in one of his dark, turbulent moods.

She hadn't said a word since they'd driven out the gate, heading for his condo. He'd taken a circuitous route to make sure they weren't being tailed, but the police were working the area, and he figured whoever had been up on that hill had gone to ground, at least for a while.

His place was just up ahead, a town house in the hills that gave him a feeling of privacy in the sea of people around him.

He glanced over at Haley, thought of the man or men who had tried to kill her, and another shot of adrenaline rolled through him.

He was jacked up and rolling, and just looking at her made him hard. If she didn't stop him now, it was going to be too late.

"You sure you're ready for this?"

She ran her hands nervously over the front of her jeans, and he wondered if she was feeling some of the same tension that was coursing through him.

Her eyes locked with his. "More than ready," she said.

Hunger gnawed at him, hot and fierce. He pulled into the garage, turned off the engine and hit the button on the automatic door, sealing them inside. As he got out of the truck and started around to the passenger side, Haley jumped down from the seat. Ty reached her, swung her up in his arms, slammed the truck door and carried her into the house.

He was breathing a little too fast when he set her on her feet in the kitchen, walked over and reset the alarm, giving her a last few seconds to change her mind. When she made no move, just stood there looking at him as if she dared him to take her, he laced his fingers in all that golden hair and dragged her mouth up to his for a deep, wet, ravaging kiss. Haley gripped his shoulders. With a soft moan, she opened for him, slipped her tongue into his mouth and kissed him back with the same hot need he was feeling. Surprise lasted only an instant, then he was deepening the kiss, sinking into those soft, full lips, driving his tongue into her mouth and taking what he wanted.

Her fingers dug into the muscles across his shoulders as he walked her backward to the kitchen counter. Peeling her little pink flowered top over her head, he reached for the hook at the front of her white lace bra and unsnapped it, tore the bra off and tossed it away.

His gaze ran over her breasts, apple-round and tilted slightly upward, the rosy tip contracting beneath his hot stare. Haley reached for him, took his face between her palms and kissed him, kissed him like she'd die if she didn't.

A low growl came from his throat. Breaking the kiss, he bent and flicked his tongue over her nipple, opened to take in the fullness, suckled and tasted, bit down a little harder than he should have on the tight bud at the crest.

A soft gasp slipped out and she pressed herself more fully against him, rubbed herself like a sexy kitten over the erection throbbing beneath his zipper.

She wanted it. Wanted him, and he was more than ready to give her what she wanted. He popped the button on the front of her jeans, unzipped and dragged them down over her hips. Lifting her up, he set her down on the kitchen counter and stripped off the rest of her clothes.

Haley jerked his T-shirt over his head and kissed him, a hot, deep, erotic kiss that begged him to take her.

Jesus, he was so ready.

Buzzing down his zipper, he freed himself, gripped her hips and dragged her to the edge of the counter. When she locked her arms around his neck and wrapped those long legs around his waist, he buried himself to the hilt.

For an instant, he just stood there, heat burning through him, his erection turning to steel. Fighting for control, he slid himself out and thrust hard back in. Out and then in, setting up a rhythm, hunger driving him, lust pouring through every cell in his body. He needed this. Needed her.

He drove into her again and again, pounding hard, gripping her hips, taking her until she cried out and her slender body shook with the force of her climax.

Still he drove into her, taking her and taking her until

the hunger exploded inside him and he couldn't wait a moment more. Haley climaxed again at the same time he did, and they clung together, both of them trembling with the loss of control.

For long seconds he held her against him, absorbing the warmth of her body, feeling the rightness of being inside her. Time slipped past. With a sigh, he set her on her feet, turned and dealt with the condom he didn't really remember putting on. Breathing hard, Haley watched him, her pretty face still flushed with pleasure.

Standing naked in his kitchen, those beautiful blue eyes languid and yet still burning with heat, she looked so damned sexy.

He wanted more. Dragging her back into his arms, he kissed her again. He'd warned her, told her what would happen. "I'm not done with you yet," he said, his voice deep and rusty, and a soft little whimper came from her throat. Lifting her high against his chest, he carried her upstairs to the bedroom and lowered her to the middle of his bed. It only took a moment to strip off the rest of his clothes and sheath himself again.

Ty drove deeply, felt her arch to take more of him. In seconds, Haley had reached another shaking climax, but Ty didn't stop, just kissed her and kissed her and fought to hang on to his control. But the hunger was driving him, forcing him to the crest and pushing him over. He thrust into her a couple more times, then came with a rush of pleasure so fierce, so sharp, every muscle in his body tightened and seized.

Slowly he relaxed, slumping for an instant on top of her, his mind completely empty, his body still pulsing with the warm feel of her gloving him so sweetly.

With a long, slow breath, he pushed himself up on

his elbows, lifted away and settled beside her on the bed. The hunger was gone, the need pushed back into the dark place it had come from. Haley had done that, helped drive away the angry frustration inside him. He looked into her softly feminine features and felt a rush of guilt for treating her so roughly.

With a long, slow breath, he shook his head. "I'm sorry. I didn't mean to hurt you. I don't know what else to say."

Haley turned to him, her eyes lambent and her body relaxed. "I know what to say." She ran a finger down his cheek. Then she smiled so wide her dimples popped out. "Thank you. That was amazing, Ty."

He laughed, relief and admiration sweeping through him. He drew her back against him, spoon fashion, content in a way he hadn't expected.

"Sometimes after a mission, I'd be this way, you know? Still working off an adrenaline high, jacked up and ready for more. Seeing you out there on the hill taking fire, it was like being in the war all over again."

"When I saw you running toward me, I knew everything was going to be okay. I saw you coming and I wasn't afraid anymore."

He kissed the top of her head, thinking of the things he had told her, things that were part of the darkness inside that little by little was fading.

"I'll be there from now on," he promised, though he wasn't sure how long that would be. All he knew was his demons were gone and that Haley had been there when he needed her, had matched him in his passion.

"You're something," he said. "You know that?"

She made no reply, but he could feel her smiling as she snuggled a little closer against him.

It was the memory of gunshots echoing down the hill that had his arms tightening around her.

Nathan Silverman walked out on the deck of his Swiss chalet, the smallest, yet favorite of the three homes he owned in different parts of the world. Built in the twenties, the house had vaulted wooden ceilings and a warm rock fireplace. A deck ran the length of the cozy living room that looked out over the water.

Lake Lucerne stretched for miles in front of him, ice-blue and as smooth as glass. In the distance, the Swiss landscape rose up from the valley floor, brilliant green, grass-covered grazing land dotted with tiny yellow flowers, rising to sharp white alpine peaks still deeply buried in snow.

He loved this home, a place to get away from the studios and make-believe world he lived in. A place where even his wife and the two children he adored were excluded. Here there was silence and room to think.

Nathan did his best creative work in the house, read scripts, chose which films he would produce. Which would be small, independent movies; which would become the blockbuster Oscar winners for which he was famous. Time had cloaked Nathan in success, and he wore it like a kingly robe.

He thought of the phone call he had received. With a sigh, he turned away from the stunning view of the lake and mountains and walked back into the chalet. Above the antique desk, a priceless Renoir added life and color to the overstuffed sofa and chairs, the heavy carved wooden tables and lively Aubusson carpets.

A picnic scene from the nineteenth century, one of the artist's favorite subjects, an impressionist work in warm, textured pastels and vibrant scarlets, yellows and blues.

It was worth tens of millions, a price too extravagant even for someone with the impressive net worth he had accumulated over the years. He owned other beautiful paintings, of course, had collected for years and displayed them proudly in his Beverly Hills mansion and also his beach house in Barbados. But once he had seen the Renoir, he'd known he had to have it.

And since it had come at what most would call a bargain price, and since few people were invited to visit him in the home where he kept it, the risk was a small one.

Or it had been.

Nathan pulled his gaze away from the painting and walked down the hall to his study. He had a great deal of work to do and he refused to waste time worrying—not while he was here. It was a rule he adhered to and would continue to do.

Things would work out; all would be well. Sometimes he'd had to play hardball, but Nathan had always come out the winner.

That wasn't going to change anytime soon.

Haley stirred. For an instant, she panicked, not quite sure where she was, then the feel of a hard male body cocooning her in warmth reminded her of the wild sex she'd had with Tyler Brodie.

Embarrassment slipped through her. Had she really initiated the encounter, practically demanded he take her to his home and make love to her? She refused to think of it as less than that, even though he'd warned her it would be nothing more than a way to satisfy his needs.

The truth was she'd had needs of her own.

"I know what you're thinking," came the rumble of a familiar deep voice from over her shoulder. "You're freaking out over what we did."

She turned onto her back so she could look at him. "Maybe a little. I can't believe I was so...you know, aggressive."

He sat up in bed, scooted back against the headboard and drew her up beside him. "Someone tried to kill you. When something like that happens, it puts everything in perspective, shows us how fragile our existence really is. It makes us want to hang on for all it's worth, take everything life has to offer."

"It was just...umm...sex. You said so yourself."

His mouth edged up at the corner. "Maybe that's what I said, but it wasn't the truth. I wanted you. I'd been aching to have you again. What we shared...it was wild and hot, but it was more than just sex. At least for me."

She leaned over and kissed him softly on the lips. "I've never done anything quite so..."

"Much fun?"

She laughed.

Ty grinned. "Stick with me and it won't be the last time."

The tightness eased inside her. There was something about Ty Brodie that always reassured her. It was okay to be wild, he made it seem. At least when she was with him.

He unwound his lanky frame, got up and padded over to retrieve his T-shirt, tossed it to her on the bed.

"I need a shower." He flashed her a grin. "We could save water if we took one together."

But she was completely wrung out, still trying to

FREE Merchandise is 'in the Cards' for you!

Dear Reader,

We're giving away FREE MERCHANDISE!

Seriously, we'd like to reward you for reading this novel by giving you **FREE MERCHANDISE** worth over $25. And no purchase is necessary!

You see the Jack of Hearts sticker above? Paste that sticker in the box on the Free Merchandise Voucher inside. Return the Voucher promptly...and we'll send you valuable Free Merchandise!

Thanks again for reading one of our novels—and enjoy your Free Merchandise with our compliments!

Pam Powers

Pam Powers

P.S. Look inside to see what Free Merchandise is **"in the cards"** for you!

FM-ROM-13

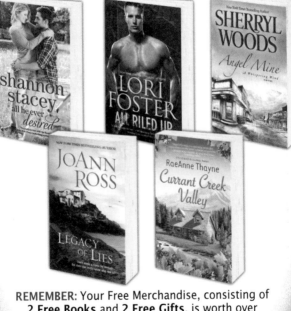

deal with the shooting, the hot sex and her uncertain feelings for Ty.

She pulled on his T-shirt and shook her head. "I don't think so."

Ty seemed to understand. "In that case, you can use the bathroom at the end of the hall."

"Thanks." She watched him amble off naked, not the least bit self-conscious, the muscles in his sexy behind tightening as he walked out of the room. With a sigh, she climbed out of bed, made her way downstairs to retrieve her clothes, then came back up to shower and dress.

Ten minutes later, they both walked into the hall at the same time and headed downstairs.

"You still haven't told me what happened last night at the Kitty Cat Club," Haley said when they reached the kitchen. "What did Ray Farrell have to say?"

Ty walked over and started a pot of coffee, taking down a bag of Starbucks and measuring it into the machine.

"Farrell said he met with your father the second time about a week before he was killed. He'd heard rumors. Word on the street was there'd been another theft. Three paintings, this time. All of them priceless."

Her hand froze as she reached for a pair of mugs. "Oh, my God. Were they stolen from the Scarsdale Center?"

"Farrell didn't think so."

She took the mugs down and set them on the counter. "Three more stolen paintings. Since we haven't heard anything about it, they must have been replaced with forgeries that haven't yet been discovered."

"That would be my guess."

"Three paintings. Three names scribbled on Dad's

iPad. I wonder if they could be the men who bought them."

"It's kind of a stretch, don't you think?"

"Farrell told Dad about the burglary. Once he knew, he would have been looking for the men who bought the pieces."

"I guess it's possible."

"So what do we do next?"

"We still have two ways to go. Find out who's painting the forgeries. Or find out who bought them—which would include running down those names."

"We need to talk to Jules Weaver," Haley said.

Ty looked at his watch. "We've missed visiting hours again today. We'll have to try to see him tomorrow."

She looked up at him, felt a little shiver of renewed sexual awareness. It was insane. She had never really been a passionate woman. At least she hadn't thought she was.

"We could drive up tonight," she heard herself saying. "Talk to Weaver in the morning."

Hazel eyes zeroed in on her blue ones. "If we were careful, made sure we weren't followed, we could get a nice room someplace, have the evening to ourselves."

"We could," she said a little breathlessly.

"We'd take it slow, this time. No hurry."

She knew what he meant, knew this time it would be lovemaking, not just sex. But she had recently discovered she liked both ways. "We could order room service instead of going out."

"Yeah." His eyes looked darker, hotter. "Have an... uh...*appetizer* first. Then dinner. Then uh...*dessert* when we finish the meal." Ty pulled her against him, kissed her softly. "You need to get permission to visit an inmate, but I know someone up there. I'll call her, make arrangements to see Weaver tomorrow morning."

"Her?"

"Carol Foster. Not a girlfriend, just a friend."

Haley slid her arms around his neck. "I need a few things. Do you think it's safe for me to go back home?"

"No one followed us here. We'll make sure no one's watching your place when we leave. We need to tell your aunt where we're going and let Stryker know you won't be needing him till sometime tomorrow."

"Don't tell him where we're going, okay?"

A dark eyebrow went up. "You don't trust him?"

"It isn't that. I just…the fewer people who know where I am, the safer I'll feel."

A muscle jumped in Ty's cheek. "The game's changed now. We know for sure they're coming after you. They come again, we'll be ready."

Haley didn't say more. She trusted Ty to keep her safe. The problem was, where he was concerned, she wasn't sure how far she could trust herself.

Twenty

As usual, Ellie rose early the next morning. Feeling a little stiff, she glanced longingly out the window toward the hillside north of the house, but after the shooting yesterday, she decided to forgo a morning run.

She found herself smiling. Last night, Haley and Ty had driven to San Luis Obispo. This morning they would be speaking to Jules Weaver, the man in prison for forgery.

They were sleeping together, she knew. She would never divulge that she had been matchmaking when she'd introduced them, but she had always been good at reading people and she'd had a hunch they would be good for each other.

Still, there were lots of obstacles to overcome and she wasn't arrogant enough to be certain things would work out between them. But finding happiness, she believed, was worth the risk.

Heading into the expensive marble bathroom that Harry had had custom designed for her, she showered and put on a little makeup. She was towel-drying her short silver hair when the phone started ringing.

Ellie walked over and picked up the receiver. "Good morning."

"Mrs. Stiles?"

"Yes, this is Eleanor Stiles. May I help you?"

"This is Betty Jean Warren. I hope I'm not calling too early. I forgot about the time difference until I'd already dialed."

"I'm always up early. I hope you're feeling better."

"Yes, much better. I'd like to speak to Haley…if it's convenient."

"I'm afraid Haley isn't in at the moment. Perhaps I could help you, Mrs. Warren?"

"Oh, please call me Betty Jean. You see, the police just phoned…a Detective Cogan? He's the policeman who looked into my husband's death. He called to follow up on a shooting that occurred at your house yesterday. He said he believed it was just an accident, someone hunting deer or something, but I… Is Haley all right?"

"She's safe, if that's what you mean."

"I don't believe it was an accident, Mrs. Stiles. I think someone was trying to kill her. I can't let that happen. I'm coming back to Los Angeles. I'm catching a flight first thing in the morning—I already have my ticket. I'm the one who got Haley involved in this, and now she's in danger. I've got to talk to her, convince her to stop her investigation."

"I don't think there's anything you can say that will stop her. She has her mind set and she can be very stubborn." Ellie thought of her late sister, Haley's grandmother on her mother's side. Stubbornness definitely ran in the family.

"Either way, I'm coming back. I can't let her handle this alone."

"You'd be safer if you stayed in Michigan."

"I'm coming back. Please tell Haley."

"Wait!" Ellie's fingers tightened on the phone. "Don't hang up, Betty Jean. I have an idea. We have two body-guards working here at the house. This morning, I hired a security company to patrol the grounds. The house is quite large, so why don't you stay here? You would have your own room and bath and complete privacy. You would be safe here as you might not be in your home."

"I couldn't possibly intrude on you that way."

"You wouldn't be intruding. You're Haley's step-mother. You're family."

"I don't think... I don't think Haley would like it."

Definitely not. At least not at first. "You two don't really know each other. But I know one thing for cer-tain. Haley wouldn't want anything to happen to you. If you're here, you'll be safe."

A long pause ensued. "I'd love for Haley and me to get to know each other. It's what her father always wanted."

"Staying here would give you a chance to make that happen."

"Yes, I guess it would. All right, then, I accept your hospitality, Mrs. Stiles."

"It's just Ellie, and I'll have a car waiting for you at the airport when you arrive. A man named Kurt Stryker will be driving. He's a bodyguard. He's quite...impres-sive. You'll know it's him right away."

"Thank you. I look forward to seeing you tomorrow."

With a smile, Ellie hung up the phone. She always knew when she had made a good decision—a feeling of rightness settled deep in her bones. Haley would get to know the woman who had loved her father, and Betty Jean would be safe in Ellie's house.

She turned back to the mirror to finish putting on her makeup. She had a lunch date today. Jonathan Hammond would be picking her up at eleven forty-five. They had met at a meeting of the Botanical Society. Since then, they had been seeing each other at least twice a week.

She had never thought she would ever find someone who could replace Harry. They had loved each other so much. But time had passed, and she had become a different, more self-sufficient woman.

Ellie smiled at her image in the mirror. It was time to let that woman have the chance for a life of her own.

Haley woke up in bed next to Ty. He was sleeping soundly, his dark hair mussed and tumbled across his forehead, his muscled chest moving steadily up and down.

They had ended up staying at the Cliffs Resort in Pismo Beach, just a ten-minute drive from San Luis. Ty had booked a lovely room that overlooked the sea. Lying next to him, Haley could hear the gulls screeching above the water, the sound of breakers beating against the shore. Peaceful sounds, yet her heart throbbed oddly, in contrast to the calmness around her.

She thought of last night, an evening that had been everything she could have hoped for. Sitting on the deck watching the sunset, making love, ordering room service, making love again after supper and again during the night.

It was perfect. Too perfect.

She wasn't good at relationships. Sooner or later, she would say the wrong thing, do something Ty wouldn't like. Or she would find out something she didn't like about him.

Even if that didn't happen, as soon as they caught the people who had killed her father—the men who had tried to kill her—she would be leaving, returning to her life in Chicago.

Long-distance relationships never worked out. All they ever led to was heartache. And marriage…? She thought of her mother and the terrible years after the divorce. Better to stay single, avoid the pain of a doomed relationship.

In the meantime, she had to be careful, had to keep her distance or she was going to fall in love with Ty, and that would be a disaster.

As if to prove the point, his cell phone started ringing. Ty groaned and stirred, reached over to where the phone rested on the bedside table and picked it up, cracked open one eye and looked at the caller ID.

He shoved the phone under his pillow, letting the call go to voice mail, but the damage was done. The caller was clearly a woman, a reminder of the uncertain relationship she and Ty shared.

Haley got out of bed and headed for the shower. As the water rained down on her, she told herself she knew the kind of man Ty was, that he would do his best not to hurt her. But the only fidelity he truly owed her was for the time they were together.

The bathroom door opened and Ty walked in, but instead of inviting him to join her, she turned off the spray and stepped out, grabbed a towel off the rack and wrapped it around her, tucked it beneath her arms.

"I need to get dressed," she said brusquely and left him in the bathroom.

She heard the shower running again as she put on her

makeup in the mirror above the dresser, brushed out her hair and plaited it into a loose braid. Ty appeared with a towel riding low on his hips, his jaw set and his features dark. He hadn't bothered to shave, and he looked like sin personified. Haley ignored a shot of lust that was beginning to feel downright familiar.

Ty walked over and caught her shoulders, turned her around to face him. "I'm sorry about the call. I should have picked up. It was a girl named Tiffany. I should have told her not to call again. I should have said I was seeing someone."

Haley glanced away. "It doesn't matter. Sooner or later this'll all be over, and your life will go back to normal."

"It *does* matter. And now that I've met you, I'm not sure what normal is anymore." Bending his head, he very thoroughly kissed her. "We need to ride this out, darlin', see where it leads. Nothing in life is ever a sure thing."

"I have a life in Chicago, Ty. A life I enjoy. I'll be leaving. You'll be staying. That's as sure as it gets."

Ty made no reply, but she could tell he wasn't happy. He pulled on a clean pair of Levi's and a light blue, short-sleeved, button-down shirt while Haley dressed in beige slacks and a turquoise silk blouse.

They didn't talk as they left the hotel. Haley told herself it didn't matter that he was the pied piper of women. That she would be heading back to Chicago, back to the life she'd made there. But it didn't make her feel any better.

Ty tossed their overnight bags into the truck. Before he'd left L.A., he'd shoved a Winchester—short-barreled, tactical shotgun—a .45 Nighthawk and a Glock 9 mm behind the seat. Along with the Beretta he carried, he was prepared if the men came after Haley again.

She didn't say anything as he drove north on the freeway. Nothing as they neared the San Luis Obispo Men's Colony, situated among the rolling green hills off Highway 1. The place was huge, with thousands of inmates housed in dozens of cell blocks arranged by different levels of crime.

Jules Weaver was housed in the minimum security West Facility. But even in that side of the prison, there were strict rules about visitors. Fortunately, Ty's friend in the system helped them cut through some of the paperwork and arranged their visit with Weaver.

Carol Foster had worked in the penal system in L.A. before her transfer to San Luis. She held a high-level position in the prison administration department, and she was good at her job. Ty had taken her out a couple of times before she'd relocated, and they had wound up friends.

He flicked a glance at Haley, who had finally relaxed back in her seat. He had a lot of women friends, not all of them former lovers. No matter what happened with Haley that probably wouldn't change.

The difference was, if he was involved with a woman, he was completely and totally committed. Cheating wasn't an option. True, he had never found a woman he was willing to make a lifetime commitment to, but he hoped that would happen someday.

His glance went back to Haley. Maybe it already had.

Ty forced the thought away. It was too soon to be thinking like that. Way too soon.

"Are we okay?" he asked her.

She turned, and a faint smile tipped up the corners of those pouty lips. "We're okay. I was being an idiot this

morning. Last night was really terrific. This morning…
maybe I was feeling a little…umm…jealous. I'm not usually that way."

He liked her honesty. Feeling a little jealous? He took
it as a good sign. "That's okay. I'm not crazy about you
being with Stryker."

She laughed. "Stryker? That's almost funny."

"Yeah, how's that?"

She just smiled and shook her head.

The prison appeared up ahead. He slowed and sig-
naled a left turn just as his phone started ringing. Praying it wasn't another of his former girlfriends, Ty pulled
over to the side of the road and dragged out his cell.
Recognizing the number as one he'd called yesterday,
he pressed the phone against his ear.

"Brodie."

"Ty, this is Carol. Weaver's in the hospital. He was
stabbed early this morning. He's in critical condition
and they don't know if he's going to make it."

Son of a bitch. "I thought he was in the minimum security section? How could that happen? Did they catch
the guy who did it?"

"We don't know how it happened. Someone found
him lying on the floor in the laundry this morning."

"I need to see him, Carol. Can you get me in?"

"Sorry, Ty, only family."

He glanced over at Haley. "I've got his…uh…sister
with me. If he doesn't have much time, she needs to see
him."

"What's her name?"

"Haley Warren. She's his half sister."

"All right, I'll get her in. Bring her directly to the
hospital. It's in the East Facility."

"I know where it is. We're almost there now." Ty ended the call.

"I'm his half sister?" Haley said, lifting a dark gold eyebrow.

"If we want to see him, you are. Weaver was shanked this morning. They don't know if he's going to live."

"Oh, my God!"

Ty began weaving his way around the long rows of bland, stucco, three-story buildings, found the one that housed the hospital and pulled the pickup into an empty parking space.

Carol was waiting for them when they got to the door. A little redhead, she was a few pounds heavier than when he'd last seen her, but smart and very pretty. The look Haley was giving him made him glad he'd never taken Carol to bed.

She started leading them down the hall. "We don't have much time," she said.

"Is he conscious?" Ty asked.

"Yes. After you called yesterday, he agreed to meet you. Believe it or not, he's been asking for you."

Ty and Haley exchanged a glance. They followed Carol to the ICU, and one of the nurses led them inside.

Jules Weaver was a thin man in his forties with salt-and-pepper hair. He was lying beneath a sheet on the hospital bed, his eyes closed. Tubes ran into both arms, and an oxygen mask covered his nose and mouth. The only thing exceptional about him were his long, thin fingers. *The hands of an artist,* Ty thought.

Weaver's eyes slowly opened. His arm shook as he reached up and pulled the mask off a face as white as the sheet on his bed. His watery blue eyes went straight to Haley.

"You're Warren's…daughter?"

She moved to his bedside. "That's right. This is Ty Brodie. He's a private investigator. We're trying to find out who painted the forgeries that were found in the Scarsdale Center. My father talked to you about it. Now he's dead."

He just nodded. His eyes slid closed again. He was so quiet that for a moment Ty thought he'd stopped breathing.

Then he opened his eyes and looked directly at Haley. "Abigail…McQueen," he wheezed. "She…painted them. I would have…kept her secret. But I won't…die for her." Then his eyes closed and a doctor strode forward while a nurse started pushing them out the door.

Carol waited in the hallway. "Did you get what you needed?"

Ty thought of the man lying near death and shook his head. "Weaver didn't know anything, after all."

"We really appreciate your help," Haley said, managing to smile.

Carol nodded, started leading them back to the front of the building. "Better luck next time," she said. Ty gave her a wave as he pushed open the door, and he and Haley walked outside.

Ty led Haley out to the parking lot and helped her into the truck.

"Do you think Weaver's going to die?" she asked.

"He didn't look good." He closed her door, walked around to his side of the pickup and climbed up behind the wheel. "From what I could find out, if he lives, with good behavior, he'll be out in less than a year."

"You tried to protect him."

He shrugged. "He did what was right. That's worth

protecting." Ty said nothing more. Finding Abigail Mc-
Queen was his first order of business. He pulled the
pickup onto the freeway and started back to L.A.

Twenty-One

By the time Haley got back to her aunt's house, she was exhausted. Weaver had been near death. The attempt on his life had obviously been an effort to silence him. Yesterday someone had tried to kill her to stop her from investigating the case. Odds were, whoever had done it would try again.

Things were heating up, the danger increasing, and yet she could not stop.

She sighed as Aunt Ellie opened the front door and stepped back to welcome her and Ty inside.

"You made it. I was starting to worry."

"I'm sorry, Aunt Ellie. I should have called."

"Weaver was stabbed this morning," Ty explained as they walked through the entry. "The good news is, he gave us the name of the artist who painted the forgeries."

"Oh, my, that is good news."

"Ever heard of an artist named Abigail McQueen?" he asked.

Ellie thought a moment, shook her head. "No, I don't think so."

"I need to go down to the office, do some digging, see if I can find her."

"You look tired, Tyler. Why don't you come into the living room and join us. Johnnie and Amy are here with Rick and Rachael. At least have a glass of iced tea before you go back to work."

Haley reached over and took his hand, felt the tension running through him, the eagerness to move forward on the case. "Come on," she urged softly, figuring he needed a minute to recuperate as much as she did. "You can introduce me."

Ty finally nodded. Haley led him down the hall to the living room at the rear of the house, which was massive, with twelve-foot ceilings and a wall of glass windows that overlooked the city. The room should have been cold, but with the layout broken into cozy conversation areas, each with a comfortable sofa and chairs, the space was almost cozy. Sleek dark wood and thick glass coffee tables, modern lamps and geometrically patterned throw rugs made it a relaxing room to sit in and converse.

Haley noticed the slatted blinds had been partly drawn, giving them privacy.

"We'd be out on the deck on such a nice day," Ellie said, "but Kurt says we'd make too easy a target. Better to be safe than sorry."

"Oh, Aunt Ellie." Haley leaned over and hugged her. "I've caused you so much trouble. Now I'm putting you and your friends in danger."

Johnnie sauntered up just then in his usual black T-shirt and jeans, his chest and arms bulging with muscle. "The kind of work we do, danger's part of the equation. We're all used to it. Even Ellie."

"Come on," Ty urged her gently. "You can say hello to Amy, and I'll introduce you to Rick and Rachael."

Haley stopped as they entered the living room and she spotted the attractive couple standing at the window next to Johnnie's petite blond wife. Rick Vega was an incredibly handsome Hispanic man. And Rachael... With her long dark hair and pale green eyes, Rachael Brewer was, quite simply, one of the most beautiful women Haley had ever seen.

"Rick and Rachael," Ty said, leading her toward them. "This is Haley. It's past time you all met each other. Especially since Haley's going to be my date for your wedding."

Haley's gaze shot to his, and she caught his sexy grin. "Right, darlin'?"

The endearment sent a curl of heat into her stomach. "When...when is it?"

Rachael walked over and took her hand. "It's only two weeks away and we'd love to have you. Amy's my maid of honor and Johnnie's Rick's best man. Of course your aunt will be there, too, so you'll know plenty of people."

Two weeks. Was there any chance all of this would be over and she would be back in Chicago? She doubted it. "I'd love to come. And it's wonderful to meet you and Rick. Congratulations."

Vega set a hand protectively at his future wife's slim waist. They made an amazingly attractive pair.

"I hear you've been having some trouble," Vega said to Haley.

"Rick's a homicide detective," Ty explained, turning his attention to his friend. "I guess Ellie's told you what's going on."

"She's been keeping me informed. I hear Cogan's working the homicide case."

"According to Cogan there is no homicide. Warren's death was an accident. Betty Jean's assault was a home invasion. And the shooting here yesterday was a hunter trying to poach a deer."

"Cogan's riding out his last weeks on the force. He wants to leave with a clean record."

"I get that. But what about Rollins?"

"Rollins is a slacker. Always has been. From now on, keep me in the loop. This doesn't fall in my jurisdiction, but if there's any way I can help, you know I will."

"I know. Thanks, Rick."

The men began making small talk while Haley, Amy and Rachael got acquainted. All the while, Vega kept Rachael in his line of sight, watching over her as if he were her guardian angel.

And clearly Rachael adored him. The secret smiles they shared couldn't be mistaken for anything but a deep and abiding love.

Still, marriages rarely worked. At least in Haley's estimation. She had always been sure getting married wasn't for her.

But watching these people, feeling their joy…she hoped it worked for them.

"If you have a moment," her aunt said as her guests departed and Ty walked them to the door. "I've asked Dolores to bring us some tea in the library. I have some news, dear, and it's nice and quiet in there."

Haley sighed. "All right, but I hope it's good news for a change."

Aunt Ellie led the way down the hall to the wood-paneled library, and they sat down on the brown leather sofa in front of the fireplace. It wasn't lit this time of year, but held a vase of large yellow chrysanthemums.

Dolores, a small Hispanic woman who had worked for Ellie for years, arrived with a silver tea tray. Apparently, news of the shooting hadn't been enough to keep her away. Dolores set the tea tray down on the coffee table and disappeared silently out of the room.

"So what's going on?" Haley asked as Aunt Ellie poured tea into a pair of gold-rimmed porcelain teacups.

"Your stepmother called me this morning."

Haley straightened, worry slipping through her. "Betty Jean? Is she okay?"

Ellie handed her a cup that held a cube of sugar and a little cream. The fragrant scent of jasmine floated into the air. "She's fine, just worried. She's coming back to Los Angeles, darling. Apparently Detective Cogan called to talk to her about the shooting. She was very upset. She wants you to call off the investigation."

Haley balanced the teacup on her knee. She was used to the afternoon ritual that was among her mother's favorites. "I'm not stopping. And to tell you the truth, Aunt Ellie, after what happened to Jules Weaver, I'm not sure it would matter."

A noise sounded in the doorway as Ty walked in. "Haley's right. We're in too deep to stop now. Jimmy Warren's dead. Betty Jean was nearly killed and Jules Weaver's in critical condition in the prison hospital. We need answers. This won't be over until we get them."

Ellie poured a cup of tea for Ty, adding cream and sugar and handing it over. The delicate cup looked ridiculously out of place in his strong, calloused hand.

"I had a feeling you'd say something like that," Ellie

said to him. "And that is the reason I invited Betty Jean to stay here at the house."

"What!" Haley nearly spilled her tea. "You can't do that. If my mother found out, she'd never forgive me."

"Would you be able to forgive yourself if something happened to Betty Jean?"

Haley felt a stab of guilt. Approving of Betty Jean— the woman who had caused her mother so much pain— would be a betrayal of the very worst sort. But Betty Jean had suffered more than enough already.

"It's the only logical solution," Ellie continued. "Aside from Tyler, Mr. Stryker is also here to protect us, and we have a security company patrolling the grounds. Betty Jean will be safe, and you and Tyler will be free to continue your investigation."

Some of Haley's tension eased. As usual, Aunt Ellie was right. It was only logical the woman should stay where she would be safe. Even her mother would be able to see the reasoning in that. "I'm sorry—of course this is where she should be."

"Besides, this will give the two of you the chance to get to know each other."

The cup in Haley's hand froze midway to her lips. She wanted the woman safe. That didn't mean she had to like her. "I don't want to know her any better than I do already. She caused my mother incredible heart-break. I feel disloyal just talking to her."

One of Ellie's silver eyebrows arched up. "Betty Jean caused your mother heartbreak? Or did your mother cause her own?"

Haley's hand trembled. Very carefully, she set the cup and saucer down on the coffee table. "What are you saying?"

"I'm saying that you're looking for the truth about

your father's murder. Perhaps there are other truths you need to discover, as well."

"And you think I can find them with Betty Jean?"

"Perhaps."

Haley didn't say more. She looked over at Ty, who had finished his tea far too quickly to be polite.

"I've got to go," he said. "I need to find Abigail McQueen." He walked over and hauled Haley to her feet, pressed a quick kiss on her mouth. "Don't go anywhere by yourself."

"A-all right."

"I'll let you know what I find out."

Haley just nodded. Her gaze followed him out of the room, and she realized her heart was beating a little too fast. He was so unbelievably handsome, and she was so damned attracted to him.

"I can see the two of you are getting along."

Her eyes swung back to her aunt, the words sobering. "He's…umm…very good at his job," she said vaguely. "A little unconventional, but he seems to get things done."

"Yes, he does. And it's clear he cares a great deal about you."

She shrugged, a memory surfacing of the look on Carol Foster's face as she gazed up at him. As if she would place the world at his feet if she thought it would do her any good. "Ty is very good at pleasing women."

"Does that include you?"

Thinking of the afternoon she had spent in his bed, she flushed. "For as long as it lasts."

"You don't think it will?"

She ignored the pinch in her chest. "Nothing lasts forever" was all she said.

* * *

Stephen Carlson stood next to the rail, his eyes fixed on the pair of Thoroughbreds pounding around the track in front of him. Speed and beauty, perfectly matched, the pair thundering neck and neck toward the finish line.

The bay, Jezebel's Son, won by little more than a nose. The sorrel, King's Joy, would find his stride in the longer stretch tomorrow.

Stephen smiled. He owned a stable full of prize Thoroughbreds. The two prancing on the track as their jockeys blew them out before taking them back to the stable were his current favorites.

He loved horse racing. Loved the pageantry and excitement of the sport, the thrill of winning, the beauty and grace of the animals. In fact, Stephen loved a number of beautiful things and one of them walked toward him now. Maria St. Vincent was tall and slender, with long, flowing black hair and enormous dark eyes.

He had spotted her in a gallery admiring a particularly interesting piece of contemporary art. Twenty-five years his junior, naive and impressed by a man of his wealth and reputation, Maria had been easy prey.

Stephen had never wanted a woman more than her, and now she was his. He didn't think he would tire of her soon.

Which made him think of another of his prized possessions. The Van Gogh might not appeal to some the way it did to him. The crudeness of the drawing, the anger and frustration, the torment that exploded on the canvas in every thick, distorted line of the artist's brush.

He had admired Van Gogh's work for years. When

the opportunity arose to own one, there had been no hesitation, not even a moment's, not even at the cost.

It belonged to him as surely as did Maria. As completely as the horses he bred. He couldn't put the priceless painting on display, but whenever he felt frustrated and overwhelmed, whenever the pressure built until it seemed unbearable, he could go into his private showroom and gaze at the masterpiece that reflected his deepest emotions.

The recent problems that had surfaced didn't matter. There were always problems to solve. He had his horses and his women, and now he had the painting. Soon all would be well.

"Got ya!" Turning away from the computer screen, Ty grinned at Haley over his shoulder. On the monitor, Abigail's photo next to one of her paintings lit up the screen.

"She certainly wasn't hard to find." Leaning down to study the monitor, her soft breasts pressed against him. The scent of her perfume made him think of sex, but there were more important matters to resolve.

They had walked down to the office that afternoon to do the search. Abigail McQueen's name had popped up on Google the minute he had typed it in.

Ty looked down at the information on the Wikipedia website. "'Born in Salinas, California in 1967, Abigail McQueen obtained a Bachelors Degree in Art History from the University of California at Santa Cruz. In the years following, she studied at the Sorbonne in Paris, and also in Italy at the Florence Academy of Art.'"

"She certainly has the right background."

"Here's the good part. 'Works by Ms. McQueen can

be seen at the Windswept Gallery in Carmel, California."' He turned to Haley. "Looks like I'm off to Carmel."

"I'm going with you. Don't even think about telling me I have to stay here."

He'd known this was coming. The thing of it was, he felt better having her with him than leaving her for Stryker to protect. And Haley knew the art world. She could be a very big help.

He kept his expression unreadable. "If I say yes, what do I get in return?"

Haley gave him a slow, sexy smile. Bending down, she bit the lobe of his ear. "I'll think of something," she whispered.

Ty hissed in a breath as his blood began to head south. "Not good enough." He pulled her down on his lap and kissed her. "I've got this fantasy— It involves you and the arm of my sofa. That's what I want."

Haley blushed. "I don't know what you're talking about."

"Good. Then you can imagine all the things I might do to you. You want to come with me to Carmel? Agree to my fantasy." He grinned. "A simple yes will do." It was blackmail of a sort, but it was also a lot of fun.

Haley glanced away, her cheeks still pink. "All right, fine. You can have your fantasy."

His mind went straight to the gutter. *Jesus God.*

"First, Carmel," she said primly. "What's the best way to get there?"

"Private plane. I use Reliable Air Charter out of Burbank. We'll leave first thing in the morning. In the meantime, we need to find out everything we can about Abigail McQueen."

Twenty-Two

Carmel-by-the-Sea was a sleepy little California coastal village that had become a tourist favorite. Located on a forested hillside, with its tiny shops, gourmet restaurants, charming seaside homes and beautiful ocean vistas, the town had somehow been able to retain its old world charm. It remained a desirable place for locals, attracted artisans of varying passions and degrees of talent, and travelers who wanted to get out of San Francisco.

The village itself was a Mecca for art enthusiasts, with over a hundred galleries in the area. The Windswept, on Ocean Avenue, the town's main street, specialized in seascapes and currently featured the work of six different painters.

One of them was Abigail McQueen.

The shop had opened at ten o'clock that morning. It was still quiet at eleven when Haley and Ty walked through the door. The gallery itself was fairly small, but the track lighting was well directed to highlight the gilt-framed seascapes against the stark white walls.

The charcoal carpeting and the small overstuffed dove-gray sofa in the reception area gave the place an air of elegance without being intimidating.

"Over here," Haley said, calling Ty over to a grouping in a front corner of the showroom. Since she worked in the field, they had agreed she should take the lead.

She stopped in front of a 36 x 24 oil-on-canvas titled *Ocean Rage.* It was a violent painting of the sea curling onto a barren stretch of rocky shoreline during a storm. The waves were a deep, cobalt-blue that slowly changed to sapphire, then azure, with a fierce, foaming white at the crest. The sky was streaked with ominous blue-gray clouds, a hint of sunlight fighting to pierce the turbulent weather.

It was an incredible painting, stunning in its intensity, framed in weathered barn wood instead of ornate gold, matching the mood of the piece. As good as it was, the price tag read only fifteen hundred dollars.

It was the common plight of an undiscovered artist. Unless you found a patron with enough clout to promote you, becoming famous or even well-known took years. And the pay wasn't much. If *Ocean Rage* found a buyer, the gallery would take fifty percent, leaving the artist with seven hundred fifty dollars. After the cost of materials, it wasn't much for all the hours of hard work.

"Good morning." A well-dressed woman in a yellow linen suit and low-heeled pumps walked toward them. Early forties, auburn hair pulled into a neat chignon, well-defined features and a warm smile made her attractive. "I'm Sara Browning. Welcome to the Windswept Gallery."

Haley returned the smile. "I'm Haley and this is Tyler. We're both art lovers and we couldn't help noticing this particular artist's work. Could you tell us a little about her?"

The woman's interest sharpened. "Why, yes, of course. Abigail McQueen is one of the gallery's finest painters. She works in oil, as opposed to acrylic. As you probably know, oil is a much more difficult medium, but Abigail handles it beautifully. She's been painting for more than twenty years, but it was only six years ago that she began to exhibit her work."

The woman pointed to the seascape, one of half a dozen large paintings that included several sunset ocean scenes, one of the water beneath a waning moon, one of the sea pounding against an arctic wall of ice at the base of the mountains, the others portraying the ocean in its various moods.

"I'm interested in the one called *Ocean Rage*," Ty said. "I wonder if there's a way we could meet the artist."

Sara Browning took in the cut of their clothes. Ty was in jeans and low-topped leather boots. But Haley was wearing the beige slacks and turquoise silk blouse she had worn to the prison, clothes her mother had purchased as a gift from Neiman Marcus in Chicago. Not inexpensive clothes.

"If you're seriously interested in the painting," Sara Browning said, "I'm sure I can arrange a meeting. How long will you be staying in Carmel?"

"We need to get back to Los Angeles," Ty said, "so we won't be here that long. We'd like to meet the artist as soon as possible." He had found the McQueen woman's home address on the internet, but he wanted to see her in a business setting before they went to her house.

Sara smiled. "Well, then, why don't I call her? I'll be right back."

While the woman returned to her desk to use the phone, Haley and Ty wandered the gallery.

"Most of the paintings in here are more expensive than the ones Abigail painted," Ty said as they strolled along, "but I don't think any of them are as good."

"Not even close," Haley agreed, surprised he would notice what could be fairly subtle differences. "But a lot of it's marketing. One artist has been painting longer than another. He may have developed a bigger following. It isn't just the caliber of the work."

"But you think McQueen is good—very good, right?"

She thought of the incredible seascapes. "I think she's amazing."

"Good enough to paint a Caravaggio or a Titian?"

She'd been pondering that same question. "There's a lot more to it than just replicating the piece, of course, and seascapes are different from portraits. But from what I can see, if she knew how to age the canvas to make it appear to have been painted in the correct time period, it's possible she could do it."

"Aging a piece has got to be damned tricky."

"Yes, but the thing is, after the provenance was checked and the original painting scrutinized and hung on the wall, no one would be looking that closely."

"Exactly," Ty said. "In a way it was genius. There was no reason to suspect the original had been replaced with a forgery."

Sara Browning walked up just then. "Ms. McQueen says she can meet you here in an hour. Would that work for you?" She leaned closer, spoke softly. "Abigail has been spending a good deal of time at the hospital. Her daughter has cystic fibrosis. It flares up now and again."

"We'll make it work," Ty said, flashing Haley a look. "We'll be back here at noon."

They left the gallery and headed down the street. The tourist crowd had begun to build, meandering aimlessly down the block. Still, compared to the throng who frequented the village in summer, it wasn't that crowded yet.

"Did you hear what she said?" Haley paused in front of a candle shop, where tiny flames flickered through the glass-paned window. "Abigail's daughter has cystic fibrosis. That can be deadly in children. Hospital stays are very expensive. That could be the reason she agreed to paint the forgeries."

"Makes sense. I didn't run across that little tidbit on the internet, just that she was widowed and had a child."

Haley's gaze strayed back to the gallery. "I wonder what Abigail's like."

Ty glanced at his heavy stainless-steel wristwatch. "We'll find out in forty-five minutes." As they walked along the sidewalk, he grabbed her hand and tugged her into a little sandwich shop. "In the meantime, I'm starving. Let's get something to eat."

Haley's stomach growled and she smiled. They'd left early for the charter flight out of the Burbank Airport and hadn't had time for anything but coffee and a packaged blueberry muffin.

Walking up to the counter, they ordered chicken paninis and iced tea, then sat down at one of the outdoor picnic tables to eat. The weather in Carmel was warmer than usual for May, and Haley was enjoying the view in the distance of blue sky and azure sea.

At least until she thought of the seascapes Abigail McQueen had painted, and the forgeries, and the men who had tried to kill her.

"Are you going to ask Abigail flat-out if she knows Jules Weaver?" She took a bite of her sandwich, which smelled delicious and tasted even better.

Ty wiped his mouth with a paper napkin. "Maybe. I'll have to see where the conversation leads."

Her nerves on edge, Haley only ate half her sandwich, then waited while Ty finished his and most of her leftover half. Picking up their paper plates, she carried them over to the trash. "I'm ready if you are."

Far more relaxed than she, Ty sauntered out of the sandwich shop in his loose-limbed gait and started along the sidewalk. He was wearing a nylon windbreaker over his T-shirt, his pistol clipped to the waistband of his jeans.

As he waited for the time to pass, he stopped at a couple of galleries and asked about Abigail McQueen, and though some of the people knew her and others had heard of her, he didn't come up with any useful information.

Abigail McQueen was waiting when they got back to the Windswept Gallery, a thin, fragile-looking woman of average height, her posture slightly brittle, with short light brown hair and mud-brown eyes. She was about the same age as the gallery owner but not nearly as well dressed, wearing loose-fitting jeans and a short-sleeved sweatshirt with spots of yellow paint on the front.

Sara Browning made the introductions then left the three of them to talk.

"We love your paintings, Ms. McQueen," Haley said, meaning it. "You're an amazing talent."

The woman softened, relaxing a little with the compliment. "Thank you."

"I plan to buy *Ocean Rage*," Ty said, to Haley's surprise. "But I was wondering if you painted anything other than seascapes."

"I paint portraits by commission. I used to do still-life pieces, but there wasn't much call for them. The seascapes seem to sell best...at least in Carmel."

"Have you ever heard of an artist named Jules Weaver?" Ty asked casually.

The woman's expression changed, turned wary. The brittleness was back in her posture. "I met him a few years back. I haven't heard his name in years. Why do you ask?"

"I bought a couple of his paintings. He's kind of disappeared. I just thought you might know him."

"As I said, it was years ago and I hardly remember him." Her cell phone started to ring, and she dug it out of her purse like a drowning man grabbing a rope. "If you'll excuse me, I have to take this call."

"No problem." Ty walked over to Sara Browning. "I want the painting. I'd like it shipped to my house." He gave her his American Express card and his home address. "Tell Ms. McQueen we appreciate her time."

"I certainly will." Sara Browning was still smiling as Ty led Haley out the door.

"That was interesting," Ty said, heading for the rental car he had picked up at the Monterey Airport. It was parked on the street just a block from the gallery.

"I can't believe you bought that painting."

"Why not? You said yourself it was incredible."

"It is. Seascapes aren't usually my style, but that was really a powerful work. It was also fifteen hundred dollars."

"What, you don't think I can afford it?"

"Can you?"

He shrugged. "Buying it won't put me in the poorhouse." Fact was, he had enough money to buy every piece in the place if he wanted to. But money wasn't important to him. He hoped it wasn't that important to Haley.

She flicked him a sideways glance as they walked, Ty keeping her on the inside in case there was trouble.

"In a way that painting suits you," she said.

"How's that?"

But she just shook her head and changed the subject. "So what's your theory so far?"

Ty thought of their meeting with Abigail McQueen. "McQueen knew Weaver. My guess, she and Weaver were a pair at one time. He's maybe a few years older, not bad-looking before someone tried to kill him. Weaver was willing to protect her, but only to a point."

"At least he's still alive."

Ty had called Carol at the prison that morning, found out Weaver was still breathing, but his outcome remained uncertain. They reached the rental car, a nice little silver Audi, and both of them climbed inside.

Ty stuck the key in the ignition. "If Abigail McQueen painted the first two forgeries and the three that haven't been discovered, she was paid a boatload to do it."

"You wouldn't know that from the way she was dressed."

"Hospitals soak up money like a blackjack table in Vegas. We need to take a look at her bank accounts, see what's going in and out."

Haley lifted an eyebrow. "How exactly do you plan to do that?"

"I know someone in Houston. He's a real whiz at that kind of thing."

"You mean illegally hacking into someone's bank account?"

"Did I say that?"

"No, but—"

"The way it works is I don't ask, and Sol doesn't tell. Keeps everything simple."

Ty made the call. Sol was busy working on another project, but he agreed to take a look. Ty ended the call and pulled the rental car out on the street.

"So I guess we're spending the night in Carmel," Haley said.

"That's right. I want to talk to Abigail again. I'd like to do it at her house."

She flicked him a glance. "So…umm…are you planning to collect on your fantasy?"

Ty fought not to let his mind go there. "Not that particular fantasy. I told you, that one involves the arm of my sofa. But you don't have to worry—I can come up with something equally creative."

Haley tapped her lush bottom lip. "I don't think so. I think tonight we live out my fantasy. What do you say to that, cowboy?"

He was already getting hard. "I say *yippee-ki-yay*— ride 'em, cowgirl."

Haley laughed, but there was a twinkle in her pretty blue eyes that made him a little nervous.

"I'm not letting you tie me up. No way! Forget it! I'm supposed to be protecting you. How can I do that if my hands are tied to the headboard?"

Haley started laughing. She couldn't help it. They'd been arguing for the past ten minutes. Ty was so serious. He was standing there in his briefs, his hands propped on his hips, looking like God's gift to women. Haley was wearing her little shortie lavender nightgown with nothing underneath, running a silk scarf back and forth over her palm and telling him bondage was her fantasy.

She was only teasing—she had no intention of actually tying him up—but Ty was completely convinced.

And he was freaking out.

She laughed harder, and he finally realized she was just having fun.

"You're kidding, right?"

She grinned so wide her eyes teared and she had to wipe away the wetness.

"You think that's funny, huh? You think making me feel like a fool is funny." He started stalking her, and the look in his eyes sobered her.

She had seen him in one of his dark moods, and the memory drove her a couple of steps backward. "It was just a joke, okay?"

"A joke? I'm worried someone might break through the door and shoot us while I'm tied to the bed, and you think it's a joke?"

She took another step backward. His eyes had changed from green to a smoky brown. He moved toward her as silently as the leopard she'd once called him. He wasn't smiling or laughing as she had imagined, and she was growing more and more uneasy. "I didn't mean to upset you."

"You think I'm upset?"

She squealed as he grabbed her, dragged her over to the bed, sat down and pulled her across his lap. Jerking up her shortie nightgown, he delivered three hard smacks to her bare bottom, and fury rolled through her.

When he let her go, she sprang to her feet, and Ty casually stood up, too. The fact he was grinning like an idiot only made her madder.

"You...you... How dare you spank me!" She swung back to slap him, but Ty caught her wrist, his grin spread even wider across his face.

"I guess we were doing my fantasy, after all."

Her bottom was still stinging, and it suddenly occurred to her that her entire body was humming with lust. With a soft feline growl, she leaped toward him, grabbed his face between her hands and dragged his mouth down to hers for a scorching wet kiss.

Ty groaned deep in his throat, lifted her up, and she wrapped her legs around his waist. Haley drove her tongue into his mouth, and they fell on the bed in a tangle of arms and legs. All she could think of was having him inside her. She wanted to climb on top of him, wanted to rub her nipples against that muscular chest. She wanted to ride him until she climaxed, then start all over again.

She felt his hands on her breasts, felt him lifting her astride him as if he had read her thoughts, then suddenly he went still.

"Someone's here," he said softly. Silently, he lifted her away, tension thrumming through every muscle in his lean, hard body. "Get in the bathroom and don't come out till I say." He nudged her in that direction, and she hurried inside, pulled the door mostly closed but left it cracked open enough to see.

Her heart was racing, threatening to pound its way out of her chest. Ty pulled his short-barreled shotgun out from under the bed, moved to the right of the door and held the weapon in his hand with an ease that said he had done it a hundred times before.

His pistol lay in easy reach on the nightstand. She wasn't sure what had alarmed him until she heard the creak of footsteps in the hall. Their room was on the second floor of the motel so there was only one way inside.

Haley screamed as a blast of gunfire splintered the wood and the door crashed open. A heavyset man, bull-necked and ugly, fired a barrage of shots into the room and Ty pulled the trigger on the shotgun. It roared and the man flew backward, his chest covered in blood.

Ty ducked and rolled, at the same time pumping another shell into the chamber. Haley stifled a cry as a second man, shaved head and just as ugly, fired a deadly spray of bullets into the room, and Ty's shotgun roared again.

The man with the shaved head went down, blood flying as he hit the floor. The room fell silent. Haley couldn't breathe. *Ty's alive,* she thought, trying to control the fear for him that threatened to choke her. *He's alive. He's alive.*

She watched him make his way to the door and look out into the hall, checking to be sure the threat was gone and no one else was there. Stepping over one of the bodies, he walked back into the room.

The acrid smell of gunpowder filled the air as Haley shoved the bathroom door all the way open, burst out and ran straight into Ty's arms.

Twenty-Three

Ty caught Haley hard against him. His adrenaline was pumping, the shotgun still in his hand. "It's okay, baby. It's over."

"Oh God, oh God, oh God." She pressed her face into his shoulder, shaking so hard he could hear her teeth chattering. His jaw hardened. The dark mood was on him, the bloodlust. They could have died in this room.

He drew Haley a little closer and the warmth of her body penetrated the haze of his rage. "It's all right, they can't hurt us now." He took a couple of deep, calming breaths, inhaled her soft, sweet scent, and some of his tension eased. They were safe. It was over.

Haley trembled. Fear and adrenaline made her legs go weak and she sagged against him. Ty eased her over to the bed, sat her down and pushed her head between her knees.

"Take a couple of deep breaths, honey, and you'll feel better." Grabbing his cell phone off the bedside table, he punched in 911. He could hear doors opening and closing down the hall, people beginning to talk in whispers as he gave police dispatch the details of the shooting, then set the phone back down on the nightstand.

Still trembling, Haley looked up at him, her eyes glistening with tears. "They could have killed you."

Some of his anger returned. If he hadn't heard them coming, he and Haley would both be dead.

Ty drew her up from the bed and into his arms. "They tried. Now they're dead."

"How…how did they find us? Did they follow us from L.A.?"

He shook his head. "I'd have spotted a tail on the way to the airport. They must have had the gallery staked out. We only drove a couple of blocks from there to the motel. It would have been easy to follow us in the traffic."

Word had gotten out about their visit to Weaver. Someone on the inside had relayed the information. He should have figured they might put someone on the gallery. The bad news was whoever had hired the two men to kill them would be panicking now, scrambling to find a way to get to them before it was too late.

As bad as things were already, the danger had just ratcheted up another notch.

The sound of sirens reached him. "Cops'll be here any minute. We'd better put on some clothes."

She looked down at herself as if she had forgotten the sexy lavender nightgown she wore, then hurried over to her suitcase. "What…what should we say?"

"We tell them the truth. That's what we've been doing all along." For all the good it had done. "Two men are dead. We don't have any other choice."

By one in the morning, they had given the police their statements and were sitting in the small office behind the check-in counter of the Fireside Inn, waiting to talk to detectives from nearby Monterey. Ten more minutes passed before the door opened and two men in suits walked in.

"You Brodie?"

"That's right. I'm a private investigator from L.A." Ty pulled out his badge wallet and flipped it open. "This is Haley Warren, my client."

"I'm Detective Margolin and this is Detective Salazar." Margolin was tall and fit. Salazar was Hispanic with straight black hair cut short and obsidian eyes.

"Your forensic guys have my shotgun," Ty said. "Officer Whittaker has my pistol." He didn't mention the two semiautomatics that were still behind the seat in his truck. He wasn't sure how this was all going to play out, and he might end up needing them.

They seated themselves at a small round table in a corner of the office. The door was closed, but the motel manager had been awakened and sat in the lobby outside.

"I read your statement," Margolin said to Ty. "You believe this is connected to an attempt on Ms. Warren's life made at her home in Los Angeles two days ago."

"That's right. A detective named Cogan is in charge of the case." Not that he was doing his job.

"I think it would be best if you start from the beginning. Detective Salazar will speak to Ms. Warren."

She flashed Ty a worried glance, but let the detective lead her out of the room. The police were making sure their stories matched. Which they would, though Ty's version might be a little more colorful.

He ran back through the details, beginning with James Warren's death in a powerboat explosion and finishing with the shooters who had burst into his motel room.

"So your theory is, the people who stole valuable

paintings from the Scarsdale Center killed James Warren and are trying to stop you and his daughter from finding out their names."

"That's about it."

"And you think Abigail McQueen is the woman who painted the forgeries, but you don't have any proof."

"So far, so good."

"On top of that, you think there may have been another theft sometime this year, but you don't know what was stolen, where it happened, and you have no proof of that, either."

"Home run," Ty said.

Margolin flicked him an irritated glance and left the office, leaving Ty to wait impatiently and worry about Haley. She was safe, at least for now. That was all that mattered.

Half an hour later, Margolin walked back in, closing the door carefully behind him. "I did a little digging. According to the police here in Carmel, Abigail McQueen is a model citizen. She has an eight-year-old daughter, lives very modestly in a small house at the edge of town. Seems to me, the likelihood of her involvement in a multimillion dollar art heist is slim to none."

He'd figured it would look that way. Didn't mean it wasn't true.

"You got any idea how she's paying her daughter's hospital bills?" he asked.

Margolin frowned. "We'll talk to her, do a little more digging, but according to what I've been told, the McQueen woman has a lot of friends in the area. They've even held fund-raisers for her little girl."

Maybe so, but odds were the money they'd raised wasn't nearly enough.

"What about the shooters? Have they been ID'd?"

"We're working on it. They don't look like locals. Probably got rap sheets a mile long. You got any enemies, Brodie? Someone you sent to prison? Someone who might want you dead?"

"I've got enemies. Comes with the job. None of them knew I was staying in Carmel."

Margolin shrugged his shoulders. His dark suit was slightly rumpled, as if he'd climbed out of bed and put on the one he'd worn during the day. As late as it was, Ty didn't blame him.

"So they followed you up here," Margolin suggested.

"We flew in on a charter."

"Could have got your flight plan."

"I guess they could have—but they didn't. They staked out the gallery. They wanted both of us dead. That would have put an end to the investigation."

The detective raked a hand through his hair, which looked as rumpled as his suit. "We'll talk to Ms. McQueen, but don't get your hopes up. Be smarter to look closer to home."

Detective Salazar opened the door. "You finished in here?"

"For now." Margolin rose from his chair and Salazar ushered Haley back into the room. "You two can go, but don't leave the state. We may have more questions."

"Soon as you get those names, I'd appreciate a call."

Margolin nodded. "Shouldn't take long. We'll get your shotgun back to you as soon as ballistics is through with it."

"Thanks."

Margolin handed him his Beretta. Ty shoved it into the holster clipped to the waistband of his jeans. Setting a hand at Haley's waist, he guided her out of the office.

He had called the charter pilot and had the twin Cessna waiting. He wanted to talk to Abigail McQueen, but now was not the time. Not with detectives banging on her door. Odds were she would clam up tight when she saw them, and there wasn't enough evidence for a warrant to search her house.

"Where are we going?" Haley asked when they reached the rental car and he had her belted into her seat.

"Home."

Her head came up. "What about Abigail McQueen?"

"We need to talk to her, but not today. The cops'll be asking her questions, but I don't think they'll push it since they don't believe she was involved. We need to let things die down for a while."

Besides, he needed to get Haley back home. She still looked pale, her features drawn. She hadn't said much since the shooting, just answered the detectives' questions in a dull monotone that told him how shaken she really was. It wasn't every day you saw two men blown in half in front of you.

"What if she gets scared and runs?"

"Her kid's in the hospital. She isn't going anywhere." She could call the people she worked for, assuming she really was the forger, but there was nothing new she could tell them.

They already knew he and Haley had been to see Weaver. Once the two of them had shown up at the gallery, they knew Weaver had given them Abigail's name. The question was, what information did the McQueen woman have that might lead to the men who had set up the burglaries.

Haley turned in the passenger seat. "You don't think

whoever came after us…you don't think they'd hurt her?"

"It's possible. Depends on how much she knows. But if she painted those forgeries, she's a gold mine. That kind of talent isn't something you find down at the local artisans' center."

"No. She has a very special talent. Her skill as a painter combined with the knowledge it would take to age a canvas to the correct time period makes her extremely unique."

As the car rolled toward the airport, Ty checked his rearview mirror, made another couple of turns and checked again. He drove several miles out of the way, made a few more turns, but saw nothing that looked like a tail. It took a while longer to reach the airport, but the extra time was worth it and they encountered no trouble along the way.

"You okay?" Ty asked as they boarded the plane and settled themselves in their seats.

"I've had better days." Haley fastened the buckle on her belt, and Ty fastened his.

"Yeah, me too." He caught her hand, noticed her skin felt cold and clammy. "The sun'll be up pretty soon. Why don't you try to get some sleep?"

Haley looked up at him. "I'm scared, Ty."

His jaw hardened. Of course she was scared. She'd damned near been killed twice in the past two days. "I won't let anything happen to you."

But the cold truth was, something could always go wrong. After dozens of missions, he knew that for sure.

"I'd stop if I thought they'd leave us alone," Haley said.

"They won't. Not now. We've got to keep going till we find out who's behind all this."

She just nodded. As the plane taxied down the runway, she leaned her head back and closed her eyes.

Ty figured there wasn't a snowball's chance in hell she'd be able to sleep.

The bell on a streetcar rang as the heavy vehicle rumbled up the hill. The fog was lifting a little and the sky was beginning to gray. Peter Danoff turned on the lights in the gallery, but didn't unlock the front door.

The streets outside were still empty. Danoff Fine Arts didn't open till ten. But after he had heard the morning news about the shooting in Carmel that left two men dead, he'd had to get out of the house. He had left his wife in bed, forgone his usual breakfast of oatmeal, a banana and toast, and driven into the city early.

The gallery always comforted him, the paintings on the walls, the way the lighting brought out the richness and textures, the brilliant colors and softer hues. He had a well-deserved reputation for discovering exceptional artists, for knowing which work would go up in value and which would never amount to more than a pretty picture to hang over the fireplace.

He had a nearly flawless record for picking winners and was well-known as an art critic of repute. Some of the wealthiest collectors in the world came to Peter Danoff for advice.

And yet, no matter how much he earned in commissions, it was never enough. With the recession, sales were down, and keeping the gallery open in lean times was expensive. He and his wife both had extravagant tastes. It seemed they were always short of money. So far he had been able to keep the wolf from the door, but it hadn't been easy.

Peter turned at the sound of the phone ringing on

his desk. He had known his boss would be calling. His hand shook as he picked up the receiver.

"Did you take care of the problem?"

His stomach began to churn. "I'm afraid not, sir. The men I hired… Well, they're dead, sir. Both of them. Brodie killed them." His voice faintly trembled. "I thought they could handle it. I had someone watching the gallery. He followed Brodie and the girl to the motel. I relayed the information, told the men where they were staying. They said they would take care of everything."

"Instead they're dead. You're a fool, Danoff. I don't have time for fools. I told you to hire someone competent, someone who could get the job done. You should have called Sloan—he's an expert—not some gangsters off the street."

"Sloan costs a fortune."

"Yes, and he's worth it. Call him. Tell him what we need."

"What…what about Abigail McQueen? What if she goes to the police, gives them my name?"

"She won't talk. She knows what will happen to her kid if she does. Now call Sloan and finish it." The phone went dead, and Danoff plucked a tissue out of the box on his desk to wipe the sweat off his forehead.

Sloan. It wasn't even the man's real name. He was a ghost, a mercenary of some kind. He was also an expert. Quentin Sloan had rigged the explosion that had killed James Warren and done it without leaving a trace.

But a hundred thousand dollars was a lot of money, and Peter would be expected to come up with a good portion of it. His share of the profits was a lot smaller than his boss's, and much of it had already been spent.

The Bellamy brothers had tried to kill the girl in L.A. but bungled the job. Now they had botched things again.

Peter couldn't afford to wait any longer. He thought of what could happen and how much he had to lose. He shuddered to think he could end up in prison. Peter picked up the phone.

Twenty-Four

H aley sat out on the deck behind her aunt's house, a quiet spot around the corner, a place Stryker said would be out of the line of fire if anyone was on the hill. She hadn't seen Ty since they got home from Carmel yesterday.

He had gone to work, she knew. Ty was talking to his contacts on the street, trying to dig up information about the men who had attacked them.

The Bellamy brothers. Detective Margolin had called yesterday with their names. Two-bit hired criminals, the detective had said.

Ty was trying to come up with information that could link the brothers to the first art theft, or to Abigail McQueen, or to a second theft that hadn't yet been discovered.

She knew he planned to talk to Ray Farrell, the guy with part of his ear missing, but Ty had warned her that he didn't think Farrell would be much help.

Haley hadn't pressed him to take her along. She needed time to recover from the horror of the shoot-

ing, the awful images her mind hung on to and refused
to let go of. The echo of gunfire, blood on the floor and
bodies sprawled in the hallway. Police sirens, and those
moments when she'd thought Ty was going to die. That
both of them were going to die.

Something inside her had shifted in those moments.
Something that allowed her to glimpse, just for an instant, her deep feelings for Ty. She was falling in love
with him. Until that night, she'd been able to pretend
it was something else, something that didn't threaten
the life she had built for herself, her happiness, her entire future.

But those moments of clarity could not be undone,
and she needed time to figure things out.

Exhausted, Haley closed her eyes, but the minute
she did, she saw images of blood and death. She hadn't
slept on the plane, nor when she got home, nor even last
night beneath the fluffy down comforter on her bed.

It didn't help that there were so many people around.
Ty was gone, but Stryker was there, looming like a vil-
lain in a low-budget movie. Aunt Ellie had been hover-
ing. And there was Betty Jean.

So far Haley had been able to avoid her, but as she
glanced across the deck, she saw that was about to
change.

Setting her coffee mug down on the round glass-
topped table next to her chair, she studied her stepmother as she hadn't allowed herself before. The woman
looked far better than when Haley had seen her lying
battered and pale in a hospital bed.

Today her color was back to normal, the bruises on
her face mostly faded. She was pretty, Haley realized,
in her inexpensive bright blue paisley blouse and blue
polyester pants. Short blond hair curled softly around

a smooth, nearly unlined face. Instead of detracting from her appearance, her full figure gave her a hint of sensuality.

For the first time, Haley saw beneath the surface, beneath the prejudices that had colored her vision to the woman who had appealed so strongly to her handsome, successful father.

"Haley, it's so good to see you." Betty Jean sat down in the chair on the other side of the table, perched nervously on the edge as if she might need to run. "After what happened, your aunt said you needed a little time to yourself so I didn't want to intrude."

"I'm all right. Just a little tired is all."

"Oh, Haley, I'm so sorry I got you involved in all this. If I could do it over, I would leave everything alone."

"It wasn't your fault, Betty Jean. If you want to blame someone, blame my dad." She managed to smile. "It was his bulldog attitude that started all this. If he'd given up finding the people who stole those paintings like anyone else, none of this would have happened."

Betty Jean's lips curved. "Your father believed in justice."

"So do I. But the truth is, I'd stop if I thought it would keep all of us safe. Ty doesn't think it will, and neither do I."

Betty Jean glanced off toward the city spread out below them. "The two of you have made a great deal of progress, but the cost has been high."

"Yes, it has. Unfortunately, we can't stop now." Haley leaned back in her chair, her gaze going to the woman beside her. Her aunt had hinted that Betty Jean had the answers to questions about her father. Maybe it was time to find out.

"There's something I've been wanting to ask you,

Betty Jean. I haven't had the courage until now. What happened to my dad's retirement? I'd really like to know."

Betty Jean looked surprised by the question. "I thought I told you. We bought a motor home and traveled. We went on some cruises. Your father took extra weeks off work so we could do things together."

"You spent millions of dollars on traveling?"

Betty Jean laughed. "Of course not. Your father's divorce was expensive. He wanted to make a clean break, so he made a lot of concessions. And he had you to think about. He wanted you to have money enough to continue your schooling if that's what you decided to do."

Haley's chest felt tight. "You said the divorce was expensive. Are you telling me my mother got Dad's retirement money?"

"Most of it." She smiled. "He thought it was only fair since she had to put up with him for all those years. That's what he said, anyway."

Her stomach was churning. "My mother led me to believe you married my dad for his money."

Betty Jean just shook her head, a soft look coming into her pale blue eyes. "I married your father because I loved him. I loved him almost from the moment I met him. The strange thing was, he told me once that was the way he felt about me."

A lump began to form in Haley's throat. She'd been unfair to Betty Jean. And to her father. "I'm sorry for thinking the worst of you. I should have given you and Dad a chance to explain."

Betty Jean reached over and patted her hand. "It's all right, dear. That's all in the past."

"Dad and my mother weren't happy. I think Dad had

been wanting to leave her for years. Maybe he would have if it hadn't been for me. Meeting you gave him the courage to do what he wanted."

Betty Jean wiped a tear from her cheek. "He was happy while we were together. We both were." She sighed. "Perhaps if Jimmy had married your mother under different circumstances, they would have had a better chance at happiness."

Haley frowned. "Dad met Mother at college. What do you mean?"

The color slowly drained from Betty Jean's face. "I'm sorry. I—I didn't say that right. What I meant was that if they had…you know…come from more similar backgrounds, then things might have been different." She glanced down at her watch and rose from the chair. "My, look at the time. I'd better go. I didn't mean to stay this long. Please promise me you and Ty will be careful."

Haley just nodded. Her mind was replaying the stricken look on Betty Jean's face. What circumstances was she talking about?

What else had happened that her mother had never bothered to tell her?

Ty pulled his worn Lakers T-shirt over his head as he started across his living room toward the stairs. He'd worked all night again last night and well into the morning. He needed to shower and get a couple hours of sleep before he went to see Haley.

He was worried about her. The shooting had to have been traumatic. He'd been in battle. He knew how she must be feeling. He hadn't seen her since they got back from Carmel. He needed to talk to her, find out how she was dealing with what had happened.

Hell, he just needed to see her.

Though Stryker seemed capable of protecting her, Ty was glad Johnnie had decided to stay in town. He was providing backup so Haley had protection 24/7 while Ty worked the streets. He wasn't sure how he felt about Stryker, but he trusted his best friend to keep Haley safe.

And the good news was, after the shooting in Carmel, Charlie Cogan had finally stepped up to the plate and started doing his job.

"I hate being wrong," the LAPD detective had grumbled, "but it's beginning to look that way. I've posted an officer on the street in front of the gate to Mrs. Stiles' house, and beefed up patrols. I'm not sure how long I can get the city to spring for the costs, but for now we're covered. We need to figure this out, Brodie, and get these a-holes off the street."

Good idea, Ty thought sarcastically.

Yesterday, he had talked to Detective Margolin. According to the police, the Bellamy brothers were San Francisco area scumbags, lowlifes who hired out for whatever dirty job needed to be done.

Ty had spent the past two nights prowling the streets, trying to come up with something that might connect the brothers to the theft at the Scarsdale Center, or the explosion that had killed James Warren, or the gunfire at Ellie's house. So far, he'd come up with zilch.

He needed to go back to Carmel, talk to Abigail McQueen. He needed to go to San Francisco, see if he could find any leads there.

Ty scrubbed a hand over his two days' growth of beard and wearily started up the stairs to his bedroom. He tried not to wish Haley was there, to wish she'd be sharing the shower with him, lying next to him in bed as he slept. He tried to ignore the heat that settled in his groin when he thought of making love to her.

He'd feel better after a little rest, he told himself as he reached the top of the stairs. He was heading for the bathroom when the doorbell started to ring.

Ty softly cursed. With a weary sigh, he turned and went back down to the living room. The last person he expected to see through the peephole in his front door was his cousin, Dylan Brodie.

Ty opened the door, took in the tall, dark-haired man who was a blue-eyed, harder, more rugged-looking version of himself. Dylan's gaze ran over him, returned to his weary face.

"Jesus, you look like something my dog dragged in."

Ty grinned. "It's good to see you, too, cousin."

Haley couldn't summon the energy to move off the deck. Instead, she picked up the sketch pad she had brought out with her that morning, and curled up in her chair.

She hadn't worked on the picture of Ty since the day she had finished it. She had never been satisfied with the drawing. The mouth wasn't right, she knew. Something about the curve, or the way the corners hinted at a smile that wasn't quite there. She had never been able to get it right.

Haley closed her eyes and imagined his face, imagined him smiling. She imagined the way his eyes darkened when he pulled her into his arms, then let the memory of his kiss sweep over her. The softness of his lips, the sexy way he coaxed her to open for him, the feel of his tongue sliding over hers, the way her breath hitched as she sank into the kiss.

For a moment she savored the sensations that had her heartbeat picking up. When she opened her eyes, she began to redraw that portion of his face, letting her feelings take control of her hands, letting the hot memories sweep through her.

She didn't know how much time had passed before she looked down at his portrait and smiled. She'd done it. Captured exactly the shape and softness of that incredibly sexy mouth, the hint of firmness in the curve of his lips that spoke of confidence and control, the faint lift that hinted at some secret amusement.

"It's good to see you smiling," Lane said as she walked toward Haley across the deck. Her friend looked beautiful, as always, in cream ankle-length pants, a tiger-print, off-the-shoulder top and high heels, silky red hair around her shoulders, nails perfectly manicured in a frosty tangerine.

"Your aunt called and told me what happened in Carmel. She thought you might need a friend to talk to about it."

Haley set the sketch pad aside, got up from the chair and went to Lane for a hug. "God, I'm glad to see you."

Lane hugged her back. "You want to talk about it or would you rather just try to forget?"

"I'd rather forget, but so far that hasn't happened."

And so she told her friend in detail about the clues they had pieced together that led them to Carmel, about Abigail McQueen's stunning artwork and the bloody shoot-out that had ended with two men dead.

As the story came to a close they poured themselves glasses of iced tea from the pitcher Dolores brought out and set on the table. Then Haley added a last few details she had forgotten.

"From what you're telling me," Lane said when Haley was finished, "Ty didn't have any choice. He had to shoot those men."

"That's right. It was completely self-defense. They broke into our room with the sole intention of killing us. They would have, if it hadn't been for Ty."

"I knew I was going to like him." Lane set her glass of tea on the table and picked up the drawing Haley had set aside. "My God, you're right. He's even more handsome the way you've redrawn him." Lane's green eyes turned shrewd. "But maybe you're seeing him in a different light—now that you've fallen in love with him."

Haley's smile faded. "I—I'm not in love with him. Why would you say that?"

"Because I've been sitting here listening to you talk about him for the past half hour. There's no mistaking the way you feel."

Haley glanced away. Lane was right. She was in love with Ty. She'd fought against it, tried to deny it, determinedly ignored it, but it was completely true.

"It doesn't matter. First of all, I have no idea what Ty feels for me. He has more women than he can count. He doesn't need another one."

"Has he been seeing anyone else?"

"He hasn't really had time."

"Do you think he wants to?"

Haley sighed. "I don't know. I don't think so. He's very protective. And I think when he's with someone, he's completely loyal. But the thing is, Lane, I have a life in Chicago. A career. It's a completely different kind of life than Ty has here in L.A. My mother is there. My friends."

"If you love someone, you work around it."

"And if I stayed? How long would it last? Sooner or later, Ty would be ready to move on. It's just the way life is."

Lane didn't argue, though she looked as if she wanted to. "If you really love him," she said, "when it's over, it's going to hurt."

Haley's gaze fixed on her friend. Lane knew about pain. She had never really gotten over the death of Jason Russell, the man she had loved.

"I'll deal with it when it happens. Right now we need to find the men who stole those paintings and killed my father. Until we do, none of us are truly safe."

Ty came back down the stairs towel-drying his hair. He'd meant to shave, but now his cousin was here and he was anxious to see Haley.

"I thought you were in Alaska," Ty said, picking up the conversation where they'd left it before he'd brewed a pot of coffee, poured a cup for his cousin and gone up to shower and change. "What the hell are you doing in L.A.?"

"The deal closed on that fishing lodge I've been wanting to buy." Dylan smiled, tiny lines fanning out at the corners of his blue eyes. "I'm the proud owner of five hundred acres in the middle of Nowhere Alaska and an old hunting lodge that's barely standing. I'm finally in business for myself, and I'm here to buy a plane."

Dylan was a bush pilot. Owning a float plane, running his own guided fishing business, was a lifelong dream. Three years older than Ty, Dylan and his two brothers, Rafe and Nick, lived in Alaska. Their father, Ty's uncle Clay, had been the first partner in the Brodie family's two-hundred-thousand-acre Texas ranch to pass away. It wasn't until the last partner, Ty's dad,

Seth, had died last year that the ranch had been sold and the cousins had all come into money.

None of the Brodie boys had been raised with wealth, but all of them were way more than comfortable now.

Fortunately, they'd also inherited a strong set of values that included hard work, loyalty to friends and family, and a belief in controlling your own destiny.

And all three of the Alaska branch of the Brodies were tough as nails.

They talked for a while, Ty filling his cousin in on his current case and the leads he'd been following that had led him to Carmel and almost gotten him killed.

"Sounds like you're in this one up to your ears—and unless I'm reading you wrong, the lady you're protecting is a lot more to you than a client."

Ty took a drink of coffee from the mug he'd just poured. "I'm heading up there now. If you've got time, I'd like you to meet her."

One of Dylan's dark eyebrows went up. "Sounds like this could be serious."

"Could be—if I can manage to keep both of us alive and catch the bastards trying to kill us."

Dylan's wide shoulders straightened. He was wearing a pair of jeans and a red plaid flannel shirt, though the weather in L.A. was a whole lot warmer than Alaska. "I'll be in town for a while. Maybe I can help."

Ty downed the last of his coffee and set the mug on the counter. One thing about the Brodie clan, they were always there if you needed them. Dylan was smart and tough, and Ty trusted him completely. His cousin knew his offer would be putting him in danger. Ty wasn't about to turn him down.

"Come on, I'll drive." He pulled open the kitchen door and led Dylan into the garage. They climbed into the pickup truck. "If we run into trouble, there's a Night-hawk .45 behind my seat and Glock nine mil behind yours. You don't have a permit to carry, but—"

"But it's better to have a weapon than be dead?"

Ty grinned. "You got it. Let's go."

Twenty-Five

$\rightsquigarrow$

Lane looked out over the L.A. Basin as she sat quietly next to Haley and finished her iced tea. The sun was shining and the air was crystal clear. The afternoon had been pleasant, two close friends sharing their thoughts and concerns, helping each other through whatever problems they were facing.

Haley's bodyguard, Kurt Stryker, had come out to check on them every now and then. Lane had noticed him prowling the grounds below, keeping an eye out for trouble. He seemed to keep a professional distance, which told her he was probably good at his job.

Lane hoped so. Clearly, her friend was in danger. If it weren't for Ty Brodie she could be dead.

Of course, if it weren't for Ty Brodie, she wouldn't be knee-deep in an investigation that might end up getting her killed.

Lane looked up at the sound of heavy footsteps on the deck, expecting to see Stryker, spotting two other men instead. Both of them were tall, at least six-two, with rangy builds and dark brown hair. Their features were similar enough to tell her they were related: straight nose, strong jaw, white teeth, all nicely put together.

She recognized Tyler Brodie immediately from Haley's drawing, the man her friend had fallen in love with. Even unshaven, he was amazingly handsome. It was the hard look in his eyes that warned he was no pretty boy. This was a man who could handle himself, one who knew his capabilities and wasn't afraid to use them.

Still, as attractive as he was, it was the man with him who snagged her attention. In a different, more hard-edged way, he was equally handsome. His features were more chiseled, the tanned forearms showing beneath his rolled-up sleeves looked rawhide-tough, as if he spent a good deal of time outdoors.

The men stopped, and Ty's hazel eyes went straight to Haley. His hard look softened as she came to her feet, and Lane stood up, too.

"I've missed you," Ty said a little gruffly, then he hauled Haley into his arms and kissed her as if he'd been gone two months instead of only two days. Just watching the heat ignite between them made Lane's stomach contract.

"I'm Dylan Brodie," the other man said with a hint of amusement. "You'll have to ignore my cousin. He's got other things on his mind than remembering his manners."

Lane smiled and extended a hand. "I'm Lane Bishop. I'm a friend of Haley's."

"Pleased to meet you," Dylan said. She could feel his eyes on her, as blue as the sky. They made his suntanned face look even darker.

"Nice meeting you, too," Lane said.

Ty ended the kiss, and faint color rose beneath the bones in his cheeks. "Sorry about that. I was just… I've been worried about her. I'm Ty Brodie. I guess you met my cousin."

"Yes."

"Dylan lives in Alaska. He's here looking to buy an airplane."

"You're a pilot?" Lane asked him.

"That's right. I own a fishing lodge near a little town on the inside passage. The plan is to fly people into the lodge and take them out on guided hunting and fishing trips."

"Sounds interesting. I've never been to Alaska. From the pictures I've seen, it's beautiful." She didn't mean to stare at him, but she couldn't seem to look away. There was something compelling about him. The remoteness in his eyes, his guarded expression said he was a man with secrets. She found herself wondering what they were.

"Lane's an interior designer," Haley said, nudging her a little, reminding her other people were there. "She owns a company called Modern Design in Beverly Hills."

Laser blue eyes zeroed in on her. "That so?"

"Umm…yes. We work mostly by commission. People hire us to come out and refit their homes."

His hard mouth edged up. "I could use someone like that. The place I just bought was built in the twenties. It needs just about everything."

Lane forced a smile. "Beverly Hills is a long way from Alaska."

"That it is."

More footsteps sounded and Lane pulled her gaze

away a second time. She had never been so glad to hear someone coming. When she turned, she saw Haley's aunt Ellie hurrying toward them.

"Amy just phoned, Tyler. She said your cell isn't working. You got a call from that woman in Carmel... the artist."

"Abigail McQueen?"

"That's right. According to Amy, the woman couldn't reach you on your cell, so she called your office. She wants you to call her back."

He pulled out his cell, saw the battery was dead. "Son of a bitch."

"Why don't you use the phone in the library? It's nice and quiet in there."

Ty grabbed Haley's hand and tugged her off toward the house. Lane glanced back at Ty's cousin standing a few feet away. There was something in the way he looked at her, something that made him seem dark and forbidden, like eating chocolate at midnight. She had never felt such a shot of lust in her life.

"Why don't I bring us out a fresh pitcher of tea?" Ellie asked, glancing between them. Lane wondered if she could feel the heat.

Lane shook her head. "I've got to run. I should have been back hours ago." She turned. "It was nice meeting you, Dylan."

"You, too." His gaze ran over her. "I'm in town for a while. Maybe our paths will cross again."

"Maybe." But Lane was determined that wasn't going to happen. This man was trouble. She could see it in those blue, blue eyes. In the past few years, she'd had more than her share of trouble.

Lane hurried through the house as if the hounds of

hell were on her heels. She didn't take an easy breath until she was in her car, driving back down to her studio in Beverly Hills.

The library was quiet and dimly lit, just an amber glass lamp on the big walnut desk. The room was wood-paneled and filled with books. Both Ellie and her late husband had been serious readers.

Ty picked up the phone. Haley stood next to him, looking anxious and hopeful. "This could be interesting," he said. Haley just nodded. Ty punched in the number Ellie had given him and tried to imagine why Abigail McQueen might have called.

She picked up on the second ring. "Hello."

"Ms. McQueen? It's Tyler Brodie. I'm sorry I missed you. What can I do for you?"

"I appreciate your returning my call."

"No problem. I guess you got my number from your boss." He had left his contact information when he'd bought the painting.

"That's right. I need to ask you a question, Mr. Brodie, and I want you to tell me the truth."

"All right."

"Did you buy my painting because you liked it, or were you just trying to get information?"

Ty flicked a glance at Haley. "I bought it because it was an amazing piece of art and I found it…I found it personally moving. But the truth is, I came to the gallery to get information."

There was a long pause on the other end of the line. "The police came to see me," Abigail finally said. "They told me about the shooting at the motel, that men broke into your room and tried to kill you and the young woman who was with you. They told me you

were a private investigator. They said those men may
have been trying to stop you from looking into the theft
of some paintings that were stolen a few years back."

"That's right."

"They said the paintings were replaced with forgeries.
They said you thought I was the one who painted them."

"Did you?"

Another long pause. "I need your help, Mr. Brodie.
You bought my painting. I need someone who under-
stands me at least a little."

"So how can I help you?"

"After the police left, I looked you up on the internet. I found your address in Los Angeles. I'm staying at
a motel not far from your office. I need to talk to you,
Mr. Brodie. How soon can we meet?"

He glanced over at Haley, whose blue eyes looked
big and intense. "I've got Ms. Warren here with me.
She was with me in that motel room. I'm bringing her
along. Where are you?"

"I'm at the Sunset Motel. Do you know where it is?"

"I know where it is. What room?"

"Number 123. It's down at the end."

"We can be there in twenty minutes. Are you sure
you weren't followed?"

"I don't think so."

"Stay inside. We'll be there as fast as we can."

"Be careful," Abigail McQueen said. "You don't
know what these men are capable of."

His fingers tightened around the receiver. "Actually,
I do." Ty hung up the phone.

Haley grabbed hold of Ty's arm. "Oh, my God, Abigail's here in L.A.?"

Ty nodded. "Sunset Motel. It's just down the hill."
He started leading her toward the door.

"You want me to come with you?"

"That's right." He stopped in the hallway, turned her to face him. "You don't have to go. I just figured, after what you've been through, you deserved to be there. If you want to stay here, it's probably a better idea."

"No way. I'm going."

"I figured. Come on." Ty led her on down the hall, but instead of heading for the door, he turned toward the deck and they walked back outside.

"I see you ran off the redhead," Ty said to his cousin, who turned away from his conversation with Ellie. Lane was nowhere to be seen.

"She's gone," Dylan said. "For now."

Haley had no trouble reading the hot look in his eyes. Lane always had that effect on men.

"You mean what you said about helping?" Ty asked.

"You know I did."

"I could use some backup. The McQueen woman is in L.A. A motel not far away. Sounds like she's ready to talk."

Dylan gestured toward the sliding-glass doors. "Lead the way."

Johnnie was out following a lead. That left Stryker to watch the house. Haley noticed Ty didn't tell him where they were going. She wondered why he had taken his cousin instead of the big, tough bodyguard. Then again, his cousin looked plenty tough himself.

Ty helped Haley into the pickup and went around to the driver's side. Dylan reached behind the passenger seat, pulled out a big black handgun, stuffed it into the waistband of his jeans and pulled his flannel shirt out to cover it.

Ty plugged his cell phone into the car charger as they drove toward the automatic gate. He waited for the gate to swing open, drove through, then waved at the officer in the patrol car parked on the opposite side of the street.

As they drove down the hill, he and Dylan both watched closely for anyone who might be following. Ty made a number of turns, blew through a yellow light and kept on driving.

"Far as I can tell we're in the clear," Dylan said.

"Looks that way."

It didn't take long to reach the Sunset Motel. Ty pulled into one of the spaces in front of room 123 and all of them got out. Dylan settled himself near the edge of the building where he had a clear view of anyone coming into the parking lot but could still keep the room in sight.

Haley's nerves were jumping. She could feel Ty right behind her, shielding her with his body. Images popped into her head of the door flying open and gunfire spraying into the room. She remembered the fear for Ty that had nearly overwhelmed her. As he reached up to knock on the door, a wave of dizziness hit her and her knees felt suddenly weak.

"You okay?"

Haley took a deep breath, pulled herself under control. "I'm all right. Go ahead."

The door opened from the inside and the woman stepped back to let them in. Ty walked in first, checked to be sure there was no one else inside, then pulled Haley in and closed the door.

Abigail McQueen looked even more frail than she had the last time Haley had seen her, her eyes slightly sunken, the skin bruised underneath.

"You came a long way to see us," Ty said. "What can we do for you, Ms. McQueen?"

She tried to smile. "I think it's time we used first names, don't you?"

Ty smiled back, but there wasn't any warmth. "All right, Abigail. Why don't we sit down and you can tell us why you're here."

Haley took his cue, and she and Abigail sat down at the cheap Formica-topped table that only had two chairs, while Ty sat down on the edge of the bed a few feet away.

Abigail fidgeted with a wrinkle on the front of her black slacks. There were traces of paint around her cuticles.

"You asked me on the phone if I painted those forgeries. I think we both know I did. I'm here because I don't want to go to prison. I can give you the name of the man who commissioned those paintings, but I need you to keep searching, find the men behind all of this."

"Why not give the name to the police, let them handle it? You might be able to make a deal for clemency, maybe even turn state's evidence and walk if you testify against them."

"I'm hoping to do that eventually. At the moment, it wouldn't work."

"Why not?"

"Because the man who commissioned the paintings doesn't know who's behind the theft. He told me he has no idea who set all of it up. He just talks to a voice on the phone and follows instructions. He's paid a commission for handling the sales."

"So he knows the buyers but not the people at the top, the ones who set up the heist."

"That's right. Will you help me?"

"If the guy who brokered the sales doesn't know who's behind the thefts, I don't have any choice. The man at the top is the one who's calling the shots. Until we find him, none of us is safe. What's the name of the man who commissioned the paintings?"

Abigail hesitated. "Will you help me make a deal?"

"When the time comes, I'll do what I can."

"His name is Peter Danoff. He owns a gallery in San Francisco. It's the only name I know besides Jules. The problem is Peter Danoff died of a heart attack this morning."

The room fell silent.

"I didn't want to do them," Abigail rushed on. "My daughter needed medical attention and I had no money. I was desperate. I didn't know what else to do."

"There are programs for that kind of thing, Abigail. They wouldn't have just let her die."

"Maybe, but I wanted the best care possible for her. Elizabeth deserves the best."

Ty got up and paced, took a few minutes before he walked back to the bed and sat down. "All right, I can understand your thinking. Why don't you start from the beginning? Tell us exactly how all of this happened."

Abigail looked pale but resigned. She took a shaky breath. "It started way back, I guess. I've always loved art. I knew I was good, but I never really expected to earn a lot of money. It was always just about the work. In college, I loved art history. I was fascinated by the old masters. Painting them became a hobby of mine. Harmless. Seeing how closely I could match the skill of a great master like Rembrandt or Da Vinci, making the painting look real."

"You had to be good. No one in the gallery suspected the paintings were forgeries."

"Back then, I was proud of my work. The pieces were beautiful. I enjoyed just looking at them. I sold a few. I never signed them. They were just copies, you know? Jules knew about it. He was the one who showed me how to age the canvas, make the paint and varnish look real. It was amazing what it did to the look of the painting, how authentic it made it seem."

"Go on."

"Jules and I used to see each other. For a while we thought we were in love. When it didn't work out, we ended our relationship. I married my husband, Thomas, and we had Elizabeth. Then Thomas died and I was back on my own."

"You started showing your work at the gallery in Carmel," Ty guessed.

"That's right. Then one day, Jules paid me a visit. He brought a man with him. Jules had told him about the old masters I sometimes painted and the man said he was interested in seeing them. I showed him a Velazquez and a Paul Cezanne I had done, and he was impressed."

"Those works are by very different artists," Haley said. "Painted in completely different styles."

"Yes, but remember, I'm copying what someone else has already created, not imagining the scene myself."

"The man who came was Danoff?" Ty asked.

"Yes. He commissioned a couple of pieces. A Caravaggio and a Titian. He brought pictures. He wanted exact copies. By then, I was desperate for money. My daughter's disease had flared up and she was in the hospital. I didn't know what to do, so I agreed to paint them."

"What happened then?"

"After I read about the theft, I knew the pieces were mine, but I had my daughter to think of. She needed me so I kept silent, as they knew I would. Then last year,

Danoff came back. He wanted three pieces this time. The Rembrandt would be extremely difficult, but the Renoir and Van Gogh wouldn't be quite so hard. He offered me even more money but this time I refused. That's when he threatened Beth. He said the man who wanted the paintings would kill my little girl if I didn't paint them. I took the money and did the forgeries. I had no other choice."

"I need the names of the pieces you painted."

Tears welled in Abigail's eyes and began to slide into the hollows of her cheeks. "If I had known what would happen, I never would have done it. People are dead." She looked at Haley. "Your father. Those men in the motel. Now they've threatened my daughter again. If I go to the police, those men will kill her—just like they did your father." She turned to Ty, her eyes glistening. "You have to find the people behind this."

"Write down the names of the paintings." He walked over and grabbed a notepad and pen off the nightstand, brought it back and tossed it down on the table.

Abigail's hand shook as she wrote down the titles of the priceless artwork she had copied and pushed the notepad back across the table.

Haley picked it up. "Rembrandt, *Old Man in Shadows.* Renoir, *Fête dans le Jardin.* Van Gogh, *Self-Portrait in Front of the Mirror.*" She stuck the paper into her purse.

"I don't know what happened to them," Abigail said, wiping away the wetness on her cheeks. "I don't know if the real ones were actually stolen. If they were, I don't know who bought them."

Ty caught the woman's thin shoulders, forcing her to look up at him. "Listen to me, Abigail. Here's what I want you to do. You go back home to your daughter.

You pretend you were never in L.A. and hope to hell they don't find out you were."

She started nodding. "I—I've got a flight back this afternoon. I was going to catch a cab to the airport."

"All right. Is there somewhere you can go, a place far enough away you and your daughter will be safe?"

"I've got friends in Arizona. They live in an artists' colony. It's way off the grid. Elizabeth is being released tomorrow. I've already talked to my friends about a visit."

"Go as soon as you can, and don't leave a trail. Once you're out of town, go to the market and buy a disposable phone."

Haley listened as Ty explained that Abigail should purchase a throwaway phone then call him with the number. She was to use that phone whenever she talked to anyone so no one would be able to trace her whereabouts through the calls.

He told her he would be in touch if he had any new information.

As they stood up to leave, Abigail turned to Haley. "I'm sorry for what happened to your father. I know it isn't enough, but I am."

Haley just nodded. Abigail had done what she had to do in order to save her daughter's life. It wasn't right, but the woman was a mother, not a murderer.

Haley flashed her a sympathetic glance as Ty led her out the door.

Twenty-Six

Ty led Haley over to the pickup, where Dylan joined them.

"Peter Danoff," Ty said to his cousin, helping Haley into the truck, seating her in the middle between the two men. "He's the one who brokered the sales. The bad news is Danoff's dead, and even if he were alive, according to Abigail, he didn't know the name of the guy who set up the heist."

"The security in an art gallery that exhibits priceless art has to be top-notch," Haley said as she fastened her seat belt across her lap. "Stealing it would require an amazing amount of preparation."

"And not just by a single person," Dylan said, "but a whole group of operators."

"And a money man," Ty added. "Someone to finance the deal. Someone with brains and connections. That's the guy who's running the show. Until we find him, going to the cops with what little we know is only going to muddy the waters."

"And maybe put Abigail and her daughter in danger," Haley added.

Ty flicked her a glance. Yeah, maybe he and Haley, too. They needed to stay below the radar as much as possible until they came up with something concrete.

"So what do we do next?" she asked as Ty pulled out of the parking lot.

"We need the names of Danoff's buyers. He's bound to keep a list of his clients. We need to see that list."

"How do we get it?"

"His gallery's in San Francisco. I need to go back and see if I can find it."

Dylan flashed him a look. Ty was talking about breaking and entering, which his cousin clearly understood. Ty wasn't about to tell that to Haley.

"You might need some help," Dylan said. "I'll go with you."

Ty just nodded, glad to have the backup.

As the pickup rolled down Sunset Boulevard, Haley shot him a glance. "You don't think there's a chance Danoff's heart attack was…you know…murder?"

"If it wasn't, it's damn coincidental."

"Danoff knew the names of the buyers," Dylan said. "They're guilty of receiving stolen property at the very least."

"And the amount of money involved makes it an extremely serious offense," Haley said. "Killing Danoff would protect them."

"Which means his client list is liable to turn up missing," Dylan finished, a fact Ty had already considered.

They hadn't gone a block when Ty's cell phone started ringing. Ty pulled the pickup over to the side of the road, grabbed the half-charged phone off the dash and checked the caller ID—Sol Greenway returning the call Ty had made in Carmel.

He pressed the phone against his ear. "Hey, buddy, you got something for me?"

"McQueen's been banking at Crocker National for the past ten years," Sol said. "In 2007, a quarter of a million dollars was deposited into her account. Nine months ago, she got another three hundred thou. Most of it's gone. Bill Pay to St. Agnes Children's Hospital."

"I figured. Any way to know where the money came from?"

"Came from a bank in the Caymans, or routed through there, at least. I haven't been able to find where it originated. These guys are pros."

"Thanks, Sol. I really appreciate the help."

"After the way you stepped up for Iceman, I figure I owe you." Ty had helped a friend of Sol's, Ben Slocum, rescue his son. "If there's anything else you need—" Sol said.

"Actually, there is one more little thing."

Sol chuckled. "Always is."

"There's a place in San Francisco. The Danoff Gallery. Peter Danoff just died, but I'm wondering if he might have been keeping records online. It's the thing to do these days, you know?"

"You mean in the Cloud?"

"That's right. I'm looking for a list of Danoff's clients. The guy was involved in moving some very heavyweight merchandise. I figure he might have used the Cloud as a way to store information he wanted to keep secret. That list might be the key to a couple of murders—maybe even his own."

"Interesting. Okay, stay cool, I'm on it." Sol hung up the phone.

"I take it that was your hacker friend," Haley said.

Ty grinned. "He prefers to be called an Internet Investigator."

She rolled her pretty blue eyes.

"Listen, baby. I've got to get going. I've got some work to do."

"So do I," Dylan said. "I've got to see a man about a plane."

Haley smiled at Ty. "I'll be busy, too. Abigail gave us the names of the paintings she forged. I'll find out where they are—or at least where they're supposed to be. See what else I can find out."

"Great. We'll drop Dylan back at my house so he can pick up his rental car and then I'll take you home."

Ty drove the short distance from the motel to his condo, pulled into his garage and closed the door behind them. Haley waited while he made a quick check to be sure no one had been in the condo, then he walked Dylan out to his rented SUV.

"You're welcome to stay here," Ty said to him as he pulled open the door of a dark brown Ford Explorer. "But it might be smarter if you stayed somewhere else till this is over."

"Good call. You might try taking your own advice."

"I'll be staying at my office. Good security up there and—"

"And you're close to your lady in case there's trouble."

Ty grinned. "That, too."

"I like her."

He nodded. "And her friend, Lane, I'm thinking."

"Her, too." Dylan opened the door of the Explorer. "Call if you're going to San Francisco."

"Will do. Thanks, cuz." Turning, Ty went back inside, stuffed some clean clothes into a canvas bag, grabbed Haley and headed for the truck. A few minutes later, he was pulling through the wrought-iron gate, driving up the hill to the parking area outside his office.

"You might as well use the extra computer in my office to dig up those names," Ty said. "Could save time if you turn up something interesting."

"All right." While Haley got to work on the computer, Ty went upstairs in search of Johnnie. Dressed in his usual black jeans, a black T-shirt stretched over his barrel chest, Riggs was striding down the hall when Ty spotted him.

"Got a minute?" Ty asked.

"Sure thing. I saw you pull in. I need to talk to you, too."

"You first."

"I got a lead on that case I've been working in San Diego. I need to get down there, but I wanted to make sure everything was covered here before I left."

"I'll be staying in the office till this is over, so you're good to go."

Johnnie nodded. "This shouldn't take long. With any luck, I'll be back tomorrow. Your turn."

Ty spent the next few minutes updating his partner on the case and his conversation with Abigail McQueen. "I've got Sol working on getting a list of Danoff's clients. But I can't afford to wait. I'm heading up to Frisco myself."

"What else?"

"Haley's downstairs locating the paintings Abigail says she copied. A Rembrandt, a Renoir and a Van Gogh. Haley says they won't be hard to find."

"Paintings of that value…probably find them on Google."

"Probably. But it's important to Haley to be involved, and this is something she can do to help."

"Amy's at work," Johnnie said. "Keep an eye on her while I'm gone, will you?"

"You got it."

Johnnie waved as he headed out to his flashy black Mustang, and Ty headed back downstairs. He still hadn't had any sleep, but he felt too restless to try. He rubbed his face as he reached the bottom of the stairs, saw Haley sitting in the chair in front of the extra computer. For a moment, he just stared.

God, she was beautiful. With her full lips and dimples, her shiny, honey-gold hair. He liked so many things about her. Her intelligence, her tenacity, her toughness. Her femininity. Her passion.

The last thought drove a hot flood of memories into his head, and his blood began to simmer. He hadn't had her in days, not since before they went to Carmel. He had forced himself to leave her alone, to focus on protecting her.

But the security alarm was set, and no one was home upstairs. His body was pulsing, need rolling through him. Hunger for her clawed at his insides. She turned as he moved silently toward her, his blood hot, his erection throbbing, pressing against the fly of his jeans.

Her eyes widened as she read the look on his face, and she came up out of her chair. "I thought you said your fantasy had something to do with your sofa."

Ty reached for her, drew her into his arms. "Baby, you're all the fantasy I need. I just want you." He kissed her softly, letting her know how much she meant to him, that what he wanted from her went deeper than just playing games.

Haley moved into his embrace, slid her arms around

his neck and kissed him back. Ty deepened the kiss, tasting her sweetness, savoring it. Scooping her into his arms, he carried her over to the thick gym mat in the corner. The blanket he had spread out the last time he slept over was still there.

The corner was out of sight of the windows. No one could see them there.

"I've missed you," Haley said as he stripped off her clothes and his own.

"I've missed you, too, darlin'." Ty ran his hands over her pretty breasts, cupped them, lowered his head to taste them. Her nipples hardened beneath his tongue, and she made a soft little mewling sound that turned him on like crazy. In minutes, he was inside her, and it felt so good, so perfect, exactly the right place to be.

He was getting in deep. In more ways than one. Ty kissed her and started to move.

Heat swept through her, desire so hot and thick Haley could barely breathe. Only Ty could make her feel this way, only Ty could give her this kind of pleasure.

Until she had met him, she had never known this all-consuming need for another person.

The feelings terrified her, reminded her of the dangerous path she traveled and where it would lead. For an instant, the heat turned cold and a shiver ran through her. Then he was kissing her again, lifting her hips and moving deeper inside. Sensation burned through her, shut down all but the thought of him. Ty drove into her, taking what he wanted, giving her what she wanted, too. The hunger returned, sweeping in, devouring her.

Haley arched beneath him, taking him deeper still, her nails digging into the muscles across his shoulders. Ty's heavy thrusts quickened as he pounded into her, taking her with him, both of them climbing toward the peak.

"Come for me, baby," he whispered. "Let yourself go."

His words pushed her over the edge, her muscles seizing, sensation washing through her, pleasure so sweet she could taste it on her tongue.

Haley didn't fight it. Once she was home, she might never know this depth of passion again. She told herself that after they parted and she was back in her old life in Chicago, she would have something to remember. Something no one could ever take from her.

She didn't realize she was crying until Ty moved off her and eased her into his arms.

His hand ran gently over her hair. "It's all right, baby, what is it? I didn't hurt you, did I?"

She shook her head. He hadn't hurt her. Not in that way. It was leaving that would hurt her. And yet she knew she could not stay.

She managed to smile. "It was wonderful. *You* were wonderful."

He drew a finger down her cheek. "You mean a lot to me, Haley. More than a lot. I want you to know that."

"You mean a lot to me, too, Ty. I owe you my life."

He frowned. "That's not what I'm talking about."

"I know that."

"What is it, then? Why were you crying?"

She rolled to her feet and picked up her clothes, carried them into the bathroom. When she came back out, Ty was dressed and pacing the floor in front of the windows.

"You didn't answer my question," he said, his hands coming to rest on his hips.

She didn't want to answer. She'd been hoping he

would leave it alone, let things go on as they had been. She could see that wasn't going to happen.

"It's just…everything is so uncertain. We need to solve this and put these people in jail, and yet, once we do, everything is going to change."

"We don't know what's going to happen. Not with the investigation. Not with you and me."

"I don't want to talk about it, Ty. I don't want to spoil the time we have together."

He clenched his jaw as he strode toward her. "Your mind's already made up, isn't it? That's what's got you upset. You're convinced it can't work between us."

"Please, Ty—"

"I'm right, aren't I? You're going back no matter what."

Her chin inched up. "I told you that from the start. My life is in Chicago. Everything I've worked for is there. My family, my friends. And even if that weren't true, you and I would never make it."

"Why the hell not?"

"For the same reason it didn't work with my mother and father. We're just too different."

A muscle flexed in Ty's jaw. "We aren't so different, Haley. Not in the things that matter." He paced back to the window, stopped and turned. "But you're right. For now we need to focus on catching the bad guys— before someone else gets killed."

Twenty-Seven

~~~~~~~~~~~~~~~~~~~~~~~~~

Once Haley got on the computer, it didn't take long to find the paintings. *Old Man in Shadows,* by Rembrandt van Rijn. Renoir's *Fête dans le Jardin.* And the Van Gogh self-portrait with a mirror. *Portrait de l'Artiste,* important because it was the last work he painted before he severed his ear.

The answer to where each was located came up the same. "They're all owned by the Fizer Foundation." Haley studied the screen, the blue-and-gold website, FizerFoundation.com. "It's on Wilshire Boulevard. Gallery Row, it says, between Fairfax and Highland. You know where that is?"

"They call it The Miracle Mile. L.A. County Museum of Art is there. Same area as the Scarsdale Center, a number of others."

"It fits that the paintings would all be in one place. That was the way they did it before."

"That's right. They can put their team in place, make the exchange and steal the paintings whenever they're ready."

"So what should we do?"

"First, we talk to the staff, find out if the paintings are real or Abigail's forgeries. But we can't do it yet. We need to make sure McQueen and her daughter are somewhere safe. That might take a couple of days."

"If they're fakes, the gallery is going to call the police. Maybe this time they'll be able to figure out who stole them."

"The police haven't come up with anything in the past three years," Ty said darkly. His mood had been sour since they'd argued. Her own wasn't any better. It was exactly what Haley had hoped to avoid.

"If we can't pursue the paintings, what do we do in the meantime?"

"As soon as Johnnie gets back, I'm going to San Francisco. Finding something in the Cloud is a long shot. We need to get our hands on that list of names. We can't afford to wait."

Haley didn't push to go with him. She needed some space, needed to accept the fact she was going to lose him and give her heart a chance to recover.

She didn't think Ty would mind.

She could already feel him pulling away.

Lane was working in the back of the studio when the intercom next to the front door buzzed. She and the two other designers in the shop only worked by appointment, and she wasn't expecting a client or a delivery. Leaving the fabric samples she had been studying, she crossed the studio and peered out the small paned window onto Robertson Boulevard.

Her heart jerked at the sight of the tall man in the plaid flannel shirt standing in front of the door. Unconsciously her hand crept to the base of her throat.

If he hadn't just spotted her through the window, she might have slipped into the back room and pretended she wasn't there.

With a sigh of resignation, she unlocked the dead bolt and pulled open the door.

"I wasn't sure you'd be here," Dylan Brodie said, his eyes sweeping from the top of her head to the open-toed sandals on her feet.

Lane ignored the little jolt of heat that slow perusal caused. "I usually meet clients by appointment. I work on projects here or at home. What can I do for you, Dylan?" She kept her voice brusque. She didn't want to encourage him.

"Mind if I come in?"

"I'm really busy, actually…" But he was already pushing past her, closing the door behind him.

"This won't take long."

"All right, then. What is it you need?"

He glanced around the studio, taking in the stacks of fabric in every texture, from the softest cashmere to the heaviest length of canvas, in vibrant reds, yellows, blues and a hundred pastel shades. At the samples of floor tiles, squares of granite for countertops and paint chips of every possible hue.

His gaze returned to her face. "I think I mentioned I just bought a fishing lodge."

"Yes?"

He glanced around again. With his rugged good looks, heavy leather boots and flannel shirt, he looked as though he had stepped out of another century, a man out of place and time.

"I don't suppose you do much of that kind of thing," he said. "I mean outdoor, rustic stuff. Log houses, things like that."

She couldn't help bragging. "Actually, I've done a great deal. A number of the Hollywood rich and famous own second homes in the Northwest. I did the interior design for a log home in Jackson Hole for a friend of Harrison Ford's, and a remodel of an old ranch house outside Bozeman, Montana for Dennis Quaid. I've done several mountain homes near the ski hill in Sun Valley."

"Busy girl."

"I've been at it awhile."

"You like it?"

She thought of the work she was good at and the satisfaction she got from completing a project, though she missed the leisure time she had once valued so highly. "Yes, of course."

"Got any pictures?"

She looked at that masculine face and those blue, blue eyes and felt a twinge that went straight to her womb. "What?"

"Pictures. Photos of the work you've done."

Why was it so hard to breathe? "I'm sorry. If you're asking if I might come up to Alaska to work on your lodge, I'm afraid it's simply too far away."

"Well, I wouldn't be interested in offering you the job unless you could handle it. So I guess, we'll leave it there."

Her pride kicked in and her chin went up. Turning, she walked over and picked up her portfolio, brought it back and started flipping through the pages of interior design projects she had completed.

"Nice work."

"Thank you. But as I said, I don't think I could coordinate it being so far away. I couldn't leave my business long enough to get the project completed."

"That's too bad." His hard gaze zeroed in on her mouth. "Doesn't mean we can't go out to dinner."

Her stomach lifted.

"How about it? I'll pick you up at eight."

A tremor slipped through her. "I'm sorry, I'm busy."

He moved a little closer. "How about tomorrow, then?" He was half a foot taller. She wished she were wearing high heels. His cologne reminded her of pine trees and fresh air. She couldn't pull her eyes from that intriguingly rugged face.

"I'm sorry. No."

He shrugged a set of incredibly wide shoulders. "I kind of figured you'd refuse."

"Why is that?"

He started for the door, pulled it open, turned back to look at her. "We both know why, Lane. Because you're a coward." Dylan gave her a last slow glance, and closed the door.

Lane dropped into a chair as he walked past the window, feeling as if she had just escaped a hanging. Good Lord, what was it about that man?

She released a slow breath. Whatever it was, Lane had no intention of ever finding out.

Ty was gone. He had left for San Francisco this morning. He had rented a plane and Dylan was flying them up.

Now that Haley was alone, she had no idea what to do with herself. She and Ty had been working together for days. She'd grown accustomed to being near him, accustomed to having him around. She'd grown used to the looks of appreciation he cast her way that turned hot and scorching and led to wild, unbelievable sex.

She'd grown to crave the way he touched her, kissed her, filled her so completely.

She jumped at the sound of Ellie's voice and felt a surge of embarrassment at her thoughts.

"There you are." Her aunt swept into the library, silver hair perfectly groomed, wearing a blue silk blouse, ivory slacks, a small string of pearls and matching pearl ear studs. "I wondered where you'd gone."

"I was bored. I thought I'd do a little digging on the internet, see what I could find out about the paintings. I was just getting started."

"Then maybe my timing is good." Ellie smiled. "There's someone I'd like you to meet."

Haley rose from the brown leather Eames chair behind the walnut desk as a distinguished, gray-haired man walked into the library and stopped at Ellie's side.

"This is a friend of mine, darling. Jonathan Hammond. You haven't asked, but I know you've been wondering where I've been slipping off to in the afternoons. Jonathan and I have been seeing each other for a while. I thought it was time the two of you met."

Finally. Haley had been suspicious, but it wasn't her place to ask. She smiled. "Hello, Jonathan."

Dressed in tan slacks and a light blue mock-neck sweater, expensive, well-tailored clothes, he walked toward her, accepted the hand she offered.

"Your aunt has told me a great deal about you, Haley. I'm glad she finally decided I've earned the right to an introduction."

Haley laughed. "I hope she hasn't given away any family secrets."

"Not so far."

"I'm glad to meet you, Jonathan." And very glad for her aunt. Ellie deserved to find happiness.

Haley ignored a little pang as Ty's handsome face popped into her head. Their circumstances were entirely different.

"Jonathan is escorting me to the wedding," Ellie said. "I wanted the two of you to meet before then."

The wedding. Inwardly, she groaned. "With everything that's been going on, I'd almost forgotten."

"It's this Sunday. It's a very special occasion for all of us. You'll be there, won't you? Tyler said he was bringing you along."

She managed to smile. "Yes, of course." She was going to a wedding with Ty. It was the last thing she wanted.

Ellie took Jonathan's arm. "All right then, we're off to lunch at The Ivy. We'd love for you to join us. We can bring Stryker along if you can break away."

Haley shook her head. She could hardly look at her aunt and Jonathan without thinking of Ty, and it only made her feel worse. And now there was the wedding.

"I appreciate the offer, but I really need to get some work done here."

"All right, darling. Be sure and do whatever Kurt tells you. Stay safe, and we'll be back in a couple of hours."

Haley just nodded. She smiled as she watched them leave, happy for her aunt, wishing things could be different for her and Ty.

With a sigh, she returned her attention to the computer screen and began researching the background on the three paintings hanging at the Fizer Foundation.

According to the links she found on Google, each piece had been purchased separately several years apart. It wasn't until 2007 that all of them were exhibited together at the Fizer. The Renoir and the Van Gogh were on display in the Impressionist Gallery. The Rembrandt was displayed with other of the artists' works in the Old Masters Hall next door.

The proximity of the pieces would make their removal easier. She couldn't wait to find out if the paintings had already been replaced, as Ray Farrell had told her father at the Blue Oyster, or if the theft was a work in progress.

She was pounding away on the keyboard when she heard the sound of footsteps and looked up to see Betty Jean come into the library. She was wearing her usual bold colors, a pair of mauve Capri pants with a pink flowered blouse.

"I heard you in here typing. If you aren't too busy, I was hoping you could spare a minute to talk."

"I'm not too busy." She stood up from her chair. "What is it?"

"I'm going home, dear. I've taken advantage of your aunt's hospitality far too long already, and besides, I miss being in my own house."

Haley frowned. "You can't go home. It isn't safe for you there."

"I think it is. After your trip to Carmel, whoever killed your father knows you and Ty are still investigating the crime. I wasn't able to convince you to stop. There is no reason for them to think I could do it now."

It made a certain amount of sense, and yet Haley was worried. "I'd rather you stay here, Betty Jean. I'd feel terrible if something happened."

The blond woman's smile lit up her face. "That's very nice to hear." She was a very attractive woman, Haley now realized, just in a different way from Allison Warren, her sophisticated mother.

"I enjoyed our chance to get acquainted," Betty Jean

said. "I know it's something your father would have wanted. But now it's time for me to go."

"I don't know, Betty Jean. I think we should talk to Ty first. See what he has to say."

"It's my decision, dear, and I've already spoken to your aunt, thanked her for everything she's done. I'm anxious to get back home."

Haley ignored a thread of worry. "If you're sure it's what you want, I suppose there's nothing I can say to stop you. But there is one thing before you go."

"What is it, dear?"

"The last time we talked, you said something about the circumstances of my parents' marriage. You said if things had been different, they might have had a better chance for happiness. What did you mean?"

Betty Jean nervously bit her lip. "I didn't mean to say anything. I think this is a subject that would be better left alone."

"I'm asking you to tell me. I won't ever tell anyone how I found out, but I have a feeling it's important."

"Haley, please—"

"I need to know, Betty Jean. My father is dead. There are things I need to work out, things I could have asked him or maybe he would have told me himself. I think this is one of them."

Betty Jean sighed. "I suppose he might have told you. He wanted so very much for you to understand."

"Then tell me."

When Betty Jean nodded, Haley led her over to the leather sofa in front of the empty hearth, and both of them sat down.

Betty Jean twisted a crease in the front of her mauve polyester pants. "You were partly right—your father and mother met in college, just as you said. They dated for a while. Your mother was beautiful and your father was extremely handsome." She smiled. "Good lord, the man could make my heart start pounding just by walking into a room." She sat up a little straighter. "I'm sorry, where was I?"

"My mother and father were dating."

"Yes, but after a while, Jimmy began to see that the two of them were not well suited. Your mother's family was extremely wealthy. They were quite involved in society. Your father wasn't interested in that kind of thing. He wanted to go into law enforcement. He believed he had a talent for that sort of work and that was where he could do the most good."

"So why did he ask her to marry him?"

"Because your mother got pregnant. For a young woman from that kind of family, a fatherless child would have been unthinkable. Jimmy believed it was his duty to marry her."

"I don't have a brother or sister. What happened? Did my mother lose the child?"

"That was the problem. You see, there never was a baby. Your mother was determined James Warren was the man she wanted to marry. She made up the story, then after the wedding, pretended to have a miscarriage. By the time Jimmy found out, the course of his life had changed. He was working for your grandfather, immersed in your mother's world. Then you came along. That was the reason he stayed."

Haley's eyes burned. She swallowed past the tightness in her throat. So many secrets. So much pain.

She leaned over and hugged Betty Jean. "Thank you for telling me."

"I hope I did the right thing."

"You did what my dad would have wanted. I know

it all now. I understand. I can't tell you how much that means to me."

Betty Jean gripped her hand. "Try to understand your mother, too, dear. She loved your father. She was spoiled and selfish, but she was also very young. Sometimes when we're young we do foolish things."

Haley just nodded. "I'll remember that." Betty Jean rose from the sofa, and Haley walked her out to the entry where her suitcase was already packed and ready. They waited together for the cab to reach the gate, then Haley punched in the code and let the cab drive up the hill.

"Please stay in touch," Haley said. "Promise you'll call every day and let us know you're okay."

"I will." The women hugged one last time. Betty Jean got into the cab and it rolled off down the hill. Haley thought of her parents' marriage, how terribly unhappy it had been.

Love and marriage. It just wasn't worth the risk.

Twenty-Eight

❦

A heavy fog rolled in off the bay, blanketing the steep hills of San Francisco. The sounds of traffic moving along the slick city streets were muted and dim. A distant foghorn moaned somewhere offshore.

"You picked a good night for it," Dylan said as they walked beneath the opaque light cast by streetlamps along the way. The cab had dropped them three blocks from the gallery, which was just up ahead.

Ty pulled up the collar on his raincoat. "Guess we got lucky." Only a couple of people passed them on the sidewalk, hurrying to get in out of the weather.

He checked his watch. Just past midnight. Earlier he had reconned the area around the Danoff Gallery, made a search of the alley behind, taken a look at the back entrance. The security system wasn't that new. Even if it were, during his years as a Special Ops Marine he had learned to get in and out of pretty much anyplace he wanted without being seen.

Not that he could break into the Scarsdale Center or

the Fizer Foundation. It took a whole crew of thieves to manage a B and E like that.

They reached the alley that led to the rear of the gallery, and he spotted the big gray metal door up ahead.

"You sure you can get in without setting off the alarm?" Dylan asked.

Ty just grinned. "Piece of cake." A few minutes later, the lock on the back door turned and the door swung open. He and Dylan slipped silently into the back room of the gallery. Pausing only long enough to disengage the alarm system, they headed for the office.

Ty moved off to the computer while Dylan crossed the room to a bank of metal file cabinets and began pulling open drawers. Thumbing through manila file folders, he searched for anything that might contain a list of Danoff's clients.

Ty booted up the computer and started pounding away on the keyboard, watching hopefully as file names began to pop up.

He frowned. "Son of a bitch. All the files on this computer are only a few days old. This damned thing is brand-new."

"Figures. Somebody crashed the old one with the client list on it. Whoever's running the gallery must have had to replace it."

"So much for Danoff's heart attack."

"The guy was murdered to shut him up, and whoever did it destroyed the computer to get rid of the list of names."

Ty shut down the machine. Both of them made a quick search of the rest of the file drawers but didn't expect to find anything.

"You think he might have kept records at home?" Dylan asked as they finished.

"If he did, good bet they're gone, too. Let's get out of here." Ty checked the office to make sure they'd left it the way they found it and started for the door, Dylan falling in behind him. He reset the alarm near the back door and they slipped quietly outside.

They'd gone only a couple of feet before the sound of footsteps echoed in the alley, coming in their direction. Ty warned Dylan with a touch, drew his Beretta from the holster on his belt, and both of them stepped back into the shadows behind a Dumpster next to the back door.

The footfalls grew louder. From his crouched position, Ty could only see a portion of the man's legs, his tan pants and heavy black shoes. The guy reached the back door and shoved a key into the lock just as a noise sounded in the darkness beside the Dumpster, drawing his attention back to where Ty crouched against the wall.

Deadly calm settled over him. His Beretta felt comfortable in his hand. He didn't plan to use it unless he had no choice, but these men were killers. He wasn't about to give this one a chance. He positioned himself to take the man down, started to move, then caught the glint of metal on the man's wide chest.

Security guard, he realized, forcing himself to stand down, to ignore the adrenaline pumping like hot liquid through his veins. *Just a night watchman making his rounds.*

Of course he could have been involved in destroying the computer, but the odds were against it. The less people who knew what was going on, the safer for the men behind the theft.

The guard took a couple more steps, and Ty stood immobile, making himself invisible in the shadows. A few feet away, Dylan was no more than a dark outline among a dozen other shadows in the alley. The guard swept his flashlight over the Dumpster, then around the area to the right and left. When the beam of light landed on a black-and-white cat licking the insides of an empty tuna can, he chuckled and aimed his light back toward the door.

A few minutes later, the gallery door opened, the man disappeared inside and Ty released the breath he had been holding. As soon as the back door closed, he and Dylan headed off down the alley in the opposite direction.

His cousin gave a sigh of relief. "I was afraid you were going to take him out," Dylan said.

Ty smiled. "I try not to kill the good guys."

Dylan chuckled. "Good thinking." He turned serious. "We didn't find the list."

No, and they needed that information badly. "There's still a chance it's in the Cloud."

"And you think if it is, your friend can get in and get it?"

"Maybe. I'll call Sol in the morning. You ready to get us home?"

"Ready when you are."

"Let's go."

Morning sunlight streamed in through the wall of windows in the office. At the sound of Alabama fiddling on his cell, Ty forced his eyes open and groped for the phone lying on the floor next to the gym mat where he'd been sleeping.

He rubbed a hand over his face, trying to recover from his late-night adventure in San Francisco and another night of very little sleep.

"Brodie."

"Wake up, cowboy, daylight's burnin'." *Sol Greenway.*

He chuckled. "Tell me you got into the Cloud and found Danoff's client list or at least got the password. Something."

"Sorry. He didn't store anything on the internet."

"Fuck."

"He stored it in his computer. I was digging around in there when it crashed."

Ty's hold tightened on the phone. "Tell me you got the file before it went down."

There was a smile in Sol's voice. "I got the file. Finished copying it just as the whole thing went belly-up."

Ty couldn't stop a grin. "Yes, yes, yes!"

"Problem is the file's encrypted. I haven't been able to come up with the password to get in."

His smile faded. "Any chance of that happening?"

"I'll get it sooner or later. Unfortunately, something's come up. Missing eight-year-old kid. Trace is on it. I've got to work the case full-time till we find her or...not."

"I understand. You get something, let me know."

"Will do." Sol signed off and Ty hung up the phone. With a yawn, he rolled to his feet and headed for the shower. The hot water felt good washing over his skin. He turned it to cool to wake himself up and stop thinking of Haley, wishing she was in there with him. A few minutes later, he was dressed in his jeans and a clean, dark blue T-shirt. Grabbing his Dodgers ball cap, he headed for the door.

As he made his way up the hill toward the big house, part of him was eager to see Haley and bring her up to speed. Another part wished he didn't have to see her at all.

After they'd argued, he had realized his feelings for her ran a whole lot deeper than he'd wanted to admit. Hell, the truth was, he was more than half in love with her. But Haley's feelings for him didn't run that deep.

If he let himself get any more involved, he was going to get hurt. He had to be careful, keep things on an even keel.

Still, she was involved in the investigation. She had almost died trying to find the man responsible for her father's death. She deserved to know what was going on.

Ty blew out a tired breath as he walked up on Ellie's front porch.

Haley heard the knock at the door and hurried to open it. Betty Jean was gone and her aunt was out with Jonathan. Stryker appeared like a specter in the hall and stepped in front of her. He looked through the peephole, pulled open the door and stepped back out of the way.

Haley's heart jerked as Ty walked into the entry. He was freshly showered and shaved. His dark hair still needed a trim. Her gaze shot to his and for a moment, neither of them moved. God, she had missed him so much. It wasn't fair a man could dominate her thoughts the way he did.

Ty glanced over her shoulder at the big, burly man who stood behind her. "Everything all right?"

"Nice and quiet," Stryker said. "I'll be outside if you need me."

Ty just nodded, returned his gaze to her face. Her heart was pounding like a battering ram and her palms felt damp. She wanted him to kiss her more than she wanted to breathe.

"Goddammit," he said, then his mouth was on hers, and he was pulling her hard against him, kissing her deeply, and she was kissing him back. He tasted like sin and felt like home.

"Ty," she whispered as he nibbled the side of her neck, bit down gently on her earlobe.

"Someone crashed Danoff's computer," he whispered, and kissed her again, softly this time, letting the moment play out before he stepped back, took a deep breath and returned to business.

"So you didn't…umm…get the list?" she said, her mind still foggy, desire still hot in her veins.

"Sol got it before the computer went down."

"That's…that's great."

"Trouble is, it's encrypted and he hasn't been able to figure out the password yet."

"Oh." She was disappointed, but all she could think of was how glad she was to see him again. Dear God, it was insane.

"He says he thinks he can get it, but at the moment, he's working a child kidnapping and that has to take precedence."

"Of course it does." She just kept looking at him.

"I really missed you," he said.

"I missed you, too."

"If I kiss you again, I won't want to stop."

She swallowed, nodded. "I know."

"We need to work this case."

She released a slow breath, turned and walked a few feet away. "Okay, we don't have the list—"

"Yet."

"We don't have the list yet. So what do we do in the meantime?"

"We need to find out if the three paintings in the Fizer have already been stolen. The good news is, before

I came over, Abigail phoned. She and her daughter are on their way to Arizona. They'll be there by tonight."

"Great. If Abigail's safe, we can go to the gallery, have the staff take a look at the paintings."

"If they're fakes," Ty said, "all hell is going to break loose."

Haley nodded. "This could be an interesting afternoon."

The Fizer Foundation on Wilshire Boulevard was a big triangular building without windows, the inside broken into large airy spaces. Various marble-floored rooms housed different periods of artwork, from Medieval manuscripts through the Renaissance and Baroque periods, to Pablo Picasso and the Art Deco period of the twenties and thirties.

Ty checked the floor plan and headed straight for the Old Masters Hall in search of the Rembrandt. Spotting a large, gilt-framed canvas, he recognized *Old Man in Shadows* from the pictures he had seen on the internet, an ancient man with long gray hair, stoop-shouldered, a brown robe belted by a scarlet sash. Though the wooden staff in his gnarled hand helped bear his weight, there was a quiet dignity and strength in his carriage that said he was wise far beyond his years.

"It's magnificent," Ty said. "Fake or not."

Next to him, Haley stood transfixed, her eyes riveted on the painting, admiring the soft flesh tones of the wrinkled face, the bold red of the sash. "It looks completely real."

"Maybe it is." Ty reached down and caught her hand. "Let's go take a look at the Renoir and the Van Gogh."

"They're in the Impressionist Gallery just next door."

He let her guide him, liking the feel of her hand

in his. It was only a short walk to the Impressionist Gallery.

"Same floor, same hallway. Very handy if you want to snatch them all at once."

"You think that's what they did?"

"It's what I'd do."

She flashed him a look.

He grinned. "Not that I'd do anything like that, of course. But the chance of getting caught is multiplied every time you break in."

"According to the provenance, all three paintings have been in the gallery since 2007."

"That works. Three years ago, the first heist went down at the Scarsdale without a hitch. They had plenty of time to make plans for a second."

He led her into the Impressionist Gallery toward an ornate gold-framed picture on the wall behind a red velvet rope. Renoir's *Fête dans le Jardin*. It was beautiful and to his untrained eye, looked like an original. The Van Gogh self-portrait was also an incredible work of art.

"If Abigail painted all three paintings," Haley said, "she's even more amazing than I thought."

"Yeah." Ty tugged on her hand, leading her out of the gallery toward the museum offices. "Why don't we find out?"

As it turned out, it wasn't that easy. They were finally allowed to speak to the Foundation Director, but getting him to cooperate seemed a monumental task.

"Who did you say you are again?" The director's name was Oliver Stilton, like the cheese and nearly as old, slightly shrunken, with only a few thin wisps of white hair combed over his bald pate.

"I'm Tyler Brodie. I'm a private investigator. We've

been working on the theft three years ago of a Titian and Caravaggio stolen from the Scarsdale Center. I imagine you're familiar with that incident."

"Quite familiar, yes. A tragedy, certainly, but what does that have to do with the pieces you mentioned?"

"We think the same people may have stolen a Renoir, a Van Gogh and a Rembrandt from the Fizer and replaced them with exceptionally good forgeries. We need one of your experts to examine the paintings, see if they're genuine."

"That is preposterous. You walk in here out of the blue and expect us to expend our time and energy trying to prove three of our masterpieces are fakes? We have one of the best security systems in the world. Our paintings are under surveillance twenty-four hours a day. The pieces you named are priceless and they are perfectly safe at the Fizer."

Ty exchanged a glance with Haley, who picked up the conversation. "My father was an investigator with Allied Global, Mr. Stilton. We're following discoveries he made before he was killed. His investigation has led us to believe the paintings have already been stolen— or soon will be. I should think it would be in your best interests to find out."

Stilton just shook his head. "The Fizer has a sterling reputation. I am not about to tarnish it with absurd claims that can only make our patrons uneasy. Now, if you will excuse me, I have important matters to attend."

Ty watched the old man walk away. "As if the theft of three priceless paintings wasn't important."

"I had a feeling this might happen. The last thing the gallery wants is to lose three pieces of irreplaceable art. They might be insured, but if they aren't recovered, they're lost to the world." She led Ty a little way away, her heels clicking on the marble floors as she dug out her cell phone and punched in a number.

"Aunt Ellie? It's Haley. We're at the Fizer. We need them to examine the paintings, but they refuse to do it. We're hoping you can help."

Ty couldn't hear her aunt's reply. But when she hung up, Haley was smiling.

"There's a coffee shop in the basement," she said. "Let's go get a cup while we're waiting for Ellie and her new beau."

"They're coming here?"

"My aunt knows everyone who's anyone in this town. Turns out Jonathan is a major donor to the Fizer Foundation."

Ty just grinned. "You gotta love that woman."

Twenty-Nine

Conversation rumbled around them. Seated across from Ty at a small white, wire mesh table at the Café Parisienne in the basement of the Fizer, Haley sat drinking a tall cappuccino. Ty upended his paper cup, draining the last of a plain French roast coffee.

Behind them, a line of people stood at the counter, ordering snacks and bakery goodies, taking a quick break from wandering the gallery floors above. Haley finished the last of her drink, picked up Ty's empty paper cup, walked over and tossed them in the trash can.

She had just returned to the table when Aunt Ellie walked into the snack shop holding the hand of the handsome, distinguished Jonathan Hammond.

"I take it that's Ellie's new boyfriend," Ty said as he stood up.

Haley smiled. "About time, don't you think?"

He watched them approach. "Past time."

The pair stopped in front of their table, Aunt Ellie smiling like a schoolgirl. "Tyler, this is my good friend, Jonathan Hammond."

Ty extended a hand. "Good to meet you. Thanks for coming."

Jonathan returned the handshake, turned and made a slight nod to Haley. "Good to see you, Haley. I'm happy to help if I can."

"The director's name is Oliver Stilton," Ty said. "I guess he runs the place."

"Yes, I've known Ollie for quite some years," Jonathan replied. "Your aunt has kept me informed as to what's been going on with your investigation. Why don't we have a little chat with Oliver?"

Ty looked relieved. "That'd be great."

They headed back to Stilton's office and this time, with Jonathan there—an obviously wealthy and extremely influential donor—the atmosphere subtly changed.

Jonathan hit the high points of the case and summed it up by saying, "The deuce of it is, Ollie, the theft of the first two paintings has, perhaps, already caused the murder of several individuals."

Stilton cleared his throat. "I didn't realize that."

"Yes, and to make matters worse, the investigation has put the life of Eleanor's niece in jeopardy. We need to bring this problem to a close, and the fastest way we can do that is to find out if a second theft has occurred."

"But surely—"

"You owe it to your patrons, Ollie. They need to be certain the foundation deserves their support. We need to know the pieces you're exhibiting are indeed the originals."

Stilton's hands trembled.

"Perhaps I should phone some of the others, perhaps talk to the members of the board."

The director stiffened. "That won't be necessary. We

have staff on site who are perfectly capable of evaluating the work on display. Which of the three pieces would you like us to examine?"

Jonathan turned to Ty. "Do you have a preference?"

Haley caught his eye. She didn't think they would get another chance. And there was always a possibility only one piece had been stolen.

"The Rembrandt is valued the highest," she answered, recalling the research she had done. "If I'm correct, it's worth over a hundred and fifty million. Why don't we start with that one?"

She smiled at Ty's wink, noticed perspiration had broken out on Oliver Stilton's forehead.

"We'll need a little time," the older man said. "Why don't I get back to you by the end of next week?"

"Today would be better," Jonathan said firmly, handing him a white business card. "I'll expect to hear from you later this afternoon."

Some of Haley's tension eased. One way or another, they would know today if at least one of the paintings had been stolen. As they walked outside the gallery, Ty extended his hand to Jonathan a second time.

"Thanks again. You were great in there."

"If I understand your theory," Jonathan said, "the idea was to replace the art that had already been examined and accepted as genuine."

"That's the way it looks."

"If that's the case, once they take the canvas out of the frame, the forgery should be easy enough to detect."

Ty glanced back toward the director's office. "I guess we'll soon find out. Whatever happens, thanks again."

"I'll let you know as soon as I get word." Jonathan waved as he and Ellie headed back to the parking lot, where his turquoise Jaguar convertible gleamed in the afternoon sunshine.

Standing at the exit door, Ty moved in front of Haley as they started back to the truck. She'd grown used to the slight lump beneath his T-shirt where a pistol rode at his waist. She paused as he opened the passenger door and helped her inside the truck.

"I guess we'll know something today," she said.

Ty made another survey of their surroundings, searching for any sign of trouble. His gaze ran over the parking lot, moved up and over the rooftops surrounding them.

"Can't be soon enough for me."

"Shouldn't we have heard something by now?"

Ty glanced over to where Haley sat working in his office at the extra computer. The afternoon was slipping away and still no word from Jonathan Hammond. She turned as Ty walked up behind her.

"They've got to be very careful," he said. "They'll need to be a hundred percent sure before they call in the police."

"I suppose."

"You realize what this could mean?" he said. "If those paintings are forgeries, it's big news—over a hundred million dollars big. It'll hit the media like a bombshell, and the police'll have no choice but to jump on it."

Her eyes widened. "That's good for us, right? We won't be a threat to the thieves anymore because the cops will be taking over the investigation. There'll be no reason for the men to kill us."

"Exactly." He leaned down and kissed her. "Let's just hope and pray they've already made the exchange, because if they haven't, the bad guys will be after us with both barrels. They'll have to shut us up before they can steal the paintings."

"They won't be able to do it right away. They'll have to wait until things cool down."

"That's right. And all the time, we'll be in the crosshairs of their gun sights."

She turned back to the computer. "Take a look at this website. It shows how you can tell if a painting is authentic. I knew some of it already, but this goes into detail."

He leaned closer, scanned the first paragraph, began to read, "'*Craquelure.* In older paintings, cracks will appear in the canvas. In oil paintings, this starts to happen after sixty to a hundred years. All authentic cracks run parallel to the inside of the wooden frame. Cracks appearing directly over the wooden frame have most likely been created artificially.'"

"Another thing is the pigment," Haley said. "The old paint colors were ground by hand. The lumps in the color were bigger. The smaller the grains of pigment, the newer the painting."

"Says here, you can also test the varnish."

"That's right. Forgers spray a dark colored liquid over the surface to make it look old, but it's easy to remove and the paint underneath is too bright to be that old." She looked up at him. "I wonder how long it's going to take them to do the tests."

Ty checked the time on the computer. "It's almost five. The gallery will be closing soon."

"I was hoping we'd know something today."

He pulled her up from her chair and into his arms, bent his head and kissed her. "Maybe I can find a way to distract you."

In silent agreement, Haley wound her arms around

his neck and leaned into him. His body was beginning to heat when his cell phone started to fiddle. With a soft oath, he dragged the phone out of his pocket and checked the caller ID.

"It's Sol," he said, then pressed the phone against his ear. "Tell me you found the password."

"Norman Rockwell."

"You're kidding."

Sol chuckled. "*N Rockwell One* to be exact. I sent you an email with the list. Hope it helps."

"You rule, buddy. I owe you, big-time."

"I'd say we're even. Take care, my brother." Sol hung up the phone.

Ty strode over to his computer and booted it up, went into his mail and found the attachment from Sol. He opened it to find a list of two hundred names in alphabetical order, each with a phone number beside it.

"Danoff had a ton of clients," Ty said.

"He must have been good at his job," said Haley.

Reaching for the paper on his desk with the names that had been scribbled on Jimmy Warren's iPad, he looked down at the names. Something that might be Tamara or Tenada, Carlson and Silverman. He compared them to the list on the screen.

"There's a Carlson," Haley said excitedly.

"Stephen Carlson. Silverman's first name is Nathan." His pulse was beginning to ratchet up, but there was no one on the list named Tamara or Tenada.

"Tanaka," Haley said excitedly, pointing a finger at the screen. "That must be it."

Ty grabbed the paper with the partial phone numbers he'd gotten from Ian Whitlow at the lab. "There— 63-7764 matches the last six digits of the number next to Aguri Tanaka."

"And 12-4356 is a partial match to Silverman." She looked up at him. "Oh, my God, I knew it! Three names—all three Danoff's clients. Three paintings at the Fizer. Dad figured out who bought them. That's the reason they killed him."

"Hold on. We don't know for sure those pieces have been stolen. Could be the men were part of the original heist."

Haley shook her head. "Timing isn't right. After Ray Farrell told Dad about the second burglary, he would have focused his efforts there. Add to that, Abigail's three forgeries. It's them. I know it."

Ty grabbed her hand and drew her down on his lap. "I recognize one of the names. Aguri Tanaka owns Kobashi. It's one of the biggest electronics companies in the world. The guy is worth billions."

"Enough to buy a priceless painting."

They typed his name into Google, found out Tanaka lived in Kamakura, Japan, a small city by the sea near Tokyo. But he also maintained a residence in San Francisco.

"San Francisco," Haley said. "That's his connection to Danoff."

"Yeah. So let's find out who these other guys are." Returning to Google, he typed in Nathan Silverman.

"Look at that." Haley tapped the screen. "I knew that name sounded familiar. Nathan Silverman is like Spielberg. He's one of the biggest producers in Hollywood. Movies, TV. The guy's into everything."

"Not that unusual a name. There are a bunch of them listed. Could be a different guy." He clicked on the names that popped up, but didn't recognize any of them, and none had the internet presence the famous producer had, with page after page of links.

"Silverman lives in Hollywood," Haley said. "The Fizer is here in L.A. That puts him in the right area, and Silverman's movies make a fortune. He'd be able to afford a multimillion-dollar painting."

Ty pounded the keyboard, typing in the third name on her father's list. Stephen Carlson. A dozen links to the name popped up, but like Silverman, none had the massive web presence that Stephen Carlson, owner of Carlson Breeding Farms, had on the internet.

"Carlson raises Thoroughbreds in Malibu," Ty said. "Some of the property's right on the ocean. That land costs a fortune."

"He's quite the socialite." Haley squirmed a little on his lap, sending his blood pumping south. *Not now, dumb-ass.*

"Here's a photo of him and a woman at the Beverly Hilton Hotel," she said. "A fund-raiser for breast cancer."

"Who's the woman?"

"It doesn't say, but she's stunning." Tall, elegantly slender, with long black hair, an exotic face and jet-black eyes. She could have been a model for any fashion magazine.

"She's in a couple of other shots," Ty said. "Maybe she's his girlfriend."

"She's not his wife. The article says he's divorced."

Ty lifted her off his lap and stood up. Haley grinned at the bulge in the front of his jeans, and Ty's mouth edged up.

"Okay—so? I'm a man, and you've got the sexiest little ass I've ever seen." Fleeting thoughts of his sofa fantasy tickled the back of his mind and he wished he was in the living room of his condo. Still, the mat was comfortable and no one was home.

He bent his head and kissed her. "How about that distraction? Seems like we've earned it."

Haley went up on her toes and deepened the kiss. Heat poured through him, and he went harder than he was already. Unfortunately, it was a workday and his cell phone started up again. He sighed, checked caller ID, but didn't recognize the number.

He pressed the phone against his ear. "Brodie."

"It's Jonathan. You might want to turn on the news."

He motioned for Haley to turn on the TV in the corner above the treadmill. "What is it?"

"The Rembrandt was a forgery. So were the Renoir and the Van Gogh. Stilton went crazy. He called the police, and the media got wind of it. Stilton gave them your name, told them you and Haley brought the theft of the paintings to his attention. The media is going to be hounding you both for a story."

"That's actually good news."

"Is it? Oh, I see. Once the police are involved, you're out of it. You're no longer a danger to the men who committed the robbery."

"That's the theory. We'll give everything we've got to the police. Once we're out of it, they've got no reason to kill us. Thanks for everything, Jonathan. Oh, and by the way, Ellie is a great lady. You're a very lucky man."

"And don't I know it. I'll see you at the wedding."

By the time Ty hung up, Haley had the TV tuned to KTLA and was watching Breaking News about the just-discovered theft of priceless paintings from the Fizer Foundation.

Police Chief Edward Tisdale, a tall, slender man with close-cropped silver hair, was ending a press conference from the steps of the LAPD Administration building downtown. Cameras were rolling and reporters were everywhere. There was even a news chopper circling above the crowd.

Tisdale adjusted the microphone on the podium in front of him. "As I said, we've only begun our investigation. But rest assured the Los Angeles Police Department will be doing everything in its power to find the criminals responsible for the theft of these valuable paintings and return them to their rightful owner, the Fizer Foundation. Thank you for your time."

Chief Tisdale stepped down and the reporters began to disperse. The cameras returned to the studio and switched to the story of a murder in La Brea.

Haley turned off the TV. "Well, at least we know we were right."

"That's something."

"What about the list of buyers? Do we give it to the police?"

"If we do, they'll want to know how we got it. Best just to give them the three names off your dad's iPad and tell them he was working on a connection between them and Peter Danoff. We tell them our suspicions, let them take it from there. Cogan knows a lot of this already. We tell them everything we know—we just don't say how we found out."

"What about Abigail?"

Ty raked a hand through his hair. "She needs a good attorney. Ellie might know someone who'll take the case pro bono, try to get her a deal."

"I hope so."

Just then someone knocked on the office door. Ty walked over to open it, found Kurt Stryker's hulking frame filling the stoop on the other side.

"The phones are ringing off the hook. The cops are

coming up the driveway, and there's a bunch of TV vans outside the gate. What do you want to do?"

Before he could answer, Ty's cell started fiddling and Haley's started ringing.

Ty just grinned. "Looks like it's showtime." He settled a hand at Haley's waist. "Come on, darlin', time for your debut."

It was dark outside. Maria would be waiting for him in bed. Sitting at the desk in his wood-paneled study, Stephen watched the TV screen, his anger building with every second.

On the ten o'clock news, the Chief of Police was holding another press conference. This time, Tyler Brodie and the Warren girl were in front of the cameras. Brodie was talking to the media about the theft of the paintings at the Fizer, telling them how it all began with his investigation into the death of James Warren, how that investigation had led him to the unsolved robbery, three years ago, of a priceless Titian and Caravaggio from the Scarsdale Center.

Further clues, Brodie explained, pointed to a similar theft at the Fizer Foundation. This time the thieves had stolen a Rembrandt, a Renoir and a Van Gogh.

"Mr. Oliver Stilton," Brodie said, "Director of the Foundation, verified that the originals had been replaced with forgeries."

The interview was being conducted in front of the Los Angeles Police Station, where cameras rolled in a media frenzy, covering what had become a major news event.

A bald man thrust a microphone toward the podium. "Will you be continuing the investigation, Mr. Brodie?"

"Ms. Warren and I have turned all the evidence

we've accumulated over to the police. We believe they'll pursue the matter diligently and efficiently and bring the thieves to justice."

A good-looking brunette reporter pushed the bald man aside. "Did your investigation turn up any suspects, Ty?"

Brodie smiled. "Sorry, Heather, I'm afraid I'm not at liberty to say. I will say we believe we've given the police some very solid leads in the case."

A reporter Stephen recognized from Channel 5 News spoke to the Warren girl. "You began your investigation to find out what happened to your father. Do you believe the men who stole these valuable paintings were responsible for the death of James Warren?"

"Yes, I do." She was blond, younger and prettier than he would have guessed. "There are a number of factors that indicate the powerboat explosion that killed my father was intentional. My father was well on his way to finding the men who stole those paintings— both the two from the Scarsdale and the three from the Fizer. The police now have that information. I'm certain they'll be able to bring the case to a close."

A detective named Cogan who had introduced Brodie and the girl at the beginning of the press conference, brought the interview to an end. "That's all for now, ladies and gentlemen. We'll keep you posted as the investigation continues." He moved in front of the cameras, giving Brodie and the Warren girl a chance to escape the sea of reporters. "Thank you for your time."

Stephen's hand tightened around the remote until the keypad dug into his palm. Clicking off the TV, he hurled the remote across the room, smashing it against the wall. Reaching into the bottom drawer of his desk, he took out the disposable phone he used for personal matters and punched in a number he knew by heart.

"What progress have you made?"

"I've seen the news. I've been expecting your call."

If Quentin Sloan had figured the connection between the burglary and the job he'd been hired to do, he had too much information.

"You want to call it off?" Sloan asked in his deep, slightly raspy voice.

He should, Stephen knew. Brodie and the girl no longer posed a threat. The police were taking over the investigation. Brodie had given them whatever information he had uncovered.

Stephen smiled darkly. He wasn't worried about the cops. Even if Brodie had somehow stumbled across his name during the investigation, there was no way to link him to the burglary and no way for them to find the painting he had kept for himself.

"Yes or no?" Sloan pressed.

Stephen thought of the trouble the pair had caused, how much time and money this could wind up costing him if he had to involve attorneys and answer questions. He thought of the other buyers and how unhappy they would be.

Not that they posed any danger to him, either.

The only connection they had with the paintings was through Danoff, and Danoff was dead.

No, it wasn't about the danger. It was about winning. He wasn't a man who allowed himself to be beaten. Brodie and the girl had interfered and now they would pay the price.

"Finish it," Stephen said, and hung up the phone.

Thirty

~~~~~~~~~

Iridescent clouds floated over an azure sky. A soft breeze rolled in off the ocean, leaving the air crystal clear, the mountains surrounding the valley visible in the distance.

Haley sat next to Ty in the front seat of Ellie's Mercedes, the engine purring as they rolled effortlessly along the road. Her aunt had already left with Jonathan in his sexy turquoise Jaguar.

Until this morning, Haley hadn't known Rachael's wedding was supposed to have been held around the swimming pool on the manicured grounds of Ellie's house. After the shooting, those plans had changed.

Now, at her aunt's insistence, the small affair was being held in an intimate garden at the posh Beverly Hills Hotel. Aunt Ellie had made all the arrangements and would be picking up the tab. Which, with only fifty guests, would be expensive, but not completely outrageous.

Ellie had adopted Ty and Johnnie, Amy, Rachael and Rick Vega, as part of her extended family. She could afford to give Rachael the wedding of her dreams, and she was doing exactly that.

Ty pulled the Mercedes up the winding drive of the hotel. Cocooned in tropical foliage, the wide leaves of banana plants waving in the breeze, the sprawling pink structure frequented by the rich and famous had been an L.A. landmark since 1912. Haley had seen photos but wasn't prepared for the old-fashioned elegance that seemed rooted in the very walls of the building.

Ty stepped on the brakes at the front entrance, and a white-coated valet pulled open Haley's door.

"Welcome to the Beverly Hills Hotel," he said with a smile.

"Thank you." She took a steadying breath as the young man helped her out of the car and ushered her around to where her handsome escort waited. She looked up at Ty and managed to put a curve in her lips. She hadn't wanted to come to the wedding. It only reminded her of her feelings for Ty and the life she would never have.

She tried not to think how little time they had left together. The investigation was in the hands of the police. She and Ty had done their best, given them the evidence she hoped would lead them to the men responsible for her father's murder.

It was time she went back home.

"You're supposed to be happy," Ty said as he guided her along the carpeted, covered walkway into the lavish yet understated lobby beneath a circular lighted ceiling. "I guess you don't like weddings." His eyes remained on hers.

"I'm happy for Rachael. I just... I hope it works out for them."

Ty didn't say more, but his shoulders tightened. She

had told him she didn't believe in marriage. Didn't believe in happy endings.

And yet as she looked at him in his dark blue suit and crisp white shirt, the French cuffs and elegant gold cuff links he wore with an ease she hadn't expected, a sharp pang cut through her. Just standing beside him made her chest ache.

He spotted the signs for the Brewer-Vega wedding, and they began to follow them out to the area in the lush gardens where the ceremony and reception would be held. She wouldn't allow herself to think what it might feel like to be the bride if Ty were the groom.

When he took her arm and wove it through his, when he looked at her the way he was now, it made her long to share a life with him. It would never work, she knew. It never did.

"I haven't told you how beautiful you are," he said, his hazel gaze running over her as he walked beside her down one of the cement paths that wove through the garden.

She smoothed the front of her pink, tea-length dress, the soft chiffon floating over her hips and fluttering around her knees. The matching pink high heels clicked with every step. The wide brim of a white straw hat decorated with pink silk flowers dipped in front of one eye.

"Thank you." Haley smiled up at him. "You look pretty amazing yourself."

He grinned. "You like it?" He flashed his cuffs. "It's the cuff links. Women love 'em."

She laughed, swatted him with her clutch bag, even though it was true. She had seen him mostly in jeans and T-shirts. In his suit and tie, he looked incredible.

They turned a corner, spotted the intimate group gathered for the ceremony being held beneath a white lattice arch entwined with pink roses. Rows of white chairs in two sections formed an aisle in between. At the opposite end of the garden beneath a green-and-white-striped canopy, a lacy, tiered wedding cake with real pink roses sat next to buckets of chilled champagne.

Walking next to Ty, Haley's steps slowed in surprise as she spotted Lane Bishop heading toward her, gorgeous in an ivory suit with a short, slim skirt, and gold, open-toed heels. Her bright auburn hair curled softly around her shoulders, and a big smile lit her face.

Haley leaned over and hugged her. "I didn't know you were going to be here. I'm so glad you came."

"Your aunt called. She asked me to come. She said you wouldn't know that many people and she wanted me to meet Rachael and Rick."

Haley laughed. "I think she plans to adopt you into her extended family. It keeps growing every year."

"Your aunt is great. She's inside with the bride and Rachael's mom. She introduced me to Jonathan, I gather he helped you at the Fizer?"

Ty grinned. "He had old Ollie Stilton jumping through hoops. Without his help, uncovering the theft would have taken a helluva lot longer."

"So you think the danger is over?"

"The way the robbery headlined the news, the bad guys know we've turned everything over to the cops. There's no reason for them to come after us."

"And just when the fun was starting," Dylan drawled as he strode toward them, tall, lean and ruggedly handsome. His amazing blue eyes went straight to Lane.

She spotted him and unconsciously took a step backward. "I didn't…didn't realize you'd be here," Lane said to him.

"Haley's aunt invited me. I guess she figures I'm part of the family being Ty's cousin."

Ty chuckled and Haley grinned. Lane cast her a beseeching glance that made Haley's grin widen until her dimples popped out. Her friend might not believe it, but Haley had no doubt Lane could handle Ty's dangerously attractive cousin—who no longer looked like a twenty-first-century Paul Bunyan, but was as well dressed as Ty.

The organ music began to play, indicating it was time for them to take their seats.

Ty escorted her along one of the rows and they sat down on the aisle. Dylan walked Lane to seats next to theirs, while Aunt Ellie sat in the front row next to Jonathan. Rick's parents took a front row seat and a few minutes later, an usher escorted Rachael's mother down the aisle to a seat in the front row next to Aunt Ellie.

As the time approached for the arrival of the bride, Haley's nerves began to build. What was it about weddings that made her happy and sad at the same time?

Johnnie Riggs, Rick's best man, walked out with Rick, and they took their places on one side of the rose-covered arch. In their black tuxedos, both men were astonishingly handsome, Johnnie, a dark, powerful force, and Rick, confident and classy, with his high cheekbones and Hispanic good looks.

She slanted a glance at Ty. He was smiling, clearly happy for his friends. The music started. Rachael's sister, Amy, the maid of honor, appeared in a rose silk gown with a slim skirt that ended above her knees and showed off her perfect curves. A circle of pink roses rested on her long straight blond hair, a silky curtain past her shoulders.

Then Rachael appeared at the head of the aisle. She

was so beautiful, Haley's throat tightened. Gowned in white silk overlaid with organdy, her smooth shoulders bare above the strapless bodice, a long slim skirt that worked perfectly with her slender figure, she was every woman's dream of the perfect bride.

Until that moment, Haley hadn't realized that deep in her heart, she carried that same dream. But she had given up on happy endings long ago, afraid to go after what she believed was impossible.

Her eyes misted and her heart began to throb. A tear escaped down her cheek, but she wiped it away before anyone could see. She felt Ty's hand slide into hers as the wedding march began and they all stood up for the bride's entrance.

Carrying a nosegay of pink roses, Rachael walked past them down the aisle on the arm of a man in his fifties.

"Who's that?" Haley whispered to Ty.

"Marvin Bixler. He's the producer of *LAPD Blue*. He's the one who hired Rachael for the show. Rachael's dad died some years back. Bixler's kind of taken his place."

Ty had told her a little about how Rachael and Rick had met, that Rachael had been kidnapped and Detective Vega had helped Johnnie and Amy find her in a search that took them all the way to Belize. Rick had fallen in love with Rachael, who couldn't resist his sexy, Latin charm.

As they reached the arch and Bixler handed the bride over to the man who would soon be her husband, the tightness returned to Haley's chest. Ty's hand squeezed hers as if he understood how hard this was for her.

As much as she wanted to believe in the forever kind of love, no couple she had ever known had truly been happy, not her parents, not any of their friends. Perhaps her father had finally found happiness. She truly hoped that he had.

What she would never tell Ty and she hoped he would never find out was that she had fallen deeply in love with him. She had no idea how deep his feelings were for her, but it didn't really matter. It could never work and surely he knew it.

Still, watching these two people join their lives together made her realize how much she would be losing when she returned to Chicago. The thought made Haley's throat ache. She forced herself to concentrate on the couple repeating their vows, Rick smiling into Rachael's beautiful, veiled face.

"I, Rick, take thee, Rachael to be my wedded wife. To have and to hold from this day forward, for better, for worse, for richer, for poorer, in sickness and in health, to love and to cherish till death do us part."

Rachael trembled as she looked at her handsome husband and repeated those same vows.

The service continued with the exchanging of rings, simple gold bands that seemed to hold some special meaning, and Haley swallowed past the lump in her throat.

A friend of Rachael's sang the Carpenters' "We've Only Just Begun" and there wasn't a dry eye in the audience. Many of the people knew the story of Rachael's abduction, and all of them were happy for her.

The minister smiled, a short, silver-haired man with kind blue eyes. "For as much as you, Rachael, and you, Rick, have consented together in holy wedlock, now, by the power vested in me, I pronounce you man and wife." His smile widened. "You may kiss your bride."

Rick lifted the veil and made a show of it, dipping

Rachael, kissing her deeply and drawing it out. The guys in the audience whooped and cheered, and Ty whistled.

As music played the retreat, they raced, laughing, back down the aisle, and at last Haley found herself smiling. Whatever happened, she hoped these two people would find the happiness they deserved.

Everyone adjourned to the tent for the reception. Champagne corks popped and waiters rushed around with silver trays heavy with long-stemmed flutes filled with the bubby golden liquid. Haley and Lane were chatting, Dylan and Ty beside them, when a group of uniformed policemen raced through the crowd beneath the tent. Haley stiffened, but Ty just laughed.

"It's all right, darlin'. Those guys are part of the cast of *LAPD Blue,* Rachael's TV show."

As the police approached the bride and groom, handcuffs at the ready and big grins on their faces, Ty's gaze shifted to a cop who had separated from the others and was moving fast through the crowd in their direction.

Something flashed in the sunlight.

"Gun!" Stryker's roar came from the roof. Haley screamed as Ty shoved her to the ground and gunfire erupted. Ty jerked his pistol and fired at the same time as Dylan forced Lane down on the grass beneath him and bullets slammed into the ground just inches from their heads.

Pulling off another two rounds, Ty shoved to his feet. "Take care of the women!" he shouted to Dylan as he took off running, moving in a zigzag pattern after the uniformed gunman racing out of the garden.

Guests were screaming, scrambling away in panic. Dylan jerked Lane to her feet, grabbed Haley and urged them toward the hotel's rear entrance, moving them rapidly toward safety. Haley caught a last glimpse of Ty racing into the bushes after the gunman, taking a shortcut through the dense foliage, leaping a hedge as he headed for the parking lot.

A few feet away, Rick Vega had pulled his off-duty pistol from an ankle holster and was shepherding his bride and Amy toward the door. Jonathan hurried Ellie along the path, and Stryker fell in behind them, pistol in hand. Johnnie was nowhere to be seen.

Haley's heart pounded and a loud roaring filled her ears. "Ty," she whispered, her gaze still fixed on the place he had been. Fear for him sent a wave of nausea rolling through her.

"Easy," Dylan said as they reached the back door and he urged them all inside. Security guards streamed past them, headed in the opposite direction. Haley glanced at Lane, whose face was as pale as her own.

"I thought…thought we were safe," Haley said. "What if something happens to him?"

Dylan's jaw hardened. In that moment, he looked exactly like a slightly older version of Ty. "He's a Brodie," he said darkly. "He'll be all right."

They were all inside the hotel when Haley heard Lane gasp, "Oh, my God, Dylan, you've been shot!"

And chaos erupted again.

For several seconds, Ty thought he'd lost him, then he spotted the shooter running across the parking lot. About six feet tall, blond hair now instead of brown, his wig tossed somewhere in the bushes. His dark blue police jacket was gone, but he still wore the uniform pants. He ducked into a brown Chevy Malibu, and the vehicle roared to life. The car screamed toward the exit, and Ty raced for the Mercedes. He jumped inside, fastened his seat belt and fired up the engine.

The wheels spun as he stomped on the gas. The car shot forward and he nearly ran over Johnnie, who raced up to the passenger-side door. Ty slammed on the brakes, Johnnie jumped in and Ty's foot came down hard on the pedal again.

The tires screamed. "Vega and Dylan are with the women," Johnnie said as the car lurched forward. Beretta in hand, he strapped himself into the seat.

Weaving in and out between parked cars, Ty cut a glance toward his friend's big semiautomatic, his own in easy reach on the center console. "I guess none of us were completely convinced it was over."

Johnnie grunted. "Better safe than sorry." He fixed his attention on the Chevy fishtailing out of the lot. It careened into the street and roared off up the road, Ty right behind it.

"Hard right on Hartford!" Johnnie shouted, and Ty spun the wheel in that direction. The Mercedes squealed and slid into the turn, screaming with power as it roared up the two-lane road. He swung around a little silver Prius. The driver leaned on the horn as Ty cut back into the right lane in front of him.

He took a couple of turns, followed the Chevy onto Cove, then floored it on a straightaway, trying to catch up. The shooter fired two quick pops out the window, Ty braked and swerved, avoiding the hit, then the shooter bore down hard on the accelerator and Ty gunned the powerful engine.

The Mercedes was faster, better on the curves, but the shooter had the route planned out, and as they shot around another corner, Ty was beginning to think there was more under the hood of the Chevy than a V-6 engine.

On a sharp curve, Johnnie leaned out the window, fired a shot at the vehicle that shattered the rear window. A return shot took out the front window of the Mercedes. Johnnie hunkered down, Ty ducked and they roared off again in hot pursuit.

"He's got to be headed for Mulholland Drive." Ty slid the car around another curve.

"There's a dozen ways to get there, and you'd better believe he's figured every one."

They blew through a stop sign. Horns blasted from two different directions. Ty swung the car around a corner and took a hard left, then made a sharp right onto Summit Ridge. One minute the Chevy was there, just ahead of them. Two more curves, and the vehicle was gone.

"Jesus! You see him?" Ty slowed the Mercedes, scanning the streets and houses on the hillsides.

"We must have missed a turn," Johnnie said. "Goddammit."

Ty slowed the car a little more, his palms damp on the wheel, his adrenaline pumping. "If we go back, try to retrace our steps, we'll lose him for sure."

"Head for Mulholland. Best way for him to disappear. Maybe we'll get lucky."

But when they pulled onto Mulholland Drive, the traffic was light and there was no sign of the shooter.

"The guy was a real pro," Johnnie said. Blowing out a breath, he leaned back in his seat. "If it hadn't been for Stryker, he'd have made at least one clean shot."

Ty's jaw hardened. "Yeah. I wasn't sure about Stryker until today. I guess I owe him one."

Johnnie scanned the area one last time. "Let's head back. Maybe the cops'll find something at the scene."

"Maybe." But Ty didn't think the shooter was the

amateur who had taken potshots at Haley off the hill. More likely that was the Bellamy brothers, and both of them were dead. This guy had done his homework. He had known about the wedding, known the time and place. Known the actors from *LAPD Blue* were planning to fake a raid.

A guy like that wasn't going to leave a clue.

Thirty-One

❧❧❧

Lane could hear sirens screaming in the distance. Dylan's protest that the wound was only a scratch didn't convince the hotel manager, who insisted it was policy to make certain a guest injured on the property was properly cared for, and immediately called an ambulance.

Lane sat next to Dylan in a comfortable room off the lobby while he waited for the EMTs. He had removed his black sport coat and blood-covered light blue dress shirt, and sat with a bandage pressed against the crease the bullet had made across his ribs.

Lane worked to keep her gaze from straying to the hard muscles in his shoulders, the bands of muscle beneath the patch of curly dark hair on his chest, the thick biceps that clearly came from hard work.

"I'll let them clean me up and put on a bandage," he grumbled, "but I'm not going to the hospital."

"You've been shot," she said. "You need to be sure you're okay."

"I've had worse scrapes cutting wood."

Lane blew out a frustrated breath. "Typical male."

Dylan just smiled. "I'm glad you noticed."

She'd noticed far more than his masculinity. She'd noticed he had risked his life protecting her. No one had ever done anything like that for her before. Not even Jason.

Lane refused to let Dylan know how it had touched her. Instead she lifted her chin. "You wouldn't have been shot if you hadn't been playing hero."

The corner of his hard mouth edged up. "Where I come from, honey, it's a man's job to protect a woman."

Ignoring the endearment, Lane glanced away. "Things are different here."

He grunted. "They shouldn't be."

Her eyes returned to his, caught and held. For a moment, she couldn't look away. "Thank you," she said softly.

Dylan's gaze sharpened. "You want to thank me? Help me remodel my fishing lodge."

"What? You want to talk about that *now?*"

"I checked you out. You're damned good at what you do. When I hire someone, I want the best."

"I told you, it's too far away. I have responsibilities here. I wouldn't be able to—"

"Think about it. That's all I ask."

She wouldn't. She didn't dare. Where this man was concerned, she was too susceptible. And yet she owed him for saving her from a bullet. Perhaps saving her life.

The door of the room burst open and the EMTs rushed in, pushing a stretcher in front of them. Haley hurried in behind them.

"Is Dylan going to be okay?" she asked Lane worriedly.

"It's really not that bad," Dylan said. "No broken ribs. Bullet just nicked my side."

"Maybe so," Lane argued, "but if it'd been over a few inches more, it could have hit your heart. You might have been—" Her voice cracked. She couldn't bear to think what might have happened.

Haley hugged her. "I'm so sorry." Lane caught a flash of tears in her friend's blue eyes. "If I hadn't come to L.A. in the first place, none of this would have happened."

"You thought it was over," Lane said. "You aren't investigating the case anymore. It should have been." She glanced behind Haley, looking for Ty. "Ty isn't back yet?"

Haley shook her head, her features lined with worry. "Not yet."

"Ty knows how to handle himself," Dylan said. "Johnnie's with him. He'll be okay."

But Haley was frightened for him just the same. Lane sighed with relief when a few minutes later, Ty walked through the door. Haley gave a soft little sob, flew across the room and into his arms. She held on to him as if she'd never let him go.

Lane's heart squeezed. Her friend was clearly in love. Lane understood better than most the pain of losing someone you loved.

"Did you catch him?" Haley asked.

Ty reached out and wiped a tear from her cheek. His eyes were dark, his features hard. He shook his head. "The guy was a pro. He had his escape route completely planned, all his ducks in a row. He didn't count on Stryker, or some of us being armed. At that, he damned near got the job done." For the first time he noticed the bloody bandage on Dylan's side.

Ty frowned. "You're hit? How bad is it?"

"Just a scratch. Not enough to warrant a hospital visit." The EMTs were cleaning the wound and asking him questions. Dylan started arguing and shaking his head.

Ty pulled Haley a little ways away, but didn't leave her side. He looked different, harder, Lane thought, nothing like the smiling man who had escorted Haley to the wedding.

"We ruined Rachael's day," Haley said, swiping at another stray tear.

"I talked to Rick. Everyone's safe, and Rachael's handling it okay. She says it's a wedding no one will ever forget. Rick offered to stay in town, but he's a husband now, and he has a wife who needs him. He and Rachael are off to the airport. They're catching a plane to Paris tonight. They won't be back for three weeks."

Haley shook her head. "I thought this was over. I thought we were safe."

A muscle ticked in Ty's cheek. He looked at her hard. "From now on, you're with me. Understand? And that means 24/7."

"But—"

"It's nonnegotiable." He turned to Dylan. "You'll be okay?"

"I told you—it's nothing."

Ty flashed a dark look at Lane. "Take care of him."

She opened her mouth to argue, tell him Dylan Brodie wasn't her problem, but he was already guiding Haley out of the room. When Lane looked back at Dylan, he was pretending to listen to what the EMTs were saying, but she didn't trust him—not for a minute.

Not when those hard blue, sexy eyes swung in her direction. *Take care of me,* they said, *and I promise I'll take care of you.*

The dark mood was on him. Ty took a deep breath and worked to control the tension humming through him. Keeping a hand at Haley's waist, he went in search of Ellie, rounded a corner and spotted her. Head held high, silver hair perfectly groomed, she walked purposely in their direction, Jonathan at her side.

"Your car's a mess," Ty said. "Shooter took out the front window."

Ellie's chin firmed. "I hope you gave him what-for."

"We did our best. Johnnie got off a couple of rounds. Unfortunately the bastard got away. I'm sorry about the car."

"Don't be silly. It's just a piece of metal. Your lives are what's important."

A fresh wave of anger washed through him. "We need to get out of here before the cops track us down and insist on statements. Haley's with me from now till this is over."

"I thought that's what you'd say." Ellie pressed a key into his hand, along with a scrap of paper with numbers written on it. "Jonathan has a second home, a place where you'll be safe."

Ty looked down at the paper, saw an address on Pacific Coast Highway.

"It's on Latigo Shore Drive," Jonathan told him. "On the ocean side of the road. The house is fully stocked. Everything's clean. The housekeeper was just there so she won't be back for two weeks. There's WiFi and a computer. You won't be out of touch. I keep a car in the garage for guests. Take a cab to the house, then use the car. It'll be safer that way."

Ty's fingers tightened into a fist around the keys. He nodded, couldn't think exactly what to say. "Thank you."

He turned back at Ellie, fought to control his temper. It wasn't time yet to analyze, try to figure where he had gone wrong. "I'll keep Haley safe. I promise you."

"I know you will."

"We'll be in touch." Ty slipped an arm around Haley's shoulders and led her down the corridor. He met Stryker along the way.

"Ellie told me you were going to be up there," Ty said. "I'm damned glad you were."

Stryker tugged on the silver hoop in his ear. "Just doing my job."

"Keep doing it. Make sure there aren't any problems at Ellie's house."

"You got it."

At the front door of the hotel, Ty paused to look around, make sure the shooter wasn't somewhere outside, waiting to finish the job.

In the taxi zone, a line of yellow cabs sat empty, ready to take hotel guests to the airport. As he started in that direction, Johnnie came up beside him, shoved a cell phone into his hand.

"It's a throwaway. I keep it in the car for emergencies."

Ty didn't have to ask what those emergencies were. There were times it was important to stay off the grid. He took out his iPhone, disabled it and turned to Haley.

"Give me your cell. It's got GPS. We don't want them tracking us." He disabled her phone and handed it back.

"I'll follow the cab a ways," Johnnie said, "make sure you aren't tailed."

"Thanks."

"I'll be all over this," Johnnie promised. "We need to stay in touch. Work things out."

"I'll let you know when we get settled in."

Johnnie nodded. "Take care, partner." He slapped Ty on the shoulder, reached over and squeezed Haley's hand. "Do what he tells you."

Haley just nodded. Which told Ty exactly how scared she was.

The dark mood surged inside him. Who still wanted them dead? What the hell was the motive?

He loosened his tie and unbuttoned the top few buttons on his white shirt, then helped Haley into the back of a yellow cab, climbed in behind her and told the driver to take them the long way to the Beverly Hilton. Through the rear window, he caught an occasional glimpse of Johnnie's black Mustang, weaving in and out of traffic, making sure they weren't being followed.

At the Beverly Hilton, they went inside, exited out another door and got into another taxi. This one took them down Santa Monica to Pacific Coast Highway. There was a lot of beach traffic. Ty gave the driver an extra twenty bucks to get them to Latigo Shore Drive as fast as possible. Cutting in and out of traffic made them even harder to follow.

They got out two blocks from the house and walked to the address Ellie had written on the note, Ty's jaw tight as he noticed a spot of Dylan's blood on Haley's pink high heels.

"Do you think we'll be safe here?" she asked as he shoved the key into the lock on the front door.

"We weren't tailed. Not many people even know Ellie's seeing Jonathan, let alone that he has a second home or that we're in it. We're safe for now."

"We can't stay hidden forever. What are we going to do?"

His eyes narrowed as he glanced back toward the city. "Find the bastards trying to kill us. That's what we're going to do."

Thirty-Two

⦿━━∽⧼⧽∽━━⦿

The house wasn't as large as some of the mansions in the neighborhood, but it fronted the water, and when Haley walked inside, she could see a spectacular view of the ocean from the opposite side of the living room. The interior was charming, decorated in light woods and pastel colors, with hooked rugs over golden hardwood floors, a modern fireplace built into one wall.

Haley followed Ty as he made an inspection of the house, the compact galley kitchen and laundry room, two guest bedrooms, each with its own bath, a master bedroom and bath and a small study at the end of the hall.

Since Jonathan's personal items were in the master, Ty led her into one of the guest rooms. "We'll take this one. It's got a sliding-glass door onto the deck. Gives us two ways out."

Haley felt a shiver. "I don't have anything with me. No clothes, nothing."

"We've got wheels. There's shopping nearby. Tomorrow we'll pick up whatever we need."

"I wish I had a gun." She didn't know where that came from. She had never shot a gun in her life.

Ty caught her shoulders, his eyes dark and stormy. "You don't need a weapon. I've got my Beretta and a couple of extra clips. I won't let him hurt you, baby. Do you believe me?"

The tension between her shoulders eased. There wasn't a doubt in her mind that Ty would keep her safe. "I believe you."

His gaze fixed on her mouth and for a moment, she thought he was going to kiss her. Instead, he turned away and headed for the study, his long strides carrying him off down the hall.

With every step he took, she felt his turbulent mood, knew their brush with death and his failed pursuit had put him in the dark place he had been before. She wished she knew what to do to bring him back into the light, but she didn't think he was ready for that, and in a way she wasn't, either.

"What are you doing?" she asked as he stripped off his navy suit coat and the tie hanging loose around his neck, slung them over the back of a chair.

"What I hope the police have been doing—looking at the security company that handled the Scarsdale Center. Then cross-checking, looking for any connection to the company who's currently in charge of the Fizer Foundation."

Rolling up the sleeves of his dress shirt, he sat down at the desk and turned on the computer, typed *museum security* and *Scarsdale* into the search engine. Haley watched as half a dozen links popped up.

"Here it is," Ty said. "Hi-Tech Security. It's in an old newspaper article written after the Titian and Caravaggio went missing. Someone interviewed the president of the company."

She smiled. "God, I love Google."

Ty skimmed the article, but apparently found nothing of interest, went back and typed in *museum security* and *Fizer*.

With the robbery so recent and such big news, dozens of articles with a Fizer link popped up. Ty scrolled down, looking for something that mentioned security. Finally found the name Sentry Security Service and popped up the website with the SSS logo.

"That was fairly easy," Haley said.

"Yeah. But what we need is a list of employees for both companies. The Hi-Tech list needs to go back at least three years. By now some of the people will have quit, some will have gone to work somewhere else. The cops might have the info, but they aren't going to want to share."

"You're looking for someone who worked for Hi-Tech at the time of the first robbery, then moved to Sentry before the second."

"That's the idea, but it won't be just one. It would take several people on the inside to pull off sophisticated heists like these."

"I'm surprised my father wasn't investigating that angle."

"He might have gotten there after the second burglary if he'd had more time."

If only he had. Haley ignored a wave of sadness at the time with him she had missed. "So how do we get the names?"

"I've got a friend in the department. Might be able to get hold of them that way."

"What about—"

"Sol Greenway," Ty and Haley both said at the same time. "Worth a try."

Ty pulled the disposable phone out of his pocket and started punching in numbers. He told Sol about the shooting, told him where they stood in the investigation and gave him the names of the security firms that handled the museums.

"We don't know the exact date of the burglaries," Ty said, "just the dates the thefts were discovered. We need something that links the two companies. There had to be someone on the inside, more than one person, and I'm thinking they could be the same people, moved from one place to another."

Haley couldn't hear what Sol said, but Ty was nodding. "Thanks, buddy." He hung up the phone. "Sol isn't sure what he can find. He's going to give it a try, but it's gonna take some time."

"How long?"

He raked a hand through his hair, shoving a few of the heavy dark strands back from his forehead. "Too long." He blew out a breath. "A day or two maybe." He walked over and began to pace in front of the window in the study. "Even then, he might not be able to get what we need."

He stopped in front of the window, stood staring out at the ocean that stretched to the horizon.

"We're going to catch them, Ty. We're getting closer all the time."

He just kept staring, his jaw a hard line. "I made a mistake today. That mistake could have cost us our lives. I missed something. I just don't know what it is."

Haley walked up to him. When he turned, she slid her arms around his neck.

Ty caught her wrists. "Don't," he said. "Not now."

He let her go and she stepped away from him. He thought it was his fault, but there was no way he could have guessed what would happen. She wished there was something she could do to make him feel better.

She studied the hard lines of his face. Sex had helped before, and they hadn't been together in days.

Haley glanced around the study, her gaze coming to rest on the comfortable-looking, overstuffed sofa. An idea slipped into her head. She walked over to where he stood at the window, reached behind her and unzipped her pink chiffon dress, let it fall in a pool at her feet.

Ty's eyes darkened, turned a scorching brown. "What do you think you're doing?"

"Remember that fantasy I owe you? The one that involves your sofa? This isn't your house, but there's a sofa right over—"

He grabbed her, hauled her hard against him. "You know how I am when I'm like this. You don't want to do this, Haley."

She felt a moment of unease. "You wouldn't…you wouldn't hurt me, would you?"

For an instant, his hard look softened, the first crack in his armor. "I'd never hurt you, honey."

She unfastened her lacy pink bra, let it join the dress at her feet. "We made a deal. I don't welch on a deal."

His dark gaze followed her to the sofa. Turning, she faced him in nothing but her pink thong and pink high heels. "Tell me your fantasy."

"Jesus, Haley."

"Okay, maybe I can guess." She studied the overstuffed sofa, tried to imagine what would really turn him on. "Let's see…you sit on the couch and I get on my knees on the floor in front of you, and—"

"No, but that does sound tempting." He strode toward her. The dark mood was still there, but it was flickering, growing lighter.

"You want to guess again?" he asked.

"Let's see…you've already spanked me. And handcuffs don't appeal to you."

His mouth started to curve. "Why don't I just show you?" Ty hauled her into his arms and started kissing her. It wasn't the slow, seductive kiss he was so good at. It was a hard, taking kiss, deep, wet and erotic. Her nipples peaked and her womb melted. In an instant, her body was weeping for him and she was moaning.

He cupped a breast, bent and took the fullness into his mouth. Her knees were trembling, her mind spinning with erotic thoughts, when he turned around and bent her over the arm of the sofa. She heard the buzz of his zipper, felt his hand moving her thong aside, felt his hardness the instant before he slid himself deep inside.

Haley gasped at the hot, thick feel of him, the dense burst of pleasure. Arching her back, she took him even deeper, heard him groan. Ty gripped her hips and started to move, drove deeply, slid out and then in, took her and took her.

It was fierce, hot sex, and it was delicious. She started coming and couldn't seem to stop. Came again before Ty reached his own release.

He was breathing hard when he eased her up and turned her into his arms. Ty kissed her softly, nuzzled the side of her neck. "You make me crazy," he said.

Completely relaxed for the first time that day, Haley smiled up at him. "Feeling better?"

Ty smiled back. "A lot better." He stared at the sofa with an odd look of regret. "I guess your debt is paid."

Haley laughed. *I love you, Ty Brodie,* she almost blurted out. Instead, she sobered, managed to fix a smile in place. "We'll have to make another bet, okay?"

Ty grinned. "Good idea. Give me a little time I'm sure I can think of something."

But time was slipping away. Every clue they discovered brought them closer to the day she'd be going back to Chicago.

Haley's smile faded. She loved him and she was going to lose him. But there wasn't time to think of that now. They needed to focus on finding a killer.

Before the killer found them.

Thanks to Haley, Ty's dark mood had lifted. She had a way of reading him, knowing just how far to push, how to tempt him back from the edge. He smiled at the memory even as he paced restlessly on the deck outside the living room.

The afternoon was gone, the sun sitting low on the horizon. Below him, at the bottom of the cliffs, waves rushed toward shore, the violent crash and roll doing nothing to soothe his frustration.

Wearing one of Jonathan's T-shirts, Haley sat in a deck chair, sketching on a yellow pad she had found in the study. She paused, set the pad on the table next to her chair. "You know, I've been thinking…"

He arched a sardonic brow. "That so?" Seemed like that was all they'd been doing for days, but so far it wasn't enough.

"If the man at the top knows we've stopped our investigation—which, with all the media coverage, he must—there has to be another reason he wants us dead. What other motives are there for murder?"

Ty turned away from the view of the sea and walked over to the table next to where she sat. "Greed's high on the list. But he's already sold the paintings, presumably gotten his money."

"Fear—but he has to know we're no longer a threat."

"Power," Ty said, beginning to follow her train of thought. "If we'd been killed, it would have given him a sense of control, proved how much power he has."

"Yes, I like that. What about revenge? He would have paid us back for all the trouble we've caused him."

"Power and revenge." Ty picked up the yellow pad Haley had been doodling on and looked down at the picture. "Not bad," he said, distracted by the sketch of a bride and groom that closely resembled Rachael and Rick. "I didn't know you were an artist."

"Not much of one. It's just a hobby."

Ty stared down at the drawing. "This couple looks happy. I thought you didn't believe in marriage."

"I don't, but it…it was a very romantic wedding."

He glanced back at Haley, noticed the way the sunlight gilded her honey-gold hair, felt the kick he always felt. She would be leaving. And she was going to break his heart.

He steeled himself. Worrying about it wasn't going to change things. Turning to a clean page, he wrote down the names of the three buyers, set the pad back down on the table.

"Silverman, Tanaka and Carlson," Haley read. They had given the names to the police, but the fact they were Danoff's clients and their names were scribbled on Jimmy Warren's iPad wasn't enough to prove they were connected to the theft.

"By now the buyers know the forged paintings have been discovered," Ty said. "Which of these men would feel the need for control and want revenge against us?"

Haley looked up at him. "You think one of the buyers is the man at the top?"

He shrugged. "It's a gut feeling. I could be wrong. It could be someone else entirely. The thing is, the first time they stole two pieces. This time they took three. Two would be easier to handle, easier to fence. Why take three?"

"More money for three than two. A lot more."

"Could be you're right. It's just…both burglaries follow a strict pattern. People on the inside. Same artist did the forgeries. Everything's the same except the number of paintings that were stolen."

"All right, let's go with it," Haley said. "After we found Danoff's list and connected three of the names to the names on Dad's iPad, I mentioned them to Aunt Ellie. She didn't know Tanaka or Carlson, but she's known Nathan Silverman since before Uncle Harry died. He's in the movie business. Ellie says he's a creative genius, kind of a soft-spoken guy, a real family man. She likes him."

"Doesn't fit our profile."

"Tanaka's a businessman," Haley said. "He's used to being in control, but I can't see a guy like that wanting revenge."

"Neither can I. Tanaka's negotiated hundreds of deals. He's used to the give and take. It wouldn't be personal for him. It would just be about the money or the painting or both."

"That leaves Carlson. He owns race horses. He likes control, likes to win. I read an article about him that said he was very difficult to work for. He expects complete loyalty, goes after anyone who says anything against him."

Ty tapped the paper. "Race horses and beautiful women. Your father believed he was one of the buyers, so we know he likes art. He likes power and he's into paybacks. Could be our man."

"If your theory is correct."

Ty rubbed a hand over his face. "Yeah."

The disposable rang just then. Ty dug it out of his pocket, heard Sol's voice on the end of the line.

"I got something you're gonna like."

"Yeah? I could use something."

Haley came out of her chair and he held the phone so that both of them could hear.

"You said you needed a connection between Hi-Tech and Sentry," Sol said.

"And?"

"I couldn't find the employee records so I dug into the ownership of both companies. Went into the corporate documents, went real deep. Guess what name came up in an umbrella corporation that's distantly connected to both firms?" Haley leaned closer. "Stephen Carlson," Sol said.

Ty pumped his fist as adrenaline shot through him. "You're the best, kid. This one's on me. Send me the bill." Ty hung up the phone.

Haley's eyes sparkled. "Oh, my God—you were

right. Carlson's the one calling the shots. He's the man at the top."

"Doesn't mean he's got the painting. That's still just a theory."

"One my father seemed to agree with."

Ty grinned. "Good point. And it's turning out your daddy was no fool."

Haley smiled. "No, he wasn't."

"Yeah, and he didn't raise one, either." Dragging her into his arms, Ty kissed her, long and deep.

Thirty-Three

"We need a plan," Haley said the next day.

They'd been on the internet all morning, finally decided to take a break, leave the computer and their brainstorming, and go get some of the things they needed—like something to put on besides their dress clothes.

They were just pulling into the garage in Jonathan's little white Prius, back from a shopping trip to the Sun and Sand Boutique off Pacific Coast Highway, the nearest place that sold clothing—mostly beach stuff, swimsuits, beach towels, blow-up rafts.

But the shop had a few pairs of jeans and lots of T-shirts. They each bought cheap canvas sneakers and socks, and changed in a dressing room at the back of the store. Haley was wearing jeans and a pink T-shirt with a mermaid on the front.

Ty's shirt was navy blue and said What Happens in Zuma Stays in Zuma, the name of a nearby beach. Haley felt the heat sweeping into her cheeks as she re-

membered the hot sex they'd had in Jonathan's study.
Ty noticed and grinned.

They bought windbreakers, stopped at the grocery
store for some food and additional supplies, then headed
back to the house. There was no trouble along the way,
and Ty seemed sure no one had followed them to or
from the beach house.

When they got out of the car in the garage, Haley
picked up the conversation where she had left off.
"We've got to tell the police about Carlson's connection to the security companies."

He nodded. "I'll call Cogan on the disposable, tell
him where to look, but it still might take weeks or
even months to collect enough evidence to build a case
against him."

"We can't afford to wait that long. We could be dead
by then."

"Yeah." Ty led her through the laundry room, into the
kitchen. Setting the grocery bags on the counter, they
started putting the few items they'd purchased away:
a quart of milk, a loaf of bread and meat and cheese to
make sandwiches, some cereal and bananas for breakfast. Ty had bought a couple of steaks for supper, but at
the moment, Haley was too worried to think about food.

"I've…umm…got an idea," she said, working up the
courage to say what she had been thinking all the way
back from the store.

Ty smiled. "Sure you do. You've always got an idea."

"You're really going to hate this one."

That seemed to intrigue him. "Yeah? What is it?"

"Carlson Farms is up Bonsall Drive, right?" They
had dug up as much information as they could on the
net before they'd left for the store. "The breeding farm,
stable and race horses."

"So?"

"His ranch is in the hills, but his house is on the ocean side of the road, on the cliffs above the water. It's just a little ways from here."

"Point Dume. So what?"

"If we could get into the house and find the painting—"

"You're kidding, right? We'd be lucky to get through the security fences. You could tell from the satellite photos, the place is protected like Fort Knox."

"The grounds, maybe. I doubt he has his own personal army, just guards from his own company."

"Probably. Still, the house sits way back on a big chunk of land. It's all open space around it. We'd be spotted before we even got close."

"I'm not suggesting we go through the fence." Haley looked up at him. "I'm suggesting we glide in."

Ty opened his mouth, closed it again and just stood there, staring.

At the sound of three familiar quick raps on the door, Ty walked over and pulled it open.

"Any problems?" he asked as Johnnie Riggs walked into the beach house late that afternoon, a six-pack under one powerful arm, a rolled-up set of plans under the other.

Johnnie shook his head, his jaw already dark with an afternoon's growth of beard. "No sign of a tail. No trouble at Ellie's house."

"Dylan okay?"

"He's fine. EMTs patched him up and let him go. He's recouping at Ellie's."

Ty chuckled. "Figures."

"The good news is the cameras at the hotel got a pic-

ture of the shooter. Facial recognition got a hit. Name's
Max Slovinski, alias Dirk Waller, alias Quentin Sloan.
He's wanted by Interpol. Real bad SOB. Cops have a
BOLO out on him."

Thinking of the planning the shooter had done, Ty
wasn't surprised.

Johnnie set the six-pack down on the light oak dining table, set the plans down beside it. "This is crazy—
you know that, right?"

"Completely lunatic. That's what I told her."

Johnnie turned a hard look on Haley. "This is nuts.
You get that, right?"

"It's going to work," she said stubbornly.

"Carlson's men will probably shoot you on sight."

"They're not going to see us. We're going to get inside the house and find the painting."

"If it's actually there," Johnnie grumbled.

Ty exchanged a glance with Haley, hoping like hell
he was right about Carlson and the painting and every
other damn thing.

"I see you got the plans," Ty said.

Haley joined them at the table. "Are those the building plans for Carlson's house? How in the world did
you get them?"

"Ty's got a friend in the building department owes
him a favor," Johnnie said.

"Lady friend?" Haley asked. Johnnie just shrugged
his thick shoulders.

Glancing away from Haley's accusing look, Ty
rolled open the pages, flipped to the page showing the
floor plan. The house was ten thousand square feet, a
showy, modern design, with vaulted ceilings and lots
of windows looking out over the ocean. There was a

guest wing on one side, a master wing on the other. He pointed to a small enclosed room in the master wing.

"That's gotta be it," Ty said.

Johnnie nodded. "That'd be my guess. I took a look at the plans earlier." He pulled a bottle of Bud Light out of the six-pack and handed it to Ty, handed one to Haley and took one for himself. He twisted off the cap and took a swallow.

Haley leaned over the drawing. "What are you two looking at?"

"See this?" Ty pointed to a square on the page. "It's an interior room off the study. There's no hallway, no windows. It's just there behind a wall."

Haley stared at the page. "What is it? A security vault of some kind?"

"The walls aren't thick enough for that. I figure if he has the painting, he wants to see it. Could be his own personal art gallery."

"It's fifteen feet by twenty." Johnnie took a pull on his beer. "Not large, but big enough to house a small private collection."

"Including one of the stolen paintings," Haley said. She cracked open her beer and took a sip.

"Assuming you're lucky enough to get in the house," Johnnie said, "you'll still have to find a way inside that room."

Ty started turning the pages, came to the cabinet layout. "There's a wall of bookshelves in front, bookshelves on most of the study walls."

"So how does Carlson get in?" Haley asked.

Ty flipped to the mechanical drawing, saw the sliding mechanism that moved the wall to one side, providing an entrance.

"Wow," Haley said, "just like James Bond."

Ty chuckled, started flipping through the pages till he came to the electrical plan. "Here's the switch. Nothing complicated. It's probably hidden behind some books."

"From what I've read," Haley said, "this guy's got an ego the size of New York. He isn't worried about anyone breaking in. He thinks he's untouchable."

"Maybe he is," Johnnie said. "Remember, Carlson's in the security business."

"Too bad there isn't a plan that shows the alarm system," Haley said glumly.

"I've been working on that." Ty walked over and picked up the printouts he had made off the computer in Jonathan's study. "High-Tec sells Ademco as its top-of-the-line product. Sentry sells DSC. Both are good, but the thing is, when you strip away all the bullshit gadgets, all alarm systems that have the same UL listing perform exactly the same. What makes the difference is the number of zones, types of keypads, X-10 compatibility, monitors and private/residential reporting."

Haley stared up at him. "I can't believe you know all that stuff. It's kind of scary."

Ty grinned. "Stick with me, kid."

"So you figure you can get in without a hitch," Johnnie said.

"I won't have a problem disarming the primary panel. The problem is…disabling the primary triggers a second sensor, which sends an alarm to the monitoring station. You have to take both sensors out at once."

Johnnie took a swallow of beer. "That's not a problem. I'll go in with you. We'll take them out together."

"Have you ever done any paragliding?" Haley asked.

"I was a Ranger. I've jumped hundreds of times."

"It's not the same. You were trying to get down as

fast as you could, not working the wind gusts, trying to stay in the air, maneuvering the chute to catch the thermals."

"I'm going to need you on the ground, partner," Ty said before Johnnie could argue. "Someone's got to handle the security guards if they become a problem. I can handle the system on my own."

"What are you talking about?" Haley's face flushed beet-red. "You won't have to do it on your own. I'll be there to help you."

Ty straightened away from the table. "I've been doing my best to postpone this conversation, but I guess it can't wait any longer. I'm not taking you with me, darlin'. It's just too dangerous."

Haley propped a hand on her hip. "You're taking me, *darlin'*. I'm going. I didn't come up with this idea to be left behind. It's nonnegotiable."

Johnnie's dark eyes widened. He tipped his head toward Ty. "Is she good enough?"

She was good at a lot of things, he thought, his mind heading to sex. He had no idea how well she could use a wing.

He stared at her hard. "Are you?"

"I'm better than good enough. I'm damned good. You need me and I'm going."

"It would sure be a help to have a partner on the inside," Johnnie said.

Ty raked a hand through his hair. "I don't like it. Not a damn bit."

Haley caught his arm. "I was almost killed at Aunt Ellie's. They tried again at the wedding. If we don't stop Carlson and his hit man, sooner or later, they're going to succeed."

Silence fell.

"She's got a point," Johnnie said.

"I've been checking the weather," Haley rushed on. "It looks good all week, warm with a slight ocean breeze, no storms in sight. It'll take a couple of days to get our gear together, find a jump site, try to get some idea of Carlson's schedule, figure the timing."

He didn't want to take her, but after all she'd been through, she deserved the chance to go. And the fact was, he needed her.

"The jump site's easy," he said. "There's a local spot on the cliffs right down the road. We need to do some recon, time the security guards' rounds, plan an escape route. Assuming we get all the info we need, we can buy the gear tomorrow and be ready to go in the day after." He turned to Johnnie. "We'll need you to get us out of there."

"Not a problem."

"We need to strategize," Ty said, "work out the details."

"So I'm going," Haley said, just to be clear.

Ty looked into her pretty face, wished he didn't have to put her in that kind of danger, thought how tough it was to deny her damned near anything. "You're going. And you'd better do exactly what I say."

Haley grinned so wide, her dimples popped out. Ty's heart expanded with the same emotion he'd been fighting since the day he'd met her. Dammit, how could he have been so stupid as to fall in love with her?

Thirty-Four

The night was black as ink, perfect for gliding in undiscovered. The day had been warm, leaving the thermals just right for the lift they needed to travel the short distance to the site.

Dressed completely in black, black greasepaint on her face, Haley shoved her hair up under a black-knit cap and tugged it down around her ears. Her heart was throbbing, her nerves jumping, but she was ready to go.

She was standing in the living room next to Johnnie as Ty walked out of the bedroom, also dressed in black. Beneath the greasepaint, his features looked hard, his mouth a thin, grim line. She recognized the place he had gone, his battle zone, saw the competence and control reflected in the lines of his face.

This was a man who knew exactly what he was doing and was ready to handle the job. As he crossed the room, every long stride was filled with purpose. Just watching the confident way he moved lessened some of the tension inside her.

In black fatigues and heavy leather boots, a big

knife strapped to his thigh, he looked dangerous, hard and every inch a man. When he pulled his pistol and checked the load, shoved the clip back in and resettled the gun in the holster on his tactical belt, Haley felt a shot of lust unlike any she had ever known.

Embarrassed, she glanced away, glad for the grease-paint that hid her pink cheeks and completely inappropriate thoughts.

"Everything's set." Ty checked the time on his heavy black wristwatch. "It's zero one hundred. Our countdown starts now. We're on target in forty minutes. If our info is correct, we're out in twenty." He turned to Haley. "You ready?"

Her mouth was dry, her heart racing. The best she could do was nod.

"All right, let's go."

They climbed into Johnnie's black Mustang, already loaded with their gear, and headed for the jump site on the cliffs above the ocean farther up the highway. At this late hour and as dark as it was, when they pulled into the lot, not a soul was around. They unpacked their gear and spread their canopies out on the flat spot above the cliffs.

Ty spoke to her through the earbuds all three of them were wearing. "Testing, one, two three."

"Loud and clear," Haley said into her mic.

"Roger that," Johnnie said.

Ty made the necessary thermal lift calculations and checked to be sure his variometer was working. In paragliding, it was used to keep track of rising or sinking air, provided a GPS and did a jillion other useful little tricks.

"Everything looks good," Ty said. "Let's do a pre-flight and we're out of here."

They strapped on their harnesses. Johnnie helped

them check for any tangled lines and make a final check of all their equipment.

Ty glanced at his watch. "We're right on schedule. You ready?"

Haley took a deep breath. She knew how to do this, she reminded herself. And Ty was going to need her help. "I'm ready."

He built a wall behind him, the term used for filling the canopy with air, and Haley prepared to do the same.

"Count to ten, then follow me." He tugged on the lines took a few steps and swooped up into the breeze. A ten-count and Haley was in the air, climbing up behind him.

The thermals were lifting just right. She headed out over the water, followed as he aimed for Dume Point. The night was dark but she could see a few lights in houses along the shore. At the target location, perimeter lighting around the Carlson house would help them locate the place they had chosen to land.

She moved up on Ty's right, just as they'd planned. At their current airspeed of roughly twenty miles an hour, the four-mile flight to the house wouldn't take very long. Haley took a deep breath and reminded herself to relax, to trust Ty and the plan they'd come up with.

She hit a couple patches of turbulence, not enough to be worrisome. Keeping Ty in sight, Haley maneuvered the canopy over the water, her nerves steadying as she settled into the flight.

They were going to do this. She just prayed it was going to work.

Ty kept a sharp eye on his airspeed indicator. They needed to time the landing just right, in between the security guards' twenty-minute rounds. He prayed Plan A would come together exactly the way it should.

Since that never happened, he went over plan B—what to do in case of a total clusterfuck—and saw Haley coming up on his right. So far so good. She was handling the wing like a pro. He'd figured she would. She was smart and capable, and in those tight black, Catwoman pants and turtleneck top, sexy as hell. He glanced her way, felt his heart throbbing deep inside his chest.

He had plans for that woman—if their crazy scheme worked and didn't land both of them in jail—or get them killed.

He studied the coastline, checked his variometer, checked his altitude. The coastline was expanding toward the west, beginning to form the V-shape into the ocean that was Dume Point. He moved toward land, saw Haley do the same.

His GPS directed them straight ahead. He looked at his watch. The area around the house was lit with small solar lamps. Cameras covered the walkways and doors, but there was plenty of open space inside the perimeter fencing just to the south and east where they could land without being seen.

Ty adjusted his mic. "Raptor, you in place?"

Johnnie's deep voice came back. "Everything's hunky-dory."

"Catbird, how you doing?"

He could almost see her smile. "Fine as wine," she said, and he relaxed a little at the confidence in her voice. "How about you, Buzzard?"

For the first time that night, he laughed. "That's Vulture, not Buzzard, and we're right on time. Target's below. Get ready to land."

"Roger that." The serious tone was back in her voice. At the landing site, Ty dropped down, put on the brakes, steered into the zone, flared, and his feet hit the ground. He did a running stop, released his harness and began to gather up his canopy. He pulled a rucksack from his backpack and stuffed the fabric inside.

Haley made a very pretty, walk-away landing right beside him. He gave her a quick smile and a thumbs-up as she dropped her harness and began to stuff the chute into her rucksack.

Ty motioned toward the house and they moved silently into the shadows. They dumped the bags in the darkness next to the house, each pulled out a pair of surgical latex gloves and tugged them on. Ty pulled a pair of plastic face masks out of his backpack and handed one to Haley.

She stared down at the mask, then back up at him. "You're kidding, right?"

Ty just grinned and pulled on his mask. Haley did the same. Roy Rogers and Dale Evans moved toward the window in the breakfast room. According to the electrical plan, there was power to a panel just inside the utility room door. The relay sensor would be somewhere nearby, designed to send an alarm if the first sensor was disabled.

The trick was taking both of them out at once. But first he needed to get inside the house.

Haley stood next to him as he worked on a window in the breakfast room that would provide easy access. A magnet was in place on each side of the sliding-glass pane. The minute contact between the magnets was broken, the alarm would go off. Ty reached into his bag and took out a thin, magnetic strip, custom-designed to fool the device into thinking the window was closed.

He slipped it between the panes, taped it in place and slid the window open.

A motion detector hung down from the ceiling a few feet away, but it was aimed toward the door. Unrolling a length of black cloth, he draped it over a telescoping rod, extended the rod toward the device and draped the cloth over the detector.

Haley joined him in the kitchen and they made their way into the utility room. He covered the motion detector there, located the security panel, then went in search of the second sensor.

He found it on a nearby wall and pointed to Haley, pressed a pair of cutters into her hand. Returning to the main panel, he opened it and studied the wires, found the one he wanted.

"Red, on one," he said softly into the mic.

"Red, on one," Haley repeated.

"Three, two, one." Ty nipped the wire, and at the same instant Haley did the same. The power went off in the house. Ty clipped the yellow wire, turning off the outside cameras but left the perimeter lights on.

He turned the power back on but the alarms remained deactivated, allowing them to move freely around the house. With the floor plan in his head, Ty headed for the study. First item on the agenda, find a way into Carlson's private gallery and hopefully find the painting.

They went into the study and he walked straight to the bookcase, removed two leather-bound volumes, found the switch on the wall and flipped it on.

The bookshelves slid silently open. He'd more than half expected to find a separate security system inside the room, laser beams or something movement-sensitive, but the room hadn't been designed as a vault to hide priceless stolen artwork, just a place for Carlson to view his collection.

They stepped inside, and Ty shone his flashlight along the walls. Haley did the same. The paintings in the room were all high-quality pieces, some early California Impressionist works. He recognized a pair of Picasso line drawings. A Salvador Dalí. Haley probably knew the names of some of the other artists. He didn't figure any were as valuable at the Van Gogh.

"There," Haley said, shining her light on a painting at the far end of the room, the only piece on that wall. "The Van Gogh," she said with soft reverence.

Damn. He hadn't been completely sure they would find it. Now that he saw it, he had to admit it was impressive. Just not enough to steal or kill for.

"We found it. Let's go." Time for the next part of the plan. Johnnie had managed to find out that Carlson would be home all week. Ty didn't ask him how. They left the painting behind and made their way silently out of the study, easing quietly down the hall to the master bedroom.

The door wasn't locked. Ty drew out his pistol, turned the knob, and the door swung silently open. Two people slept in a big king-size bed beneath a dark brown satin comforter. Haley ran her light over their sleeping forms, and Ty saw the woman next to Carlson was black-haired and beautiful.

The drapes were pulled. He reached over and flipped on the light. "Wake up, Carlson. You've got visitors."

The man stirred. The light glinted on the silver streaks in his dark hair and a face beginning to show his fifty years of hard living. Spotting the two of them, he bolted upright, and so did the woman, exposing a very pretty breast she quickly covered. Ty recognized

Maria St. Vincent from the photos he had found of her on the net.

"Who the hell are you?" Carlson asked, staring at Roy and Dale. He was naked to the waist, gray patches visible in the curly brown hair on his chest.

"Get out of bed," Ty said. "Both of you. Do it now."

Haley walked over and grabbed a blue satin robe lying on a nearby chair and tossed it to the woman, who hurriedly slipped it on and tied the sash.

Carlson grabbed a thick white terry-cloth robe and shrugged it on. "Whoever you are, you're going to be sorry you were ever born."

"What are going to do, Carlson? Kill us?"

Haley's mask muffled a laugh.

"Let's go," Ty said.

Carlson walked in front of the woman, leaving her to trail behind him down the hall. Ty wasn't surprised. "Into the study."

Carlson's eyes widened at the sight of the gallery door standing open. "You'll pay for this."

"I think it's clear you're the one who's going to pay." Ty dragged a couple of chairs out from around the gaming table in the corner, spun them around and placed them back-to-back in front of the open door. "Sit down."

"You'd better think this through. There's no way you can fence the painting and get the money it's worth. Leave it, and I'll give you cash right now—a hundred thousand dollars. You can go and no one will ever be the wiser."

Ty pointed his weapon at Carlson's chest. "I said sit down."

Carlson's mouth flattened into an ugly line, but he did as he was told. As the pair sat down back-to-back in the chairs, Ty retrieved a length of rope from his backpack along with a handful of plastic ties. He bound Carlson's hands behind him, tied Maria's in front of her, then bound their legs to the chairs and secured the chairs together with the rope.

Carlson shifted his weight, testing the line. "I know who you are. I'm not a fool."

"You're worse than a fool. You're a thief and a murderer."

"You can't prove a thing."

"I don't have to. Proof's on the wall behind you." And Haley had posted a sign below it: VAN GOGH STOLEN FROM THE FIZER, just to be sure it was found.

"You're finished, Carlson. You and your hit man." Ty leaned over him. "One more thing. If you know who I am, you've read my file. If you have, you know what I can do. You're lucky I'm leaving you alive."

Carlson's face paled.

Ty slapped a strip of duct tape over the man's mouth, and a strip over Maria's. He pulled his backpack back on. "Let's get out of here."

Haley didn't hesitate, just hurried ahead of him down the hall toward the back door.

"We're on our way, Raptor," he said through his mic.

"I'm right out front. You'd better hurry. Company's on the way."

"Roger that."

They went out the back door, leaving it open for the police, grabbed their rucksacks so their gear couldn't be traced back to them, and ran to the front of the house. The engine on the Mustang was purring as they tossed their bags into the trunk and jumped into the car.

The masks and gloves came off as Johnnie stepped on the gas and the Mustang rolled off down the road.

"Cops are on the way," he said, having made an

anonymous call to the police about a burglary in progress at the Carlson residence.

"No problem with the guards?" Ty asked.

Johnnie grunted. "One of them is napping," he said and Ty smiled.

Sirens sounded in the distance. Carlson might know who was responsible for the break-in, but since Ty had given Detective Cogan a heads-up on the man's involvement in the two security firms and the theory that he was behind the heists, the detective had, by unspoken agreement, promised to look the other way.

After all was said and done, Detective Charlie Cogan would be retiring a hero for solving the heist of the decade, and the investigation into who had been in the house would wind up going nowhere.

It was almost over.

The wail of sirens grew closer as police cars raced toward the mansion. Looked like for once Plan A had actually worked.

Ty flicked a glance at Haley and both of them grinned.

Thirty-Five

Sunlight poured in through the bedroom window. Haley slanted a look at the digital clock, saw it was after 10:00 a.m. She and Ty had spent the night making love in his big king-size bed, gotten up and showered together.

Two days had passed since the break-in at the Carlson house. Two days, and so much had happened.

After Johnnie's anonymous call, the police had arrived exactly on time. The cops had found the painting, freed Maria St. Vincent, and arrested Stephen Carlson for possession of stolen property and suspicion of burglary, among a vast array of other charges.

So far, Carlson had confessed to the possession charge, but denied any involvement in the burglary. The bad news was he had lawyered-up and there was a good chance he was going to get out on bail.

Haley and Ty had been interviewed by the police, each given a statement in regard to the shooting at the wedding, but claimed no knowledge of the B and E at the Carlson house. Since there was no way to prove they were there, only Carlson's ravings that they were the two masked assailants responsible for breaking in and tying him up, the questioning had ceased.

The media was calling it a Robin Hood–style escapade that had uncovered priceless stolen art and the man allegedly behind the theft.

The police were searching for Quentin Sloan, who was, they were sure, doing his best to leave the country.

Last night, they had returned to Ty's condo, spent the night in bed and made slow, incredible love. It wasn't until this morning that Haley's despair had begun to set in.

The danger was over. The case was on its way to being resolved. It was time for her to go home.

As she pulled on her jeans and white cotton blouse, she thought about spending the day with Ty, but the longer she stayed with him, the harder it was going to be to leave him. It made her heart hurt just to think of it, and yet there was no other choice.

Ty had just pulled on his jeans when a knock sounded at the door.

"What the hell…" He flashed a look at the digital clock. "Damn, it's later than I thought."

While Ty went downstairs to answer the door, Haley finished dressing then headed downstairs behind him. A woman was standing in the doorway. Smooth olive complexion and a pretty face, thick, nearly black hair curling softly past her shoulders, a lush, sexy figure.

"Tiffany," Ty said, standing in front of her, barechested in only his jeans. "What are you doing here? I thought I told you I was seeing someone."

"It's been over a month, Ty. I figured by now you'd be a free man again. I thought maybe you'd want to go out."

Haley's heart squeezed.

"Look, Tiffany. I'm involved, okay?" He looked over his shoulder, saw Haley standing near the stairs, turned back to the woman. "We're friends. That's all we ever have been."

"But what we had was good, Ty. You said so yourself."

"Go home, Tiff. I'm sorry. It's over." Ty shut the door, turned and started walking toward her.

"I'm sorry that happened," Ty said. "I told her a while back I was seeing someone."

"At least the phone calls stopped."

Ty started frowning. "I've dated other women. You know that. But that was in the past. I'm not seeing anyone but you."

She nodded, felt her eyes begin to well. "I know that. You've been great, Ty. No woman could ask for more than you've given. But it's time for me to go back to my life in Chicago. My mother is there, my friends."

Ty caught her shoulders. "You have friends and family here, Haley. Your aunt's here. I'm here. I love you, baby. I don't want you to leave."

Haley's throat closed up. He had never said those words to her before. "I'm going, Ty. It's better for both of us. We had a fling and it was great, but now it's time to go."

"Bullshit. You're just afraid."

She glanced at the door, her mind still filled with images of the woman who had been standing there offering herself to Ty. "Can't you see? I'm doing you a favor. If we let this go any further, we're only going to hurt each other."

He caught her shoulders. "Don't say that. It isn't true. I love you, Haley. Doesn't that mean anything to you?"

She swallowed past the lump in her throat. "It means

everything. More than you'll ever know. But it doesn't change things. I'm going back to Chicago. That's where I belong."

"That isn't where you belong. You belong here with me. I want you to marry me."

"What...what are you talking about?"

"That's right. I want it all, Haley. A home, a wife, a family. I want kids and grandkids. I want to have them with you."

The tears in her eyes slipped over onto her cheeks. "It wouldn't work, Ty."

"Why? Because you don't love me?"

"Because I do."

He shook his head. "That makes no sense."

"Ask my mother. It makes perfect sense." Turning, she ran back up the stairs and grabbed her purse, threw the rest of her clothes into the overnight bag she'd brought with her.

When she came back down, Ty said nothing, just took her bag and loaded it into the pickup. He drove her back to Ellie's in silence. He didn't say a word as she climbed out of the truck and walked up on the porch.

Haley's chest clamped down as he drove away. She was going home. It was over.

She was fighting a fresh round of tears when she walked into the house and found her mother standing in the foyer.

"Hello, darling. I'm so glad to see you." Allison Warren was blond and statuesque, taller than Haley, her complexion without a wrinkle or blemish. The most expensive plastic surgeon in Chicago had seen to that.

Haley turned away, wiped the tears from her eyes so her mother wouldn't see. "I didn't...didn't know you were coming."

They embraced lightly and exchanged air kisses. Haley thought how different the greeting was from the warm hugs she received from Betty Jean.

"I didn't really know it myself until the last minute. I called Eleanor when I arrived at the airport. I thought if she didn't have room for me here, I could always take a suite at the Bel-Air." Her mother's favorite place to stay on the coast, the ultimate luxury hotel.

"You wasted a trip," Haley said. "I was planning to come home as soon as I could get a ticket."

Her mother smiled. "Well, that is good news. Ellie mentioned you were seeing someone. I was afraid you might decide to stay."

She was only a little surprised Aunt Ellie had mentioned her relationship with Ty. But her aunt was honest to a fault and always trying to help the people she cared about. Maybe she thought Haley would want to stay with Ty, and she was trying to help smooth the way.

She swallowed past the lump in her throat. "My life is in Chicago."

"Of course it is. We'll fly back together. I can only imagine how much you must have missed your friends. And your job. The Seymour is quite a prestigious gallery."

Haley nodded, but the truth was, the only friend she had ever really missed was Lane Bishop. And Lane was living in L.A. Her gallery work was important, too. She loved art and always would, and she was good at her job. She was surprised she hadn't missed the gallery more than she had.

Haley's chest tightened. She hadn't missed Chicago, but she missed Ty already. She wondered if she always would.

"The Brighton's daughter, Whitney, got married last

week," her mother said as Haley carried her bags down the hall to her room in the guest wing. "Geoffrey was there. He's quite a handsome young man."

"He's also the most boring guy on the planet."

"Darling, don't be silly. The man is set to inherit a very sizable fortune. How could he possibly be boring?"

"You're right," she said. "What was I thinking?" The sarcasm went unnoticed by her mother. Haley squeezed her eyes shut, trying to block images of Ty. "I need to ask you something, Mother."

"Of course, dear, what is it?"

"You've always said how much you loved Dad. From the day you first met him—that's what you said. It was love at first sight. But if you really loved him, why would you trick him into marrying you?"

Her mother frowned. "What are you talking about?"

"It's true, isn't it? You told him you were pregnant, but you weren't. You didn't care about his happiness, only your own. That doesn't sound like love to me."

"Where did you hear that? That harlot your father married? I can't believe you would listen to a word that woman said."

"Betty Jean is actually a really good person, Mother. The kind of person who would have done anything for Dad. She loved him. Really loved him."

"She was a harlot. A tramp who broke up our marriage. How can you defend her?"

"It's true, though, isn't it? You made up that story to get Dad to marry you. You were never pregnant at all."

"So what? I brought him into the family. My father made him a millionaire. He owed all that to me."

Haley's chest clamped down. "Excuse me, Mother. I've got a terrible headache. If you don't mind, I think I'll lie down for a while."

Allison sniffed. "Well, maybe you should. I'm sure you'll feel better when you wake up. In the meantime, I'll find us a flight back to Chicago. We can leave in the morning."

Haley didn't argue. Suddenly she felt exhausted. She was going home. She should be happy to be getting her life back. She should be looking forward to returning to work, to seeing all of her friends.

Instead all she could think of was Ty and how lonely she was going to be without him.

Ty paced the floor of his living room. The painting he had purchased in Carmel, *Ocean Rage,* hung on the wall above the sofa. Violent, white-capped waves crashed against a desolate shore and the day was bleak and lonely.

Haley had said the painting somehow fit him. As he felt the anger inside him, mixed with unbearable sadness, he understood what she had meant.

But it wasn't the dark mood he faced now, it was a feeling of aching loss. He was in love with Haley Warren as he had never been with another woman. She had won his heart with her intelligence, her loyalty and her courage. She fit him perfectly. He didn't think he would ever meet another woman so exactly right for him.

But Haley didn't love him in return. At least not enough.

If she did, she would stay. She would marry him. Have his children. The hard truth was, she didn't trust him enough to believe it could work between them.

He turned at the sound of a knock at his door, paced over to pull it open. His cousin Dylan stood on the porch.

"I thought I'd stop and say goodbye. I'm flying my

new plane back home. I'm just on my way to the air-port."

"How's your side? You feeling okay?"

Unconsciously he touched the bandage over his bullet wound. "I heal pretty fast."

Ty almost smiled. "Especially with a sweet little red-head to take care of you."

Dylan glanced away. "She was nothing but trouble."

Ty thought of Haley and felt a soft pang. "Aren't they all."

Dylan clapped him on the shoulder. "I gotta go. When I get the lodge up and running, you and Haley'll have to come up and see me."

Ty shook his head. "Haley's going back to Chicago. It's over between us."

"You didn't ask her to stay? I kind of thought that was a given."

"I asked. She doesn't want what I've got to offer."

Dylan scoffed. "Then she's a fool."

Ty managed to smile. "Thanks for all the help. Fly high, cuz."

Dylan waved as he walked away.

Ty told himself he needed to go to the office, get busy working, dredge up a few new clients. Instead he sat down on the sofa beneath the painting, feeling as if a heavy weight had settled on his chest.

He'd feel better tomorrow or the day after. Better once Haley was gone. But he couldn't make himself believe it.

After a sleepless night of tossing and turning, Haley finally gave up and climbed out of bed. All night she'd thought of Ty, remembered their passionate lovemaking, the danger they had shared, the closeness.

He had asked her to marry him. He had told her he loved her. She'd been too afraid to tell him how deeply she loved him.

The shower renewed some of her energy. She dressed in jeans and a soft pink sleeveless sweater and headed for the kitchen. She wasn't surprised to find her aunt already up, drinking a cup of the coffee Dolores had brewed that morning.

"Join me? There's a fresh pot on the counter. I guess your mother's still in bed."

"She never was an early riser." Not like Haley's dad. She wondered if her parents ever had anything at all in common. She glanced toward the door, anxious now that her course was set.

"There's something I need to do. Any chance I could borrow a car?"

"Of course, dear." Ellie smiled. "Take the Triumph. It'll get you there faster."

Haley wasn't sure where her aunt thought she was headed. She probably wouldn't have guessed she was going to see Betty Jean.

Since it was still too early for a visit, Haley pulled the Triumph into a drive-through coffee kiosk and got her morning fix, then drove aimlessly around the city, waiting for it to get late enough for her to talk to her stepmother.

At eight o'clock, her nerves were too jumpy to wait any longer. Parking the little red Triumph at the curb, she walked up on the porch and rapped on the door.

"Coming!"

Haley heard the shuffle of feet and an instant later, the door swung open. In a fluffy yellow robe and a pair of fuzzy yellow slippers, Betty Jean smiled.

"Haley! What a lovely surprise."

"I know it's early. I should have called first, but I just…I really needed to see you."

Betty Jean gave her a warm hug. "You don't need to call. You're welcome here anytime. Would you like a cup of tea, dear? I ran out of coffee and haven't had a chance to go to the store."

"Tea sounds great." Haley followed Betty Jean into the kitchen, and the woman busied herself filling a kettle and setting it on the stove. When it started whistling, she poured the water into a china pot, added tea, then poured each of them a cup.

The scent of cinnamon filled the kitchen as Betty Jean set the cup down in front of her.

"You looked troubled, dear." Betty Jean sat down across from her. "Is there anything I can do to help?"

Haley wrapped her fingers around the teacup, the warmth soothing her nerves. "I hope so. I came here to ask you about my father."

Betty Jean stirred a lump of sugar into her tea. "What would you like to know?"

"I know you loved him. I can see it in your eyes whenever you talk about him. But in the beginning, how did you know it wasn't…you know, just physical attraction?"

Betty Jean smiled, her blond hair still slightly tousled from sleep. "I suppose at first that's what it was. He was just so handsome, you know? Every time he looked at me, my insides just melted."

"So how could you be sure he was the right man for you? A man you could trust and love for the rest of your life?"

Betty Jean's smile softened. "Oh, that's easy. I knew it the first time he kissed me. It was magical. Like an electrical shock in every cell in my body. I could hardly catch my breath. For a moment, I actually thought I was going to faint."

"You did?"

She nodded. "You probably think that's silly, but I knew right then what we had was special, something that would last a lifetime. And it would have. Our love grew deeper every year."

Haley's hands were trembling, her heart squeezing. She remembered the first time Ty had kissed her and how amazing it had been, blazing hot and at the same time so wonderfully tender. She thought how that single kiss had changed her, helped her free the passionate woman she was inside.

Tears filled her eyes. "Oh, God, Betty Jean, Ty asked me to marry him and I said no. I told him I was going back to Chicago."

"But I thought you loved him. It looked that way to me."

Her lips trembled. "I love him. I love him with everything inside me."

"Then why didn't you tell him?"

She brushed at the wetness on her cheeks. "Because I was afraid it wouldn't work. I told him I didn't believe in marriage, but the truth is, I just didn't want to wind up like my mother."

Betty Jean's hand covered hers on the table. "You're nothing like your mother. You love Ty and he loves you. That's something far different than what your parents felt for each other."

"I know that now."

Betty Jean squeezed her hand. "You've already trusted Ty with your life. Don't you think you can trust him with your heart?"

Her throat tightened. Could she trust him to make

her happy? The painful truth was she couldn't be happy without him.

A feeling of rightness settled over her, so strong fresh tears welled in her eyes. "I know I can."

Betty Jean rose from the table. "Then you had better go and find him. You had better tell him what you feel and when he asks again, you had better say yes this time."

Haley got up from her chair, leaned over and hugged the woman her father had loved. "Thank you, Betty Jean. Thank you so much. I'm glad my father found you."

Betty Jean's eyes glistened as Haley walked away.

She knew her heart now, knew what she wanted. But as she headed back down the walkway to the Triumph, her nerves kicked in.

What would Ty say? Would he forgive her? Would he still want her now that she had turned him down?

By the time she got to his house, she was a nervous wreck.

Worse than that, Ty wasn't home.

Thirty-Six

❧❧❧

Ty's cell phone fiddled for the tenth time that day, but he continued to ignore it. Just like he'd ignored the knock at his door. He didn't want to talk to anyone, didn't want to see anyone. He just wanted to be left alone.

It was late afternoon when the phone started ringing again, the fiddling ringtone grating on his already strained nerves. With a sigh, he picked it up. Hell, he couldn't hide out for the rest of his life.

"Ty?"

The sound of Haley's voice made his chest ache. He hardened his heart. "What is it, Haley? What do you want?"

Someone took the phone from her hand. A man's voice spoke in his ear. "Hey, buddy. Seems I got something that belongs to you."

Ty sat up straighter on the sofa, his stomach knotting. "Stryker? What the hell's going on?"

"Carlson's out on bail. He wants to see you and your woman. He's got a proposition for the two of you. He's waiting for you at the old Kenmore Aggregate Mine. It's up Haines Canyon Road. You think you can find it?"

Fury rolled through him. And a terrible fear for Haley. Ty clamped down hard to stay in control. "So now you're working for Carlson?"

Stryker's voice turned hard. "I asked if you know how to get to the goddamn mine."

Ty knew the place. He'd worked a missing-persons case that had led him into the canyon. He and Johnnie had found the missing woman's body near the abandoned mine. "I know where it is."

"You've got an hour to get there and you'd better come alone."

"You motherfucker. You lay a hand on Haley and you're dead."

Stryker just grunted. "I wouldn't be late if I were you." The phone disconnected.

For several seconds, Ty fought his anger and his fear for Haley. With a calming breath, he pulled himself together and hit Johnnie's cell number.

His friend answered on the first ring. "Hey, partner."

"Stryker's got Haley. Carlson's out on bail. He's waiting for us at the old Kenmore mine. I'm headed up there. I could use some backup."

"You got it. I'll meet you at the first turnout at the bottom of the hill."

The call ended and Ty went to retrieve his weapons and gear. He wasn't sure exactly who'd be attending this little party, but he hadn't forgotten that Quentin Sloan was still out there.

His tactical shotgun had been returned. He pushed in a handful of shells and set it aside, checked the load on his Beretta, shoved it back into its holster and clipped it onto his belt beneath his T-shirt. He strapped on his ankle holster, eased in his .38 revolver, pulled his pant leg down to cover it.

Grabbing his gear bag, he tossed in some extra ammunition clips, a couple of flash grenades and his Nighthawk .45.

As soon as his pickup was loaded and he was on the road, he checked the time. He needed to push it to get there.

If Stryker or anyone else had touched Haley, he'd be a dead man when Ty arrived.

Stephen Carlson was tall and still attractive at fifty, with light blue eyes and a hint of silver in his dark brown hair. Dressed in expensive tan gabardine slacks and a blue short-sleeved shirt, his hair perfectly groomed, his manners were impeccable as he welcomed Haley on her arrival.

"We meet again," Carlson said.

"Where's Ty?" She glanced around, saw no one, felt a rush of fear. "Stryker said he was here. He said you wanted to make a deal." And Stryker had said Carlson would kill Ty if she didn't come.

"I'm sure he'll be here shortly."

Fear and adrenaline pumped through her. This was the man who had tried to kill them. After his arrest, she had believed he would leave them alone.

"I don't know what you think you're going to accomplish with this. You're going to prison, Carlson. Whatever deal you think you're going to make, that isn't going to change."

"I guess we'll just have to see."

"So far there's no proof linking you to my father's murder. If you kill us, there will be."

One of his dark eyebrows went up. "I'm not going to kill you. What gave you that impression?"

He sounded sincere. Her hands trembled. She prayed he was telling the truth. "Then what do you want?"

He turned his attention to the big man standing a few feet away, legs splayed, hands clasped in front of him in bodyguard mode.

"You've got your money, Stryker. Brodie's on the way. Your part in this is over."

Stryker looked uneasy. The open-pit mine was abandoned, the rocky landscape overgrown with scrub brush, sage and cactus, nothing else around for miles.

When she had returned home from Betty Jean's that morning, he had come to her, told her Carlson had phoned, said he was holding Ty and that if she didn't go with him, Carlson was going to kill him.

"He wants to make a deal," Stryker had said. "He doesn't want to go to prison. Just agree to do whatever he wants and he'll let you both go."

"Screw him," Haley had said, but she had gone with him. Her aunt had already left to meet Jonathan. Her mother had taken a cab—alone—to the airport. Haley had been going crazy trying to figure out where Ty was, since he wasn't answering his phone. Trying not to imagine he had gone to Tiffany, or another of his lady friends for comfort, now that she had left him.

She glanced over at Stryker. She'd been a fool to trust him when her instincts had been warning her all along. He had used her as bait to lure Ty into a trap, and it was all her fault.

She read the uncertainty on his face. At least he had a slim thread of conscience.

"Maybe I should wait till Brodie gets here," Stryker said.

Carlson's features hardened. "You've been paid. A

quarter of a million compensates for a multitude of sins. Now go."

Stryker checked his watch, looked at Haley. "Don't worry, he'll come. He'll be here any minute."

Haley flicked him a disgusted glance. "You really think Ty's going to take Carlson's blood money the way you did? You think either of us is going to?"

"Use your head. He just doesn't want you to testify, keep stirring things up. You agree and you won't have a problem."

Carlson reached into the canvas bag on the battered wooden table beside him, pulled out a big black, semi-automatic pistol. "Get out, Stryker. Now."

Kurt's hands fisted. He gazed down at the bag filled with money Carlson had tossed at his feet. Reaching for it, he picked it up and hoisted it over a brawny shoulder, started walking toward his flashy yellow Camaro. Sand flew up beneath the wheels as the car fishtailed out of the abandoned mining yard. In minutes, he was gone.

Haley glanced at Carlson and thought of running, but she didn't doubt for a moment that Ty was on his way. If she wasn't there when he arrived, Carlson might shoot him.

"I don't think we'll have long to wait," Carlson said, his gun pointed in her direction. "Why don't we sit down, make ourselves comfortable?" Brushing dirt off a rough wooden bench, he sat down at a battered wooden table, used the barrel of the gun to indicate she should sit down on the bench opposite him.

Haley steeled herself, walked over and took a seat.

"Let me out here," Johnnie said, his features set in hard lines.

Ty pulled the pickup over to the side of the narrow canyon road leading up to the mine. Johnnie got out and grabbed his rifle from where it rested behind the seat. His nine mil rode in his shoulder holster, his KA-BAR knife was strapped to his thigh. Like Ty, he was armed to the teeth.

"Give me five minutes to get in position before you go in." As expected, Johnnie had been parked in the turnoff when Ty started up the canyon road. They'd driven up together, using the time it took to reach the mine to go over their plan.

"Will do."

"Take care, partner," Johnnie said as he walked away.

"You, too."

Ty let a couple of minutes pass, then pulled on down the dirt road into the abandoned, open-pit mine. Aside from a couple of falling-down wooden buildings and some rusted-out heavy equipment covered in graffiti, there was nothing around. As he drew near, he spotted Stephen Carlson sitting at an overturned cable spool turned into a rough wooden table.

Haley sat across from him. Ty breathed a sigh of relief that she was still alive.

Both of them rose as Ty pulled the pickup into the empty yard, turned off the engine and got out of the truck.

"Might have been easier if you'd just called," he said as he shortened the distance between them.

Carlson's lips stretched into a smile that wasn't. His gun pointed at Haley. "I think this is going to work out much better."

"Where's Stryker?"

"He had an appointment."

Haley spoke up. "Carlson paid him to get us out here. I shouldn't have trusted him. I'm sorry, Ty."

"Not your fault, honey." He turned to Carlson. "We're here. What is it you want?"

"That's easy. I want you dead. That's what I've wanted since you started prying into my life, destroying everything I've worked for."

Haley stared at Carlson's weapon. "You said you weren't going to kill us."

"I'm not. But I wanted to be here when it happened. I wanted to see you both in a pool of blood. Mr. Sloan is going to take care of that for me."

Carlson pulled Haley in front of him and pressed his pistol against the side of her head, while Sloan appeared in the window of an empty wooden shack, a big semi-automatic in his hand. Only a heartbeat passed. Sloan fired at the same instant Ty dropped and rolled, pulled his weapon and fired. Bullets pinged off the side of the pickup. Ty caught the flash of metal on the hillside. Sloan fired again before Johnnie took him out with a rifle shot to the heart.

His Beretta leveled on Carlson, Ty rolled to his feet. Carlson steadied the barrel of his semiautomatic against Haley's temple.

"Let her go." From the corner of his eye, he saw Johnnie moving, trying to get into position for another shot.

Carlson's smile looked demonic. "You think I'm going to let you both just walk away? You've taken everything from me. Maria's left me. The painting's gone. It's only a matter of time until they connect me to the robbery, maybe even to Warren's murder. You can shoot me, but I'm taking her with me. If I lose the things I love—so do you."

Carlson was going to kill her. It was there in his eyes. Johnnie didn't have a clear shot and there wasn't time to wait. With Haley in front of him, taking Carlson out wouldn't be easy, but it was a shot Ty had to make.

Carlson's features hardened and his grip tightened. Ty looked at Haley's beautiful face, thought how much he loved her and squeezed the trigger on his Beretta. The roar of the gunshot echoed over the canyon and Carlson's body hit the dirt.

Haley felt Carlson's weight fall away from her. A scream caught in her throat as she looked down and saw him, his eyes blankly staring, a perfectly round hole in the middle of his forehead.

Then Ty was there, his hard arms wrapping around her, holding her as her body shook and she sobbed against his chest.

"It's over, baby. I've got you. Everything's all right."

He held her as she trembled, adrenaline still pumping through her veins. "I came to your house," she said brokenly, wiping at the wetness on her cheeks. "I had to see you, talk to you, but you weren't home."

He kissed the top of her head. "I was home. I didn't know it was you, and I wasn't in the mood for company." He dialed 911 as he led her away from the carnage, over to his truck.

"I shouldn't have gone with Stryker. I almost got us killed."

"It wasn't your fault. It was Stryker's."

"He took Carlson's money, but he's not…not a killer."

"He made a bad choice, baby. Now he'll have to pay."

Johnnie came jogging up just then, the rifle casually gripped in one hand. "You both okay?"

Ty nodded. "Thanks, partner."

"Looks like this is finally over."

Ty nodded. "Yeah, looks like." His eyes found hers,

and Haley thought he wanted to say something more, but he didn't. There were a million things she wanted to say to him.

It wasn't going to happen here, not with death all around them, not with the police on their way up the hill.

It was getting dark by the time Detective Cogan had finished taking their statements and was finally ready to let them go home.

"You need to stay close until all this is sorted out," the detective said.

"We'll be where you can find us," Ty told him.

Cogan's partner, Matt Rollins, walked away from where the crime scene people were working over the bodies, over to where they stood getting ready to leave.

"You and I may not like each other, Brodie, but I shouldn't have let that interfere with my job. I'm glad this went down the way it did."

Ty nodded. "Thanks." He helped Haley into the pickup and they rolled off down the hill, the silence thick between them as they made their way out of the canyon.

"I don't want to go back to Aunt Ellie's," Haley said. "I need to talk to you. There are things I want to say, and I'm asking you to give me a chance to say them."

Ty cast her a sideways glance but made no reply, just drove back down to his condo, parked in the garage and led her inside. Both of them were exhausted, Ty in the dark place he always went to after he'd been in action. But Haley had waited all day to have her say, and at last it was time.

Ty tossed his gear bag up on the kitchen table, unclipped his holstered weapon and set it down next to the canvas bag. He took off his ankle gun and the knife strapped to his thigh, put them in the bag.

"I'm sorry you had to see that," he said. "Fuck, I'm sorry it happened. I read Carlson wrong all along. I didn't think he'd involve himself personally. I've been wrong about a lot of things lately."

She wanted to touch him so badly she ached. "You couldn't have known what would happen, and I've been wrong about a lot of things, too."

His eyes found hers. "Is that right?"

"I wanted to tell you. I called a dozen times, but you didn't pick up. I thought…I was afraid you were with Tiffany."

He scoffed. "I'm not interested in Tiffany. I thought you at least knew that much."

Her heart squeezed. "I do. I just… I should have trusted you, believed in you. Then Stryker said you were with Carlson and that Carlson was threatening to kill you. I couldn't…couldn't let anything happen to you. I love you too much for that."

Ty stood immobile as she walked toward him, slid her arms around his neck, leaned into him. "I love you so much, Ty. I thought we were going to die today. But I'd already figured out I didn't want to live without you."

The darkness slowly faded from his eyes. Ty cupped her face between his hands, bent his head and very softly kissed her.

"I want to marry you, baby. I want that more than anything. But while you were gone, I had time to think. If you're not ready for that, I'm willing to wait. Just say you'll stay here and not go back to Chicago."

A thick lump swelled in her throat. "I'm not going back. And I don't want to wait. I want us to get married. I want to have your babies. I was just afraid."

Ty's arms came around her, drew her closer. "We're gonna make it. You believe that, don't you?"

"I believe it. I know it in my heart."

"Are you sure about this, Haley? Because I'm only doing it once."

"I'm not my mother. I know what real love is, and I know I've found it with you. I love you, Ty Brodie." She looked up at him, let him see all the feelings there in her heart. "Let's get married."

Ty started grinning. "When?"

"Whenever you say."

"Your aunt's gonna want to do the whole wedding bit all over. Can you handle it?"

"This time without the shooting?"

He just kept grinning. "Yeah."

"Then I can definitely handle it."

Ty kissed her, slow and deep. "You know what, baby? After the last few days, I think you can handle just about anything."

Haley laughed and kissed him.

Epilogue

They'd been married three weeks, just home from a honeymoon in Hawaii, a week of lounging on the beach, catamaran sailing, hiking and paragliding off the cliffs. They were already looking forward to snowboarding this winter.

Ty was back at work, and Haley had accepted Lane Bishop's offer to come aboard as a partner in her design firm. Haley was in charge of the art acquisitions for her friend's wealthy clients' homes. Haley was also busy adding feminine touches here and there to his condo. Ty hadn't realized how much he'd missed having a place that felt like a real home.

The past was slowly fading. Stephen Carlson was dead and so was Quentin Sloan. Stryker had turned himself in and made a plea bargain, returning Carlson's money in exchange for a three-year prison sentence.

Abigail McQueen had also come in voluntarily. No longer afraid for her daughter's life or her own, she'd agreed to assist the police in any way she could. Ellie had helped her find a good lawyer, and he was in the process of negotiating a deal.

Jules Weaver's condition was improving. Looked like he'd be out of jail before the end of the year.

Three security guards, recently employed at the Fizer but formerly employed at the Scarsdale Center had also been arrested, charged with burglary, grand theft and myriad other charges.

On learning about James Warren's murder and the other deaths related to the theft of the paintings, Nathan Silverman had a change of heart and voluntarily returned the Renoir in exchange for any charges against him being dropped.

A search warrant for Aguri Tanaka's San Francisco residence turned up nothing. As the owner of several homes, including one in Japan, it was thought the Rembrandt had been shipped out of the country. Ty didn't think it would ever be recovered.

So far nothing had revealed the whereabouts of the Titian and Caravaggio stolen in the original heist.

But Jimmy Warren's killers had been found and faced a harsh justice. The rest would be up to the police.

Ty looked up at the sound of the doorbell. Haley was upstairs comparing paint chips, trying to decide what color to paint the guest room. There was no doubt she was happy. Ty grinned to think he was the beneficiary of all the love she'd once been afraid to show him.

The doorbell rang again, and he glanced through the peephole, spotted Betty Jean on the porch. She and Haley had bonded, brought together by the love they shared for Haley's dad.

He pulled open the door to welcome her in, leaned over and hugged her. "How you doin', darlin'?"

"Oh, it's a glorious day, and I'm doing just fine." In

emerald-green polyester pants and a matching print top, she bustled into the room. "I was going to call but I wasn't that far away. I found something I thought you might want to see."

Haley came bounding down the stairs, ponytail swinging, and flew into his arms. "Hey, cowboy." She gave him a quick kiss on the lips. "Hi, Betty Jean. I found just the right color for the guest room. It's sort of a soft butter-yellow. It could work for a nursery when the time comes."

He grinned. God, he loved this woman. "Sounds perfect." He kissed her back, returned his attention to their visitor. "So what did you bring us?"

She opened her purse and pulled out a key ring. "I found Jimmy's car keys. I stumbled onto them out in the yard near the back door. He must have used the spare set the morning he drove to the dock. Jimmy was always losing his keys."

Ty took the key chain from Betty Jean's hand, noticed a silver medallion with the picture of a boat on the front, keys to the Jeep, a house key and a rabbit's foot.

"That was Jimmy's lucky charm," Betty Jean said.

Ty recognized the rabbit's foot for what it was, reached out and gently pulled it apart. "It's a flash drive."

"Oh, wow," Haley said. "You don't think—"

"You never know. Let's see what's on it."

They went into the room Ty used as an office, and he booted up the computer. He plugged in the furry little flash drive, watched as rows and rows of numbers started popping up.

"What is that?" Betty Jean asked.

Interest trickled through him. "Account numbers." He raised his eyebrows. "Well, would you look at that?

Bank of Grand Cayman. The name on the account is Stephen Carlson." Ty flicked a glance at Haley. "Looks like your dad found the money Carlson got paid for the first two paintings. He was building one helluva case."

"Maybe the cops'll be able to track down the buyers and recover the stolen art."

"Danoff would have brokered the deal, but if they follow the money, there's no telling where it might lead."

Haley smiled. "I'm glad you sent me that first email, Betty Jean. If you hadn't, I wouldn't have come to California. We wouldn't have found the men who killed my dad." She looked up at Ty, and he didn't miss the quick flash of tears in her pretty blue eyes. "And I wouldn't have met the man I fell in love with."

Never tired of hearing the words, Ty leaned down and kissed her. He wondered if James Warren was watching his wife and daughter from somewhere above.

If he was, Ty figured Jimmy would definitely approve.

* * * * *

Author's Note

I hope you enjoyed Ty and Haley in *Against the Mark*. They were such fun characters to write. If you haven't read the rest of my Raines of Wind Canyon series, I hope you'll look for the Raines brothers in *Against the Wind, Against the Fire, Against the Law,* as well as their friends in *Against the Storm, Against the Night, Against the Sun, Against the Odds* and *Against the Edge*.

Until next time, very best wishes and happy reading.

Kat

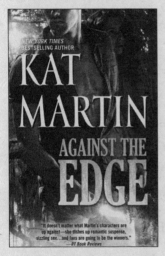

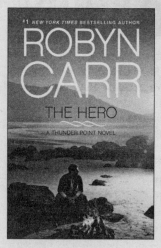

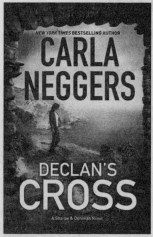

REQUEST YOUR
FREE BOOKS!

2 FREE NOVELS
FROM THE ROMANCE COLLECTION
PLUS 2 FREE GIFTS!

YES! Please send me 2 FREE novels from the Romance Collection and my 2 FREE gifts (gifts are worth about $10). After receiving them, if I don't wish to receive any more books, I can return the shipping statement marked "cancel." If I don't cancel, I will receive 4 brand-new novels every month and be billed just $6.24 per book in the U.S. or $6.74 per book in Canada. That's a savings of at least 22% off the cover price. It's quite a bargain! Shipping and handling is just 50¢ per book in the U.S. and 75¢ per book in Canada.* I understand that accepting the 2 free books and gifts places me under no obligation to buy anything. I can always return a shipment and cancel at any time. Even if I never buy another book, the two free books and gifts are mine to keep forever.

194/394 MDN F4XY

Name	(PLEASE PRINT)

Address	Apt. #

City	State/Prov.	Zip/Postal Code

Signature (if under 18, a parent or guardian must sign)

Mail to the Harlequin® Reader Service:
IN U.S.A.: P.O. Box 1867, Buffalo, NY 14240-1867
IN CANADA: P.O. Box 609, Fort Erie, Ontario L2A 5X3

Want to try two free books from another line?
Call 1-800-873-8635 or visit www.ReaderService.com.

* Terms and prices subject to change without notice. Prices do not include applicable taxes. Sales tax applicable in N.Y. Canadian residents will be charged applicable taxes. Offer not valid in Quebec. This offer is limited to one order per household. Not valid for current subscribers to the Romance Collection or the Romance/Suspense Collection. All orders subject to credit approval. Credit or debit balances in a customer's account(s) may be offset by any other outstanding balance owed by or to the customer. Please allow 4 to 6 weeks for delivery. Offer available while quantities last.

Your Privacy—The Harlequin® Reader Service is committed to protecting your privacy. Our Privacy Policy is available online at www.ReaderService.com or upon request from the Harlequin Reader Service.

We make a portion of our mailing list available to reputable third parties that offer products we believe may interest you. If you prefer that we not exchange your name with third parties, or if you wish to clarify or modify your communication preferences, please visit us at www.ReaderService.com/consumerschoice or write to us at Harlequin Reader Service Preference Service, P.O. Box 9062, Buffalo, NY 14269. Include your complete name and address.

ROM13R

KAT MARTIN

32940	AGAINST THE LAW	___ $7.99 U.S.	___ $9.99 CAN.
32930	AGAINST THE FIRE	___ $7.99 U.S.	___ $9.99 CAN.
32919	AGAINST THE WIND	___ $7.99 U.S.	___ $9.99 CAN.
32874	THE HANDMAIDEN'S NECKLACE	___ $7.99 U.S.	___ $9.99 CAN.
32867	THE BRIDE'S NECKLACE	___ $7.99 U.S.	___ $9.99 CAN.
32642	ROYAL'S BRIDE	___ $7.99 U.S.	___ $8.99 CAN.
31443	AGAINST THE EDGE	___ $7.99 U.S.	___ $9.99 CAN.
31422	AGAINST THE ODDS	___ $7.99 U.S.	___ $9.99 CAN.
31319	AGAINST THE NIGHT	___ $7.99 U.S.	___ $9.99 CAN.
31292	AGAINST THE STORM	___ $7.99 U.S.	___ $9.99 CAN.

(limited quantities available)

TOTAL AMOUNT	$ _____
POSTAGE & HANDLING	$ _____
($1.00 for 1 book, 50¢ for each additional)	
APPLICABLE TAXES*	$ _____
TOTAL PAYABLE	$ _____

(check or money order—please do not send cash)

To order, complete this form and send it, along with a check or money order for the total above, payable to MIRA Books, to: **In the U.S.:** 3010 Walden Avenue, P.O. Box 9077, Buffalo, NY 14269-9077; **In Canada:** P.O. Box 636, Fort Erie, Ontario, L2A 5X3.

Name: _____
Address: _____ City: _____
State/Prov.: _____ Zip/Postal Code: _____
Account Number (if applicable): _____
075 CSAS

*New York residents remit applicable sales taxes.
*Canadian residents remit applicable GST and provincial taxes.

31901055190930

HARLEQUIN® MIRA®
www.Harlequin.com

MKM0913BL

THIS TALE IS INSCRIBED
TO THE
LORD JOHN RUSSELL
IN REMEMBRANCE OF
MANY PUBLIC SERVICES AND
PRIVATE KINDNESSES

CONTENTS

BOOK THE FIRST
RECALLED TO LIFE

BOOK THE SECOND
THE GOLDEN THREAD

CONTENTS

THE FIRST EDITION

WHEN I was acting, with my children and friends, in Mr. Wilkie Collins's drama of *The Frozen Deep*, I first conceived the main idea of this story. A strong desire was upon me then to embody it in my own person; and I traced out in my fancy the state of mind of which it would necessitate the presentation to an observant spectator, with particular care and interest.

As the idea became familiar to me, it gradually shaped itself into its present form. Throughout its execution, it has had complete possession of me; I have so far verified what is done and suffered in these pages, as that I have certainly done and suffered it all myself.

Whenever any reference (however slight) is made here to the condition of the French people before or during the Revolution, it is truly made, on the faith of trustworthy witnesses. It has been one of my hopes to add something to the popular and picturesque means of understanding that terrible time, though no one can hope to add anything to the philosophy of Mr. Carlyle's wonderful book.

TAVISTOCK HOUSE, LONDON
November, 1859

BOOK THE FIRST

Recalled to Life

1 The Period

IT WAS the best of times, it was the worst of times, it was the age of wisdom, it was the age of foolishness, it was the epoch of belief, it was the epoch of incredulity, it was the season of Light, it was the season of Darkness, it was the spring of hope, it was the winter of despair, we had everything before us, we had nothing before us, we were all going direct to Heaven, we were all going direct the other way—in short, the period was so far like the present period, that some of its noisiest authorities insisted on its being received, for good or for evil, in the superlative degree of comparison only.

There were a king with a large jaw, and a queen with a plain face, on the throne of England; there were a king with a large jaw, and a queen with a fair face, on the throne of France. In both countries it was clearer than crystal to the lords of the State preserves of loaves and fishes, that things in general were settled for ever.

It was the year of Our Lord one thousand seven hundred and seventy-five. Spiritual revelations were conceded to England at that favoured period, as at this. Mrs. South-cott had recently attained her five-and-twentieth blessed birthday, of whom a prophetic private in the Life Guards had heralded the sublime appearance by announcing that arrangements were made for the swallowing up of London and Westminster. Even the Cock-lane ghost had been laid only a round dozen of years, after rapping out its messages, as the spirits of this very year last past (supernaturally deficient in originality) rapped out theirs. Mere messages in the earthly order of events had lately come to the English Crown and People, from a congress of British subjects in America: which, strange to relate, have proved more important to the human race than any communications yet received through any of the chickens of the Cock-lane brood.

France, less favoured on the whole as to matters spiritual than her sister of the shield and trident, rolled with exceeding smoothness down hill, making paper money and spending it. Under the guidance of her Christian pastors, she entertained herself, besides, with such humane achievements as sentencing a youth to have his hands cut off, his tongue torn out with pincers, and his body burned alive, because he had not kneeled down in the rain to do honour to a dirty procession of monks which passed within his view, at a distance of some fifty or sixty yards. It is likely enough that, rooted in the woods of France and Norway, there were growing trees, when that sufferer was put to death, already marked by the Woodman, Fate, to come down and be sawn into boards, to make a certain movable framework with a sack and a knife in it, terrible in history. It is likely enough that in the rough outhouses of some tillers of the heavy lands adjacent to Paris, there were sheltered from the weather that very day, rude carts, bespattered with rustic mire, snuffed about by pigs, and roosted in by poultry, which the Farmer, Death, had already set apart to be his tumbrils of the Revolution. But that Woodman and that Farmer, though they work unceasingly, work silently, and no one heard them as they went about with muffled tread: the rather, forasmuch as to entertain any suspicion that they were awake, was to be atheistical and traitorous.

In England, there was scarcely an amount of order and protection to justify much national boasting. Daring burglaries by armed men, and highway robberies, took place in the capital itself every night; families were publicly cautioned not to go out of town without removing their furniture to upholsterers' warehouses for security; the highwayman in the dark was a City tradesman in the light, and, being recognised and challenged by his fellow-tradesman whom he stopped in his character of "the Captain," gallantly shot him through the head and rode away; the mail was waylaid by seven robbers, and the guard shot three dead, and then got shot dead himself by the other four, "in consequence of the failure of his ammunition": after which the mail was robbed in peace; that magnificent potentate, the Lord Mayor of London, was made to stand and deliver on Turnham Green by one highwayman, who despoiled the illustrious creature in sight of all his retinue; prisoners in London gaols fought battles with their turnkeys, and the majesty of the law fired blunderbusses in among them, loaded with rounds of shot and ball; thieves snipped off diamond crosses from the necks of noble lords at Court drawing-rooms; musketeers went into St. Giles's, to search for contraband goods, and the mob fired on the musketeers, and the musketeers fired on the mob, and nobody thought any of these occurrences much out of the common way. In the midst of them, the hangman, ever busy and ever worse than useless, was in constant requisition; now, stringing up long rows of miscellaneous criminals; now, hanging a housebreaker on Saturday who had been taken on Tuesday; now, burning people in the hand at Newgate by the dozen, and now, burning pamphlets at the door of Westminster Hall; to-day, taking the life of an atrocious murderer, and to-morrow of a wretched pilferer who had robbed a farmer's boy of sixpence.

All these things, and a thousand like them, came to pass in and close upon the dear old year one thousand seven hundred and seventy-five. Environed by them, while the Woodman and the Farmer worked unheeded, those two of the large jaws, and those other two of the plain and the fair faces, trod with stir enough, and carried their divine rights with a high hand. Thus did the year one thousand seven hundred and seventy-five conduct their Greatnesses, and myriads of small creatures—the creatures of this chronicle among the rest—along the roads that lay before them.

2 The Mail

IT WAS the Dover road that lay, on a Friday night late in November, before the first of the persons with whom this history has business. The Dover road lay, as to him, beyond the Dover mail, as it lumbered up Shooter's Hill. He walked uphill in the mire by the side of the mail, as the rest of the passengers did; not because they had the least relish for walking exercise, under the circumstances, but because the hill, and the harness, and the mud, and the mail, were all so heavy, that the horses had three times already come to a stop, besides once drawing the coach across the road, with the mutinous intent of taking it back to Blackheath. Reins and whip and coachman and guard, however, in combination, had read that article of war which forbade a purpose otherwise strongly in favour of the argument, that some brute animals are endued with Reason; and the team had capitulated and returned to their duty.

With drooping heads and tremulous tails, they mashed their way through the thick mud, floundering and stumbling between whiles, as if they were falling to pieces at the larger joints. As often as the driver rested them and brought them to a stand, with a wary "Wo-ho! so-ho then!" the near leader violently shook his head and everything upon it—like an unusually emphatic horse, denying that the coach could be got up the hill. Whenever the leader made this rattle, the passenger started, as a nervous passenger might, and was disturbed in mind.

There was a steaming mist in all the hollows, and it had roamed in its forlornness up the hill, like an evil spirit, seeking rest and finding none. A clammy and intensely cold mist, it made its slow way through the air in ripples that visibly followed and overspread one another, as the waves of an unwholesome sea might do. It was dense enough to shut out everything from the light of the coach-lamps but these its own workings, and a few yards of road; and the reek of the labouring horses steamed into it, as if they had made it all.

Two other passengers, besides the one, were plodding up the hill by the side of the mail. All three were wrapped to the cheek-bones and over the ears, and wore jack-boots. Not one of the three could have said, from anything he saw, what either of the other two was like; and each was hidden under almost as many wrappers from the eyes of the mind, as from the eyes of the body, of his two companions. In those days, travellers were very shy of being confidential on a short notice, for anybody on the road might be a robber or in league with robbers. As to the latter, when every posting-house and ale-house could produce somebody in "the Captain's" pay, ranging from the landlord to the lowest stable nondescript, it was the likeliest thing upon the cards. So the guard of the Dover mail thought to himself, that Friday night in November, one thousand seven hundred and seventy-five, lumbering up Shooter's Hill, as he stood on his own particular perch behind the mail, beating his feet, and keeping an eye and a hand on the arm-chest before him, where a loaded blunderbuss lay at the top of six or eight loaded horse-pistols, deposited on a substratum of cutlass.

The Dover mail was in its usual genial position that the guard suspected the passengers, the passengers suspected one another and the guard, they all suspected everybody else, and the coachman was sure of nothing but the horses; as to which cattle he could with a clear conscience have taken his oath on the two Testaments that they were not fit for the journey.

"Wo-ho!" said the coachman. "So, then! One more pull and you're at the top and be damned to you, for I have had trouble enough to get you to it!—Joe!"

"Halloa!" the guard replied.

"What o'clock do you make it, Joe?"

"Ten minutes, good, past eleven."

"My blood!" ejaculated the vexed coachman, "and not atop of Shooter's yet! Tst! Yah! Get on with you!"

The emphatic horse, cut short by the whip in a most decided negative, made a decided scramble for it, and the three other horses followed suit. Once more, the Dover mail struggled on, with the jack-boots of its passengers squashing along by its side. They had stopped when the coach stopped, and they kept close company with it. If any one of the three had had the hardihood to propose to another to walk on a little ahead into the mist and darkness, he would have put himself in a fair way of getting shot instantly as a highwayman.

The last burst carried the mail to the summit of the hill. The horses stopped to breathe again, and the guard got down to skid the wheel for the descent, and open the coach-door to let the passengers in.

"Tst! Joe!" cried the coachman in a warning voice, looking down from his box.

"What do you say, Tom?"

They both listened.

"I say a horse at a canter coming up, Joe."

"*I* say a horse at a gallop, Tom," returned the guard,

leaving his hold of the door, and mounting nimbly to his place. "Gentlemen! In the king's name, all of you!"

With this hurried adjuration, he cocked his blunderbuss, and stood on the offensive.

The passenger booked by this history was on the coachstep, getting in; the two other passengers were close behind him, and about to follow. He remained on the step, half in the coach and half out of it; they remained in the road below him. They all looked from the coachman to the guard, and from the guard to the coachman, and listened. The coachman looked back and the guard looked back, and even the emphatic leader pricked up his ears and looked back, without contradicting.

The stillness consequent on the cessation of the rumbling and labouring of the coach, added to the stillness of the night, made it very quiet indeed. The panting of the horses communicated a tremulous motion to the coach, as if it were in a state of agitation. The hearts of the passengers beat loud enough perhaps to be heard; but at any rate, the quiet pause was audibly expressive of people out of breath, and holding the breath, and having the pulses quickened by expectation.

The sound of a horse at a gallop came fast and furiously up the hill.

"So-ho!" the guard sang out, as loud as he could roar. "Yo there! Stand! I shall fire!"

The pace was suddenly checked, and, with much splashing and floundering, a man's voice called from the mist, "Is that the Dover mail?"

"Never you mind what it is!" the guard retorted. "What are you?"

"*Is* that the Dover mail?"

"Why do you want to know?"

"I want a passenger, if it is."

"What passenger?"

"Mr. Jarvis Lorry."

Our booked passenger showed in a moment that it was his name. The guard, the coachman, and the two other passengers eyed him distrustfully.

"Keep where you are," the guard called to the voice in the mist, "because, if I should make a mistake, it could never be set right in your lifetime. Gentleman of the name of Lorry answer straight."

"What is the matter?" asked the passenger, then, with mildly quavering speech. "Who wants me? Is it Jerry?"

("I don't like Jerry's voice, if it is Jerry," growled the guard to himself. "He's hoarser than suits me, is Jerry.")

"Yes, Mr. Lorry."

"What is the matter?"

"A despatch sent after you from over yonder. T. and Co."

"I know this messenger, guard," said Mr. Lorry, getting down into the road—assisted from behind more swiftly than politely by the other two passengers, who immediately scrambled into the coach, shut the door, and pulled up the window. "He may come close; there's nothing wrong."

"I hope there ain't, but I can't make so 'Nation sure of that," said the guard, in gruff soliloquy. "Hallo you!"

"Well! And hallo you!" said Jerry, more hoarsely than before.

"Come on at a footpace, d'ye mind me? And if you've got holsters to that saddle o' yourn, don't let me see your hand go nigh 'em. For I'm a devil at a quick mistake, and when I make one it takes the form of Lead. So now let's look at you."

The figures of a horse and rider came slowly through the eddying mist, and came to the side of the mail, where the passenger stood. The rider stooped, and, casting up his eyes at the guard, handed the passenger a small folded paper. The rider's horse was blown, and both horse and rider were covered with mud, from the hoofs of the horse to the hat of the man.

"Guard!" said the passenger, in a tone of quiet business confidence.

The watchful guard, with his right hand at the stock of his raised blunderbuss, his left at the barrel, and his eye on the horseman, answered curtly, "Sir."

"There is nothing to apprehend. I belong to Tellson's Bank. You must know Tellson's Bank in London. I am going to Paris on business. A crown to drink. I may read this?"

"If so be as you're quick, sir."

He opened it in the light of the coach-lamp on that side, and read—first to himself and then aloud: " 'Wait at Dover for Mam'selle.' It's not long, you see, guard. Jerry, say that my answer was, RECALLED TO LIFE."

Jerry started in his saddle. "That's a Blazing strange answer, too," said he, at his hoarsest.

"Take that message back, and they will know that I received this, as well as if I wrote. Make the best of your way. Good night."

With those words the passenger opened the coach-door and got in; not at all assisted by his fellow-passengers, who had expeditiously secreted their watches and purses in their boots, and were now making a general pretence of being asleep. With no more definite purpose than to escape the hazard of originating any other kind of action.

The coach lumbered on again, with heavier wreaths of mist closing round it as it began the descent. The guard soon replaced his blunderbuss in his arm-chest, and, having looked to the rest of its contents, and having looked to the supplementary pistols that he wore in his belt, looked to a smaller chest beneath his seat, in which there were a few smith's tools, a couple of torches, and a tinder-box. For he was furnished with that completeness that if the coach-lamps had been blown and stormed out, which did occasionally happen, he had only to shut himself up inside, keep the flint and steel sparks well off the straw, and get a light with tolerable safety and ease (if he were lucky) in five minutes.

"Tom!" softly over the coach-roof.

"Hallo, Joe."

"Did you hear the message?"

"I did, Joe."

"What did you make of it, Tom?"

"Nothing at all, Joe."

"That's coin*cid*ence, too," the guard mused, "for I made the same of it myself."

Jerry, left alone in the mist and darkness, dismounted meanwhile, not only to ease his spent horse, but to wipe the mud from his face, and shake the wet out of his hat-brim, which might be capable of holding about half a gallon. After standing with the bridle over his heavily-splashed arm, until the wheels of the mail were no longer within hearing and the night was quite still again, he turned to walk down the hill.

"After that there gallop from Temple Bar, old lady, I won't trust your fore-legs till I get you on the level," said this hoarse messenger, glancing at his mare. " 'Recalled to life.' That's a Blazing strange message. Much of that wouldn't do for you, Jerry! I say, Jerry! You'd be in a Blazing bad way, if recalling to life was to come into fashion, Jerry!"

3 *The Night Shadows*

A WONDERFUL fact to reflect upon, that every human creature is constituted to be that profound secret and mystery to every other. A solemn consideration, when I enter a great city by night, that every one of those darkly clustered houses encloses its own secret; that every room in every one of them encloses its own secret; that every beating heart in the hundreds of thousands of breasts there is, in some of its imaginings, a secret to the heart nearest it! Something of the awfulness, even of Death itself, is referable to this. No more can I turn the leaves of this dear book that I loved, and vainly hope in time to read it all. No more can I look into the depths of this unfathomable water, wherein, as momentary lights glanced into it, I have had glimpses of buried treasure and other things submerged. It was appointed that the book should shut with a spring, for ever and for ever, when I had read but a page. It was appointed that the water should be locked in an eternal frost, when the light was playing on its surface, and I stood in ignorance on the shore. My friend is dead, my neighbour is dead, my love, the darling of my soul, is dead; it is the inexorable consolation and perpetuation of the secret that was always in that individuality, and which I shall carry in mine to my life's end. In any of the burial-places of this city through which I pass, is there a sleeper more inscrutable than its busy inhabitants are, in their innermost personality, to me, or than I am to them?

As to this, his natural and not to be alienated inheritance, the messenger on horseback had exactly the same possessions as the King, the first Minister of State, or the richest merchant in London. So with the three passengers shut up in the narrow compass of one lumbering old mail coach; they were mysteries to one another, as complete as if each had been in his own coach and six, or his own coach and sixty, with the breadth of a county between him and the next.

The messenger rode back at an easy trot, stopping pretty often at ale-houses by the way to drink, but evincing a tendency to keep his own counsel, and to keep his hat cocked over his eyes. He had eyes that assorted very well with that decoration, being of a surface black, with no depth in the colour or form, and much too near together —as if they were afraid of being found out in something, singly, if they kept too far apart. They had a sinister expression, under an old cocked-hat like a three-cornered spittoon, and over a great muffler for the chin and throat, which descended nearly to the wearer's knees. When he stopped for drink, he moved this muffler with his left hand, only while he poured his liquor in with his right; as soon as that was done, he muffled again.

"No, Jerry, no!" said the messenger, harping on one theme as he rode. "It wouldn't do for you, Jerry. Jerry, you honest tradesman, it wouldn't suit *your* line of business! Recalled—! Bust me if I don't think he'd been a drinking!"

His message perplexed his mind to that degree that he was fain, several times, to take off his hat to scratch his head. Except on the crown, which was raggedly bald, he had stiff, black hair, standing jaggedly all over it, and growing downhill almost to his broad, blunt nose. It was so like smith's work, so much more like the top of a strongly spiked wall than a head of hair, that the best of players at leap-frog might have declined him, as the most dangerous man in the world to go over.

While he trotted back with the message he was to deliver to the night watchman in his box at the door of Tellson's Bank, by Temple Bar, who was to deliver it to greater authorities within, the shadows of the night took such shapes to him as arose out of the message, and took such shapes to the mare as arose out of *her* private topics of uneasiness. They seemed to be numerous, for she shied at every shadow on the road.

What time, the mail-coach lumbered, jolted, rattled, and bumped upon its tedious way, with its three fellow-inscrutables inside. To whom, likewise, the shadows of the night revealed themselves, in the forms their dozing eyes and wandering thoughts suggested.

Tellson's Bank had a run upon it in the mail. As the bank passenger—with an arm drawn through the leathern strap, which did what lay in it to keep him from pounding against the next passenger, and driving him into his corner, whenever the coach got a special jolt—nodded in his place, with half-shut eyes, the little coach-windows, and the coach-lamp dimly gleaming through them, and the bulky bundle of opposite passenger, became the bank, and did a great stroke of business. The rattle of the harness was the chink of money, and more drafts were honoured in five minutes than even Tellson's, with all its foreign and home connection, ever paid in thrice the time. Then the strong-rooms underground, at Tellson's, with such of their valuable stores and secrets as were known to the passenger (and it was not a little that he knew about them), opened before him, and he went in among them with the great keys and the feebly-burning candle, and found them safe, and strong, and sound, and still, just as he had last seen them.

But, though the bank was almost always with him, and though the coach (in a confused way, like the presence of pain under an opiate) was always with him, there was another current of impression that never ceased to run, all through the night. He was on his way to dig some one out of a grave.

Now, which of the multitude of faces that showed themselves before him was the true face of the buried person, the shadows of the night did not indicate; but they were all the faces of a man of five-and-forty by years, and they differed principally in the passions they expressed, and in the ghastliness of their worn and wasted state. Pride, contempt, defiance, stubbornness, submission, lamentation, succeeded one another; so did varieties of sunken cheek, cadaverous colour, emaciated hands and figures. But the face was in the main one face, and every head was prematurely white. A hundred times the dozing passenger inquired of this spectre:

"Buried how long?"

The answer was always the same: "Almost eighteen years."

"You had abandoned all hope of being dug out?"

"Long ago."

"You know that you are recalled to life?"

"They tell me so."

"I hope you care to live?"

"I can't say."

"Shall I show her to you? Will you come and see her?"

The answers to this question were various and contradictory. Sometimes the broken reply was, "Wait! It would kill me if I saw her too soon." Sometimes, it was given in a tender rain of tears, and then it was, "Take me to her." Sometimes it was staring and bewildered, and then it was, "I don't know her. I don't understand."

After such imaginary discourse, the passenger in his fancy would dig, and dig, dig—now with a spade, now with a great key, now with his hands—to dig this wretched creature out. Got out at last, with earth hanging about his face and hair, he would suddenly fall away to dust. The passenger would then start to himself, and lower the window, to get the reality of mist and rain on his cheek.

Yet even when his eyes were opened on the mist and rain, on the moving patch of light from the lamps, and the hedge at the roadside retreating by jerks, the night shadows outside the coach would fall into the train of night shadows within. The real banking-house by Temple Bar, the real business of the past day, the real strong-rooms, the real express sent after him, and the real message returned, would all be there. Out of the midst of them, the ghostly face would rise, and he would accost it again.

"Buried how long?"

"Almost eighteen years."

"I hope you care to live?"

"I can't say."

Dig—dig—dig—until an impatient movement from one of the two passengers would admonish him to pull up the window, draw his arm securely through the leathern strap, and speculate upon the two slumbering forms, until his mind lost its hold of them, and they again slid away into the bank and the grave.

"Buried how long?"

"Almost eighteen years."

"You had abandoned all hope of being dug out?"

"Long ago."

The words were still in his hearing as just spoken—distinctly in his hearing as ever spoken words had been in his life—when the weary passenger started to the consciousness of daylight, and found that the shadows of the night were gone.

He lowered the window, and looked out at the rising sun. There was a ridge of ploughed land, with a plough upon it where it had been left last night when the horses were unyoked; beyond, a quiet coppice-wood, in which many leaves of burning red and golden yellow still remained upon the trees. Though the earth was cold and wet, the sky was clear, and the sun rose bright, placid, and beautiful.

"Eighteen years!" said the passenger, looking at the sun. "Gracious Creator of day! To be buried alive for eighteen years!"

*　　*　　*　　*　　*　　*　　*　　*

4 The Preparation

WHEN THE mail got successfully to Dover, in the course of the forenoon, the head drawer at the Royal George Hotel opened the coach-door as his custom was. He did it with some flourish of ceremony, for a mail journey from London in winter was an achievement to congratulate an adventurous traveller upon.

By that time, there was only one adventurous traveller left to be congratulated; for the two others had been set down at their respective roadside destinations. The mildewy inside of the coach, with its damp and dirty straw, its disagreeable smell, and its obscurity, was rather like a larger dog-kennel. Mr. Lorry, the passenger, shaking himself out of it in chains of straw, a tangle of shaggy wrapper, flapping hat, and muddy legs, was rather like a larger sort of dog.

"There will be a packet to Calais to-morrow, drawer?"

"Yes, sir, if the weather holds and the wind sets tolerable fair. The tide will serve pretty nicely at about two in the afternoon, sir. Bed, sir?"

"I shall not go to bed till night; but I want a bedroom, and a barber."

"And then breakfast, sir? Yes, sir. That way, sir, if you please. Show Concord! Gentleman's valise and hot water to Concord. Pull off gentleman's boots in Concord. (You will find a fine sea-coal fire, sir.) Fetch barber to Concord. Stir about there, now, for Concord!"

The Concord bedchamber being always assigned to a passenger by the mail, and passengers by the mail being always heavily wrapped up from head to foot, the room had the odd interest for the establishment of the Royal George, that although but one kind of man was seen to go into it, all kinds and varieties of men came out of it. Consequently, another drawer, and two porters, and several maids and the landlady, were all loitering by accident at various points of the road between the Concord and the coffee-room, when a gentleman of sixty, formally dressed in a brown suit of clothes, pretty well worn, but very well kept, with large square cuffs and large flaps to the pockets, passed along on his way to his breakfast.

The coffee-room had no other occupant, that forenoon, than the gentleman in brown. His breakfast-table was drawn before the fire, and as he sat, with its light shining on him, waiting for the meal, he sat so still, that he might have been sitting for his portrait.

Very orderly and methodical he looked, with a hand on each knee, and a loud watch ticking a sonorous sermon under his flapped waistcoat, as though it pitted its gravity and longevity against the levity and evanescence of the brisk fire. He had a good leg, and was a little vain of it, for his brown stockings fitted sleek and close, and were of a fine texture; his shoes and buckles, too, though plain, were trim. He wore an odd little sleek crisp flaxen wig, setting very close to his head; which wig, it is to be presumed, was made of hair, but which looked far more as though it were spun from filaments of silk or glass. His linen, though not of a fineness in accordance with his stockings, was as white as the tops of the waves that broke upon the neighbouring beach, or the specks of sail that glinted in the sunlight far at sea. A face habitually suppressed and quieted was still lighted up under the quaint wig by a pair of moist bright eyes that must have cost their owner, in years gone by, some pains to drill to the composed and reserved expression of Tellson's Bank. He had a healthy colour in his cheeks, and his face, though lined, bore few traces of anxiety. But, perhaps the confidential bachelor clerks in Tellson's Bank were principally occupied with the cares of other people; and perhaps second-hand cares, like second-hand clothes, come easily off and on.

Completing his resemblance to a man who was sitting for his portrait, Mr. Lorry dropped off to sleep. The arrival of his breakfast roused him, and he said to the drawer, as he moved his chair to it:

"I wish accommodation prepared for a young lady who may come here at any time to-day. She may ask for Mr. Jarvis Lorry, or she may only ask for a gentleman from Tellson's Bank. Please to let me know."

"Yes, sir. Tellson's Bank in London, sir?"

"Yes."

"Yes, sir. We have oftentimes the honour to entertain your gentlemen in their travelling backwards and forwards betwixt London and Paris, sir. A vast deal of travelling, sir, in Tellson and Company's House."

"Yes. We are quite a French House, as well as an English one."

"Yes, sir. Not much in the habit of such travelling yourself, I think, sir?"

"Not of late years. It is fifteen years since we—since I—came last from France."

"Indeed, sir? That was before my time here, sir. Before our people's time here, sir. The George was in other hands at that time, sir."

"I believe so."

"But I would hold a pretty wager, sir, that a House like Tellson and Company was flourishing, a matter of fifty, not to speak of fifteen years ago?"

"You might treble that, and say a hundred and fifty, yet not be far from the truth."

"Indeed, sir!"

Rounding his mouth and both his eyes, as he stepped backward from the table, the waiter shifted his napkin from his right arm to his left, dropped into a comfortable attitude, and stood surveying the guest while he ate and drank, as from an observatory or watch-tower, according to the immemorial usage of waiters in all ages.

When Mr. Lorry had finished his breakfast, he went out for a stroll on the beach. The little narrow, crooked town of Dover hid itself away from the beach, and ran its head into the chalk cliffs, like a marine ostrich. The beach was a desert of heaps of sea and stones tumbling wildly about, and the sea did what it liked, and what it liked was destruction. It thundered at the town, and thundered at the cliffs, and brought the coast down, madly. The air among the houses was of so strong a piscatory flavour that one might have supposed sick fish went up to be dipped in it, as sick people went down to be dipped in the sea. A little fishing was done in the port, and a quantity of strolling about by night, and looking seaward: particularly at those times when the tide made, and was near flood. Small tradesmen, who did no business whatever, sometimes unaccountably realised large fortunes, and it was remarkable that nobody in the neighbourhood could endure a lamplighter.

As the day declined into the afternoon, and the air, which had been at intervals clear enough to allow the French coast to be seen, became again charged with mist and vapour, Mr. Lorry's thoughts seemed to cloud too. When it was dark, and he sat before the coffee-room fire, awaiting his dinner as he had awaited his breakfast, his mind was busily digging, digging, digging, in the live red coals.

A bottle of good claret after dinner does a digger in the red coals no harm, otherwise than as it has a tendency to throw him out of work. Mr. Lorry had been idle a long time, and had just poured out his last glassful of wine with as complete an appearance of satisfaction as is ever to be found in an elderly gentleman of a fresh complexion who has got to the end of a bottle, when a rattling of wheels came up the narrow street, and rumbled into the inn-yard.

He set down his glass untouched. "This is Mam'selle!" said he.

In a very few minutes the waiter came in to announce that Miss Manette had arrived from London, and would be happy to see the gentleman from Tellson's.

"So soon?"

Miss Manette had taken some refreshment on the road, and required none then, and was extremely anxious to see the gentleman from Tellson's immediately, if it suited his pleasure and convenience.

The gentleman from Tellson's had nothing left for it but to empty his glass with an air of stolid desperation, settle his odd little flaxen wig at the ears, and follow the waiter to Miss Manette's apartment. It was a large, dark room, furnished in a funereal manner with black horsehair, and loaded with heavy dark tables. These had been oiled and oiled, until the two tall candles on the table in the middle of the room were gloomily reflected on every leaf; as if *they* were buried, in deep graves of black mahogany, and no light to speak of could be expected from them until they were dug out.

The obscurity was so difficult to penetrate that Mr. Lorry, picking his way over the well-worn Turkey carpet, supposed Miss Manette to be, for the moment, in some adjacent room, until, having got past the two tall candles, he saw, standing to receive him by the table between them and the fire, a young lady of not more than seventeen, in a riding-cloak, and still holding her straw travelling-hat by its ribbon in her hand. As his eyes rested on a short, slight, pretty figure, a quantity of golden hair, a pair of blue eyes that met his own with an inquiring look, and a forehead with a singular capacity (remembering how young and smooth it was) of lifting and knitting itself into an expression that was not quite one of perplexity, or wonder, or alarm, or merely of a bright fixed attention, though it included all the four expressions—as his eyes rested on these things, a sudden vivid likeness passed before him, of a child whom he had held in his arms on the passage across that very Channel, one cold time, when the hail drifted heavily and the sea ran high. The likeness passed away, like a breath along the surface of the gaunt pier-glass behind her, on the frame of which, a hospital procession of Negro cupids, several headless and all cripples, were offering black baskets of Dead Sea fruit to black divinities of the feminine gender—and he made his formal bow to Miss Manette.

"Pray take a seat, sir." In a very clear and pleasant young voice; a little foreign in its accent, but a very little indeed.

"I kiss your hand, miss," said Mr. Lorry, with the manners of an earlier date, as he made his formal bow again, and took his seat.

"I received a letter from the Bank, sir, yesterday, informing me that some intelligence—or discovery—"

"The word is not material, miss; either word will do."

"—respecting the small property of my poor father, whom I never saw—so long dead—"

Mr. Lorry moved in his chair, and cast a troubled look towards the hospital procession of Negro cupids. As if *they* had any help for anybody in their absurd baskets!

"—render it necessary that I should go to Paris, there to communicate with a gentleman of the Bank, so good as to be despatched to Paris for the purpose."

"Myself."

"As I was prepared to hear, sir."

She curtseyed to him (young ladies made curtseys in those days), with a pretty desire to convey to him that she felt how much older and wiser he was than she. He made her another bow.

"I replied to the Bank, sir, that as it was considered necessary, by those who know, and who are so kind as to advise me, that I should go to France, and that as I am an orphan and have no friend who could go with me, I should esteem it highly if I might be permitted to place myself, during the journey, under that worthy gentleman's protection. The gentleman had left London, but I think a messenger was sent after him to beg the favour of his waiting for me here."

"I was happy," said Mr. Lorry, "to be entrusted with the charge. I shall be more happy to execute it."

"Sir, I thank you indeed. I thank you very gratefully. It was told me by the Bank that the gentleman would explain to me the details of the business, and that I must prepare myself to find them of a surprising nature. I have done my best to prepare myself, and I naturally have a strong and eager interest to know what they are."

"Naturally," said Mr. Lorry. "Yes—I—"

After a pause, he added, again settling the crisp flaxen wig at the ears:

"It is very difficult to begin."

He did not begin, but, in his indecision, met her glance. The young forehead lifted itself into that singular expression—but it was pretty and characteristic, besides being singular—and she raised her hand, as if with an involuntary action she caught at, or stayed some passing shadow.

"Are you quite a stranger to me, sir?"

"Am I not?" Mr. Lorry opened his hands, and extended them outwards with an argumentative smile.

Between the eyebrows and just over the little feminine nose, the line of which was as delicate and fine as it was possible to be, the expression deepened itself as she took her seat thoughtfully in the chair by which she had hitherto remained standing. He watched her as she mused, and the moment she raised her eyes again, went on:

"In your adopted country, I presume, I cannot do better than address you as a young English lady, Miss Manette?"

"If you please, sir."

"Miss Manette, I am a man of business. I have a business charge to acquit myself of. In your reception of it, don't heed me any more than if I was a speaking machine —truly, I am not much else. I will, with your leave, relate to you, miss, the story of one of our customers."

"Story!"

He seemed wilfully to mistake the word she had repeated, when he added, in a hurry, "Yes, customers; in the banking business we usually call our connection our customers. He was a French gentleman; a scientific gentleman; a man of great acquirements—a Doctor."

"Not of Beauvais?"

"Why, yes, of Beauvais. Like Monsieur Manette, your father, the gentleman was of Beauvais. Like Monsieur Manette, your father, the gentleman was of repute in Paris. I had the honour of knowing him there. Our relations were business relations, but confidential. I was at that time in our French House, and had been—oh! twenty years."

"At that time—I may ask, at what time, sir?"

"I speak, miss, of twenty years ago. He married—an English lady—and I was one of the trustees. His affairs, like the affairs of many other French gentlemen and French families, were entirely in Tellson's hands. In a similar way I am, or I have been, trustee of one kind or other for scores of our customers. These are mere business relations, miss; there is no friendship in them; no particular interest, nothing like sentiment. I have passed from one to another, in the course of my business life, just as I pass from one of our customers to another in the course of my business day; in short, I have no feelings; I am a mere machine. To go on—"

"But this is my father's story, sir; and I begin to think" —the curiously roughened forehead was very intent upon him—"that when I was left an orphan through my mother's surviving my father only two years, it was you who brought me to England. I am almost sure it was you."

Mr. Lorry took the hesitating little hand that confidingly advanced to take his, and he put it with some ceremony to his lips. He then conducted the young lady straightway to her chair again, and, holding the chair-back with his left hand, and using his right by turns to rub his chin, pull his wig at the ears, or point what he said, stood looking down into her face while she sat looking up into his.

"Miss Manette, it *was* I. And you will see how truly I spoke of myself just now, in saying I had no feelings, and that all the relations I hold with my fellow-creatures are mere business relations, when you reflect that I have never seen you since. No; you have been the ward of Tellson's House since, and I have been busy with the other business of Tellson's House since. Feelings! I have no time for them, no chance of them. I pass my whole life, miss, in turning an immense pecuniary mangle."

After this odd description of his daily routine of employment, Mr. Lorry flattened his flaxen wig upon his head with both hands (which was most unnecessary, for nothing could be flatter than its shining surface was before), and resumed his former attitude.

"So far, miss (as you have remarked), this is the story of your regretted father. Now comes the difference. If your father had not died when he did— Don't be frightened! How you start!"

She did, indeed, start. And she caught his wrist with both her hands.

"Pray," said Mr. Lorry, in a soothing tone, bringing his left hand from the back of the chair to lay it on the supplicatory fingers that clasped him in so violent a tremble: "pray control your agitation—a matter of business. As I was saying—"

Her look so discomposed him that he stopped, wandered, and began anew:

"As I was saying; if Monsieur Manette had not died; if he had suddenly and silently disappeared; if he had been spirited away; if it had not been difficult to guess to what dreadful place, though no art could trace him; if he had an enemy in some compatriot who could exercise a privilege that I in my own time have known the boldest people afraid to speak of in a whisper, across the water there; for instance, the privilege of filling up blank forms for the consignment of any one to the oblivion of a prison for any length of time; if his wife had implored the king, the queen, the court, the clergy, for any tidings of him, and all quite in vain—then the history of your father would have been the history of this unfortunate gentleman, the Doctor of Beauvais."

"I entreat you to tell me more, sir."

"I will. I am going to. You can bear it?"

"I can bear anything but the uncertainty you leave me in at this moment."

"You speak collectedly, and you—*are* collected. That's good!" (Though his manner was less satisfied than his words.) "A matter of business. Regard it as a matter of business—business that must be done. Now if this doctor's wife, though a lady of great courage and spirit, had suffered so intensely from this cause before her little child was born—"

"The little child was a daughter, sir?"

"A daughter. A—a—matter of business—don't be distressed. Miss, if the poor lady had suffered so intensely before her little child was born, that she came to the determination of sparing the poor child the inheritance of any part of the agony she had known the pains of, by rearing her in the belief that her father was dead— No, don't kneel! In Heaven's name why should you kneel to me?"

"For the truth. O dear, good, compassionate sir, for the truth!"

"A—a matter of business. You confuse me, and how can I transact business if I am confused? Let us be clearheaded. If you could kindly mention now, for instance, what nine times ninepence are, or how many shillings in twenty guineas, it would be so encouraging. I should be so much more at my ease about your state of mind."

Without directly answering to this appeal, she sat so still when he had gently raised her, and the hands that had not ceased to clasp his wrists were so much more steady than they had been, that she communicated some reassurance to Mr. Jarvis Lorry.

"That's right, that's right. Courage! Business! You have business before you; useful business. Miss Manette, your mother took this course with you. And when she died— I believe broken-hearted—having never slackened her unavailing search for your father, she left you, at two years old, to grow to be blooming, beautiful, and happy, without the dark cloud upon you of living in uncertainty whether your father soon wore his heart out in prison, or wasted there through many lingering years."

As he said the words he looked down, with admiring

pity, on the flowing golden hair; as if he pictured to himself that it might have been already tinged with gray.

"You know that your parents had no great possession, and that what they had was secured to your mother and to you. There has been no new discovery, of money, or of any other property; but—"

He felt his wrist held closer, and he stopped. The expression in the forehead, which had so particularly attracted his notice, and which was now immovable, had deepened into one of pain and horror.

"But he has been—been found. He is alive. Greatly changed, it is too probable; almost a wreck, it is possible; though we will hope the best. Still, alive. Your father has been taken to the house of an old servant in Paris, and we are going there: I, to identify him if I can: you, to restore him to life, love, duty, rest, comfort."

A shiver ran through her frame, and from it through his. She said, in a low, distinct, awe-stricken voice, as if she were saying it in a dream:

"I am going to see his ghost! It will be his ghost—not him!"

Mr. Lorry quietly chafed the hands that held his arm. "There, there, there! See now, see now! The best and the worst are known to you, now. You are well on your way to the poor wronged gentleman, and, with a fair sea voyage, and a fair land journey, you will be soon at his dear side."

She repeated in the same tone, sunk to a whisper, "I have been free, I have been happy, yet his ghost has never haunted me!"

"Only one thing more," said Mr. Lorry, laying stress upon it as a wholesome means of enforcing her attention. "He has been found under another name; his own, long forgotten or long concealed. It would be worse than useless now to inquire which; worse than useless to seek to know whether he has been for years overlooked, or always designedly held prisoner. It would be worse than useless now to make any inquiries, because it would be dangerous. Better not to mention the subject, anywhere or in any way, and to remove him—for a while at all events—out of France. Even I, safe as an Englishman, and even Tellson's, important as they are to French credit, avoid all naming of the matter. I carry about me not a scrap of writing openly referring to it. This is a secret service altogether. My credentials, entries, and memoranda are all comprehended in the one line, 'Recalled to Life,' which may mean anything. But what is the matter? She doesn't notice a word! Miss Manette!"

Perfectly still and silent, and not even fallen back in her chair, she sat under his hand, utterly insensible; with her eyes open and fixed upon him, and with that last expression looking as if it were carved or branded into her forehead. So close was her hold upon his arm, that he feared to detach himself lest he should hurt her; therefore he called out loudly for assistance without moving.

A wild-looking woman, whom, even in his agitation, Mr. Lorry observed to be all of a red colour, and to have red hair, and to be dressed in some extraordinary tight-fitting fashion, and to have on her head a most wonderful bonnet like a Grenadier wooden measure, and good measure too, or a great Stilton cheese, came running into the room in advance of the inn servants, and soon settled the question of his detachment from the poor young lady, by laying a brawny hand upon his chest, and sending him flying back against the nearest wall.

("I really think this must be a man!" was Mr. Lorry's breathless reflection, simultaneously with his coming against the wall.)

"Why, look at you all!" bawled this figure, addressing the inn servants. "Why don't you go and fetch things, instead of standing there staring at me? I am not so much to look at, am I? Why don't you go and fetch things? I'll let you know, if you don't bring smelling-salts, cold water, and vinegar, quick, I will."

There was an immediate dispersal for these restoratives, and she softly laid the patient on a sofa, and tended her with great skill and gentleness: calling her "my precious!" and "my bird!" and spreading her golden hair aside over her shoulders with great pride and care.

"And you in brown!" she said, indignantly turning to Mr. Lorry; "couldn't you tell her what you had to tell her, without frightening her to death? Look at her, with her pretty pale face and her cold hands. Do you call *that* being a banker?"

Mr. Lorry was so exceedingly disconcerted by a question so hard to answer, that he could only look on, at a distance, with much feeble sympathy and humility, while the strong woman, having banished the inn servants under the mysterious penalty of "letting them know" something not mentioned if they stayed there, staring, recovered her charge by a regular series of gradations, and coaxed her to lay her drooping head upon her shoulder.

"I hope she will do well now," said Mr. Lorry.

"No thanks to you in brown, if she does. My darling pretty!"

"I hope," said Mr. Lorry, after another pause of feeble sympathy and humility, "that you accompany Miss Manette to France?"

"A likely thing, too!" replied the strong woman. "If it was ever intended that I should go across salt water, do you suppose Providence would have cast my lot in an island?"

This being another question hard to answer, Mr. Jarvis Lorry withdrew to consider it.

* * * * * * * *

5 *The Wine-Shop*

A LARGE cask of wine had been dropped and broken, in the street. The accident had happened in getting it out of a cart; the cask had tumbled out with a run, the hoops had burst, and it lay on the stones just outside the door of the wine-shop, shattered like a walnut-shell.

All the people within reach had suspended their business, or their idleness, to run to the spot and drink the wine. The rough, irregular stones of the street, pointing every way, and designed, one might have thought, expressly to lame all living creatures that approached them, had dammed it into little pools; these were surrounded, each by its own jostling group or crowd, according to its size. Some men kneeled down, made scoops of their two hands joined, and sipped, or tried to help women, who bent over their shoulders, to sip, before the wine had all run out between their fingers. Others, men and women, dipped in the puddles with little mugs of mutilated earthenware, or even with handkerchiefs from women's heads, which were squeezed dry into infants' mouths; others made small mud embankments, to stem the wine as it ran; others, directed by lookers-on up at high windows, darted here and there, to cut off little streams of wine that started away in new directions; others devoted themselves to the sodden and lee-dyed pieces of the cask, licking, and even champing the moister wine-rotted fragments with eager relish. There was no drainage to carry off the wine, and not only did it all get taken up, but so much mud got taken up along with it, that there might have been a scavenger in the street, if anybody acquainted with it could have believed in such a miraculous presence.

A shrill sound of laughter and of amused voices—voices of men, women, and children—resounded in the street while this wine game lasted. There was little roughness in the sport, and much playfulness. There was a special companionship in it, an observable inclination on the part of every one to join some other one, which led, especially among the luckier or lighter-hearted, to frolicsome embraces, drinking of healths, shaking of hands, and even joining of hands and dancing, a dozen together. When the wine was gone, and the places where it had been most abundant were raked into a gridiron pattern by fingers, these demonstrations ceased, as suddenly as they had broken out. The man who had left his saw sticking in the firewood he was cutting, set it in motion again; the woman who had left on a doorstep the little pot of hot ashes, at which she had been trying to soften the pain in her own starved fingers and toes, or in those of her child, returned to it; men with bare arms, matted locks, and cadaverous faces, who had emerged into the winter light from cellars, moved away, to descend again; and a gloom gathered on the scene that appeared more natural to it than sunshine.

The wine was red wine, and had stained the ground of the narrow street in the suburb of Saint Antoine, in Paris, where it was spilled. It had stained many hands, too, and many faces, and many naked feet, and many wooden shoes. The hands of the man who sawed the wood left red marks on the billets; and the forehead of the woman who nursed her baby was stained with the stain of the old rag she wound about her head again. Those who had been greedy with the staves of the cask, had acquired a tigerish smear about the mouth; and one tall joker so besmirched, his head more out of a long squalid bag of a nightcap than in it, scrawled upon a wall with his finger dipped in muddy wine-lees—BLOOD.

The time was to come, when that wine too would be spilled on the street-stones, and when the stain of it would be red upon many there.

And now that the cloud settled on Saint Antoine, which a momentary gleam had driven from his sacred countenance, the darkness of it was heavy—cold, dirt, sickness, ignorance, and want, were the lords in waiting on the saintly presence—nobles of great power all of them; but, most especially, the last. Samples of a people that had undergone a terrible grinding and re-grinding in the mill, and certainly not in the fabulous mill which ground old people young, shivered at every corner, passed in and out at every doorway, looked from every window, fluttered in every vestige of a garment that the wind shook. The mill which had worked them down was the mill that grinds young people old; the children had ancient faces and grave voices; and upon them, and upon the grown faces, and ploughed into every furrow of age and coming up afresh, was the sign, Hunger. It was prevalent everywhere. Hunger was pushed out of the tall houses, in the wretched clothing that hung upon poles and lines; Hunger was patched into them with straw and rag and wood and paper; Hunger was repeated in every fragment of the small modicum of firewood that the man sawed off; Hunger stared down from the smokeless chimneys, and started up from the filthy street that had no offal, among its refuse, of anything to eat. Hunger was the inscription on the baker's shelves, written in every small loaf of his scanty stock of bad bread; at the sausage-shop, in every dead-dog preparation that was offered for sale. Hunger rattled its dry bones among the roasting chestnuts in the turned cylinder; Hunger was shred into atomies in every farthing porringer of husky chips of potato, fried with some reluctant drops of oil.

Its abiding place was in all things fitted to it. A narrow winding street, full of offence and stench, with other narrow winding streets diverging, all peopled by rags and nightcaps, and all smelling of rags and nightcaps, and all visible things with a brooding look upon them that looked ill. In the hunted air of the people there was yet some wild-beast thought of the possibility of turning at bay. Depressed and slinking though they were, eyes of fire were not wanting among them; nor compressed lips, white with what they suppressed; nor foreheads knitted into the likeness of the gallows-rope they mused about enduring, or inflicting. The trade signs (and they were almost as many as the shops) were, all, grim illustrations of Want. The butcher and the porkman painted up only the leanest scrags of meat; the baker, the coarsest of meagre loaves. The people rudely pictured as drinking in the wine-shops, croaked over their scanty measures of thin wine and beer, and were glower-ingly confidential together. Nothing was represented in a flourishing condition, save tools and weapons; but, the cutler's knives and axes were sharp and bright, the smith's hammers were heavy, and the gunmaker's stock was mur-derous. The crippling stones of the pavement, with their many little reservoirs of mud and water, had no footways, but broke off abruptly at the doors. The kennel, to make amends, ran down the middle of the street—when it ran at all: which was only after heavy rains, and then it ran, by many eccentric fits, into the houses. Across the streets, at wide intervals, one clumsy lamp was slung by a rope and pulley; at night, when the lamplighter had let these down, and lighted, and hoisted them again, a feeble grove of dim wicks swung in a sickly manner overhead, as if they were at sea. Indeed they were at sea, and the ship and crew were in peril of tempest.

For, the time was to come, when the gaunt scarecrows of that region should have watched the lamplighter, in their idleness and hunger, so long as to conceive the idea of improving on his method, and hauling up men by those ropes and pulleys, to flare upon the darkness of their condi-tion. But, the time was not come yet; and every wind that blew over France shook the rags of the scarecrows in vain, for the birds, fine of song and feather, took no warning.

The wine-shop was a corner shop, better than most others in its appearance and degree, and the master of the wine-shop had stood outside it, in a yellow waistcoat and green breeches, looking on at the struggle for the lost wine. "It's not my affair," said he, with a final shrug of the shoul-ders. "The people from the market did it. Let them bring another."

There, his eyes happening to catch the tall joker writing up his joke, he called to him across the way:

"Say, then, my Gaspard, what do you do there?"

The fellow pointed to his joke with immense signifi-cance, as is often the way with his tribe. It missed its mark, and completely failed, as is often the way with his tribe too.

"What now? Are you a subject for the mad hospital?" said the wine-shop keeper, crossing the road, and obliterating the jest with a handful of mud, picked up for the purpose, and smeared over it. "Why do you write in the public streets? Is there—tell me thou—is there no other place to write such words in?"

In his expostulation he dropped his cleaner hand (perhaps accidentally, perhaps not) upon the joker's heart. The joker rapped it with his own, took a nimble spring upward, and came down in a fantastic dancing attitude, with one of his stained shoes jerked off his foot into his hand, and held out. A joker of an extremely, not to say wolfishly practical character he looked, under those circumstances.

"Put it on, put it on," said the other. "Call wine, wine; and finish there." With that advice, he wiped his soiled hand upon the joker's dress, such as it was—quite deliberately, as having dirtied the hand on his account; and then re-crossed the road and entered the wine-shop.

This wine-shop keeper was a bull-necked, martial-looking man of thirty, and he should have been of a hot temperament, for, although it was a bitter day, he wore no coat, but carried one slung over his shoulder. His shirt-sleeves were rolled up, too, and his brown arms were bare to the elbows. Neither did he wear anything more on his head than his own crisply-curling short dark hair. He was a dark man altogether, with good eyes and a good bold breadth between them. Good-humoured looking on the whole, but implacable-looking, too; evidently a man of a strong resolution and a set purpose; a man not desirable to be met, rushing down a narrow pass with a gulf on either side, for nothing would turn the man.

Madame Defarge, his wife, sat in the shop behind the counter as he came in. Madame Defarge was a stout woman of about his own age, with a watchful eye that seldom seemed to look at anything, a large hand heavily ringed, a steady face, strong features, and great composure of manner. There was a character about Madame Defarge, from which one might have predicated that she did not often make mistakes against herself in any of the reckonings over which she presided. Madame Defarge, being sensitive to cold, was wrapped in fur, and had a quantity of bright shawl twined about her head, though not to the concealment of her large earrings. Her knitting was before her, but she had laid it down to pick her teeth with a toothpick. Thus engaged, with her right elbow supported by her left hand, Madame Defarge said nothing when her lord came in, but coughed just one grain of cough. This, in combination with the lifting of her darkly defined eyebrows over her toothpick by the breadth of a line, suggested to her husband that he would do well to look round the shop among the customers, for any new customer who had dropped in while he stepped over the way.

The wine-shop keeper accordingly rolled his eyes about, until they rested upon an elderly gentleman and a young lady, who were seated in a corner. Other company were there: two playing cards, two playing dominoes, three standing by the counter lengthening out a short supply of wine. As he passed behind the counter, he took notice that the elderly gentleman said in a look to the young lady, "This is our man."

"What the devil do *you* do in that galley there?" said Monsieur Defarge to himself; "I don't know you."

But, he feigned not to notice the two strangers, and fell into discourse with the triumvirate of customers who were drinking at the counter.

"How goes it, Jacques?" said one of these three to Monsieur Defarge. "Is all the spilt wine swallowed?"

"Every drop, Jacques," answered Monsieur Defarge.

When this interchange of Christian name was effected, Madame Defarge, picking her teeth with her toothpick, coughed another grain of cough, and raised her eyebrows by the breadth of another line.

"It is not often," said the second of the three, addressing Monsieur Defarge, "that many of these miserable beasts know the taste of wine, or of anything but black bread and death. Is it not so, Jacques?"

"It is so, Jacques," Monsieur Defarge returned.

At this second interchange of the Christian name, Madame Defarge, still using her toothpick with profound composure, coughed another grain of cough, and raised her eyebrows by the breadth of another line.

The last of the three now said his say, as he put down his empty drinking vessel, and smacked his lips.

"Ah! So much the worse! A bitter taste it is that such

poor cattle always have in their mouths, and hard lives
they live, Jacques. Am I right, Jacques?"

"You are right, Jacques," was the response of Monsieur
Defarge.

This third interchange of the Christian name was completed at the moment when Madame Defarge put her
toothpick by, kept her eyebrows up, and slightly rustled
in her seat.

"Hold then! True!" muttered her husband. "Gentlemen
—my wife!"

The three customers pulled off their hats to Madame
Defarge, with three flourishes. She acknowledged their
homage by bending her head, and giving them a quick
look. Then she glanced in a casual manner round the wine-
shop, took up her knitting with great apparent calmness
and repose of spirit, and became absorbed in it.

"Gentlemen," said her husband, who had kept his bright
eye observantly upon her, "good day. The chamber, furnished bachelor-fashion, that you wished to see, and were
inquiring for when I stepped out, is on the fifth floor. The
doorway of the staircase gives on the little courtyard close
to the left here," pointing with his hand, "near to the
window of my establishment. But, now that I remember,
one of you has already been there, and can show the way.
Gentlemen, adieu!"

They paid for their wine, and left the place. The eyes
of Monsieur Defarge were studying his wife at her knitting, when the elderly gentleman advanced from his corner, and begged the favour of a word.

"Willingly, sir," said Monsieur Defarge, and quietly
stepped with him to the door.

Their conference was very short, but very decided. Almost at the first word, Monsieur Defarge started and
became deeply attentive. It had not lasted a minute, when
he nodded and went out. The gentleman then beckoned
to the young lady, and they, too, went out. Madame Defarge knitted with nimble fingers and steady eyebrows,
and saw nothing.

Mr. Jarvis Lorry and Miss Manette, emerging from the
wine-shop thus, joined Monsieur Defarge in the doorway
to which he had directed his other company just before.
It opened from a stinking little black courtyard, and was
the general public entrance to a great pile of houses, in-
habited by a great number of people. In the gloomy tile-

paved entry to the gloomy tile-paved staircase, Monsieur Defarge bent down on one knee to the child of his old master, and put her hand to his lips. It was a gentle action, but not at all gently done; a very remarkable transformation had come over him in a few seconds. He had no good-humour in his face, nor any openness of aspect left, but had become a secret, angry, dangerous man.

"It is very high; it is a little difficult. Better to begin slowly." Thus Monsieur Defarge, in a stern voice, to Mr. Lorry, as they began ascending the stairs.

"Is he alone?" the latter whispered.

"Alone! God help him, who should be with him?" said the other, in the same low voice.

"Is he always alone, then?"

"Yes."

"Of his own desire?"

"Of his own necessity. As he was, when I first saw him after they found me and demanded to know if I would take him, and, at my peril, be discreet—as he was then, so he is now."

"He is greatly changed?"

"Changed!"

The keeper of the wine-shop stopped to strike the wall with his hand, and mutter a tremendous curse. No direct answer could have been half so forcible. Mr. Lorry's spirits grew heavier and heavier, as he and his two companions ascended higher and higher.

Such a staircase, with its accessories, in the older and more crowded parts of Paris, would be bad enough now; but, at that time, it was vile indeed to unaccustomed and unhardened senses. Every little habitation within the great foul nest of one high building—that is to say, the room or rooms within every door that opened on the general staircase—left its own heap of refuse on its own landing, besides flinging other refuse from its own windows. The uncontrollable and hopeless mass of decomposition so engendered would have polluted the air, even if poverty and deprivation had not loaded it with their intangible impurities; the two bad sources combined made it almost insupportable. Through such an atmosphere, by a steep dark shaft of dirt and poison, the way lay. Yielding to his own disturbance of mind, and to his young companion's agitation, which became greater every instant, Mr. Jarvis Lorry twice stopped to rest. Each of these stoppages was made at a doleful grating, by which any languishing good airs that were left uncorrupted seemed to escape, and all spoilt and sickly vapours seemed to crawl in. Through the rusted bars, tastes, rather than glimpses, were caught of the jumbled neighbourhood; and nothing within range, nearer or lower than the summits of the two great towers of Notre Dame, had any promise on it of healthy life or wholesome aspirations.

At last, the top of the staircase was gained, and they stopped for the third time. There was yet an upper staircase, of a steeper inclination and of contracted dimensions, to be ascended, before the garret story was reached. The keeper of the wine-shop, always going a little in advance, and always going on the side which Mr. Lorry took, as though he dreaded to be asked any questions by the young lady, turned himself about here, and, carefully feeling in the pockets of the coat he carried over his shoulder, took out a key.

"The door is locked then, my friend?" said Mr. Lorry, surprised.

"Ay. Yes," was the grim reply of Monsieur Defarge.

"You think it necessary to keep the unfortunate gentleman so retired?"

"I think it necessary to turn the key." Monsieur Defarge whispered it closer in his ear, and frowned heavily.

"Why?"

"Why! Because he has lived so long, locked up, that he would be frightened—rave—tear himself to pieces—die—come to I know not what harm—if his door was left open."

"Is it possible?" exclaimed Mr. Lorry.

"Is it possible?" repeated Defarge, bitterly. "Yes. And a beautiful world we live in, when it *is* possible, and when many other such things are possible, and not only possible, but done—done, see you!—under that sky there, every day. Long live the Devil. Let us go on."

This dialogue had been held in so very low a whisper, that not a word of it had reached the young lady's ears. But, by this time she trembled under such strong emotion, and her face expressed such deep anxiety, and, above all, such dread and terror, that Mr. Lorry felt it incumbent on him to speak a word or two of reassurance.

"Courage, dear miss! Courage! Business! The worst will be over in a moment; it is but passing the room-door, and the worst is over. Then, all the good you bring to him, all the relief, all the happiness you bring to him, begin. Let our good friend here assist you on that side. That's well, friend Defarge. Come, now. Business, business!"

They went up slowly and softly. The staircase was short, and they were soon at the top. There, as it had an abrupt turn in it, they came all at once in sight of three men, whose heads were bent down close together at the side of a door, and who were intently looking into the room to which the door belonged, through some chinks or holes in the wall. On hearing footsteps close at hand, these three turned, and rose, and showed themselves to be the three of one name who had been drinking in the wine-shop.

"I forgot them in the surprise of your visit," explained Monsieur Defarge. "Leave us, good boys; we have business here."

The three glided by, and went silently down.

There appearing to be no other door on that floor, and the keeper of the wine-shop going straight to this one when they were left alone, Mr. Lorry asked him in a whisper, with a little anger:

"Do you make a show of Monsieur Manette?"

"I show him, in the way you have seen, to a chosen few."

"Is that well?"

"*I* think it is well."

"Who are the few? How do you choose them?"

"I choose them as real men, of my name—Jacques is my name—to whom the sight is likely to do good. Enough: you are English; that is another thing. Stay there, if you please, a little moment."

With an admonitory gesture to keep them back, he stooped, and looked in through the crevice in the wall. Soon raising his head again, he struck twice or thrice upon the door—evidently with no other object than to make a noise there. With the same intention, he drew the key across it, three or four times, before he put it clumsily into the lock, and turned it as heavily as he could.

The door slowly opened inward under his hand, and he looked into the room and said something. A faint voice answered something. Little more than a single syllable could have been spoken on either side.

He looked back over his shoulder, and beckoned them to enter. Mr. Lorry got his arm securely round the daughter's waist, and held her; for he felt that she was sinking.

"A—a—a—business, business!" he urged, with a moisture that was not of business shining on his cheek. "Come in, come in!"

"I am afraid of it," she answered, shuddering.

"Of it? What?"

"I mean of him. Of my father."

Rendered in a manner desperate, by her state and by the beckoning of their conductor, he drew over his neck the arm that shook upon his shoulder, lifted her a little, and hurried her into the room. He set her down just within the door, and held her, clinging to him.

Defarge drew out the key, closed the door, locked it on the inside, took out the key again, and held it in his hand. All this he did, methodically, and with as loud and harsh an accompaniment of noise as he could make. Finally, he walked across the room with a measured tread to where the window was. He stopped there, and faced around.

The garret, built to be a depository for firewood and the like, was dim and dark: for the window of dormer shape was in truth a door in the roof, with a little crane over it for the hoisting up of stores from the street: unglazed, and closing up the middle in two pieces, like any other door of French construction. To exclude the cold, one half of this door was fast closed, and the other was opened but a very little way. Such a scanty portion of light was admitted through these means, that it was difficult, on first coming in, to see anything; and long habit alone could have slowly formed in any one, the ability to do any work requiring nicety in such obscurity. Yet, work of that kind was being done in the garret; for, with his back towards the door, and his face towards the window where the keeper of the wine-shop stood looking at him, a white-haired man sat on a low bench, stooping forward and very busy, making shoes.

*　　*　　*　　*　　*　　*　　*　　*

6 *The Shoemaker*

"GOOD DAY!" said Monsieur Defarge, looking down at the white head that bent low over the shoemaking.

It was raised for a moment, and a very faint voice responded to the salutation, as if it were at a distance:

"Good day!"

"You are still hard at work, I see?"

After a long silence, the head was lifted for another moment, and the voice replied, "Yes—I am working." This time, a pair of haggard eyes had looked at the questioner, before the face had dropped again.

The faintness of the voice was pitiable and dreadful. It was not the faintness of physical weakness, though confinement and hard fare no doubt had their part in it. Its deplorable peculiarity was, that it was the faintness of solitude and disuse. It was like the last feeble echo of a sound made long and long ago. So entirely had it lost the life and resonance of the human voice, that it affected the senses like a once beautiful colour faded away into a poor weak stain. So sunken and suppressed it was, that it was like a voice underground. So expressive it was, of a hopeless and lost creature, that a famished traveller, wearied out by lonely wandering in a wilderness, would have remembered home and friends in such a tone before lying down to die.

Some minutes of silent work had passed, and the haggard eyes had looked up again; not with any interest or curiosity, but with a dull mechanical perception, beforehand, that the spot where the only visitor they were aware of had stood, was not yet empty.

"I want," said Defarge, who had not removed his gaze from the shoemaker, "to let in a little more light here. You can bear a little more?"

The shoemaker stopped his work; looked with a vacant air of listening, at the floor on one side of him; then similarly, at the floor on the other side of him; then upward at the speaker.

"What did you say?"

"You can bear a little more light?"

"I must bear it, if you let it in." (Laying the palest shadow of a stress upon the second word.)

The opened half-door was opened a little further, and secured at that angle for the time. A broad ray of light fell into the garret, and showed the workman with an unfinished shoe upon his lap, pausing in his labour. His few common tools and various scraps of leather were at his feet and on his bench. He had a white beard, raggedly cut, but not very long, a hollow face, and exceedingly bright eyes. The hollowness and thinness of his face would have caused them to look large, under his yet dark eyebrows and his confused white hair, though they had been really otherwise; but, they were naturally large, and looked unnaturally so. His yellow rags of shirt lay open at the throat, and showed his body to be withered and worn. He, and his old canvas frock, and his loose stockings, and all his poor tatters of clothes, had, in a long seclusion from direct light and air, faded down to such a dull uniformity of parchment-yellow, that it would have been hard to say which was which.

He had put up a hand between his eyes and the light, and the very bones of it seemed transparent. So he sat, with a steadfastly vacant gaze, pausing in his work. He never looked at the figure before him, without first looking down on this side of himself, then on that, as if he had lost the habit of associating place with sound; he never spoke, without first wandering in this manner, and forgetting to speak.

"Are you going to finish that pair of shoes to-day?" asked Defarge, motioning to Mr. Lorry to come forward.

"What did you say?"

"Do you mean to finish that pair of shoes to-day?"

"I can't say that I mean to. I suppose so. I don't know."

But, the question reminded him of his work, and he bent over it again.

Mr. Lorry came silently forward, leaving the daughter by the door. When he had stood, for a minute or two, by the side of Defarge, the shoemaker looked up. He showed no surprise at seeing another figure, but the unsteady fingers of one of his hands strayed to his lips as he looked at it (his lips and his nails were of the same pale lead-colour), and then the hand dropped to his work, and he once more bent over the shoe. The look and the action had occupied but an instant.

"You have a visitor, you see," said Monsieur Defarge.

"What did you say?"

"Here is a visitor."

The shoemaker looked up as before, but without removing a hand from his work.

"Come!" said Defarge. "Here is monsieur, who knows a well-made shoe when he sees one. Show him that shoe you are working at. Take it, monsieur."

Mr. Lorry took it in his hand.

"Tell monsieur what kind of shoe it is, and the maker's name."

There was a longer pause than usual, before the shoemaker replied:

"I forget what it was you asked me. What did you say?"

"I said, couldn't you describe the kind of shoe, for monsieur's information?"

"It is a lady's shoe. It is a young lady's walking-shoe. It is in the present mode. I never saw the mode. I have had a pattern in my hand." He glanced at the shoe with some little passing touch of pride.

"And the maker's name?" said Defarge.

Now that he had no work to hold, he laid the knuckles of the right hand in the hollow of the left, and then the knuckles of the left hand in the hollow of the right, and then passed a hand across his bearded chin, and so on in regular changes, without a moment's intermission. The task of recalling him from the vacancy into which he always sank when he had spoken was like recalling some very weak person from a swoon, or endeavouring, in the hope of some disclosure, to stay the spirit of a fast-dying man.

"Did you ask me for my name?"

"Assuredly I did."

"One Hundred and Five, North Tower."

"Is that all?"

"One Hundred and Five, North Tower."

With a weary sound that was not a sigh, nor a groan, he bent to work again, until the silence was again broken.

"You are not a shoemaker by trade?" said Mr. Lorry, looking steadfastly at him.

His haggard eyes turned to Defarge as if he would have

transferred the question to him: but as no help came from that quarter, they turned back on the questioner when they had sought the ground.

"I am not a shoemaker by trade? No, I was not a shoemaker by trade. I—I learnt it here. I taught myself. I asked leave to—"

He lapsed away, even for minutes, ringing those measured changes on his hands the whole time. His eyes came slowly back, at last, to the face from which they had wandered; when they rested on it, he started, and resumed, in the manner of a sleeper that moment awake, reverting to a subject of last night.

"I asked leave to teach myself, and I got it with much difficulty after a long while, and I have made shoes ever since."

As he held out his hand for the shoe that had been taken from him, Mr. Lorry said, still looking steadfastly in his face:

"Monsieur Manette, do you remember nothing of me?"

The shoe dropped to the ground, and he sat looking fixedly at the questioner.

"Monsieur Manette"—Mr. Lorry laid his hand upon Defarge's arm—"do you remember nothing of this man? Look at him. Look at me. Is there no old banker, no old business, no old servant, no old time, rising in your mind, Monsieur Manette?"

As the captive of many years sat looking fixedly, by turns, at Mr. Lorry and Defarge, some long-obliterated marks of an actively intent intelligence in the middle of the forehead, gradually forced themselves through the black mist that had fallen on him. They were overclouded again, they were fainter, they were gone; but they had been there. And so exactly was the expression repeated on the fair young face of her who had crept along the wall to a point where she could see him, and where she now stood looking at him, with hands which at first had been only raised in frightened compassion, if not even to keep him off and shut out the sight of him, but which were now extending towards him, trembling with eagerness to lay the spectral face upon her warm young breast, and love it back to life and hope—so exactly was the expression repeated (though in stronger characters) on her fair young face, that it looked as though it had passed like a moving light, from him to her.

Darkness had fallen on him in its place. He looked at the two, less and less attentively, and his eyes in gloomy abstraction sought the ground and looked about him in the old way. Finally, with a deep long sigh, he took the shoe up, and resumed his work.

"Have you recognised him, monsieur?" asked Defarge in a whisper.

"Yes; for a moment. At first I thought it quite hopeless, but I have unquestionably seen, for a single moment, the face that I once knew so well. Hush! Let us draw further back. Hush!"

She had moved from the wall of the garret, very near to the bench on which he sat. There was something awful in his unconsciousness of the figure that could have put out its hand and touched him as he stooped over his labour.

Not a word was spoken, not a sound was made. She stood, like a spirit, beside him, and he bent over his work.

It happened, at length, that he had occasion to change the instrument in his hand, for his shoemaker's knife. It lay on that side of him which was not the side on which she stood. He had taken it up, and was stooping to work again, when his eyes caught the skirt of her dress. He raised them, and saw her face. The two spectators started forward, but she stayed them with a motion of her hand. She had no fear of his striking at her with the knife, though they had.

He stared at her with a fearful look, and after a while his lips began to form some words, though no sound proceeded from them. By degrees, in the pauses of his quick and laboured breathing, he was heard to say:

"What is this?"

With the tears streaming down her face, she put her two hands to her lips, and kissed them to him; then clasped them on her breast, as if she laid his ruined head there.

"You are not the gaoler's daughter?"

She sighed, "No."

"Who are you?"

Not yet trusting the tones of her voice, she sat down on the bench beside him. He recoiled, but she laid her hand upon his arm. A strange thrill struck him when she did so, and visibly passed over his frame; he laid the knife down softly, as he sat staring at her.

Her golden hair, which she wore in long curls, had been hurriedly pushed aside, and fell down over her neck. Advancing his hand by little and little, he took it up and looked at it. In the midst of the action he went astray, and, with another deep sigh, fell to work at his shoemaking.

But not for long. Releasing his arm, she laid her hand upon his shoulder. After looking doubtfully at it, two or three times, as if to be sure that it was really there, he laid down his work, put his hand to his neck, and took off a blackened string with a scrap of folded rag attached to it. He opened this, carefully, on his knee, and it contained a very little quantity of hair: not more than one or two long golden hairs, which he had, in some old day, wound off upon his finger.

He took her hair into his hand again, and looked closely at it. "It is the same. How can it be! When was it! How was it!"

As the concentrating expression returned to his forehead, he seemed to become conscious that it was in hers too. He turned her full to the light, and looked at her.

"She had laid her head upon my shoulder, that night when I was summoned out—she had a fear of my going, though I had none—and when I was brought to the North Tower they found these upon my sleeve. 'You will leave me them? They can never help me to escape in the body, though they may in the spirit.' Those were the words I said. I remember them very well."

He formed this speech with his lips many times before he could utter it. But when he did find spoken words for it, they came to him coherently, though slowly.

"How was this?—*Was it you?*"

Once more, the two spectators started, as he turned upon her with a frightful suddenness. But she sat perfectly still in his grasp, and only said, in a low voice, "I entreat you, good gentlemen, do not come near us, do not speak, do not move!"

"Hark!" he exclaimed. "Whose voice was that?"

His hands released her as he uttered this cry, and went up to his white hair, which they tore in a frenzy. It died out, as everything but his shoemaking did die out of him, and he refolded his little packet and tried to secure it in his breast; but he still looked at her, and gloomily shook his head.

"No, no, no; you are too young, too blooming. It can't be. See what the prisoner is. These are not the hands she knew, this is not the face she knew, this is not a voice she ever heard. No, no. She was—and he was—before the slow years of the North Tower—ages ago. What is your name, my gentle angel?"

Hailing his softened tone and manner, his daughter fell upon her knees before him, with her appealing hands upon his breast.

"O, sir, at another time you shall know my name, and who my mother was, and who my father, and how I never knew their hard, hard history. But I cannot tell you at this time, and I cannot tell you here. All that I may tell you, here and now, is, that I pray to you to touch me and to bless me. Kiss me, kiss me! O my dear, my dear!"

His cold white head mingled with her radiant hair, which warmed and lighted it as though it were the light of Freedom shining on him.

"If you hear in my voice—I don't know that it is so, but I hope it is—if you hear in my voice any resemblance to a voice that once was sweet music in your ears, weep for it, weep for it! If you touch, in touching my hair, anything that recalls a beloved head that lay on your breast when you were young and free, weep for it, weep for it! If, when I hint to you of a Home that is before us, where I will be true to you with all my duty and with all my faithful service, I bring back the remembrance of a Home long desolate, while your poor heart pined away, weep for it, weep for it!"

She held him closer round the neck, and rocked him on her breast like a child.

"If, when I tell you, dearest dear, that your agony is over, and that I have come here to take you from it, and that we go to England to be at peace and at rest, I cause you to think of your useful life laid waste, and of our native France so wicked to you, weep for it, weep for it! And if, when I shall tell you of my name, and of my father who is living, and of my mother who is dead, you learn that I have to kneel to my honoured father, and implore his pardon for having never for his sake striven all day and lain awake and wept all night, because the love of my poor mother hid his torture from me, weep for it, weep for it! Weep for her, then, and for me! Good gentlemen, thank God! I feel his sacred tears upon my face, and his sobs strike against my heart. O, see! Thank God for us, thank God!"

He had sunk in her arms, and his face dropped on her

breast: a sight so touching, yet so terrible in the tremendous wrong and suffering which had gone before it, that the two beholders covered their faces.

When the quiet of the garret had been long undisturbed, and his heaving breast and shaken form had long yielded to the calm that must follow all storms—emblem to humanity, of the rest and silence into which the storm called Life must hush at last—they came forward to raise the father and daughter from the ground. He had gradually dropped to the floor, and lay there in a lethargy, worn out. She had nestled down with him, that his head might lie upon her arm; and her hair drooping over him curtained him from the light.

"If, without disturbing him," she said, raising her hand to Mr. Lorry as he stooped over them, after repeated blowings of his nose, "all could be arranged for our leaving Paris at once, so that, from the very door, he could be taken away—"

"But, consider. Is he fit for the journey?" asked Mr. Lorry.

"More fit for that, I think, than to remain in this city, so dreadful to him."

"It is true," said Defarge, who was kneeling to look on and hear. "More than that; Monsieur Manette is, for all reasons, best out of France. Say, shall I hire a carriage and post-horses?"

"That's business," said Mr. Lorry, resuming on the shortest notice his methodical manners; "and if business is to be done, I had better do it."

"Then be so kind," urged Miss Manette, "as to leave us here. You see how composed he has become, and you cannot be afraid to leave him with me now. Why should you be? If you will lock the door to secure us from interruption, I do not doubt that you will find him, when you come back, as quiet as you leave him. In any case, I will take care of him until you return, and then we will remove him straight."

Both Mr. Lorry and Defarge were rather disinclined to this course, and in favour of one of them remaining. But, as there were not only carriage and horses to be seen to, but travelling papers; and as time pressed, for the day was drawing to an end, it came at last to their hastily dividing the business that was necessary to be done, and hurrying away to do it.

Then, as the darkness closed in, the daughter laid her head down on the hard ground close at the father's side, and watched him. The darkness deepened and deepened, and they both lay quiet, until a light gleamed through the chinks in the wall.

Mr. Lorry and Monsieur Defarge had made all ready for the journey, and had brought with them, besides travelling cloaks and wrappers, bread and meat, wine, and hot coffee. Monsieur Defarge put this provender, and the lamp he carried, on the shoemaker's bench (there was nothing else in the garret but a pallet bed), and he and Mr. Lorry roused the captive, and assisted him to his feet.

No human intelligence could have read the mysteries of his mind, in the scared blank wonder of his face. Whether he knew what had happened, whether he recollected what they had said to him, whether he knew that he was free, were questions which no sagacity could have solved. They tried speaking to him; but, he was so confused, and so very slow to answer, that they took fright at his bewilderment, and agreed for the time to tamper with him no more. He had a wild, lost manner of occasionally clasping his head in his hands, that had not been seen in him before; yet, he had some pleasure in the mere sound of his daughter's voice, and invariably turned to it when she spoke.

In the submissive way of one long accustomed to obey under coercion, he ate and drank what they gave him to eat and drink, and put on the cloak and other wrappings that they gave him to wear. He readily responded to his daughter's drawing her arm through his, and took—and kept—her hand in both his own.

They began to descend; Monsieur Defarge going first with the lamp, Mr. Lorry closing the little procession. They had not traversed many steps of the long main staircase when he stopped, and stared at the roof and round at the walls.

"You remember the place, my father? You remember coming up here?"

"What did you say?"

But, before she could repeat the question, he murmured an answer as if she had repeated it.

"Remember? No, I don't remember. It was so very long ago."

That he had no recollection whatever of his having been brought from his prison to that house was apparent to them. They heard him mutter, "One Hundred and Five, North Tower"; and when he looked about him, it evidently was for the strong fortress-walls which had long encompassed him. On their reaching the courtyard he instinctively altered his tread, as being in expectation of a drawbridge; and when there was no drawbridge, and he saw the carriage waiting in the open street, he dropped his daughter's hand and clasped his head again.

No crowd was about the door; no people were discernible at any of the many windows; not even a chance passer-by was in the street. An unnatural silence and desertion reigned there. Only one soul was to be seen, and that was Madame Defarge—who leaned against the door-post, knitting, and saw nothing.

The prisoner had got into a coach, and his daughter had followed him, when Mr. Lorry's feet were arrested on the step by his asking, miserably, for his shoemaking tools and the unfinished shoes. Madame Defarge immediately called to her husband that she would get them, and went, knitting, out of the lamplight, through the courtyard. She quickly brought them down and handed them in— and immediately afterwards leaned against the door-post, knitting, and saw nothing.

Defarge got upon the box, and gave the word "To the Barrier!" The postilion cracked his whip, and they clattered away under the feeble over-swinging lamps.

Under the over-swinging lamps—swinging ever brighter in the better streets, and ever dimmer in the worse—and by lighted shops, gay crowds, illuminated coffee-houses, and theatre-doors, to one of the city gates. Soldiers with lanterns, at the guard-house there. "Your papers, travellers!" "See here then, Monsieur the Officer," said Defarge, getting down, and taking him gravely apart, "these are the papers of monsieur inside, with the white head. They were consigned to me, with him, at the—" He dropped his voice, there was a flutter among the military lanterns, and one of them being handed into the coach by an arm in uniform, the eyes connected with the arm looked, not an every-day or an every-night look, at monsieur with the white head. "It is well. Forward!" from the uniform. "Adieu!" from Defarge. And so, under a short grove of feebler and feebler over-swinging lamps, out under the great groves of stars.

Beneath that arch of unmoved and eternal lights; some,

so remote from this little earth that the learned tell us it is doubtful whether their rays have even yet discovered it, as a point in space where anything is suffered or done: the shadows of the night were broad and black. All through the cold and restless interval, until dawn, they once more whispered in the ears of Mr. Jarvis Lorry—sitting opposite the buried man who had been dug out, and wondering what subtle powers were for ever lost to him, and what were capable of restoration—the old inquiry:

"I hope you care to be recalled to life?"

And the old answer:

"I can't say."

BOOK THE SECOND

The Golden Thread

1 *Five Years Later*

TELLSON'S BANK by Temple Bar was an old-fashioned place, even in the year one thousand seven hundred and eighty. It was very small, very dark, very ugly, very incommodious. It was an old-fashioned place, moreover, in the moral attribute that the partners in the House were proud of its smallness, proud of its darkness, proud of its ugliness, proud of its incommodiousness. They were even boastful of its eminence in those particulars, and were fired by an express conviction that, if it were less objectionable, it would be less respectable. This was no passive belief, but an active weapon which they flashed at more convenient places of business. Tellson's (they said) wanted no elbow-room, Tellson's wanted no light, Tellson's wanted no embellishment. Noakes and Co.'s might, or Snooks Brothers' might; but Tellson's, thank Heaven!—

Any one of these partners would have disinherited his son on the question of rebuilding Tellson's. In this respect the House was much on a par with the Country, which did very often disinherit its sons for suggesting improvements in laws and customs that had long been highly objectionable, but were only the more respectable.

Thus it had come to pass, that Tellson's was the triumphant perfection of inconvenience. After bursting open a door of idiotic obstinacy, with a weak rattle in its throat, you fell into Tellson's down two steps, and came to your senses in a miserable little shop, with two little counters, where the oldest of men made your cheque shake as if the wind rustled it, while they examined the signature by the dingiest of windows, which were always under a shower-bath of mud from Fleet Street, and which were made the dingier by their own iron bars proper, and the heavy shadow of Temple Bar. If your business necessitated your seeing "the House," you were put into a species of Condemned Hold at the back, where you meditated on a misspent life, until the House came with its hands in its pockets, and you could hardly blink at it in the dismal twilight. Your money came out of, or went into, wormy old wooden drawers, particles of which flew up your nose and down your throat when they were opened and shut. Your bank-notes had a musty odour, as if they were fast decomposing into rags again. Your plate was stowed away among the neighbouring cesspools, and evil communications corrupted its good polish in a day or two. Your deeds got into extemporised strong-rooms made of kitchens and sculleries, and fretted all the fat out of their parchments into the banking-house air. Your lighter boxes of family papers went upstairs into a Barmecide room, that always had a great dining-table in it and never had a dinner, and where, even in the year one thousand seven hundred and eighty, the first letters written to you by your old love, or by your little children, were but newly released from the horror of being ogled through the windows, by the heads exposed on Temple Bar with an insensate brutality and ferocity worthy of Abyssinia or Ashantee.

But indeed, at that time, putting to death was a recipe much in vogue with all trades and professions, and not least of all with Tellson's. Death is Nature's remedy for all things, and why not Legislation's? Accordingly, the forger was put to Death; the utterer of a bad note was put to Death; the unlawful opener of a letter was put to Death; the purloiner of forty shillings and sixpence was put to Death; the holder of a horse at Tellson's door, who made off with it, was put to Death; the coiner of a bad shilling was put to Death; the sounders of three-fourths of the notes in the whole gamut of Crime were put to Death. Not that it did the least good in the way of prevention—it might almost have been worth remarking that the fact was exactly the reverse—but, it cleared off (as to this world) the trouble of each particular case, and left nothing else connected with it to be looked after. Thus, Tellson's, in its day, like greater places of business, its contemporaries, had taken so many lives, that, if the heads laid low before it had been ranged on Temple Bar instead of being privately disposed of, they would probably have excluded what little light the ground floor had, in a rather significant manner.

Cramped in all kinds of dim cupboards and hutches at Tellson's, the oldest of men carried on the business gravely.

When they took a young man into Tellson's London house, they hid him somewhere till he was old. They kept him in a dark place, like a cheese, until he had the full Tellson flavour and blue-mould upon him. Then only was he permitted to be seen, spectacularly poring over large books, and casting his breeches and gaiters into the general weight of the establishment.

Outside Tellson's—never by any means in it, unless called in—was an odd-job-man, an occasional porter and messenger, who served as the live sign of the house. He was never absent during business hours, unless upon an errand, and then he was represented by his son: a grisly urchin of twelve, who was his express image. People understood that Tellson's, in a stately way, tolerated the odd-job-man. The house had always tolerated some person in that capacity, and time and tide had drifted this person to the post. His surname was Cruncher, and on the youthful occasion of his renouncing by proxy the works of darkness, in the easterly parish church of Hounsditch, he had received the added appellation of Jerry.

The scene was Mr. Cruncher's private lodging in Hangingsword Alley, Whitefriars: the time, half-past seven of the clock on a windy March morning, Anno Domini seventeen hundred and eighty. (Mr. Cruncher himself always spoke of the year of our Lord as Anna Dominoes: apparently under the impression that the Christian era dated from the invention of a popular game, by a lady who had bestowed her name upon it.)

Mr. Cruncher's apartments were not in a savoury neighbourhood, and were but two in number, even if a closet with a single pane of glass in it might be counted as one. But they were very decently kept. Early as it was, on the windy March morning, the room in which he lay abed was already scrubbed throughout; and between the cups and saucers arranged for breakfast, and the lumbering deal table, a very clean white cloth was spread.

Mr. Cruncher reposed under a patchwork counterpane, like a Harlequin at home. At first, he slept heavily, but, by degrees, began to roll and surge in bed, until he rose above the surface, with his spiky hair looking as if it must tear the sheets to ribbons. At which juncture, he exclaimed, in a voice of dire exasperation:

"Bust me, if she ain't at it agin!"

A woman of orderly and industrious appearance rose

from her knees in a corner, with sufficient haste and trepidation to show that she was the person referred to.

"What!" said Mr. Cruncher, looking out of bed for a boot. "You're at it agin, are you?"

After hailing the morn with this second salutation, he threw a boot at the woman as a third. It was a very muddy boot, and may introduce the odd circumstance connected with Mr. Cruncher's domestic economy, that, whereas he often came home after banking hours with clean boots, he often got up next morning to find the same boots covered with clay.

"What," said Mr. Cruncher, varying his apostrophe after missing his mark, "what are you up to, Aggerawayter?"

"I was only saying my prayers."

"Saying your prayers! You're a nice woman! What do you mean by flopping yourself down and praying agin me?"

"I was not praying against you; I was praying for you."

"You weren't. And if you were, I won't be took the liberty with. Here! Your mother's a nice woman, young Jerry, going a praying agin your father's prosperity. You've got a dutiful mother, you have, my son. You've got a religious mother, you have, my boy: going and flopping herself down, and praying that the bread-and-butter may be snatched out of the mouth of her only child."

Master Cruncher (who was in his shirt) took this very ill, and, turning to his mother, strongly deprecated any praying away of his personal board.

"And what do you suppose, you conceited female," said Mr. Cruncher, with unconscious inconsistency, "that the worth of *your* prayers may be? Name the price that you put *your* prayers at!"

"They only come from the heart, Jerry. They are worth no more than that."

"Worth no more than that," repeated Mr. Cruncher. "They ain't worth much, then. Whether or no, I won't be prayed agin, I tell you. I can't afford it. I'm not a-going to be made unlucky by *your* sneaking. If you must go flopping yourself down, flop in favour of your husband and child, and not in opposition to 'em. If I had had any but a unnat'ral wife, and this poor boy had had any but a unnat'ral mother, I might have made some money last week instead of being counterprayed and countermined and religiously circumwented into the worst of luck. B-u-u-ust me!" said Mr. Cruncher, who all this time had been putting on his clothes, "if I ain't, what with piety and one blowed thing and another, been choused this last week into as bad luck as ever a poor devil of a honest tradesman met with! Young Jerry, dress yourself, my boy, and while I clean my boots keep a eye upon your mother now and then, and if you see any signs of more flopping, give me a call. For, I tell you," here he addressed his wife once more, "I won't be gone agin, in this manner. I am as rickety as a hackney-coach, I'm as sleepy as laudanum, my lines is strained to that degree that I shouldn't know, if it wasn't for the pain in 'em, which was me and which somebody else, yet I'm none the better for it in pocket; and it's my suspicion that you've been at it from morning to night to prevent me from being the better for it in pocket, and I won't put up with it. Aggerawayter, and what do you say now!"

Growling, in addition, such phrases as "Ah! yes! You're religious, too. You wouldn't put yourself in opposition to the interests of your husband and child, would you? Not you!" and throwing off other sarcastic sparks from the whirling grindstone of his indignation, Mr. Cruncher betook himself to his boot-cleaning and his general preparation for business. In the meantime, his son, whose head was garnished with tenderer spikes, and whose young eyes stood close by one another, as his father's did, kept the required watch upon his mother. He greatly disturbed that poor woman at intervals, by darting out of his sleeping closet, where he made his toilet, with a suppressed cry of "You are going to flop, Mother. Halloa, Father!" and, after raising this fictitious alarm, darting in again with an undutiful grin.

Mr. Cruncher's temper was not at all improved when he came to his breakfast. He resented Mrs. Cruncher's saying grace with particular animosity.

"Now, Aggerawayter! What are you up to? At it agin?"

His wife explained that she had merely "asked a blessing."

"Don't do it!" said Mr. Cruncher, looking about, as if he rather expected to see the loaf disappear under the efficacy of his wife's petitions. "I ain't a going to be blest out of house and home. I won't have my wittles blest off my table. Keep still!"

Exceedingly red-eyed and grim, as if he had been up all night at a party which had taken anything but a convivial turn, Jerry Cruncher worried his breakfast rather than ate it, growling over it like any four-footed inmate of a menagerie. Towards nine o'clock he smoothed his ruffled aspect, and, presenting as respectful and business-like an exterior as he could overlay his natural self with, issued forth to the occupation of the day.

It could scarcely be called a trade, in spite of his favourite description of himself as "a honest tradesman." His stock consisted of a wooden stool, made out of a broken-backed chair cut down, which stool young Jerry, walking at his father's side, carried every morning to beneath the banking-house window that was nearest Temple Bar; where, with the addition of the first handful of straw that could be gleaned from any passing vehicle to keep the cold and wet from the odd-job-man's feet, it formed the encampment for the day. On this post of his, Mr. Cruncher was as well known to Fleet Street and the Temple, as the Bar itself—and was almost as ill-looking.

Encamped at a quarter before nine, in good time to touch his three-cornered hat to the oldest of men as they passed in to Tellson's, Jerry took up his station on this windy March morning, with young Jerry standing by him, when not engaged in making forays through the Bar, to inflict bodily and mental injuries of an acute description on passing boys who were small enough for his amiable purpose. Father and son, extremely like each other, looking silently on at the morning traffic in Fleet Street, with their two heads as near to one another as the two eyes of each were, bore a considerable resemblance to a pair of monkeys. The resemblance was not lessened by the accidental circumstance, that the mature Jerry bit and spat out straw, while the twinkling eyes of the youthful Jerry were as restlessly watchful of him as of everything else in Fleet Street.

The head of one of the regular indoor messengers attached to Tellson's establishment was put through the door, and the word was given:

"Porter wanted!"

"Hooray, Father! Here's an early job to begin with!"

Having thus given his parent God speed, young Jerry seated himself on the stool, entered on his reversionary interest in the straw his father had been chewing, and cogitated.

"Al-ways rusty! His fingers is al-ways rusty!" muttered young Jerry. "Where does my father get all that iron rust from? He don't get no iron rust here!"

2 A Sight

"YOU KNOW the Old Bailey well, no doubt?" said one of the oldest of clerks to Jerry the messenger.

"Yes, sir," returned Jerry, in something of a dogged manner. "I *do* know the Bailey."

"Just so. And you know Mr. Lorry."

"I know Mr. Lorry, sir, much better than I know the Bailey. Much better," said Jerry, not unlike a reluctant witness at the establishment in question, "than I, as a honest tradesman, wish to know the Bailey."

"Very well. Find the door where the witnesses go in, and show the doorkeeper this note for Mr. Lorry. He will then let you in."

"Into the court, sir?"

"Into the court."

Mr. Cruncher's eyes seemed to get a little closer to one another, and to interchange the inquiry, "What do you think of this?"

"Am I to wait in the court, sir?" he asked, as the result of that conference.

"I am going to tell you. The doorkeeper will pass the note to Mr. Lorry, and do you make any gesture that will attract Mr. Lorry's attention, and show him where you stand. Then what you have to do, is, to remain there until he wants you."

"Is that all, sir?"

"That's all. He wishes to have a messenger at hand. This is to tell him you are there."

As the ancient clerk deliberately folded and super-scribed the note, Mr. Cruncher, after surveying him in silence until he came to the blotting-paper stage, remarked:

"I suppose they'll be trying Forgeries this morning?"

"Treason!"

"That's quartering," said Jerry. "Barbarous!"

"It is the law," remarked the ancient clerk, turning his surprised spectacles upon him. "It is the law."

"It's hard in the law to spile a man, I think. It's hard enough to kill him, but it's wery hard to spile him, sir."

"Not at all," returned the ancient clerk. "Speak well of the law. Take care of your chest and voice, my good friend, and leave the law to take care of itself. I give you that advice."

"It's the damp, sir, what settles on my chest and voice," said Jerry. "I leave you to judge what a damp way of earning a living mine is."

"Well, well," said the old clerk; "we all have our various ways of gaining a livelihood. Some of us have damp ways, and some of us have dry ways. Here is the letter. Go along."

Jerry took the letter, and, remarking to himself with less internal deference than he made an outward show of, "You are a lean old one, too," made his bow, informed his son, in passing, of his destination, and went his way.

They hanged at Tyburn, in those days, so the street outside Newgate had not obtained one infamous notoriety that has since attached to it. But, the gaol was a vile place in which most kinds of debauchery and villainy were practised, and where dire diseases were bred, that came into court with the prisoners, and sometimes rushed straight from the dock at my Lord Chief Justice himself, and pulled him off the bench. It had more than once happened, that the Judge in the black cap pronounced his own doom as certainly as the prisoner's, and even died before him. For the rest, the Old Bailey was famous as a kind of deadly inn-yard, from which pale travellers set out continually, in carts and coaches, on a violent passage into the other world: traversing some two miles and a half of public street and road, and shaming few good citizens, if any. So powerful is use, and so desirable to be good use in the beginning. It was famous, too, for the pillory, a wise old institution, that inflicted a punishment of which no one could foresee the extent; also, for the whipping-post, another dear old institution, very humanising and softening to behold in action; also, for extensive transactions in blood-money, another fragment of ancestral wisdom, systematically leading to the most frightful mercenary crimes that could be committed under Heaven. Altogether, the Old Bailey, at that date, was a choice illustration of the precept that "Whatever is, is right"; an aphorism that would be as final as it is lazy, did it not include the troublesome consequence, that nothing that ever was, was wrong.

Making his way through the tainted crowd, dispersed up and down this hideous scene of action, with the skill of a man accustomed to make his way quietly, the messenger found out the door he sought, and handed in his letter through a trap in it. For people then paid to see the play at the Old Bailey, just as they paid to see the play in Bedlam—only the former entertainment was much the dearer. Therefore, all the Old Bailey doors were well guarded—except, indeed, the social doors by which the criminals got there, and those were always left wide open.

After some delay and demur, the door grudgingly turned on its hinges a very little way, and allowed Mr. Jerry Cruncher to squeeze himself into court.

"What's on?" he asked, in a whisper, of the man he found himself next to.

"Nothing yet."

"What's coming on?"

"The treason case."

"The quartering one, eh?"

"Ah!" returned the man, with a relish; "he'll be drawn on a hurdle to be half hanged, and then he'll be taken down and sliced before his own face, and then his inside will be taken out and burnt while he looks on, and then his head will be chopped off, and he'll be cut into quarters. That's the sentence."

"If he's found guilty, you mean to say?" Jerry added, by way of proviso.

"Oh! they'll find him guilty," said the other. "Don't you be afraid of that."

Mr. Cruncher's attention was here diverted to the doorkeeper, whom he saw making his way to Mr. Lorry, with the note in his hand. Mr. Lorry sat at a table, among the gentlemen in wigs: not far from a wigged gentleman, the prisoner's counsel, who had a great bundle of papers, before him: and nearly opposite another wigged gentleman with his hands in his pockets, whose whole attention, when Mr. Cruncher looked at him then or afterwards, seemed to be concentrated on the ceiling of the court. After some gruff coughing and rubbing of his chin and signing with his hand, Jerry attracted the notice of Mr. Lorry, who had stood up to look for him, and who quietly nodded and sat down again.

"What's *he* got to do with this case?" asked the man he had spoken with.

"Blest if I know," said Jerry.

"What have *you* got to do with it, then, if a person may inquire?"

"Blest if I know that either," said Jerry.

The entrance of the judge, and a consequent great stir and settling down in the court, stopped the dialogue. Presently, the dock became the central point of interest. Two gaolers, who had been standing there, went out, and the prisoner was brought in, and put to the bar.

Everybody present, except the one wigged gentleman who looked at the ceiling, stared at him. All the human breath in the place rolled at him, like a sea, or a wind, or a fire. Eager faces strained round pillars and corners, to get a sight of him; spectators in back rows stood up, not to miss a hair of him; people on the floor of the court laid their hands on the shoulders of the people before them, to help themselves, at anybody's cost, to a view of him—stood a-tiptoe, got upon ledges, stood upon next to nothing, to see every inch of him. Conspicuous among these latter, like an animated bit of the spiked wall of Newgate, Jerry stood: aiming at the prisoner the beery breath of a whet he had taken as he came along, and discharging it to mingle with the waves of other beer, and gin, and tea, and coffee, and what not that flowed at him, and already broke upon the great windows behind him in an impure mist and rain.

The object of all this staring and blaring was a young man of about five-and-twenty, well-grown and well-looking, with a sunburnt cheek and a dark eye. His condition was that of a young gentleman. He was plainly dressed in black, or very dark gray, and his hair, which was long and dark, was gathered in a ribbon at the back of his neck; more to be out of his way than for ornament. As an emotion of the mind will express itself through any covering of the body, so the paleness which his situation engendered came through the brown upon his cheek, showing the soul to be stronger than the sun. He was otherwise quite self-possessed, bowed to the judge, and stood quiet.

The sort of interest with which this man was stared and breathed at was not a sort that elevated humanity. Had he stood in peril of a less horrible sentence—had there been a chance of any one of its savage details being spared —by just so much would he have lost in his fascination. The form that was to be doomed to be so shamefully mangled was the sight; the immortal creature that was to be so butchered and torn asunder, yielded the sensation. Whatever gloss the various spectators put upon the interest, according to their several arts and powers of self-deceit, the interest was, at the root of it, ogreish.

Silence in the court! Charles Darnay had yesterday pleaded not guilty to an indictment denouncing him (with infinite jingle and jangle) for that he was a false traitor to our serene, illustrious, excellent and so forth, prince, our Lord the King, by reason of his having, on divers occasions, and by divers means and ways, assisted Lewis, the French King, in his wars against our said serene, illustrious, excellent, and so forth; that was to say, by coming and going, between the dominions of our said serene, illustrious, excellent, and so forth, and those of the said French Lewis, and wickedly, falsely, traitorously, and otherwise evil-adverbiously, revealing to the said French Lewis what forces our said serene, illustrious, excellent, and so forth, had in preparation to send to Canada and North America. This much, Jerry, with his head becoming more and more spiky as the law terms bristled it, made out with huge satisfaction, and so arrived circuitously at the understanding that the aforesaid, and over and over again aforesaid, Charles Darnay, stood there before him upon his trial; that the jury were swearing in; and that Mr. Attorney-General was making ready to speak.

The accused, who was (and who knew he was) being mentally hanged, beheaded, and quartered, by everybody there, neither flinched from the situation, nor assumed any theatrical air in it. He was quiet and attentive; watched the opening proceedings with a grave interest; and stood with his hands resting on the slab of wood before him, so composedly, that they had not displaced a leaf of the herbs with which it was strewn. The court was all bestrewn with herbs and sprinkled with vinegar, as a precaution against gaol air and gaol fever.

Over the prisoner's head there was a mirror, to throw the light down upon him. Crowds of the wicked and the wretched had been reflected in it, and had passed from its surface and this earth's together. Haunted in a most ghastly manner that abominable place would have been, if the glass could ever have rendered back its reflections, as the ocean is one day to give up its dead. Some passing thought of the infamy and disgrace for which it had been reserved may have struck the prisoner's mind. Be that as it may, a change in his position making him conscious of a bar of light across his face, he looked up; and when he saw the glass his face flushed, and his right hand pushed the herbs away.

It happened, that the action turned his face to that side of the court which was on his left. About on a level with his eyes, there sat, in that corner of the Judge's bench, two persons upon whom his look immediately rested; so immediately, and so much to the changing of his aspect, that all the eyes that were turned upon him, turned to them.

The spectators saw in the two figures, a young lady of little more than twenty, and a gentleman who was evidently her father; a man of a very remarkable appearance in respect of the absolute whiteness of his hair, and a certain indescribable intensity of face: not of an active kind, but pondering and self-communing. When this expression was upon him, he looked as if he were old; but when it was stirred and broken up—as it was now, in a moment, on his speaking to his daughter—he became a handsome man, not past the prime of life.

His daughter had one of her hands drawn through his arm, as she sat by him, and the other pressed upon it. She had drawn close to him, in her dread of the scene, and in her pity for the prisoner. Her forehead had been strikingly expressive of an engrossing terror and compassion that saw nothing but the peril of the accused. This had been so very noticeable, so very powerfully and naturally shown, that starers who had had no pity for him were touched by her; and the whisper went about: "Who are they?"

Jerry, the messenger, who had made his own observations, in his own manner, and who had been sucking the rust off his fingers in his absorption, stretched his neck to hear who they were. The crowd about him had pressed and passed the inquiry on to the nearest attendant, and from him it had been more slowly pressed and passed back; at last it got to Jerry:

"Witnesses."

"For which side?"

"Against."

"Against what side?"

"The prisoner's."

The Judge, whose eyes had gone in the general direction, recalled them, leaned back in his seat, and looked steadily at the man whose life was in his hand, as Mr. Attorney-General rose to spin the rope, grind the axe, and hammer the nails into the scaffold.

*   *   *   *   *   *   *   *

3   *A Disappointment*

MR. ATTORNEY-GENERAL had to inform the jury that the prisoner before them, though young in years, was old in the treasonable practices which claimed the forfeit of his life. That this correspondence with the public enemy was not a correspondence of to-day, or of yesterday, or even of last year, or of the year before. That, it was certain the prisoner had, for longer than that, been in the habit of passing and repassing between France and England, on secret business of which he could give no honest account. That, if it were in the nature of traitorous ways to thrive (which happily it never was), the real wickedness and guilt of his business might have remained undiscovered. That Providence, however, had put it into the heart of a person who was beyond fear and beyond reproach, to ferret out the nature of the prisoner's schemes, and, struck with horror, to disclose them to his Majesty's Chief Secretary of State and most honourable Privy Council. That this patriot would be produced before them. That his position and attitude were, on the whole, sublime. That he had been the prisoner's friend, but, at once in an auspicious and an evil hour detecting his infamy, had resolved to immolate the traitor he could no longer cherish in his bosom, on the sacred altar of his country. That, if statues were decreed in Britain, as in ancient Greece and Rome, to public benefactors, this shining citizen would assuredly have had one. That, as they were not so decreed, he probably would not have one. That Virtue, as had been observed by the poets (in many passages which he well knew the jury would have, word for word, at the tips of their tongues; whereat the jury's countenances displayed a guilty consciousness that they knew nothing about the passages), was in a manner contagious; more especially the bright virtue known as patriotism, or love of country. That the lofty example of this immaculate and unimpeachable witness for the Crown, to refer to whom however unworthily was an honour, had communicated itself to the prisoner's servant, and had engendered in him a holy determination to examine his master's table-drawers and pockets, and secrete his papers. That he (Mr. Attorney-General) was prepared to hear some disparagement attempted of this admirable servant; but that, in a general way, he preferred him to his (Mr. Attorney-General's) brothers and sisters, and honoured him more than his (Mr. Attorney-General's) father and mother. That he called with confidence on the jury to come and do likewise. That the evidence of these two witnesses, coupled with the documents of their discovering that would be produced, would show the prisoner to have been furnished with lists of his Majesty's forces, and of their disposition and preparation, both by sea and land, and would leave no doubt that he had habitually conveyed such information to a hostile power. That these lists could not be proved to be in the prisoner's handwriting; but that it was all the same; that, indeed, it was rather the better for the prosecution, as showing the prisoner to be artful in his precautions. That the proof would go back five years, and would show the prisoner already engaged in these pernicious missions, within a few weeks before the date of the very first action fought between the British troops and the Americans. That, for these reasons, the jury, being a loyal jury (as he knew they were), and being a responsible jury (as *they* knew they were), must positively find the prisoner guilty, and make an end of him, whether they liked it or not. That they never could lay their heads upon their pillows; that they never could tolerate the idea of their wives laying their heads upon their pillows; that they could never endure the notion of their children laying their heads upon their pillows; in short, that there never more could be, for them or theirs, any laying of heads upon pillows at all, unless the prisoner's head was taken off. That head Mr. Attorney-General concluded by demanding of them, in the name of everything he could think of with a round turn in it, and on the faith of his solemn asseveration that he already considered the prisoner as good as dead and gone.

When the Attorney-General ceased, a buzz arose in the court as if a cloud of great blue-flies were swarming about the prisoner, in anticipation of what he was soon to become. When toned down again, the unimpeachable patriot appeared in the witness-box.

Mr. Solicitor-General then, following his leader's lead, examined the patriot: John Barsad, gentleman, by name. The story of his pure soul was exactly what Mr. Attorney-General had described it to be—perhaps, if it had a fault, a little too exactly. Having released his noble bosom of its burden, he would have modestly withdrawn himself, but that the wigged gentleman with the papers before him, sitting not far from Mr. Lorry, begged to ask him a few questions. The wigged gentleman sitting opposite, still looking at the ceiling of the court.

Had he ever been a spy himself? No, he scorned the base insinuation. What did he live upon? His property. Where was his property? He didn't precisely remember where it was. What was it? No business of anybody's. Had he inherited it? Yes, he had. From whom? Distant relation. Very distant? Rather. Ever been in prison? Certainly not. Never in a debtors' prison? Didn't see what that had to do with it. Never in a debtors' prison?—Come, once again. Never? Yes. How many times? Two or three times. Not five or six? Perhaps. Of what profession? Gentleman. Ever been kicked? Might have been. Frequently? No. Ever kicked downstairs? Decidedly not; once received a kick on the top of a staircase, and fell downstairs of his own accord. Kicked on that occasion for cheating at dice? Something to that effect was said by the intoxicated liar who committed the assault, but it was not true. Swear it was not true? Positively. Ever live by cheating at play? Never. Ever live by play? Not more than other gentlemen do. Ever borrow money of the prisoner? Yes. Ever pay him? No. Was not this intimacy with the prisoner, in reality a very slight one, forced upon the prisoner in coaches, inns, and packets? No. Sure he saw the prisoner with these lists? Certain. Knew no more about the lists? No. Had not procured them himself, for instance? No. Expect to get anything by this evidence? No. Not in regular government pay and employment to lay traps? Oh dear no. Or to do anything? Oh dear no. Swear that? Over and over again. No motives but motives of sheer patriotism? None whatever.

The virtuous servant, Roger Cly, swore his way through the case at a great rate. He had taken service with the prisoner, in good faith and simplicity, four years ago. He had asked the prisoner, aboard the Calais packet, if he wanted a handy fellow, and the prisoner had engaged him. He had not asked the prisoner to take the handy fellow as an act of charity—never thought of such a thing. He began to have suspicions of the prisoner, and to keep an eye upon him, soon afterwards. In arranging his clothes, while travelling, he had seen similar lists to these in the prisoner's pockets, over and over again. He had taken these lists from the drawer of the prisoner's desk. He had not put them there first. He had seen the prisoner show these identical lists to French gentlemen at Calais, and similar lists to French gentlemen, both at Calais and Boulogne. He loved his country, and couldn't bear it, and had given information. He had never been suspected of stealing a silver teapot; he had been maligned respecting a mustard-pot, but it turned out to be only a plated one. He had known the last witness seven or eight years; that was merely a coincidence. He didn't call it a particularly curious coincidence; most coincidences were curious. Neither did he call it a curious coincidence that true patriotism was *his* only motive too. He was a true Briton, and hoped there were many like him.

The blue-flies buzzed again, and Mr. Attorney-General called Mr. Jarvis Lorry.

"Mr. Jarvis Lorry, are you a clerk in Tellson's Bank?"

"I am."

"On a certain Friday night in November one thousand seven hundred and seventy-five, did business occasion you to travel between London and Dover by the mail?"

"It did."

"Were there any other passengers in the mail?"

"Two."

"Did they alight on the road in the course of the night?"

"They did."

"Mr. Lorry, look upon the prisoner. Was he one of those two passengers?"

"I cannot undertake to say that he was."

"Does he resemble either of these two passengers?"

"Both were so wrapped up, and the night was so dark, and we were all so reserved, that I cannot undertake to say even that."

"Mr. Lorry, look again upon the prisoner. Supposing him wrapped up as those two passengers were, is there anything in his bulk and stature to render it unlikely that he was one of them?"

"No."

"You will not swear, Mr. Lorry, that he was not one of them?"

"No."

"So at least you say he may have been one of them?"

"Yes. Except that I remember them both to have been —like myself—timorous of highwaymen, and the prisoner has not a timorous air."

"Did you ever see a counterfeit of timidity, Mr. Lorry?"

"I certainly have seen that."

"Mr. Lorry, look once more upon the prisoner. Have you seen him, to your certain knowledge, before?"

"I have."

"When?"

"I was returning from France a few days afterwards, and at Calais, the prisoner came on board the packet-ship in which I returned, and made the voyage with me."

"At what hour did he come on board?"

"At a little after midnight."

"In the dead of the night. Was he the only passenger who came on board at that untimely hour?"

"He happened to be the only one."

"Never mind about 'happening,' Mr. Lorry. He was the only passenger who came on board in the dead of the night?"

"He was."

"Were you travelling alone, Mr. Lorry, or with any companion?"

"With two companions. A gentleman and lady. They are here."

"They are here. Had you any conversation with the prisoner?"

"Hardly any. The weather was stormy, and the passage long and rough, and I lay on a sofa, almost from shore to shore."

"Miss Manette!"

The young lady, to whom all eyes had been turned before, and were now turned again, stood up where she had sat. Her father rose with her, and kept her hand drawn through his arm.

"Miss Manette, look upon the prisoner."

To be confronted with such pity, and such earnest youth and beauty, was far more trying to the accused than to be confronted with all the crowd. Standing, as it were, apart with her on the edge of his grave, not all the staring curiosity that looked on could, for the moment, nerve him to remain quite still. His hurried right hand parcelled out the herbs before him into imaginary beds of flowers in a garden: and his efforts to control and steady his breathing shook the lips from which the colour rushed to his heart. The buzz of the great flies was loud again.

"Miss Manette, have you seen the prisoner before?"

"Yes, sir."

"Where?"

"On board of the packet-ship just now referred to, sir, and on the same occasion."

"You are the young lady just now referred to?"

"O! most unhappily, I am."

The plaintive tone of her compassion merged into the less musical voice of the judge, as he said something fiercely: "Answer the questions put to you, and make no remark upon them."

"Miss Manette, had you any conversation with the prisoner on that passage across the Channel?"

"Yes, sir."

"Recall it."

In the midst of a profound stillness, she faintly began: "When the gentleman came on board—"

"Do you mean the prisoner?" inquired the judge, knitting his brows.

"Yes, my Lord."

"Then say the prisoner."

"When the prisoner came on board, he noticed that my father," turning her eyes lovingly to him as he stood beside her, "was much fatigued and in a very weak state of health. My father was so reduced that I was afraid to take him out of the air, and I had made a bed for him on the deck near the cabin steps, and I sat on the deck at his side to take care of him. There were no other passengers that night, but we four. The prisoner was so good as to beg permission to advise me how I could shelter my father from the wind and weather, better than I had done. I had not known how to do it well, not understanding how the wind would set when we were out of the harbour. He did it for me. He expressed great gentleness and kindness for my father's state, and I am sure he felt it. That was the manner of our beginning to speak together."

"Let me interrupt you for a moment. Had he come on board alone?"

"No."

"How many were with him?"

"Two French gentlemen."

"Had they conferred together?"

"They had conferred together until the last moment, when it was necessary for the French gentlemen to be landed in their boat."

"Had any papers been handed about among them, similar to these lists?"

"Some papers had been handed about among them, but I don't know what papers."

"Like these in shape and size?"

"Possibly, but indeed I don't know, although they stood whispering very near to me: because they stood at the top of the cabin steps to have the light of the lamp that was hanging there; it was a dull lamp, and they spoke very low, and I did not hear what they said, and saw only that they looked at papers."

"Now, to the prisoner's conversation, Miss Manette."

"The prisoner was as open in his confidence with me— which arose out of my helpless situation—as he was kind, and good, and useful to my father. I hope," bursting into tears, "I may not repay him by doing him harm to-day."

Buzzing from the blue-flies.

"Miss Manette, if the prisoner does not perfectly understand that you give the evidence which it is your duty to give—which you must give—and which you cannot escape from giving—with great unwillingness, he is the only person present in that condition. Please to go on."

"He told me that he was travelling on business of a delicate and difficult nature which might get people into trouble, and that he was therefore travelling under an assumed name. He said that this business had, within a few days, taken him to France, and might, at intervals, take him backwards and forwards between France and England for a long time to come."

"Did he say anything about America, Miss Manette? Be particular."

"He tried to explain to me how that quarrel had arisen, and he said that, so far as he could judge, it was a wrong and foolish one on England's part. He added, in a jesting way, that perhaps George Washington might gain almost as great a name in history as George the Third. But there was no harm in his way of saying this: it was said laughingly, and to beguile the time."

Any strongly marked expression of face on the part of a chief actor in a scene of great interest to whom many eyes are directed will be unconsciously imitated by the spectators. Her forehead was painfully anxious and intent as she gave this evidence, and, in the pauses when she stopped for the judge to write it down, watched its effect upon the counsel for and against. Among the lookers-on there was the same expression in all quarters of the court; insomuch, that a great majority of the foreheads there might have been mirrors reflecting the witness, when the judge looked up from his notes to glare at that tremendous heresy about George Washington.

Mr. Attorney-General now signified to my Lord, that he deemed it necessary, as a matter of precaution and form, to call the young lady's father, Doctor Manette. Who was called accordingly.

"Doctor Manette, look upon the prisoner. Have you ever seen him before?"

"Once. When he called at my lodgings in London. Some three years, or three years and a half ago."

"Can you identify him as your fellow-passenger on board the packet, or speak to his conversation with your daughter?"

"Sir, I can do neither."

"Is there any particular and special reason for your being unable to do either?"

He answered, in a low voice, "There is."

"Has it been your misfortune to undergo a long imprisonment, without trial, or even accusation, in your native country, Doctor Manette?"

He answered, in a tone that went to every heart, "A long imprisonment."

"Were you newly released on the occasion in question?"

"They tell me so."

"Have you no remembrance of the occasion?"